PRAISE FOR JUDITH FRENCH

Rachel's Choice
"This is a romance with plenty of action, wonderful characters, and a love story that endures social differences."
—*Romantic Times*

"Is *Rachel's Choice* a winner? Most assuredly."
—*Rendezvous*

McKenna's Bride
"A wonderful story of growing trust and love."
—*Romantic Times*

"Ms. French's portrayal of ranch life, the harshness and beauty, is vibrantly displayed page after page. This and a passionate romance with endearing characterizations are just what's needed on a cold wintry night."
—*Affaire de Coeur*

The Irish Rogue
"Ms. French knows how to make the past come alive, and our hearts sing with happiness."
—*Romantic Times*

"Judith French has penned a winner."
—*The Romance Reader*

P9-DTL-568

MAR   2001

By Judith E. French:

FORTUNE'S BRIDE
FORTUNE'S FLAME
FORTUNE'S MISTRESS
SHAWNEE MOON
SUNDANCER'S WOMAN
THIS FIERCE LOVING
McKENNA'S BRIDE*
RACHEL'S CHOICE*
MORGAN'S WOMAN*
THE IRISH ROGUE*
THE TAMING OF SHAW MacCADE*
FALCON'S ANGEL*

Published by The Ballantine Publishing Group

Falcon's Angel

Judith E. French

IVY BOOKS • NEW YORK

An Ivy Book
Published by The Ballantine Publishing Group
Copyright © 2002 by Judith E. French

www.ballantinebooks.com

ISBN 0-345-43761-6

Manufactured in the United States of America

First Edition: February 2002

10 9 8 7 6 5 4 3 2 1

For Grey Culver, with all my love.
This one's for you.

"Angels are painted fair, to look like you . . ."

—Thomas Otway

Prologue

Charleston, South Carolina
May 1810

"She's alive. I'd certainly know if she were dead," Lady Graymoor said.

"Yes, ma'am." A portly butler in silver and blue livery waded through a clutch of spaniels, set a silver tray on the gateleg table, and motioned to the maid. The girl pushed back the heavy, velvet drapes and started to open the French doors leading to the balcony that overlooked the garden.

"Leave it." The white-haired woman waved an elegant hand. "And take all this away, Griffin. You know what day this is."

"Yes, my lady." He removed a thin cotton cloth to reveal a plate laden with fresh strawberries, ·fluffy hot scones, and sweet butter. "It is the second of May, in the year of our Lord, eighteen hundred ten."

"How long have you been in my service?"

"Twenty-two, no, twenty-three years, ma'am. It will be twenty-four years exactly on—"

"Never mind. You've been with me long enough to know that the first days of May are a great sorrow to me. I remain secluded. I don't take meals. I am in mourning."

1

"Yes, my lady, you are indeed." Griffin poured cream into a porcelain teacup, added steaming amber tea, and finally three lumps of white sugar. "But you haven't eaten a bite since yesterday noon. You must keep up your strength. If you do not, who will continue looking for the little lady?"

"Don't manage me, Griffin. I may be a foolish old woman, but I will not be manipulated by my household staff." She leaned forward, sitting up in the satin-draped poster bed, and allowed her maid to tuck another pillow behind her back.

The young woman smiled and bobbed a curtsy. "Will there be anything else, madam?"

"Yes, thank you, Peggy. If you would just bring me my teakwood chest, the small one there atop the lacquer cabinet."

"You could never be foolish," Griffin said. "But you are often careless of your own health."

"Enough!" The countess clapped her hands sharply, sending the younger dogs into a frenzy of yipping. "I'll eat the bloody scones, but I shall have my box. Give it to me, and leave at once, both of you, before I get out of this bed and box your ears."

She clapped again. "Be still, you infernal puppies! Quiet, I say, or you'll be exiled below stairs with the parrot." Instantly, the dogs stopped their clamor and lay down. Ears drooped, and all but the matriarch Fanny appeared contrite.

Lady Graymoor waited until her servants were gone, the heavy door closed behind them, their footsteps clicking away down the hall, before unlocking the chest. With a deep sigh, she removed a yellowed, stained, and much creased letter, put on her spectacles, and began to read the dreadful words that she long ago had committed to memory.

Lady Graymoor
Graymoor Hall
Surrey, England

August 1, 1790

Your ladyship,
It is my sad duty to inform you of the following tragic events. On the morning of May 3, your son Henry, the Viscount Kemsley; his wife, Lady Anne; and your grandchildren, Miss Elizabeth and Master Alexander, sailed from Charleston, South Carolina, on the Content, *bound for Philadelphia and London.*
Despite clement weather and repeated sightings by passing vessels, the Content *never arrived at her destination. Weeks later, there were reports of the crew of a Virginia schooner observing a ghost ship, mysteriously empty of crew or passengers, adrift in the fog near Cape Hatteras. This claim is unsubstantiated.*
Due to our long association with your family and our ongoing responsibility for your late husband's American financial concerns, Holland, Hansen, and Russell has taken the liberty of posting a significant reward in your name. At our insistence, American authorities ordered an intensive search of the Atlantic coastline.
In June, the bodies of most of the missing, including your son, Viscount Kemsley; his wife; and their young son, washed up on North Carolina beaches. It is my sorrowful duty to tell you that no trace of five-year-old Elizabeth was ever found. . . .

Moisture blurred Lady Graymoor's vision. Tears filled her eyes, and dropped one by one onto the bold script, causing the ink to run. With a deep, soul-wrenching sigh, she allowed the letter to fall from her fingers to the satin coverlet.

"Elizabeth . . . my darling, where are you?" The only answer in the shadowed room was the whining of her spaniels and the click of her parrot's beak against the bars of his cage. Hugging her narrow chest, the old woman rocked slowly to and fro and waited for this day to pass as all the others had done.

Chapter 1

Will Falcon shielded his eyes from the driving rain and strained to see land through the darkness. Snapping sails and the fury of wind and waves made it almost impossible for his bellowed commands to be heard over the tumult of the squall. But he wasn't worried yet. His crew was seasoned, and the *Katherine* as sweet and seaworthy a ship as any clipper ever built in Baltimore. With luck, he could avoid the shifting sandbars and stay in the channel without grounding the schooner.

An unidentified island loomed on his port side, too near for comfort, and a morass of shoals and tricky currents lay between the *Katherine* and open sea. The storm had swept in fast, surprising Will with its intensity. In the space of a half hour, three-foot seas had become six-, and the shallow waters churned into a foaming maelstrom. Winds gusted to sixty knots, thunder rolled overhead, and bolts of lightning seared the heavens.

"Sweet Mother of God," Will muttered as needles of hail battered his exposed skin. No wonder these waters were a graveyard of sunken ships and wandering

5

ghosts. If the tides and weather didn't sink a ship, the pirates would.

Sailing so close to shore at night was a calculated risk. For years a ruthless band of outlaw wreckers had haunted these waters, luring unsuspecting vessels to destruction. If he and his men were to have a chance at hunting down these predators, the *Katherine* needed the cover of darkness. And tonight, she needed the relative safety of protection from the higher seas in deep water.

He'd hired a guide, a local called Stump, who swore he'd fished this area all his life and knew the sandbars, shoals, and elusive waterways between the islands like the back of his hand. If Stump turned out to be a fool or a liar, Will could lose his ship and all hands.

"Cap'n! The storm sail—" A gust ripped the sailor's shout away as two more seamen scrambled to add muscle to the taut line.

Will felt the *Katherine* shudder as she plunged into a trough between waves. Water boiled over the gunnel and washed across the sharply tilted deck, and a solid wall of churning sea rose on the leeward side.

"Come on, darlin'," Will pleaded. "You can. Yes!" Like a spirited hunter rising to the jump, the ship nosed up, slicing waves and wind. "Yes, that's it!" He laughed as spray drenched his face and hair.

Damn but his *Katherine* was a ship to boast of from Boston to New Orleans. Hamilton Shipping might possess her title, but every curve and spar of her was Will's, and someday he'd save enough to buy her back.

Lightning flashed, momentarily blinding Will, leaving a taste of burning sulfur on his tongue and filling his brain with the stench of brimstone. Hairs rose on his arms and the nape of his neck. And when he forced his eyes open, he saw tongues of blue-white fire licking at the poles atop the foremast.

A crewman swore and pointed.

"St. Elmo's fire!" First Officer Aaron Fletcher appeared at his side.

"Nice night for it." Will motioned for the younger man to take the tiller.

Aaron grinned. "My thoughts exactly," he shouted.

"Cap'n!" The cry came from mid-ship. "A bolt broke. Gun's comin' loose."

"Secure it!" Will ordered. A cannon adrift on the deck was serious trouble.

Several men rushed to tie down the heavy gun. The *Katherine* carried a crew of thirty-eight, but in a storm like this, every hand was needed.

"Cap'n!" Will recognized Isaiah. The sailor was an old salt, not likely to call for help unless he needed it.

"Want me . . ." The wind's howl ripped Aaron's question away.

Will shook his head. "I'll go. You stay at the helm." The slick deck slanted under his feet as he made his way hand over hand down the lines.

"Cap'n, I can't—" Isaiah's words were lost in another blast of lightning.

Will was an arm's length away when wood splintered and the cannon surged free, striking Isaiah. The old man slammed onto his back and slid helplessly across the deck toward the leeward gunnel. Will lunged for him, but black water swept the sailor off the deck in the blink of an eye. "Man overboard!" Will yelled.

He caught a glimpse of a pale bald head and one hand before Isaiah sank like a stone. "Man overboard!" Will screamed as he dove over the side after him.

Will's last thought before the wall of water closed over him was that trying to save Isaiah was the most stupid decision he'd ever made.

Groping blindly, Will went down until he touched

bottom. A fierce current tugged at him. Sand and mud swirled, burning his eyes, confusing his senses. Instinctively, he turned toward the surface, pushing upward with powerful stokes. He'd always considered himself a strong swimmer, but the tide and undertow tossed him like a length of driftwood.

Gasping for breath, he broke water and sucked in lungfuls of air. The stern of the *Katherine* was a dark, receding mass against a gray bowl of scudding clouds and arcing lightning. "Here!" he shouted. "I'm here!"

Had the sea carried him so far, or had the ship altered course? He couldn't tell. "Damn it! We're here!" he cried into the wind.

The storm was moving away from shore, but six-foot chops still crashed over his head. Will took in a mouthful of water and spat it out. He kicked hard with his feet, riding the crest of a wave and scanning the surface.

There! There, by God! He saw something a few yards away. "Isaiah!" he yelled. "Hold on! I'm coming!" Determined, he plowed through the whitecaps, fixing his will and body to reach that spot before the old man went under again.

The distance seemed impossible to traverse. With every two arms' lengths he went forward, the current dragged him back one. "Isaiah!"

Nothing.

Was it here he'd seen him? Had he lost his bearings? No, by damned! Here! Will gritted his teeth and dove in Stygian blackness as images of the old seaman's face flashed across his mind. He could clearly see flashes of Isaiah, sailcloth draped across his lap, patiently stitching a torn seam, and Isaiah, mother-naked, dancing a jig to a hornpipe and balancing a noggin of rum on top of his bald head. And, most vividly of all, Isaiah swinging a belaying pin and cutting a swath through a British press gang to rescue a wet-nosed Charleston runaway.

Will's chest burned. He'd been down too long. He knew he had to have air soon. Just a little—

His heart leaped as his fingers brushed something solid. He seized Isaiah's shirt and hauled him back to the surface. "Isaiah!" Will gasped, choking and drinking in the sweet air. "Are you . . ." He trailed off as his fingers touched the back of his friend's broken head.

A bolt of lightning illuminated the old man's round face and unseeing blue eyes.

"No." Will shook his head. "Isaiah?" For a moment, he hugged the limp body, then reluctantly released his grip until Isaiah slipped away and vanished.

Grief as thick as a January fog squeezed Will's chest. But seconds later, a swell broke over his head, shoving him down. This time when he fought his way back and looked for his ship, he saw nothing but waves and an angry predawn sky. He turned in the direction he believed shore to be and began to swim, stripping his mind of everything but the need to survive.

He lost all track of time. Whether he had been struggling toward shore or out to sea, he didn't know. He thought the winds and waves were weakening, but so was he. The muscles in his neck and shoulders burned; he'd long ago lost feeling from his knees down.

Over his left shoulder translucent hues of lavender and peach shimmered along the eastern horizon. Once, Will was certain he saw a line of stunted trees and sand, but then the tumbling whitecaps buried him, filling his mouth and throat with salt water and dulling his brain.

How easy it would be to give up . . . to sink as Isaiah had done . . . to rest. . . . Resolve gave way to anger and then to caustic humor.

That's the trouble with you, Will Falcon, an inner voice mocked. You don't have sense enough to stay down when you're beaten.

The beach was there. He knew it was. No man who had learned to swim at the tender age of four should drown within sight of land. He'd made a fool's decision to go into the water after a dead man, but panicking would only make his situation worse.

Breakers. He could hear surf crashing. Where there was surf, there was solid ground. But the undertow kept sweeping him out, and the numbness kept creeping up his aching limbs. His breaths came in ragged gulps . . . he was swallowing water . . . choking . . . frantically struggling.

And then . . . there was nothing but the soft, all-encompassing blackness of death.

Will opened his swollen eyes and blinked in the glare. "So this is hell," he said, clamping his eyes tight against the brilliance. But the words didn't come out. The sound he made was more of a gasping croak, before he curled on his side and coughed up salt water.

He wiped his mouth and tried to sit up, but his muscles wouldn't obey. He fell back, against what felt like lapping waves and sand . . . and something else . . . something soft and warm.

He forced his eyes open, but the light was almost more than he could bear. Colors and images swirled before his vision gradually cleared, and he found himself staring into the most beautiful face he'd ever seen.

Will gasped, unable to believe what he was seeing.

Illuminated by an unearthly light, a siren with sea-green eyes, clad in nothing but a mass of tumbling red-gold curls, bent over him. "What . . . what are you?" he stammered.

She tilted her head and smiled, revealing perfect, shell-white teeth. "Angel," she replied.

"Then . . . this must be heaven," Will managed to say. "Fancy me making it to . . ." But then the bees buzzing in his head became a roar, and he tumbled into a soundless abyss.

It seemed to Will that, as he fell, there were short periods when he felt as though he was swimming or being dragged through sea and surf . . . and finally abandoned in shallow water with solid beach beneath him and a land breeze caressing his face. He could have sworn he heard a woman's voice raised in anger, her words strangely accented but ringing as clear and pure as spring rain.

He was mistaken, of course, being dead and in the company of an angel. That he'd washed up on heaven's shore puzzled him to no end. He'd not expected to dock safely in God's golden port. Considering the liquor he'd consumed, the ladies he'd seduced, the rascals he'd helped to glory, and his spotty church attendance, he would have laid odds that he was bound for a darker harbor.

A man's guttural oath wrenched Will from his stupor. Choking, he raised his aching head and opened his eyes. For a moment, the earth seemed to sway sickeningly, but then Will's senses cleared. With a start, he found himself lying facedown on solid ground, with the shriek of seabirds in his ears and morning sun warming his back.

Standing over him was the radiant spirit he'd seen earlier. At least, he thought she must be the same angel. Now, it was obvious that he'd been mistaken. This was a flesh-and-blood woman . . . as real as the grains of sand clinging to his damp hands.

Garbed now in a thin, cotton shift, soaked by sea and spray, his barefoot guardian stood between him and two hard-faced men. The brilliant rays of the morning sun illuminated the tumbled mass of her copper-gilt hair and gleamed on the filleting knife she gripped in one hand.

"Stand aside, ye reeking notch!" the closest thug snarled as he fumbled for his own weapon at his belt. "Them boots looks prime. I mean to have'm." The pock-faced ruffian was near Will's age, somewhere in his early thirties. He stood at least six feet, with burly shoulders, legs like mooring posts, and raw hams for fists.

"Back off, Dyce," the woman warned.

"If it's the boots you want, you can have them," Will said, fighting for time. He blinked, trying to steady his wits. He had no doubt that the brute meant to kill him, but if he could just get to his feet, he might have a chance.

Dyce's shrewd eyes glittered from under a thatch of greasy, dark hair. The knife looked like a child's toy in his massive hand.

"A plague on you, Dyce Towser!" the angel flung back. "He's mine. I took him from the sea, and you'll not have him."

"He's seen our faces," Dyce said. "I won't end on the gibbet for a wench's soft heart."

"Best do as Dyce says," the second man called. "He's right. None what sees us can leave here alive. Would ye have us dance the Tyburn jig?" He was short and rail-thin, with one walleye, and a tarred pigtail that stuck out from under a seaman's striped cap.

"Are you naught but a lickspittle toad, Tom?" she replied. "You know the law. Go for the cap'n. He'll settle this before blood is spilled."

Reaching for his sword, Will struggled to his knees. He was nauseated and light-headed, but not so far gone as to lie helpless while they gutted him like a fish. He swore as his right hand closed on an empty scabbard. "Get back!" Will said to the woman. "Don't put yourself in harm's way for me!"

With an oath, the big man charged.

"No!" Will lurched up, determined to meet the attack on his feet.

Angel held her ground until the last instant, then, knife flashing, she danced between him and Dyce. With almost fluid motion, she struck so swiftly that Will couldn't be certain what he'd seen.

Dyce howled and clutched his wrist as his blade spun away and landed in the sand. A sheet of crimson dripped down the giant's arm. "Bitch!" he cried. "You'll pay fer this!" Swearing, he twisted toward his companion. "Get her, you yellow-backed—"

" 'Tis nay me what's to blame, ye niding lout," Angel cried. "He's mine, I say. Booty taken fair and square from—"

The sailor rushed at her, knotted fists drawn back to strike. Will grabbed for the discarded weapon, snatched it up, and tried to put himself between her and danger.

But she was too quick for him. In an eye-blink, she slashed Tom's shirt, tripped him, and pressed a high-arched bare foot against his Adam's apple. "Give over, Tom," she cried. "Hurt a hair of his head, and I'll send you to a narrow grave."

A shout sounded from the scrub pines, and Will's heart sank as he saw three heavily armed pirates pounding down the beach toward them.

"Ye got yer wish," Dyce shouted. "Cap'n comin'! He'll slice this dandy bow to stern and feed his guts to the sharks."

Chapter 2

Will straightened. If he had to die, it would be on his feet and fighting. More brigands spilled from the dunes and ran toward him. Will had no doubt that he'd found his outlaw wreckers. The trouble was, he'd intended to face them with his crew and the *Katherine*'s cannon at his back. Now, it seemed there was only one fallen angel to stand beside him in his final battle.

Forcing his voice to some semblance of normal, he said, "I'm Will Falcon, captain of the—"

"Nay!" Swiftly, Angel removed her foot from her prisoner's throat and turned to hiss a warning. "Hold your tongue, handsome sir. Do you wish to walk away with your head on your shoulders, you must leave the fine words to me."

Still gasping for air, Tom rolled onto his belly, coughed, and crawled crablike out of her reach. "Cap'n! Ye must do somethin'!" he croaked. Still coughing, face contorted with wrath, Tom jabbed the air in Angel's direction. "Attacked Dyce with a knife! Cut him—"

"Pay no heed to their lyin' tongues," Angel exclaimed. " 'Twas these yellow-backed curs that tried to steal my goods."

Will studied the man he assumed must be in command. Cap'n was a middling man, middle-aged, and average in height and build, with short-cropped, reddish hair graying at the sides and temples. A faint smile played over his thin lips as his gaze swept from one player to the other, missing nothing.

For the barest instant, the two men stared into each other's eyes. Then the pirate folded his arms across his chest and inclined his head in a gesture of acknowledgment. "The bitch took a knife to me," Dyce railed.

The air around Will crackled with tension as more belligerent figures swarmed around them. Not a peaceful fisherman in the lot, Will thought. Some carried muskets, others pistols. Every one, including the females, had the fierce look of predators and bore the heavy weight of knives or cutlasses belted at their hips. Their clothes and speech were strangely old-fashioned, as though they all belonged in his grandfather's time. But there was no doubt in Will's mind that his life hung by a thread.

He glanced at his defiant angel standing so boldly without a hint of fear on her beautiful face. "Stand back," he cautioned. "You're a brave wench, but I'd not have you trade your life for mine. I'm no man to hide behind a woman's petticoats."

"What are you waitin' for?" Dyce demanded. "The law is clear. He's an outsider. None can come among us and leave to bear witness."

"Aye!" cried a blond woman in a tattered yellow skirt. "What Dyce says is true. No strangers among us!" The loudmouthed jade was little older than sixteen, and far gone with child. The brass buttons on her red military waistcoat were strained to the point of popping over her swollen belly.

"Kill him!" cried a strapping ruffian behind her.

"Ye canna speak fer us, Angel!"

"Be you cap'n, now, Watt Cook?" A tall, full-bosomed

woman shouldered through the crowd. "Since when do you give orders? You're naught but a jug-bitten turd who cannot tell his arse from a hole in the sand! Was I sleepin' when ye were elected captain?"

Guffaws erupted from rogues on either side of her. More voices chimed in, some in support of Dyce's case, others opposed. An aging seaman with a harelip brandished a cutlass.

"Put that cheese knife away, Jonas," the big woman scolded as she stopped beside the captain and nudged him in the ribs with an easy familiarity. "Brother, can you not put an end to this prattle? Yon stranger's no danger to the lot of us. But they won't cease their bickerin' until ye set them down."

Standing side by side, Will could see a clear resemblance. The ample-hipped, outspoken woman had the same reddish-blond hair and gray eyes as the captain. Since she was too near in age to be either mother or daughter, Will assumed she must be his sister.

"Aye, Bett's right," agreed a muscular, one-armed man who had not yet spoken for either side. "We all know that Watt cannot tell his arse from a hole in the sand."

"That's truth, Nehemiah," the pregnant girl agreed, adding an off-color jest of her own.

Nehemiah paused long enough for his comrades' laughter to ebb before asking, "What say ye, Cap'n? What's to be done with this booty?"

"He's mine," Angel repeated firmly. "He washed in on the tide. I found him, and my claim is upheld by our code."

"A keg of ale ye may claim." Nehemiah nodded agreement. "But not a stranger. He could be the death of us all."

"I say kill him." Dyce spat on the sand. "Kill him and

give me Angel for my trouble. I'll take her to wife and put an end to her troublesome ways."

"Nay! I will not! I'd sooner wed mad King George!" Angel exclaimed.

"Hist, hist, all of ye," Bett said. "Look at'm!" She pointed at Will. "Be those the clothes of a poor sailor? He's a gent, he is. We could cut his throat, but how much profit will we see from a corpse? A lordling with such boots must have rich relatives who will pay hard silver to get him back in one piece."

"Ransom? Bett's thinking sound," cried a spare, dark-haired woman with a babe in her arms. "Are we honest wreckers or murderers?"

"Listen to Dyce," Tom whined. "Dyce thinks we oughta cut . . ." Tom trailed off as the captain raised a hand for quiet.

"What we have here is a difference of opinion," the leader said in a low, gravelly voice. "We will do what we always do."

"Vote!"

"Nay, hear Angel out."

"I say, we should—"

"Silence." Cap'n nodded to Angel. "Step away from him and sheath your blade." He motioned to two of the younger men. "Disarm the prisoner and bind his hands—"

"Will you not hear me?" Angel demanded as Will tightened his grip on his weapon. "If you mean to have a vote, at least let me—"

"You will have your chance." Cap'n glanced at Dyce. "As will you and Tom. But what will be decided will be for the good of all, not one. Drop the knife, stranger, or I'll have them put a musket ball through your heart."

"Wait!" Angel turned her back on her captain. "Do ye trust me, Will Falcon?" she asked.

Will looked into her eyes. "Should I?"

"Aye," she said. "For sure ye should. I'm all that stands between you and eternity." She was so close that he could feel her warm breath on his face, smell the clean, salt-sweet scent of her glorious hair. "Would you live, sir?"

"I would."

"Marry me, and ye shall live."

Will blinked. "What?"

"Quick!" she hissed. "A bargain. There is no time to argue. It will save your life. Will you, or will you not?"

He nodded, and she whirled on the closing circle.

"Hold!" she cried. "I claim this salvage as husband. If he weds me, he will be one of us. Outlaw. As liable to hang as any!"

"There!" Bett thrust both hands into the air. " 'Tis her right, Brother. If he takes Angel to wife, the law will build as high a gallows tree for him as fer you."

"Damn if he will!" Dyce swore. " 'Tis a trick. The wench is spoke fer. Does he wish to gainsay my claim, let him take her from me with fist and steel!"

"Aye!" Tom agreed. "Let's see whether his bullocks be brass or water."

"Nay," Angel protested. "I refused Dyce. Not once, but a dozen times. A member of the Brethren cannot be forced—"

"Ye be no full sister of the Brethren yet," Watt sputtered. "So long as you remain unwed, ye count as no woman, but a maid. Only them with a strong husband can sign the contract."

"Fie on ye," Angel retorted. "He's weak and near to dyin'. He's swallowed half the Atlantic. How can any man go into the circle and fight when—"

"He can't," Bett agreed. "Come, Brother. Be fair

about it. Give the poor soul time to get back his wind. T'will make not a smidgen of difference in the end."

"What are they talking about?" Will asked Angel. "What circle?"

"I'll give him until noon," the captain said. "Put down your weapon, stranger. No harm will come to you until then unless you bring it on yourself."

"Hell shall find him inside that circle," Dyce jeered. "I'll slit that fine white shirt from dawn till Sunday and spill his innards for the gulls."

"Cut his throat and spare the cloth," Jonah cried. "I've a mind to have them breeches."

Angel gripped Will's hand. " 'Tis the best I can do for you. You heard the cap'n. You have until the sun is high." She paused. "Two men go into the circle drawn in the sand. Each has but a knife, and only one comes out."

"The rules?" he asked.

Her eyes grew moist. "That is the pity, sir," she murmured. "There are no rules."

"You've gone mazy-headed, sweeting." Bett lowered her voice to speak privately to Angel as two of their men bound the stranger's hands behind his back and tied a length of cloth over his eyes. "In all these years you've never chosen a man. This morning you swim addle-headed into a storm surf to haul in an outlander that will bring ye naught but grief."

"Ye cannot judge him half-drowned," Angel replied. "Perhaps he's canny with a knife. Those blue eyes of his are hard as flint."

"Atch. It's his blue eyes, is it?" Bett's broad face split into a grin revealing one shiny gold incisor. "Eyes and not arse? He is fair to look at, I'll give you that. Long-legged and lovely as my first husband, Shadrack. But . . ." She sighed. "This one is a gentleman. I know them and their fancy ways. Don't pin your hopes on a rising fog. Dyce Towser may be a suck-egg knave, but he's the devil's imp with a knife." The grin became a deep belly chuckle. "Near as good as you, I reckon."

Angel shrugged. "I was lucky. And I had a good master."

"Aye, Cap'n be the master of the blade. He would not have led the Brethren so long without that skill. But you, luck be praised, ye be far too strong-headed a wench for her own good."

"So you've often told me."

Bett slipped a meaty arm around Angel's shoulder. "I wish your fine gentleman some of that fortune tomorrow. I wager Brother will shed no tear for either of them."

Angel nodded and walked down the beach to the spot where she'd left her dugout canoe. Wadded up in the bow were her striped linen skirt and short, laced waistcoat. Dressing was as simple as casting off her garments had been when she'd made the decision to save the stranger. It was May, and she'd have no need of stockings or shoes until autumn.

The Brethren had seen the schooner in trouble during the storm. Lightning strikes had illuminated the ship as she struggled to avoid the sandbars. Watt Cook had bet four bits that wind and tide would sink her.

Had the vessel gone down, Angel would have helped to salvage whatever valuables the sea brought them, but she would have no part of murder. It was Dyce and his followers she suspected of such foul tricks.

The Brethren of the Coast were wreckers, true enough. They lived on goods that washed ashore. That was fact. But what people said of them, that they lured vessels to their doom by building fires or carrying lanterns along the strand in foul weather, was untrue.

The ship and the long night of watching had been no different from many others. But something about this schooner had tugged at Angel's heart. Since she was a child she had learned to follow her instincts, no matter how unreasonable they might seem. Many of the Brethren called her fey, and more than one had whispered the word *witch*.

When the fury of the storm had passed, the urge to take her dugout and paddle out beyond the sandbars had been irresistible. She feared neither tide nor waves, and she could swim like a dolphin.

Thus, she had been out far enough to see Will Falcon's battle to keep his head above water in those first moments of dawn. And she had made the decision to save him.

The Brethren claimed it was bad cess to steal a life that the ocean had claimed. "Take what belongs to the sea, and ye will pay a terrible price," Bett had always told her.

Angel glanced out at the gray rolling waves and shivered. Quickly, she crossed herself. "St. Jonah protect me," she murmured, wondering if she'd lost her mind and didn't have the sense to realize it.

She'd known what risk she was taking when she'd turned her dugout toward Will's struggling figure. But she couldn't help herself. Knowing that it would be impossible to heave the weight of a grown man over the side of her boat without capsizing, she'd stripped off her clothing and had dived in after him.

She'd caught the outlander by his hair and dragged him back to the dugout. Whitecaps still boiled, threatening to drag them both down to the depths, but she'd managed to get both the boat and her prize to a sand spit a quarter mile off the beach.

Once there, she'd given him a sound pounding on his back to get the sea out of him and had waited until his breathing was strong and steady before bringing him back to shore.

Bett's shout broke into Angel's reverie. "Need help with your boat?"

"No, I can manage," she replied. "Go on with the others. I'll be along directly." She wanted to be alone for a while longer to collect her thoughts.

Bett waved and strode inland toward the low trees.

Angel waited for an incoming wave, then used the water's force to shove her dugout farther up onto the sand beyond the reach of the tide. Using driftwood and brush, she covered the little vessel so that it wasn't visible from the water.

Brushing the sand off her hands, she straightened and loosened her hair. It was still damp from her swim and might not dry for hours if she didn't shake it out. Combing out the tangles, she allowed Will Falcon's image to take shape in her mind's eye.

He was beautiful . . . surely, the most beautiful man she had ever seen. The combination of dark brown hair and bright blue eyes were at once striking and rare. For blue did not begin to describe the proper color of them, Angel decided. They were a raw blue, a blue such as the Almighty had mixed for sea and sky on the first day of creation. And looking into those eyes was as scary and thrilling as staring into the curl of a huge storm wave just before it broke over your boat.

And then, there was the way the man was put together. Will was tall and broad of shoulder, long of leg, flat-bellied, and firm of buttocks. His nose was straight and strong, flared just enough at the nostrils to give him boldness. His chin was firm and square, his mouth . . .

A curious ribbon of excitement twisted in the pit of Angel's stomach as she imagined what it might feel like to be kissed by those lips.

Or touched by those callused hands. . . .

Will Falcon's hands were lean and hard. She had expected a gentleman's hands to be as soft-white as fish belly, but his were not. They were the hands of a strong and lusty sailor, but one whose ringless fingers were both long and very clean. Even his nails were filed straight across, not broken off as her own. She had always been a woman to notice a man's hands, and those of her sea-gifting were pleasing indeed.

She wondered if Will's ship had survived and why, if she had, the crew hadn't returned to search for him. Did they believe him drowned, or hadn't anyone missed him? How had he been so clumsy as to tumble overboard?

She had so many questions that they were near to bursting out of her skin. The trouble was, if he came to a dreadful end under Dyce's blade, she would never find the answers to any of them.

Chapter 3

Angel followed a twisting path through the dunes to the far side of the island, which the locals called Kidd's Retreat, emerging at Haunt's Cove. She hesitated while she was still hidden from view by the vegetation and looked cautiously around her before stepping out onto the narrow beach.

To her right, three small boats belonging to the Brethren were drawn up on the sand. Directly ahead, open water stretched between Kidd's Retreat and a larger isle, Sanctuary, too far for her to see with the naked eye. The mainland lay miles west of Sanctuary.

She shielded her eyes from the sun's rays, searching for sight of a sail, but saw nothing except choppy blue-green waves and a cloudless sky. Satisfied that Will Falcon's ship hadn't circled Kidd's Retreat hunting for him, she stepped farther out into the open.

What had possessed her to offer to take him to husband? What Bett had said was true. So far, Angel had wanted no man. None to dally with and none to accept as protector or as mate. Since she had sprouted from child to maiden, she had distanced herself from all males but Cap'n. He was more father to her than friend.

So different was she from other young women that many of the Brethren called her mermaid, wave witch, or moonling. She suspected some feared her for her odd behavior, and she was content to have it so. Yet she who had never been kissed by a man had offered her bed to one she knew nothing about.

Perhaps she was sick. She might have taken a chill in the cold water, or she could be coming down with some ague. Even now, it seemed her thoughts eddied and churned like a storm tide. Her breath came ragged, and her blood ran hot. She touched her forehead, seeking some hint of fever, but found none. "Truly, I am the one bewitched," she murmured. "Beguiled by a pair of devil-blue eyes and a mouth that would tempt a saint."

Abruptly, Bett noticed her and waved. "There you are, Angel. Best ye have some of these vittles before they're gone. I've got clam fritters here, and ye know how the cap'n loves them."

"She ain't lookin' fer food," Tamsey remarked. "It's him she's got a hunger fer." Several members of the group laughed as the pregnant girl motioned toward the prisoner.

Angel's heart gave an odd little flutter as she caught sight of Will Falcon bound hand and foot, sitting with legs outstretched, his back to a scraggy pine tree. She had told herself that she had spun him out of mist, that no flesh-and-blood man could be the way she remembered him.

From here, she saw that one of his eyes was swollen. Blood trickled from the corner of his mouth, and a purple bruise marred his left cheekbone. None of these injuries had been obvious when she'd pulled him from the water, and none took away a measure of the enchantment he'd cast on her.

"Yer wastin' yer time with that'n," Tom jeered. "He's shark bait." Dyce, sprawled beside him, said nothing, but Angel saw him ogling her as he crammed a hunk of corn bread into his mouth and chewed greedily.

God rot your stinkin' bowels, Dyce Towser, Angel thought as a knot twisted in the pit of her stomach. 'Twas you who struck the outlander once he was tied and helpless. I'd bet my soul on it.

Without answering or showing any hint of her seething anger, Angel strolled to one of the boats, dipped water from a small ironbound keg in the stern, and drank. The liquid was warm and tasted faintly of vinegar, but there was no fresh water on this key. Every drop had to be brought in from the main settlement. It was drink this or go without.

Once she had satisfied her thirst, she filled the gourd to the brim and carried it to Will. "Thirsty?" she asked him.

He nodded, and she raised the gourd to his cracked lips. The bird-wing sensation in her chest had intensified, and it seemed to her that the air had become as thick as molasses. Try as she might, she couldn't hold the dipper steady, and some of the liquid spilled down Will's chin. "Had enough?" she asked.

"Thanks." His fierce gaze met hers, holding her spellbound for long seconds.

He was a clean-shaven man with a single day's growth of dark beard, and thick, silky hair. And well named, she thought as a chill rippled down her spine in spite of the growing heat of the morning sun.

"You're kind," he said.

" 'Tis nothin'." She tore free from her breathless trance and covered her unease with practicality. "Have you hunger?" she asked, trying to keep her gaze from straying to the width of his shoulders or the bulge of hard muscle in his upper arms.

He shook his head. "No, I'm not hungry."

She watched, fascinated, as the last beads of water dripped from his square chin onto his cream-colored linen shirt and wondered what it was about him that drew her so. "I'll wager you've felt better," she replied in a breathy rush. "Ye were as near to drownin' as I've seen and yet live."

"More thanks to you."

"Nay." She felt her cheeks grow warm and knew she was blushing. "You're a strong swimmer. Few men could last long in that riptide and not be swept under." A thought came to her. "We are much apart here. I . . . I know not the ways of gentlefolk. Does it trouble your pride to be pulled from the sea by a wench?"

The slightest hint of a smile tugged at his mouth. "Hardly. But, mistress, I—"

"No," she admonished, listening closely to his strangely accented English. "Do not mock me with fripperies. I am no one's mistress, and I have no titles. I am just Angel."

"Simply Angel? No surname?"

"Why would I need another? There are no other angels among the Brethren that we would need a nickname to tell us apart." She flashed him a shy smile as she gave him more water. "Some say it is unlucky to save a drowning man. Some think the sea will take revenge on both the saved and the rescuer."

"I've heard that.

"But, I put little stock in such superstitions," he concluded.

"Aye. You would think that," she agreed, "being the one with nothin' to lose and all to gain."

He gave her a wicked grin. "I give you the field, mistress. You have wit as well as nerve."

"There's many here who would argue that," she answered, but she wasn't able to resist smiling back at him. "You should eat," she advised. "Ye will need your strength to—"

"You're not like the others," he said. "Not willing to see blood shed—"

"Don't waste your breath with honey-coated words. You must enter the circle, and you must fight." She swallowed, trying to dissolve the lump in her throat. "And if . . . when," she corrected, ". . . when you best Dyce, you must take me to wife. There is no other way."

He muttered a half oath, but bit it back. "I'm the last man you'd want for a husband. Couldn't you—"

Angel shook her head. "You dinna understand, outlander. It's not me who's in need of a husband, 'tis you who must accept a partner from among us. We have our own law here. Those who do not follow it are put to death."

"So be it. If I must fight him, I will. But my muscles will cramp and stiffen if I remain tied like this. Can you loosen the ropes?"

She made a small sound of wry amusement. "Ye take me for a fool."

"No, I don't. But truth is, your Dyce looks a formidable foe. If they want fair combat, I need—"

She took a step back and shrugged. "Have you forgotten what I told you? In the circle, there are no rules."

No rules. Angel's words came back to haunt her as Dyce and Will faced each other under the glare of the noon sun. Within seconds of the start of the ordeal, Dyce launched his first attack. Moving faster than Angel would have imagined the brute was capable of, Dyce bent, scooped up a fistful of sand, and hurled it into Will Falcon's face. Temporarily blinded, Will clutched his eyes and twisted sideways, barely evading a wicked thrust of Dyce's blade.

"Mind the circle!" Angel shouted when Will's bare foot came dangerously close to the boundary line Cap'n had drawn on the cleared earth. No more than nine feet from edge to edge, the faint mark was all that stood between either opponent and the yawning gates of hell.

Will moved as quick and light as spray dancing on waves, wordlessly taunting Dyce, keeping just out of arm's range. Angel noted with approval that the foreigner seemed to know how to hold the weapon she had lent him, and that he was fast. No trace of fear showed on his handsome face.

Both men had stripped to their breeches, shedding garments, boots, and stockings, before the challenge began. What little protection a shirt or waistcoat would give the wearer would be naught compared to the ease of movement without. Leather soles might give poor footing on sand, and a man who lost his balance and fell was doomed.

Angel squeezed her fingers into knots as alternate waves of heat and ice flashed under her skin. Raw fear was an emotion she seldom experienced, but she was afraid now. Will's sleek muscles and narrow waist seemed dwarfed by Dyce's massive frame and barrel neck. It seemed impossible that he would be the one left standing when the contest was over.

And he had to be. . . .

If Will didn't survive the battle, she'd have to deal with Dyce alone. Cap'n might be able to protect her for a while, but soon he, too, would fall victim to Dyce's relentless greed. She had seen the evil in Dyce's little pig eyes. He wanted to be leader of the Brethren and he was determined to have her. Neither she nor Cap'n could sleep with both eyes shut until Dyce was dead.

She had never taken a human life. But if Will Falcon didn't kill Dyce, she was fearful she would have to do it herself.

The big wrecker charged again. Will dodged right,

then left. Dyce's knife flashed in the sunlight, and Will uttered a grunt of pain before retreating with sweat and blood glistening on his bare chest.

"Get'm!" Tom howled. "Cleave off his root, if ye can find it!"

Tamsey shrieked with excited laughter.

It seemed to Angel that everything outside the circle lost its importance. The seabirds' cries faded. The Brethren ceased to shout. She no longer felt the shell-littered beach beneath her feet, smelled the tang of salt in the air, or felt the breeze on her face. For that moment, nothing mattered but Will Falcon and his fate.

Then Dyce snarled an oath and bore down upon Will with scarlet-stained steel and clenched fist. This time the stranger didn't feint. He spun on one foot and slammed the bare sole of the other into Dyce's hairy chest.

The air burst from Dyce like a punctured bladder. He toppled backward and crashed to the earth, with Will on top of him. And somehow, in the blink of an eye, the battle had turned. Angel's knife, the one that she had lent Will, pinned Dyce's hand to the ground, while his own was pressed against Dyce's throat.

"Kill him!" Bett urged. "Kill the bastard!"

"Yield," Will ordered. "Yield or die."

"I . . . I give up," Dyce blubbered. "Don't cut me . . ."

Will looked at the captain. "Must I finish him?"

"No! Please!" Dyce begged.

Abruptly, Angel became aware of an acrid stench and saw the dark stain spreading across the front of Dyce's breeches.

"Dyce's pissed himself!" Tamsey pointed, and began to giggle.

"Kill him," Angel whispered. "If you don't . . ."

But Cap'n had already intervened, shaking his head

and gesturing for Will to let Dyce up. "You've proved yer worth. Angel's yours, if she'll still claim ye."

In one swift motion, Will yanked the blade from Dyce's mutilated hand, got to his feet, and moved far enough away so Dyce couldn't grab him.

Cap'n held out his hand for the knives. "I'll take those," he said. "We'll let ye join our company, but you'll not carry steel until we're sure of you."

Will glanced at the other men who closed in around him, expressions hard, hands reaching for their own weapons.

"Do as Cap'n says," Angel said. "It's our way."

"How do I know I'm not signing my own death warrant by trusting you?" Will asked the captain.

Cap'n chuckled. "Ye don't, laddie. An' that's gospel."

"His word's been good enough fer us since before the war," Watt Cook exclaimed. "Damn yer eyes if ye think to question our cap'n. We've hemp enough to string ye to—"

Angel stepped between Will and the captain. "Give them to me," she said, placing her hand over Will's. "It's all right. You have my word on it."

Reluctantly, he surrendered the knives to her keeping. Trying to keep from trembling, Angel handed Dyce's to Bett and bent to clean hers in the dry sand. Behind Will, she saw Dyce sitting up and cradling his injured hand against his chest. No one but Tom seemed the slightest bit interested.

"You're certain ye want to go through with this?" Bett asked. "Tom's right. We can still silence him another way."

"No, he's mine, and I'll have him," Angel said. She reached out and clasped Will's hand. "I take this man to husband," she cried. "He has passed the test of courage."

"Do it now, then, do ye mean to," Cap'n said, "but I believe it as foolish as any act I've seen. Nehemiah? Can ye remember the words?"

Will's fingers tightened on Angel's. "Him? How can he—"

"Nehemiah was a man of God in his old life," she explained. "He speaks over the dead, marries us, and christens the babes."

Will scowled down at her and hissed, "This is a farce, woman. I've no wish to wed you, and I'll take my leave at first chance."

"Mayhap you will, and mayhap you won't," she replied. "But if ye do not say the words with me, you'll not live to see the sun go down."

"That's certain," Bett agreed, shoving a bouquet of pine boughs into Angel's hands. " 'Tis no gaysome marriage, but Angel has the right to demand it."

"I do," Angel said. "Nehemiah?"

The one-armed man strode forward, red-cheeked and stiff with importance. "Have ye a wife already?" he demanded of Will. "Do ye, have sense enough to deny it or it will be the death of ye. I'll marry no man what has a wench and bairns at home."

Will glared back at him, mouth thin with anger and eyes narrowed. "I have no wife," he said between clenched teeth. "Have none and want none not of my own choosing."

"Angel be a proper maid," Bett said. "Get on with the words, Nehemiah."

"Aye." He shifted from one foot to the other before glancing at the captain. "This don't seem—"

"I, Angel, take you, Will Falcon, to be my lawful husband under God and under the law of the Brethren," she said. "Now you must ask him the same, Nehemiah."

"Do ye, Will Fallon—" Nehemiah began.

"Falcon," Will snapped. "William Randolph Falcon, of Charleston, South Carolina."

"Aye." Nehemiah cleared his throat. "Do ye, Will'm Randolph Falcon, of—"

"Stand aside, bitch, or I'll blow ye to hell with him!" Dyce shouted.

Angel whirled to see Dyce standing right behind them with a sawed-off musket.

"Get down!" Bett cried.

"Too late!" Dyce said. Grinning, he pulled the trigger.

Chapter 4

Will threw himself over Angel as the musket roared. He felt the lead ball slam into his back. And then he was falling, tumbling over and over in a white-hot blaze of pain, until after what seemed an eternity, he felt nothing more at all. Blackness . . . Rough jostling . . .

"Will. Wake up."

The soft, feminine voice tugged at his consciousness with a nagging urgency.

"Will."

He drew in a long, ragged breath. His bones ached. Every muscle in his body protested his attempts to move. His eyelids were as heavy as iron deck-cleats. He couldn't open them . . . couldn't . . .

Cold water splashed in his face. He gasped. "What the—"

"Hist, hist, sweeting. Take a little water."

Will sputtered and swore. "Are you trying to drown me?" He opened his eyes to find Angel smiling down at him. It was dark, and the room was fire-lit. He tried to sit up, but she pushed him back on the pallet with strong arms.

"Nay, nay. Ye vexed me sore, Will Falcon. I feared you had a mind to die."

He hurt all over. "How bad is it?" he rasped.

"Not so bad. That lout Dyce tried to murder you. Bett

34

feared he might, so she asked Watt Cook to foul Dyce's musket. Watt will do anything to get into Bett's bed. But our Watt is not as bright as he could be. He poured sand down the barrel. Dyce's gun blew up, and you were struck by pieces of metal instead of the musket ball."

"But . . ." Will struggled to push the fog from his mind. Firelight framed Angel's face and hair so that she was once again a heavenly vision. "I . . . I heard the—"

She shook her head, cutting off his statement. "What you heard was Cap'n's pistol, not Dyce's musket. Cap'n knew nothing of what Watt had done, so he tried to shoot the musket out of Dyce's hands. Why he didn't kill the villain, I don't know, but—"

"You're a bloodthirsty wench for one of God's messengers," he said, sinking back onto the pillow.

"Nay, I am not. And you must not blaspheme." She crossed herself before continuing. "Dyce is the devil's panderer, and you have hurt his hellish pride sore. Better you had slain him than his bile fester and he live on to cause the death of better men than he."

"Where am I?"

"My home." She laid a cool, damp cloth on his forehead. "I have washed the cuts in warm seawater, but I fear two need stitching up. T'will nay be pleasant for ye. Would you take rum?"

"No." It was becoming easier to understand her antiquated English. Under less dangerous circumstances, he might have found her speech charming. She was a beauty and a temptress with a lush and curving body and comehither eyes that a man could drown in. But at the moment her sensual charms were the farthest thing from his mind. What was important was getting off this island alive. "No rum," he said. "I'd keep my wits about me."

He already felt as though he'd drunk a tavern dry. His head was pounding. He was nauseated, and his mouth

tasted like bilge water. Gritting his teeth, he pushed up
on one elbow to ease the fire in his back, and found his
left foot tangled in something hard. "What the hell?" he
protested. Throwing off the cover, he found a rusty
manacle encircling his ankle.

Will's oath seared the rafters.

"Peace," Angel soothed as she stepped back out of
reach. "Do not—"

"Let me go!" he said. Solid iron links bound the
metal cuff to an upright post at the foot of his bed.

"Shhh." She put a finger to her lips. "Lie still. You
will start your hurts bleeding again."

"What game is this?" Will felt a tear and a sharp
pain. Warm liquid dampened his chest, and he looked
down to see the white bandage turning dark with blood.

"See. What did I warn ye about?" she admonished.
"It's a shallow gash, but even that could—"

"Unchain me, I say!" He forced himself to sit up and
wrenched the manacle with both hands. The chain
didn't budge. "What treachery is this?"

Angel folded her arms over her breasts and gave a
small sigh. "I told them ye would be angry."

"Angry? Angry?" Reason struggled with the red tide
of fury that threatened to drown caution. "Why?" he
demanded. "Why have they done this? I fought and I
won. Now you—"

"Not me, husband."

He swore fiercely. "I never spoke the vows—"

She retreated to the central fire and crouched beside
it, shifting a kettle over the glowing coals. "Mayhap ye
didn't repeat every word of the wedding lines, but you
did clasp my hand and stand before the Brethren.
You declared by your actions, before witnesses, that you
meant to take me to wife." She shrugged. " 'Tis all that
is necessary for a handhold marriage."

Shards of broken glass seemed to spear through him with each breath. Tight-mouthed, breathing hard, he lay back on one side, still glaring at her. "What now? Am I to let you sew me up so that I can fight two more of your crew tomorrow? And three the following day?"

Angel wrapped the hem of her skirt around the handle of the kettle and poured hot water into a silver teapot that would have graced any fine parlor in Charleston. "No more challenges," she assured him. "Ye are chained because Cap'n does not trust you. A wise decision, wouldn't you say?"

She rose and walked to a mahogany tea chest that sat on a gnarled section of driftwood against one wall. Rummaging through the box, she produced two small bags, opened and sniffed each one, then added pinches of the contents to the teapot. "If you don't wish to take strong drink, this will ease the discomfort and help you sleep," she said. "You'll be safe here, for now. Trust me. A day or two of rest and my potions will set you right."

"Why? Why are you doing this?"

She smiled. "I pulled you from the sea, outlander. I claimed you as my salvage, and it is in my interests to keep ye safe."

"For what purpose? Am I to be your slave? A stud horse?"

Shock registered on her face. "Do not speak so. You shame yourself and me. Can there be such talk between husband and wife? What will be, will be, and none of us can stop it. I knew that my life had taken a different turn when I first saw ye struggling to keep your head above water. When I pulled you onto the sandbar, and you opened your eyes . . ."

She stirred the brew with a wooden spoon. "Deny it, if you can, Will Falcon. We are bound together. In what way, I do not know, but your life will never be the same. And neither will mine."

For long minutes, he watched her in stony silence. As his eyes became accustomed to the firelight, he inspected the rough walls and crude furnishings of what he supposed must be a single-room hut. The floor was hard-packed earth, swept clean and free of litter. The single door, cut from a ship's hatch cover, was barred with an iron harpoon, and the window small and shuttered. The ceiling was low, and curving, causing him to suspect that the beams might also be salvage from some hapless vessel. The walls were lined with woven reed matting, and instead of a fireplace there was a pit dug in the center of the structure and surrounded by bricks. Baskets and leather sacks hung from the rafters, along with strings of dried clams and fish, onions, and herbs. Smoke from the fire drifted up to vanish through a small hole in the roof.

His pallet took up the greater part of one wall, an inlaid, walnut writing cabinet and a gatelegg oak table with elegant, turned legs the far one. There was an ornately carved chair with leather-padded seat and backrest, and a single old-fashioned stool, which looked Dutch. Two sea chests, a wooden barrel, and a gilt mirror completed the crow's nest collection of furniture. "A pirate's lair," he murmured.

"What?" Angel poured the tea into a blue and white pottery mug, tasted it, and nodded. " 'Tis ready. Drink it," she urged. "And try to understand that the Brethren are not pirates. We are honest wreckers. We take what the sea gives us and make our living from—"

"The deaths of honest men."

"Nay," she protested. " 'Tis not so. At least not under Cap'n. If Dyce Towser kills our captain and takes his place, who knows what will happen."

"You're wrong, woman. Dozens of ships have been

lured to their destruction along this stretch of shoreline. Many others have vanished. Can you deny that your people light fires along the beach to deceive the lookouts and—"

"We do not! Those are ghost lights, the fires of Indian spirits, long dead. Sometimes they glow green and sometimes red. All manner of haints walk these—"

"What?"

"Haints. Ghosts. Those dead but still among us."

He snorted in derision. "Superstitious nonsense."

She curled her fingers and made the sign for warding off the evil eye. "You a saltwater man, and you can speak so?" She shook her head. "Have ye never seen water nymphs or blue flames dancing on the sea? Have ye not heard the long-drowned singing from the ocean depths? Witnessed the sails of a ghost ship in the fog? You are either a fool or a liar if you deny that things exist that cannot be explained."

"Enough. Do you hear yourself? If you were peaceful wreckers, would your captain want me killed? Would anyone have worried that I saw your faces?"

Her lips pursed. "We are a people apart. We do not trust the mainlanders, nor they us. And ignorant folk can expect faint justice from high courts and bigwigs. It is our law that we do not mix with your kind. And rightly, as I see it. For you find us guilty of murder and piracy without a spoonful of proof."

Will shook his head. "Keep your witch's potion and sew up my wounds, if you will. Doubtless you're bloodthirsty enough to enjoy it."

"As you wish, sir," she said. "And mayhap I shall take satisfaction in every tiny stitch."

Despite her shrewish words, Angel couldn't take pleasure in her task. Her needle was fine and sharp, her thread silk. But though she knew it must be done, she had always found that sewing a wound was painful for both patient and seamstress.

He was brave, as she knew he would be. He clamped his teeth, set his jaw, and endured her ministrations without uttering a sound. Sweat broke out on his forehead, and his hands clenched into tight fists, but he did not cry out. When she was finished, his olive complexion was the color of old ivory.

Making no effort to hide the compassion she felt for his injuries, she offered Will her special tea. This time, he drank it. As she'd hoped, he grew sleepy within a few minutes.

"What have you given me?" he asked, struggling to keep his eyes open.

"A bit of this, a bit of that. Ye need have no fear. Ye are safe here. Rest awhile. I will keep watch."

Angel gathered up her ointments and bandages and busied herself until she heard the rhythm of his breathing steady and grow easier. Then, when she was certain he was in a deep sleep, she took a clean cloth, dipped it in the fresh water she'd warmed by the fire, and prepared to bathe him.

Starting with Will's face, she gently wiped away the sweat and dust, then massaged a soothing cream into his skin with featherlight strokes. He tossed his head and moaned, but did not wake.

It was curious how the simple act of washing a grown man should make her feel as though she'd been running in deep, deep sand. She tried to tell herself her discomfort was naught but foolish whimsy. Outlander or not, Will Falcon was her husband. There was no need for maidenly modesty. She would be failing in her duty to him if she didn't use all her skills to bring him back to full health, whether he approved of her or not. And it had been her experience that wounds must be kept clean to heal.

Still, she could not keep her fingers from trembling or her heart from fluttering as rapidly as that of the injured sandpiper she had found on the beach. Touching Will in such a familiar manner was both pleasing and more than a little frightening.

With a fingertip, she traced the faint scar that ran from the corner of his left eyebrow to the center of his cheekbone. So bronzed was Will by sun and sea that she had not noticed the thin mark before. It looked as though it had been made by a thin, sharp blade, such as a dueling sword.

Will's swollen and cracked lips were as goodly shaped as any she had ever seen on a man. His roguish mouth was neither over-wide nor too small for his face, and she could not help wondering if he would taste like seawater.

Without realizing she was doing so, Angel moistened her own lips. Nervously, she swallowed and took a long, slow breath. What had she done? What if the old ones were right? What if taking someone from the sea brought disaster to the rescuer? Could the odd sensations racing through her be the start of some dreadful plague?

And what if this beautiful stranger was as hard in his heart as Dyce Towser?

By marrying him, she had given him the use of her body. She shivered as a sheen of ice slid over her skin. What if Will was not kind when he took his husband's right? She had seen beasts . . . wild horses and dogs . . . even dolphins. The dolphins seemed gentle and loving, but the others had been wild, even cruel in their mating. Would Will use his man root like a weapon to cruelly tear her tender flesh?

The shivering became worse, and she locked her teeth together to keep them from chattering. No, Will Falcon

wasn't like that, she told herself. Hadn't she always
been a good judge of men and weather? Will might be
hard, but he would be fair. He would use her lightly. She
could bear the pain of losing her maidenhood. She was
no coward, but . . .

"More spinster's fancies," she murmured. How many
husbands had Bett had? Surely, if tupping were unpleasant, her mother wouldn't be forever on the watch
for another man. It must be that once a maiden was
breached, she grew tough and callused down there, so
that she could perform a wife's duty without complaint.

Will Falcon was as hard-muscled as any saltwater
sailor. Lying asleep as he was, she'd expected some soft-
ness, but he was all bone and sinew without an ounce
of fat. How did a gentleman come by such broad shoulders or such a flat, ridged belly? Seen in a ruffled shirt,
waistcoat, and dress coat, a casual observer might have
thought Will slender, almost boyish in form. When
she'd pulled him from the waves, she'd not guessed how
well formed he was beneath his clothing.

How strong these arms would be . . . how powerful
his callused hands. If he turned his might on her, what
chance would she have to protect herself?

Yet, she had done what she had done. There was no
turning back, and no unsaying the wedding lines. A
Brethren union might not last more than a few months,
but while they were together, it was a marriage.

Angel laid down the cloth and loosened her laced
bodice. It was suddenly too warm in her hut. Ordinar-
ily, both the door and window would stand open, but
she had wanted to be alone with the outlander.

She had so many questions she wanted to ask him
about the world beyond these islands. She could count
on the fingers of one hand how many strangers she had
seen in the last five years. Two of those had been

drowned sailors, and the other one she had barely glimpsed in the darkness, a mysterious man who bought the booty the Brethren gathered from the sea.

Angel carefully washed each long finger. On his right hand, Will wore a wide gold ring with a single design carved on the flattened top. She thought the mark might be the letter F, but it was as curved as an angry snake, and she had never learned to read or write. She sighed, knowing that Dyce would not have missed seeing the ring, no doubt wondering how it would look on his own hairy hand.

Angel had never owned a ring, never wanted one. Sometimes the sea yielded all manner of baubles: jeweled rings, necklaces, brooches, and crosses set with precious stones. But such fripperies were not for common folk. They were packed up and sold along with other valuables. Such money as they brought could be traded for black powder, lead, flour, and other necessities that the Brethren could not come by otherwise.

She inspected Will from tousled mane to the sprinkling of ebony hairs just above the waistband of his expensive breeches. The task was finished. There was no need to do more. Rest and food should put him right in a few days.

But she could not soothe the mischievous curiosity that bubbled in the dark corners of her mind. Will had a respectable amount of black hair on his chest and arms and none on his back. She wondered about the parts of him she hadn't examined. Were his legs heavily furred? His loins?

A grown man's bishop was generally decently covered, but she had seen a few pizzles, three to be exact. Tom was apt to wave his in the wind when he was drunk, and Dyce had deliberately exposed himself to her more than once. She'd not been impressed. Dyce's eel had been thick and purple, Tom's rather puny with a definite lean to starboard. The third man had been dead, so his shriveled root didn't count. You couldn't expect a corpse to amount to much.

She hoped that Will's pizzle wasn't purple.

Getting up, she disposed of the water, washed her hands, and started a clam stew for supper. But somehow, her heart wasn't in the cooking, and her eyes kept straying to the mound in the front of Will's breeches.

Suppose he had a hurt she wasn't aware of? The woolen cloth was torn in one spot. What if Dyce's knife had cut Will there? A puncture wound could kill a man quicker than any other. Some took the lockjaw sickness and died in agony.

Angel wondered if she was neglecting her duty to Will in not examining all of him to make certain he wasn't injured. "No need to make such a fuss," she murmured. The best thing to do was put her mind at rest about her new husband's health.

She went back to him, knelt beside the pallet, and began to gently untie his breeches' lacing. He grunted and shifted to one side, startling her. She froze, holding her breath.

Will tossed his head, muttered something she couldn't understand, and lay still again. She waited, sweat beading between her breasts, until it seemed safe to continue.

Heart racing, Angel reached out with trembling fingers to loosen the strings of his garment.

Will's powerful hand clamped around her wrist.

"Ahhh!" Her shriek of fright strangled in her throat as his fierce eyes snapped open and his gaze locked with hers.

"Lost something?"

Chapter 5

Angel tried to jerk loose, but Will held her fast in an iron grip. Her cheeks flamed.

"What exactly were you looking for?"

There was no missing the scornful amusement in his words as he fumbled with the flap on his breeches' front with the fingers of his free hand. "I'll be happy to show you—"

"Nay." Mortified, she averted her face. "Let go of me. I was not—"

"If this is a game, I need to know the rules."

"Please."

He released her, and she fled to the far side of the fire. "I saved your life."

"And you think that gives you the right to—"

She shook her head. "I wasn't—"

"Damned if you weren't."

The flush spread until the roots of her hair felt ready to burst into flame. She felt like such a fool. She wanted to run away, to get far from his taunting voice, and breathe in cool sea air. But the blood pulsed hot in her wrist where his fingers had pressed against her skin, and her heart pounded.

"Why?" he asked.

She blinked back the moisture that clouded her vision as anger replaced shame. She wanted to salvage her wounded pride, to sting Will Falcon with words as fierce as a nest of riled ground wasps.

It was on her tongue to shout, "I should have left you to drown!" But that would be untrue, and she'd had no experience at lying. Instead, she remained mute, letting the silence stretch between them until she felt she would shatter into a hundred pieces. "I wanted to see what it looked like," she confessed, her words rushing over one another like foam on a cresting breaker.

"What?"

"Your pizzle. Dyce's is purple and thick like the neck of an old sea turtle."

Will's lips curved into a near smile before he forced a scowl. He thought he knew women, but he was at a loss of what to make of this one.

Angel was no girl, but a woman grown. Yet she seemed both wantonly bold and innocent at the same time. She lived among bloodthirsty pirates and seemed unaware of their acts of violence. He wondered if she was possessed of all her senses or simply hiding a nature as vile and criminal as the rest of the Brethren.

"Ye were awake," she said. "While I washed you."

"I was."

"Cod's head!"

"Deceitful wench."

"I was not the deceitful one. You sailed under false colors, pretending to be asleep when you were not."

"Can you deny you tried to drug me? To take advantage of a helpless prisoner?"

"Helpless?" she scoffed. "You're about as helpless as a six-foot shark."

"I thought it best to learn firsthand what you were up to." He chuckled. "It turned out to be a pleasant experience." No need to tell her how enjoyable he'd found her touch, or that her herb tea had dulled the pain of his injury.

"Fie on you!"

"Fie on me? I don't mean to be ungrateful, but you have dragged me here, chained me to a post, and made free with my body. You can't expect me to—"

"Nay, I cannot." She wiped her hands on her skirt. "I want us to be friends."

"Friends don't hold each other prisoner."

"I have asked ye . . . you . . . to trust me. In time, mayhap—"

"You'll help me escape to the mainland?"

"Shhh. Folks here find it wise to hold their tongues when others may be about. The walls be thin, and some are fond of listenin' to what they should not." She crouched by the fire and cut slivers of bacon into a simmering pot. "Chowder will be done soon."

He nodded. He'd thought he wasn't hungry, but the smell of the clam broth was enticing. "Thanks, I'll—"

A knock came at the door. "Who is it?" Angel asked.

" 'Tis me. Brought you a mess of greens and hoecake hot from the griddle."

Angel lifted the bar, and the loud woman from the beach shouldered her way in, handed Angel a basket, and glared suspiciously at him.

"Thanks, Bett," Angel said. "I've a smidgen of beach plum preserves left from last summer. T'will make fine eatin' with your bread."

Bett gestured toward him with her chin. "That one givin' you trouble? I thought I heard ye cry out."

"No trouble. We're suited, I think."

Bett sniffed in obvious disbelief. She was tall and wide-hipped without being sloppily fat. Will would miss his guess if she was not near fifteen stone in weight. Huge bosoms jiggled and spilled over the neckline of her checked bodice, and her carroty-gray hair was barely contained by a beribboned mobcap that had seen better days. Her hands were as large and gnarled as a bosun's and looked capable of both rowing a longboat and throttling a hapless sailor.

"I still say this be a mistake, Angel. Since you're bound to make it, I'll hold me tongue and let ye reap the harvest."

She looked familiar, this brassy shrew. Will had seen Betts in a hundred dockside taverns from Boston to Port Royal, some willing to warm your cockles or slit your throat for whatever coin you had in your purse.

As if she were reading his mind, Bett studied him with shrewd eyes. "Don't loosen his manacles."

Angel nodded. "I will not."

"And if nature calls, good woman, what then?" he asked.

Bett shrugged. "Do he need to piss, give him a bucket." She whispered something to Angel, then hurried out.

"Quite the lady," he said.

"Hold your blather. Bett is a brave woman with a heart as big as an island. I'll not have you say a word against her." She shook her head in disgust. "A babe in leading strings would know Bett for the lady she is."

He coughed. "A little rough around the edges is your Bett."

"Mayhap, but you'll treat my mother with respect or soon rue it."

"That's your mother?" His tone echoed his shock that such a jade could give birth to the beauty beside him.

"She is," Angel replied sharply. "And what of it?"

"Truce, woman. I beg pardon if I've given offense. I didn't know she was . . ." He swallowed and shook his head. "I'd not fight with you, nor offer insult. Just give me some of that soup and let me sleep."

"Gladly. But you will give Bett her due. And remember that my name is Angel. You will please to call me that . . . or . . ." She flashed a bright smile. "Or you may call me wife. I do not fancy *woman*. It sounds much like *tree* or *dog*."

"You're an odd one."

"You're not the first to say so." She dipped a mug of the chowder and carried it to him. "Careful, 'tis hot. But it will put strength in your loins."

"We're back to my loins, again, are we?"

"Hmmp." Her forehead furrowed in a frown. "You be as touchy as—"

"You are," he corrected.

She stopped, puzzled. "Nay, 'twas you I—"

"You *are*, not you *be*, touchy."

". . . As a crab in a steam pot." She filled a wooden bowl with the soup and took it to the table. Seating herself in the chair, she began to eat and didn't speak again until she had finished. Then she took a clean pewter plate, spread two pieces of pone with preserves, and took one to him.

"Bett brought greens, but they won't be fit to eat. She cannot tell one kind from another. Tomorrow, I'll pick some that are decent and cook up a mess for our nooning. If you go too long on a diet of bread, fish, and meat, your teeth will fall out. And yours are too fine to lose."

When he looked down at his mug, he found that he'd finished the chowder. "It was good," he said. "Thank you." Angel had twisted her hair up on her head, and the bright, red-gold strands caught the firelight like a halo. She was very clean, and her skin, although tanned, was as smooth and flawless as porcelain.

With looks like hers, he mused, Angel had no need of living barefoot on a nameless key. She could make her fortune in Charleston or Savannah or any town on the shores of the Atlantic. Men would shower her with gifts for a single night, while he, he thought with wry humor, wanted nothing more than to be shed of her.

"What you said . . . before." She returned to the table, sat, and steepled her fingers thoughtfully. "You do not like the way I talk. You think 'tis backward."

"Old-fashioned, at least. And difficult to understand."

"For ye." She corrected herself. "For you. Not for the Brethren. 'Tis the only speech I have ever heard. I be nay stupid." She laughed. "Am nay stupid."

"Not."

"Good. We agree on something. It makes me gaysome that *you* find me canny."

He held up a hand, palm up. "I surrender, madam. I know when I'm defeated." He smiled at her with all the charm he could muster. "And now, you must grant me a boon. I'm in need of a private place to . . . pass water."

"You wish to go out."

"I'll be damned before I piss in a bucket."

She laughed. "You may well be damned, Will Falcon, gentleman of Charleston. But I can see that you are a prideful man, and I fear that I suffer from the same vanity." She rose and went to the door. "You will be blindfolded."

"Why the hell should I be? I've already seen all of your faces."

"Not all," she said. "And you have not seen our camp. Cap'n is a cautious man." She flashed him a smile. "Bide here, and I will see if I can find someone to guard you whilst ye do what needs be done."

"I'll wait right here."

"Patience is a virtue."

"Another I have never possessed."

"Luckily, I do, husband. Maybe ye will learn some from me."

Later, after he'd been blindfolded, and a lad with a musket had escorted him to a secluded spot, Will walked back toward Angel's hut. Although he couldn't see, there was nothing wrong with his other senses. He could feel the salt breeze on his face, smell roasting pork, and hear the chatter of people around them.

There was a myriad of other sounds that told him that this was a substantial settlement. Dogs barked, and a goat bleated. Chickens squawked and clucked. And he was certain he heard the flutter and cooing of a flock of pigeons.

It was impossible to guess how many pirates there were. Women's laughter and the wail of a babe told him there were more females here, perhaps even children. Seagulls shrieked overhead, their cries rising and falling as they dove toward land or water. He guessed the beach was close, but whether he was on an island or the mainland, he couldn't tell.

The youth with the gun had dared him to make a break, but Will had known he was too weak to try to escape. If he were given a few days to recover his strength, things would be different. He decided to pretend to go along with Angel's marriage until an opportunity presented itself.

Where was his ship? Damned if he wouldn't have the hide off someone's back for leaving him here. Even if they'd been unable to turn the *Katherine* in the storm, Aaron should have returned in daylight to continue the search. They couldn't have given up and returned to Charleston without him. If they had . . .

Will bit back an oath. If the *Katherine*'s crew had abandoned him for dead, he'd have to find his own way home. Then it would be "Devil take the hindmost." He'd come back with enough armed men to scour these islands clean of vermin.

Moving had brought back both his headache and the pain from his back and chest injuries. But the dizziness had left him, and his thoughts were clearer.

It was hard to believe that ten days ago he'd been dancing with sweet Julia Hamilton in the finest mansion on Church Street. Or that he'd promised both her and her father that he'd take a crew up the coast and clean out this nest of wreckers in two weeks' time.

"Life is full of surprises," his neighbor Lady Graymoor was wont to remark. He wondered what the old girl would think of this fine kettle of fish.

"Stop where'yar."

The muzzle of a musket poked Will hard in the back, and he winced.

"Angel. Here's yer salvage."

Will heard the creak of hinges.

"I'll take him from here," Angel said.

"Cain't. Cap'n says I gotta chain'm up like I found'm."

"Do it, then, but go easy. If ye set them wounds t'bleedin' again, I'll put the *droch shuil* on ye."

"Ye would, too, ye giddy quean."

"You'll do what to the lad?" Will asked when he was back on the pallet, and they were alone. "What was it you said?"

"The *droch shuil,* the evil eye. Surely, even in Charleston, you've heard of—"

"You said you were no witch."

"I'm not." She laughed and removed his blindfold. "But they don't know that."

He eased himself down on the mattress and stifled a groan. "I don't suppose you'll tell me where I am."

She smiled and shook her head. "In time. But I've gone to a muckle of trouble for you, and ye must pay me back by telling me of outlanders and their ways."

"You've never been away from here?"

"No, not to my rememberin'. But my poppet years are but mist."

"You were born here?"

"Mayhap." She shrugged. "I should be asking you the questions."

"You're not like these others. Why haven't you left this place to see what's out there yourself?"

"I am a child of the sea and sand. I would not flourish on stone streets or amid the babble of crowds of strangers. But I am curious, and I ask that ye buy your freedom with answers to my questions."

"Fair enough."

She brought him more of the foul-tasting tea, and he drank it without protest. "It will help the hurt," Angel said. "Or at least will do you no harm."

She waited until the potion's magic settled over him before drawing the stool close to his bed and sitting on it. "Tomorrow I will take you into the sea. The salt will sting, but it will heal you. You'll be pert as a cricket in no time at all."

Will closed his eyes and took a deep breath as the scent of fresh pine boughs drifted up from beneath him. "You said you had questions. Ask away."

"I will. I will ask until ye bid me be still."

Sleep teased at his consciousness, and he licked his lips. "Could I have water?"

"Aye. As much as you like. You have fever, and water will drown it."

"Better that than me." He drank the contents of her

dipper. The water was cool and sweet, and it soothed his raw throat. He nodded his thanks.

"I know you have a grudge against me. But I did what I had to do. The Brethren follow their law, and 'twas the only way I could think of to save you."

"Gentlefolk that your Brethren are."

"Dyce and his like are changin' our ways. And Cap'n is no longer strong enough to stand agin them." She brushed a lock of hair off his forehead, and the touch of her hand was soothing.

"You know I can't stay here, Angel."

She nodded. "Aye, but whilst you do, you belong to me." She nibbled at her lower lip and sighed. "Does your heart yearn for someone? A woman?"

"In Charleston, you mean?"

"You said you were not married. But have you a love, someone you wanted to ask to wed you?"

"Maybe."

"What is her name?"

"Julia. Julia Hamilton."

"A fine lady with fine manners?"

"The finest.

"With a good heart?"

"Yes."

"Then she will understand, Will Falcon. And she would approve of our handfasting."

"Julia?"

"Aye. For if she is full of caring, she would rather see you wed to me than floating facedown on the tide."

Chapter 6

Sunlight filtered in through the partially opened door. Will blinked, squinted, and closed his eyes as yesterday came flooding back. Without moving, he tried to take stock of his condition. His back and chest were so stiff and sore that he felt the knitting wounds with each breath. But his thought processes were clear, and he felt strength returning to his muscles.

He'd slept most of the night, his light drowsing interrupted with frequent, often disturbing dreams. He remembered, or thought he remembered, seeing Angel undressing, the curves of her sensual body illuminated by the glowing coals in the firepit. Had the vision been real or drug induced? It didn't matter. Her image was burned into his brain; just thinking about her brought a tightening in his loins that had nothing to do with healing flesh.

Will's eyes snapped open, and he looked around the shadowy room. He was alone. The fire was banked, the window still shuttered.

He could smell the sea and the damp, fresh scent of early morning.

A dull ache in his gut told him that he had to piss, but his rigid cod would make that release as difficult as breaking free from the leg manacle. He needed to go outside and find privacy.

Ignoring his injuries, he sat up and tested the chain and iron. Rusty or not, they held firm. He considered his options.

The minutes passed. He could hear gulls, the faint crash of breakers, and the rustle of tree branches. Wherever the Brethren had taken him, he was still on the beach. And where there was water, there would be boats. Give him a craft, any craft, and a sail or a pair of oars, and he would escape. They'd made a mistake when they hadn't killed him. Today, or tomorrow, or the day after that he'd get away. And he'd come back to finish the job he'd started out to do.

As for Angel, she'd risked her life to save his. He'd spare her if he could. But sympathy for her wouldn't stop him from wiping these scoundrels off the face of the map. Too many good men had died to worry about one shapely pirate lass.

A lump rose in his throat, and he swallowed. Shapely? Hell, yes. Angel was more than that. She was perfection, Eve, every man's concept of the ideal woman. But likely she was as ruthless a killer as any other in this nest of rascals.

"Will Falcon."

Angel's greeting jerked him from his reverie.

She came through the open doorway dripping wet, carrying a sea trout on the point of a spear. And for all the decency her linen shift offered, she might as well have been wearing nothing at all.

Will's mouth went dry.

Angel's breasts were high and full, her prominent nipples pressing against the thin cloth. And lower, beneath her curving waist and flat belly, he could just make out the dark shadow of her nether curls.

He barely suppressed a groan as his palms itched to cup her rosy, tight little ass.

"God's grace to ye, Will," she said. "Are you hungry?"

Her face glowed with sunshine and morning dew, but he couldn't tear his gaze away from her breasts. Round and firm as ripe apples, they thrust forward, tipped with hard little nipples that a man would trade his soul to taste.

She laughed merrily. "Did you lose the power of speech in the night?" she teased. "I've brought us a fine fish to break our fast. Have you nothin' at all to say?"

Heat flashed beneath his skin, flooding to settle in his groin, making him rock hard. "God's teeth, woman! Do you make it a habit of walking about stark naked?"

"Naked?" She laughed again. "I'm covered from mound to mound. 'Tis your eyes, sir." And before he could think of a reply, she stripped off the wet shift and dropped a calf-length skirt over her head. "Are all outlanders so—"

"Damn you, woman! Have you no modesty at all?" He felt foolish, lying chained to a post, his cock's blood pulsing for this teasing flame-haired doxy who . . .

"I am as the Lord made me," she answered, clearly puzzled by his question. "Should I be ashamed of what I cannot change?"

He blinked again, confused. He'd had his share of trollops who had little qualms about showing off the merchandise, but Angel's demeanor was different. She seemed not to know what effect her nakedness had on him.

"Customs here must be different," he said, glad for the rough coverlet that hid his full arousal. "In Charleston, no lady would—"

"Wives and husbands keep themselves covered?"

"Not all the time. But there is a time and place for . . ." He broke off, feeling tongue-tied. Lord knew he was no saint. Under different circumstances, he'd have jumped at the chance to sample her wares.

She sniffed, an amused sound that spoke more eloquently than words. "I was fishing. What fool would wear good cloth in salt water?"

"Fishing."

"Aye, spear fishing." She wiggled her prize. "Are you feverish?" She came close and laid a cool palm on his forehead. "Nay, you—"

He brushed her hand away. "You didn't consider yourself my wife when you pulled me out of the ocean yesterday morning."

Angel shrugged. "Should we both have drowned because I wished to swim in storm seas in skirts?" She removed the fish from the fire-blackened point of the spear. "I'll clean this and—"

A man's form blocked the doorway. "How fares your man?" the captain asked. "Do his wounds fester?"

"Come in and see for yourself," Angel said. "I have fresh fish. Will ye break your—"

Cap'n shook his head. "Some mutter against your stranger." He glanced down. "Have ye strength to walk?"

"I do," Will said. "If you'll loose this leg iron."

The older man's eyes narrowed. "I've a mind to send ye both to *Huskanaw* for a moon's passing to let the others get used to the idea of him bein' one of us. Be ye willin'?"

"Aye," Angel agreed. " 'Tis best."

"What—" Will began, but she silenced him with a finger to her lips.

"Trust me," she said. "T'will be better for us both on Huskanaw Isle."

By moon's rise Angel carried ashore the last bundle of necessities she had brought from the main settlement and turned to wave at Bett and the others as the sloop pulled anchor. Canvas, fishing gear, salt, and two baskets of personal belongings were heaped just above the tidemark. Her husband, still blindfolded and with bound wrists and ankles, lay on the sand just beyond. He had not uttered a word since they'd boarded the boat.

"Be well," Bett called to her.

"And you!" Angel watched as Nehemiah caught the wind and the sail billowed. The familiar figures grew smaller. Hugging herself, she walked back to where Will lay, and knelt beside him.

A half hour passed before Will spoke.

"What the hell is going on?"

A shiver rippled through her, but she smiled in spite of it. This outlander terrified her, but whatever came of knowing him, she guessed she would learn much of the world beyond her horizon.

"Angel." His tone was harsh.

She wondered if she'd made a mistake, if she should have left Huskanaw with the sloop. She had lived with hard men all her life, but in Will she sensed a strength, a sheer maleness that she had not seen before.

Will strained at the ropes. "Let me go, damn it."

She took a deep breath and pulled away his blindfold. He continued to swear as she started on the knots. "Hold still," she said. "You make it harder by wigglin'."

"Now what? Am I to be pierced with spears? Burned at the stake?"

She shook her head. "Nay. You will remain here for the space of a moon's cycle."

"Why?" Wrists free, he tore at his ankle bonds.

"You do not understand? It is our honeymoon."

He got to his feet and heaved the rope away. Standing

upright, he was taller and broader than he'd seemed in her house. His hands were strong enough to choke the life from her; his lean, muscular legs . . . his powerful thighs . . . would surely outrun hers.

Alone on Huskanaw, she was surely at his mercy.

The thought churned in her head as she backed a few steps away, not certain as to how to deal with his anger.

"Another island?"

"Aye. 'Tis Huskanaw."

"I've not seen the name on any map."

"Nay. 'Tis not likely. None live here but wild things. A herd of horses . . . deer . . . foxes and rabbits. Huskanaw is far from ships' routes and too distant from the mainland to swim ashore. There are bad currents, and some say sharks."

"So I'm to be marooned with you?"

"Not marooned. The Brethren will come for us in a month."

Without warning, his fingers closed around her upper arms, and he yanked her against his chest. "We're alone here?"

Fear turned her blood to ice. She forced herself to meet those deep blue eyes. "Aye," she murmured. Her heart was racing, and her head felt mazy.

"You're not afraid to be here with me?"

She wanted to tell him no, that she was no coward, but it wasn't true. She was afraid, more afraid than she'd ever been.

"The tables are turned. You're mine to do with as I please."

"Not if you value your life, outlander." She was trembling from head to foot, but she stiffened her spine and raised her chin defiantly. "Can you find fresh water in the sandy soil? Feed yourself? Build shelter? Make a fire to cook your food?"

"Can you?"

"Aye." She knew if she butted him hard in the chin, or punched the knife wound on his chest, even kicked him hard in the kneecap, she could break away from him. But she didn't want to cause him pain, and she didn't wish to make him even angrier. "I am not your enemy," she whispered. "Have I done aught to harm you?"

He lowered his head. For a second, their lips were almost touching, and she had the craziest notion that he might kiss her. Instead, he thrust her roughly away.

"No more ropes," he said. "And keep your clothes on around me, or I'll not be responsible for what happens."

She shook her head. "No more ropes. 'Twas only that Cap'n wished you not to know where our settlement lies or in what direction we sailed to reach Huskanaw."

"South. And east."

He was right, but she wouldn't give him the satisfaction of saying so. "We should move our things farther up, into the dunes. I've some food in that basket, but it might be cold before morning. I should gather wood for a fire."

"You know I'll escape the first chance I get."

She nodded, fighting for time to regain her senses. "I ken—I mean that I understand," she corrected. "And I'll not try to stop you. But that chance will not be tonight or tomorrow. Can we not be friends for now?"

"You claim to be my wife. That makes us rather more, wouldn't you say?"

She picked up the basket, holding it as a barrier between them. "Mayhap," she said. "But I be no halterless mare to be run down and mounted with a few bites and a kick or two. I will come to your bed on my own or not at all."

"Do you take me for a rapist? You're the one flaunting your naked body."

"If I thought you a scoundrel, you'd not be standing here drawing breath. I but warn you. You have seen that I know well what end of a knife cuts bait."

"Is that a threat?"

"No threat, but a promise." She motioned toward the remaining supplies. "If you would sleep warm this night, you can help set up camp." She turned her face away, not wanting him to see the flush in her cheeks.

His accusation shamed her. It was clear that he did not understand Brethren ways or that of the free folk. He thought her a slut. Pride would not let her say that she had never lain with a man or that her maidenhead was as untouched as that of a holy nun.

He glanced back at the ocean. "They won't be back tonight?"

"I told ye. Not for a month. It be the custom among the Brethren that a man and woman have time alone to come to an agreement between them."

"And after that?"

"After that, ye will be one of us."

"And I'll be expected to murder and rob with the best of them?"

"Mayhap ye should have stayed in Charleston."

"I came for your Brethren, Angel," he said as he picked up the rest of her things. "And whether I make it back to Charleston alive or not, others will do the same. The penalty for piracy is death. Your lawless band will end by sword and black powder or by rope."

"Blather on," she said. "Have you forgotten that only minutes ago you were fettered like a fattened shoat bound for market? The Brethren have roamed these islands for a hundred year and more. Finding them is like finding a pearl in an oyster, and catching them . . ." she scoffed. "A will-o'-the-wisp leaves more tracks than Cap'n."

Shoulders rigid, she stalked away. He was trouble, this stranger that she had taken to husband, and she hoped mightily that she wouldn't live to regret her action.

She didn't doubt that he would gladly see Bett and Nehemiah and the others dangling from a gibbet. Her as well, she supposed. Pudding-headed, Will was, for all his fine looks. Like most mainlanders, he believed the worst about the Brethren and their livelihood.

Dyce was scum, and Tom little better. But they had not grown up among the Brethren as she had. She could not, would not believe that Cap'n would sanction piracy and murder. And if he could get rid of Dyce's bunch, things would be as they always had been.

Ships sank, and someone may as well make use of what goods washed up on the beaches. Bett said that wrecking was an ancient and honorable trade, that her folk had followed the practice in Cornwall.

Underbrush tangled around Angel's ankles, and she kilted up her skirts and forged on into the beach plum and stunted pines. She'd not been on Huskanaw in two years, but her sense of direction was good. She wanted to make camp near freshwater, and she thought she could find the low spot, even in the dark.

"Do you have any idea where you're going?" Will called after they'd walked far enough that she could no longer hear the surf.

"No one asked you to follow." She let go of a branch and it swished back, producing a satisfactory smack.

"Ouch, damn it. Watch what you're doing."

"Aye, sir, I will." Off to her left, she heard the rustling

of a small creature. Clouds had passed over the moon, and she had to slow her pace so that Will was only a few steps behind her.

The breeze was from the sea, strong enough to keep away mosquitoes. She was glad of that. There were precautions a body could take from biting insects, but tonight she need not worry about them.

Being an island, Huskanaw was safe. Since she was a child, she'd liked to roam isolated beaches and forests. On the mainland were swamp bears and wild dogs. Here she need fear nothing but humans, so why was she so filled with unease and doubt?

Abruptly, the clouds parted, and moonlight dusted the trees and bushes with shimmering silver. Just ahead she glimpsed the lightning-scarred pine she'd been searching for. She angled right, went another few hundred yards, and set down her basket in a small clearing.

"Why here?" Will asked.

"Would you drink salt water?"

With swift efficiency, she brushed aside ground litter until she had a space of clean sand, gathered pine needles and twigs, and used flint and steel to strike a flame. She bent low and blew on the sparks, tenderly feeding the young fire until it grew in strength. "If you'll tend this, I'll fetch water," she said.

Dumping the items in her basket, she removed a big clamshell and a drinking gourd. She replaced the shell and the gourd in the container and carried all three a few yards away. She felt in the darkness for two lengths of log, pushed them away, and began to dig a hole.

She'd not gone more than eighteen inches down when the sand turned damp. She kept digging until she had a space deep and wide enough to hold the basket. She waited, and within a few minutes clean water had seeped into the artificial pool. She filled the gourd and returned to the fire. "Thirsty?" she asked, handing him the dipper.

"Yes." He took it from her and drank. "You're right," he said, when he was satisfied. "We're in this together. There's no need for me to blame you."

"Or I you. Ye have your ways, as I have mine. I ask only that you do not judge me without reason."

"Fair enough," he agreed.

"Shall we make a peace between us?" Her skin prickled with anticipation. Of what, she didn't know. She wanted to bolt, to run far and fast. He'd never catch her. But some force stronger than fear held her motionless.

"Yes."

Moonlight gleamed on his handsome face, and Angel's breath caught in her throat. "A bargain, then," she said huskily. "And to seal it, a kiss of peace." And, pulse racing, she stepped forward, tilted her head, and brushed her lips against his.

Chapter 7

She hadn't known she was going to kiss Will until it was too late to stop. And by then, committed to the action she'd begun, she'd expected that her caress would be swift, a mere touch of her mouth to his.

But nothing in her experience had prepared her for the array of stunning sensations that struck with the ferocity of a lightning bolt.

Or, for Will's reaction . . .

He was honey sweet and as powerful as a storm tide. When his arms closed around her and his lips parted, she was as helpless as a skiff without oars or sail caught in that gale.

Her knees went weak, and intense pleasure spiraled through her, jumbling her thoughts and making her cling to him as the kiss turned from tender hesitation to kindling desire.

Will Falcon was all hard muscle and rigid sinew, and she fitted against him so seamlessly that moonlight could not pass between them.

His male scent filled her head with every breath she drew and she sighed, reveling in the erotic glide of tongue against tongue and lips molded to lips. Shivers of excitement shimmered through her body, blocking out every shred of uncertainty.

Vaguely, she was aware of Will's voice murmuring her

name and his hands moving over her, pressing the curve of her spine . . . running intimately over her bottom. But she didn't care. All she wanted . . . needed . . . was to keep kissing him.

. . . Until Will groaned, breaking the spell. "Angel." Raw emotion rang in his voice.

Shocked, she realized Will's hand was cupping her breast; his fingers teasing her swollen nipple.

"Nay!" Breathless, she pushed away. "I did not mean to let . . ." Tears sprang to her eyes. "I only . . ." The words died in her throat as she raised trembling fingers to her lips. With a cry, she whirled and fled through the darkness.

"Angel! Come back!" Will shouted. When she didn't, he cursed.

Hours passed, and she still didn't return. He'd considered going after her, but knew he'd have little chance of catching her. And right now, he wasn't certain he wanted to.

Whatever she was up to, he couldn't fathom it. She'd come into his arms willingly, had kissed him. . . . He swore and kicked at the roll of blankets he'd carried from the beach. Angel had fired him up, and gotten him so aroused that he couldn't think straight. And then she'd backed off.

He'd been hungry on the walk from the water, but he was too angry to eat now. She was a crazy woman. Worse, she was a tease. He'd seen others like her, but most could be bought with a flash of silver. Somehow, he didn't think that would work with Angel. Whatever she wanted, he didn't think it was money.

She'd forced him into a mock wedding, come alone with him to this island, and let him think that she was willing. He could still taste her . . . still smell the wild, sweet scent of her . . . feel her in his hands.

He swore again and reached down to try to adjust his aching cod. Maybe it had just been too long since he'd been with a woman. Not since the Cuban wench in Savannah on his last voyage. What was her name? He couldn't remember any more than he could remember her face. She'd been clean and eager, and she could hold her liquor.

Out of respect for the Falcon name and position, he'd never sought out a whore in Charleston. Not that Julia or any other properly brought-up lady would have expected her husband to come innocent to her marriage bed. But his father had asked for his word that he'd sow his wild oats in other fields far from his homeport, and he'd never broken a promise to his father yet.

Nor was he about to.

Will bent and tossed another branch on the fire and unrolled a threadbare quilt. He glanced around, picked a spot where there seemed to be a thick mat of leaves, and spread out the blanket.

His father was the main reason he'd found himself in this kettle of fish. He'd vowed on his father's grave to take his revenge on the pirates who'd destroyed Falcon Shipping, and he'd not back away from the task no matter what price he had to pay.

Will sat on the blanket and stared into the fire. In the past two days, he'd given scant thought to his father's death or the loss of the company and most of their family possessions. Money could be won or lost on the turn of a card or a captain's skill, but losing his father had left a black hollowness where Will supposed his heart had once been.

Exhaling softly, he eased himself back on the blanket. Whatever happened here on this island was of little consequence. Even the girl didn't matter. His life, his future, lay in Charleston. And in the end, whether he captained

Hamilton's vessels or his own, it was much the same. So long as he had a good ship under him, he'd be content as any man had reason to expect.

This island girl intrigued him. Hell, he lusted after her body. She'd helped keep him alive, and he'd return the favor if he could. But finding joy in each other's arms was a temporary pleasure. Be damned if he'd lose any sleep over her.

Still, old habits were hard to break. On shipboard, he'd learned to nap lightly. Tonight was no exception.

After several hours, he'd come fully awake when he'd heard a twig snap. He didn't move, just lay there watching beneath lowered lids as a shadow detached itself from the trees and crept toward him.

"If you're cold, you're welcome to a blanket," he said. "But if you've come to pick up where we left off, I'm not interested."

"I'm sorry," Angel said.

"I doubt that." He sat up. "It's late. Whatever excuses you have can wait until morning."

She snatched up a blanket and retreated to the far side of the fire pit. The wood had burned down to glowing embers, but heat still radiated from the coals.

"I wanted to see what it felt like," she said. "What you felt like."

"I told you I didn't want to hear it."

"I didn't know kissing would be like that," she continued. "That I would want—"

"Enough. Go to sleep. I won't touch you. You have my word as a gentleman."

She shook out the blanket and wrapped it around her shoulders. "You're angry with me."

"Damn straight." It was a lie, and he knew it, even as the words spilled out of his mouth. He was angry with himself . . . angry and aching to have her.

"Will, I—"

"One more word out of you, and I'll—"

"I can make a camp someplace else if ye want. Ye don't have to holler at me."

"I'm a patient man. But you're trying that patience. Sleep in a futtering tree, for all I care. But stop talking, and stay over there."

"Aye, Will."

"Good night." He lay back and closed his eyes.

" 'Tis sorry I be to vex ye so, but—"

"What? What is so damned important that you can't hold your tongue until morning? That you'd rather drive me to strangle you before—"

"No need to be so nurly," she replied in a contrite voice. "I know you're tuckered, but was I you, I'd move my blanket."

"And why, Mistress Angel," he snapped. "Why might that be?"

"Because, sir, ye be lyin' on a bed of poison ivy."

Swearing, he shifted his blanket to another spot.

When Will awoke in the morning, the fire had burned out. Angel was gone again, and he was alone in the camp. He rose, studied the suspicious flattened foliage a few feet away, and inspected his exposed skin for any sign of a rash.

"Poison ivy," he muttered. She must have taken him for a fool to settle down in a bed of the stuff. He wasn't completely ignorant. As a boy, he'd spent hours roaming the fields and woods around Charleston, and he'd suffered from several bouts of severe ivy poisoning. He simply hadn't noticed the stuff in the darkness, and he wondered how it was that Angel had.

Maybe she wasn't human. Or maybe he hadn't been swept off the *Katherine* in that storm. Perhaps he'd fallen in his efforts to save Isaiah, struck his head on the deck, and this was all a bad dream.

The theory was a good one, except for the wounds on his back and chest. He couldn't remember any dreams where he'd awakened in the morning with chunks missing from his anatomy and wearing bandages and smelly poultices.

No, this was worse than a nightmare. He hadn't dreamed Angel or the Brethren or this God-forsaken island. It was all too real.

Gingerly, he removed the strips of linen around his chest and scraped off Angel's potion. To his surprise, Dyce's knife wound seemed to be healing nicely without infection. When he flexed his muscles, the crooked stitches pulled at the edges of the cut, but the gash was neither red nor swollen. He hoped his back was doing as well.

He rolled up the blanket and laid it next to Angel's. Then he helped himself to the piece of corn bread nestled in a wooden bowl and drank the rest of the water in the gourd.

When half an hour had passed without her appearing, Will decided to look for her. His first thought was to return to the beach where the wreckers had put them ashore. With a final glance around, he took his directions from the sun, and set out east.

The game path was narrow and twisting, but occasional heel marks and broken grass stems kept him on the trail, first through the sparse pine forest, and then over and between the dunes until he reached the shoreline.

He smelled and heard the ocean before he saw it. The rhythmic ebb and flow of waves and the cry of seabirds were comforting. His father had accused him of having salt water in his veins, and he supposed he did. Nothing cheered him like the feel of a sea breeze on his face.

The tide was low, the broad beach littered with shells and pieces of driftwood. He didn't see Angel anywhere, but he found her discarded clothing on the sand. Skirt, bodice, and shift lay neatly folded on the sand beside a fish spear; and dainty prints of high-arched bare feet led to the water's edge.

He scanned the water, expecting to see her. When he didn't, he looked up and down the strand before calling her name. When there was no answer, an uneasy feeling settled over him.

A shrieking gull hovered over the waves. But other than a scuttling crab and a pair of ducks winging high above, Will saw no living creature.

Fear twisted in his gut. The tide was receding. The sand was wet and smooth except for the single set of footprints. If she'd gone in here, she should have come out. . . .

"Angel!" If she was playing some trick on him . . . "Angel!"

Nothing.

Suddenly, just beyond the breakers, he saw a large creature break the surface and rise out of the water. A second shape loomed up, and then a third.

Dolphins.

As he watched, one leaped into the air, followed by another and then two more. Then a red-gold head bobbed up in the waves where he'd first seen the dolphins.

"Will!"

He let out a pent-up breath and felt relief wash over him. "What the hell are you doing out there?"

Angel waved. "Come on in!" A sleek form appeared beside her, dark beside her pale body.

Will stiffened. The dolphin dwarfed her. They were reputed to be friendly to people, but one bite of those razor-sharp teeth could take off a hand or—

She reached out and stroked the animal. It uttered a squeak and vanished in a spray of water. Angel laughed. "Don't be afraid, come on!"

"I've had swimming enough to last me. You come out."

"Nay! They won't hurt you!" She laughed and plunged under, giving him a brief but tantalizing glimpse of luscious unclad buttocks.

Dolphins be damned! Will tore off his boots and clothing, waded out until the tumbling breakers reached his chest, and began to swim toward her. The salt water was cool and stinging on his back and chest, but he didn't care. She drew him like north pulls the needle of a compass.

Angel waited, treading water, until he'd almost reached her before she ducked under. He swam to where he'd seen her last and followed her down. The water was clear and blue-green. He could make out the bottom, but saw no trace of her.

When he came up for air, she was laughing at him. She splashed water at him and dove again. He went after her, bewitched by her lithe, graceful movements and the long red hair streaming behind her like coppery seaweed.

Midway between the surface and the sand, she let him catch her around the waist. Her arms encircled his neck, and her bare breasts pressed against his chest.

His lungs ached for air, and he kicked upward, carrying them both. But when she twisted away, he couldn't hold her, and she surfaced just out of arm's reach.

He took a deep breath and reached for her. She splashed him again and retreated, laughing. "You are crazy," he said.

"Nay, I'm the only one sane."

"Swimming with dolphins."

"I like dolphins." She flashed him a glorious smile. "Ye frightened them away. I don't think they like outlanders."

Will's heart hammered against his chest wall. She was a mermaid, too beautiful to be real. Her eyes were as green as emeralds; her thick, dark lashes glistened with diamond-like drops of water. Specks of sea foam clung to one bare shoulder and frosted the tops of her breasts.

"There were six of them," she said. "Two were young ones." She paddled out a few yards. Her skin was a golden-peach, sprinkled with a few tiny freckles, her neck as slender and shapely as that he'd once seen on a statue of Diana in the governor's mansion.

"I couldn't find you. I saw your clothes on the beach."

She smiled shyly at him. "You worried about me?"

He didn't answer.

She laughed. "I don't know what was the finest sight. Those lovely beasties or you, as naked as God made you."

He took several strokes toward her. "Last night—"

"You were right to be vexed with me. But this being a wife is new to me."

"For the last time, woman, I'm not your husband."

"You agreed there would be peace between us," she reminded him.

"I did that, but I didn't agree to marry you. I'm used to being skipper of a ship, commanding men, not taking orders from a woman."

"So I see."

"If you're looking for a soft bunk, there's many a man would gladly have you."

"I displease you?"

He paddled toward her, and once again she backed off. "Angel . . . you're a beautiful woman, but you don't want me, nor I you. When I take a wife—if I take a wife—she'll be of my choosing. I'm not a fish to be hooked and hauled in."

She laughed and then became serious. "A handfasting is not forever, Will. Can you not play at being my husband for a few weeks . . . a few months at most?"

"No, I can't. And I don't know why you want me. If it's money, I haven't got any. My family house was sold on the auction block, and I'm deeply in debt. Hell, the sheriff's probably sold off my wardrobe to pay my creditors."

" 'Tis not money I want."

"What then?"

"I told ye . . . I mean *you*," she corrected herself. " 'Tis fair hard to learn a new way of speakin'." She sighed. "I know I'm ignorant, but I've no wish to stay that way. I want to know about your world. I want to see in my mind's eye the sailing ships and the far-off ports. I want to hear about Charleston and London and all those places."

"You want me to take you with me when I leave."

She shook her head. "These islands are my home. I'd be as out of place in your world as you be in mine. All I want from you be answers to my questions."

"And if I tell you, what do I get in return?"

"Whatever you wish, husband. Whatever you wish."

Chapter 8

Will's stomach clenched. They might not speak the same language, but there was no mistaking Angel's offer. Despite what had happened last night when they'd kissed, he knew that he could have her—all of her—whenever he wanted. She was his to do with as he pleased.

He could cup and fondle Angel's satin breasts, tease and suck her sweet little nipples, explore the curves of those delicious buttocks, and nibble every inch of her alluring body.

Sweat broke out on his forehead. Cool ocean water or not, just imagining the delights of parting those long legs and sheathing himself to the hilt in her soft, wet folds made him rock-hard and throbbing with need.

All he had to do was reach out. Carry her up to the beach and throw her down on the warm sand, or do it here. A thrill of anticipation bubbled up in his chest. He could do it, make love to her here in the rushing tide and breaking surf.

A black-haired Carabee girl had taught him that trick on the night of his sixteenth birthday. He'd been so drunk that he could barely walk, but he'd never forgotten the sheer intensity of that encounter. Those erotic sensations could happen again with Angel, if he wanted it.

The trouble was, the price for Angel's taking was too high.

He had no illusions about her virginity. No woman who lived among pirates could remain intact past her first bleeding. He didn't know or care how many men she'd lain with. It wasn't his right to ask or fault her for what she'd had to do to survive.

But regardless of her past, he could not escape the realization that she was an innocent. Angel didn't understand the rules he lived by. She was neither a whore nor a woman he could take home to Church Street and introduce to his friends and relatives.

A southern gentleman, a South Carolinian, a son of Nicholas Falcon, was careful where and how he took his pleasure. A trollop could be paid with silver; a man could dally with a jade, each taking joy from the moment and neither expecting anything more than a good-natured parting in the light of day. But a gentlewoman, a lady, must be protected, cared for, and honored.

When he chose a wife, if he ever did, she would be someone of his own kind. Cultured, born of an old, respected Charleston or Savannah family, she would be quality in the truest sense.

If his future bride was an heiress, so much the better, but she must possess grace, education, piety, and sterling character. Falcon women were above reproach, fit mothers for any children the Almighty might be pleased to send. Falcon wives were worthy to be introduced at the governor's palace.

Angel was not a wench he could buy off with a few coins or a silken petticoat, and she was not a woman he could consider as a partner. Taking advantage of her naïveté for his own lust, or even hers, would be an unforgivable breach of his code. Some men did use unfortunate females that way, but to his mind, they were not and never could be called gentlemen.

As much as he hungered for Angel's body, he could

not take what she was offering and live with himself. "Shit," he muttered.

"What's wrong?" Angel asked, swimming closer.

Without answering, damning his own stupidity, Will turned and swam toward shore.

"I don't understand," Angel said later as they shared a breakfast of grilled red drum and raw clams back at their campsite. "Even though we're handfasted, married according to old custom, you say you can't lay with me because I'm not a whore?"

"That's not what I said," he insisted.

She shrugged. "Trull. Trug-moldy. Draggle-tail. All are insults men fling at a poor wench who trades her favors for a living." Licking the final delicious drop of juice from the clamshell, Angel sent it spinning into a garbage pit she'd dug in the sand.

She wore a rough skirt of sailcloth that fell just below her knees, and a green linen bodice. Bare-legged and barefooted, she settled onto a fallen log well away from the small outcrop of poison ivy to enjoy her portion of the still-warm fish.

"A lady shouldn't know such words, let alone speak them," he scolded.

She laughed and fixed him with a shrewd stare. "Will Falcon. Ye are such a liar. You don't think me a gentlewoman. To you, I'm but a merry-begotten island wench."

"Merry-begotten? Speak the King's English, for God's sake."

"Briar-patch child. A bastard."

He scowled at her so fiercely that she laughed again. "Charleston must be a grand place that men hold themselves so high to tell their women how to speak." She retrieved another clam, this one no bigger than Will's thumbnail, opened it with her knife, and offered it to him.

He shook his head. "It's not personal, and you shouldn't feel offended that I can't—"

She popped the tiny clam into her mouth and chewed slowly, savoring the salty flavor. "Am I as ugly as a mud dauber?" she asked him.

"Hell, no. It's not that."

"Then what? What is it about my naked body that offends you?" It was strange that she was not the least afraid of him today, when last night she had fled his heated kisses as though the haints of hell were on her heels. "I can tell you that I find no fault with you beneath your shirt and breeches."

His face flushed red beneath the shadow of his dark beard. "I'm used to seeing women with their clothes on."

"They wear dresses when they swim?"

"Charleston ladies don't go into the water."

She found that funniest of all. "More pity if it's true," she said as she covered the pit full of clamshells and fish bones, then dusted the sand off her hands. "Proves that I could never go to such an outlandish place. I'd soon stop breathin' as stop swimming."

Will got to his feet. She could tell by the way he moved that he was still hurting, but he was on the mend. She'd gotten him into the salt water, and that was the best thing for a wound.

Old Sisi had taught her that when she was ten and had cut her foot on a clamshell. When the injury had festered until her foot swelled, Bett had taken her to Sisi's cabin back in the swamp on the mainland. Folks said that the African woman was a runaway slave and a witch. Mayhap she was. But Sisi had taught her more about healing than anybody else in her whole life. Sisi had claimed that salt water was good for the poison ivy, too. And if those red blotches on Will's forearm rose to blisters, he'd have to do a lot more swimming, lessen he wanted to suffer a powerful itch.

Will took his shirt off a branch and eased it on. "I want to explore this island," he said, "unless you have objections."

She smiled at him. "If I did?"

"I'd do it, anyway."

"Nothin' much to see. But suit yourself. You can walk around it in a day, long as you don't founder in the low spots. There's a freshwater pond near the south end. You'll likely see a few horses there, and maybe a deer."

"You'll be all right here alone?"

She nodded. "I thought to hunt for some bird eggs and maybe catch a few crabs for supper. If you get lost, follow the beach. You'll come to the place where we landed." She'd hoped they could sit and talk awhile. She had so much she wanted to ask him, and just looking at Will gave her a curious fluttering feeling in the pit of her belly. But she reckoned he was restless and still out of sorts with her. Will would be easier to handle once he'd walked a few miles and cooled the fire in his bowels.

An hour later, Will stood on the beach and looked out to sea. He'd guessed that he was a half mile or less south of the place where he and Angel had landed. He was thirsty, and would be thirstier yet by the time he returned to camp. If he hadn't been so damned determined to prove that Angel couldn't stop him from leaving, he would have brought water with him.

Worse, he was sweating, and the rash on his arm was itching. Tugging off his boots and stockings, he waded into the surf and eased his discomfort in the salt water.

A flock of red knots landed on the wet sand. He'd heard they were good eating, but without a gun he wasn't likely to find out for himself.

He didn't suppose that he and Angel would starve, but subsisting on a diet of fish and clams for a month would definitely have its drawbacks. Not that he was hungry; food was the least of his worries.

It was the woman he couldn't get off his mind. She was infuriating . . . yet she drew him like deep water draws an old sailor. He'd never met a wench to match her, not in voluptuousness, or in that sexual appeal that a man can't find words to explain—a raw feminine essence that caused his palms to sweat, his chest to tighten, and his sack to feel full and heavy.

A movement farther down the beach caught Will's eye, and he turned to see three shaggy ponies break from the dunes to trot along the water's edge. One was spotted, another white as sea foam, and the third, a chestnut foal that leaped into the spray with playful abandon.

"A pretty sight, aren't they? I told you you might see horses."

He snapped around as her honey-soft voice came from behind him. Frowning, he said, "Angel?"

He started to ask how she'd found him, but bit back the question before making even more of a fool of himself. It was obvious she'd followed him through the woods without him knowing she was there. "Keeping guard over the prisoner?" he asked.

She giggled. The sound didn't come out high and foolish as a girl's might. Instead, her rich laughter flowed over him like good whiskey, making his chest tight and an odd prickling sensation run down his spine.

Amusement danced in her green eyes. "You're free to go, Will. I know you're planning to get as far from me and this island as you can."

He scowled. "Without a boat? Where do you expect me to go?"

The stroll through the tangle of the island's interior

obviously hadn't fazed her a bit. There wasn't a drop of sweat on her face, and other than a few pine needles caught in her thick, glossy braid, she looked as though she'd been resting in the shade.

He tried to tell himself that he wanted to get away from her, but nothing could quell the rush of excitement he felt on seeing her.

This boyish infatuation troubled him. He liked women, liked talking to them, watching them. Age or race didn't matter; since he was a boy, he'd felt both protective and intrigued by them. Hell, one of his best friends was Lizzy Graymoor. And she was what? In her seventies? But Lizzy aside, he'd not lost his heart, ass over head and blind-staggering, to a woman since he'd been twenty and found out the object of his desires was already married.

Too bad the Lady Elizabeth Graymoor was too old for him. They'd be a perfect match. Lizzy never complained when he went to sea, and she welcomed him with open arms whenever he returned. Lizzy was worldly, elegant, wise, and rich. And in her day, he was certain she'd caused heads to turn at King George's court. "Maybe she'd still have me," he said only half aloud.

"Who will have you?" Angel demanded. She moved closer, looked up at him through thick lashes, and moistened her bottom lip with the tip of her tongue. "For sure, fever's come over you, if you're starting to talk to yourself."

He'd been wrong, he realized, as desire stabbed through him. She had worked up a sweat. Just above the neckline of her bodice, in the hollow between her breasts, Angel's dewy peach-gold skin shimmered with a damp sheen.

He wondered if she would taste of salt. . . .

"Not quamished are you?"

"Quamished?"

"Sick in your gut. I vow, you're fish-belly pale."

"Damn it, woman," he snapped, "quit fussing over me like a wife. I'm not feverish. All I want is to get off this God-forsaken island."

Angel dropped to the sand, crossed one leg over her knee, and inspected the sole of her left foot. "Thought so," she murmured. "Picked up a prickle." She drew her knife from the sheath at her waist and used the blade to remove the thorn. "There, got it." She sheathed the weapon and patted the ground beside her. "Sit, Will."

He considered for a moment, then settled beside her.

"You were deep in thought when I slipped up on you."

She flashed him a smile, and he noticed again how perfectly spaced and white her small teeth were.

"Musing on your lady, weren't you?"

He nodded. "A great lady, but old enough to be my grandmother. She's my neighbor . . . and friend. Lady Elizabeth Graymoor."

"Gentry?"

"More than that. Lady Graymoor is an English noblewoman, widow of an earl."

"And you know her? You've been in her house?"

"More times than I can count, and Lizzy in mine. She's a dear soul, and I think she would find you intriguing."

Angel made a small sound of derision. "Aye, she'd that. Very intrigued she'd be with the likes of me."

"I'm serious. And you'd like her. She's a great storyteller and a talented painter. She gives the best parties on Church Street. Even the governor and his lady come when they're in town."

"In Charleston."

"Yes. She still has vast estates in England, but she's lived in Charleston for many years."

"Ye must tell me everything about her, of her house and yours, and of these great parties. Has she a coach and four white horses to pull them? And does she dress in silk and wear pearls in her hair?"

He laughed. "As a matter of fact, she does wear silk and pearls. Lizzy is the soul of fashion and a fantastic dancer."

"And the coach? Is it all aglitter with gold and silver wheels and—"

"Lizzy has a fine carriage and a team of black horses to pull it, but I've not noticed any golden wheels."

Angel sighed. "Bett said the coaches in London are all golden, and I thought that . . ." She took a deep breath. "Does the lady have music at her parties and candles by the dozen?"

"Hundreds." Will grinned at her. "Lizzy has not only candles and a coach, but spaniels, a pack of them, all bathed and beribboned like spoiled children. And a parrot that sings."

"Fie on you, Will Falcon, to take me for a cod's head. Surely, you're telling me lies." She scrambled up and began running away from him down the sand.

"Wait!" he called. "I wasn't . . . Angel!" He got up and ran after her, startling the horses and sending them galloping into the thicket.

Angel sprinted along the hard-packed sand at the water's edge, her coppery braid bouncing against her back and streaming out behind her. She was fast, and his healing injuries had left him in less than prime condition. But once he'd set his mind on catching her, his longer legs began to close the distance between them.

"Angel!" he shouted. A cramp stitched through his side, but every step took him closer.

She glanced back over her shoulder, saw how near he was, and veered into the waves.

"Why are you . . ." He broke off when she whirled to face him, and he saw tears glistening on her cheeks. His annoyance faded, and he stopped a few arms' lengths away.

"I've never seen it," she said all in a rush, shouting above the crash of the surf. "Not the houses, nor coaches, nor golden streets. I'm naught but an ignorant wrecker's wench with salt water in my veins, but that gives you no right to poke fun at me. It was all I asked of you, that you tell me—"

The tears were his undoing.

He splashed through the incoming wave and seized Angel by the shoulders. She struggled, but he held her and gathered her close against him while water drenched him nearly to the waist. "I didn't mean to laugh at you," he said.

Trembling, she raised her head and looked full into his eyes. For an instant, he thought she would kiss him again, and he bent to meet her mouth, but she turned her face away.

"Is it wrong, to want to know what's out there?"

"No, Angel, it's not." He kissed the crown of her head, marveling at her wild, clean scent and the heady sensation of holding her in his arms.

She gave a small ragged cry, deep in her throat, and need thundered through him. He caught her chin in his hand, lifted it, and seared her mouth with his.

Chapter 9

She yielded to him. Her lips softened and parted. She struggled in his embrace, not to escape, but to get closer. He could feel every curve and swell of her body pressed to his, and need pulsed in his groin.

"Angel . . . Angel." He groaned as desire ignited into a flame that roared through his veins, searing through bone and sinew, destroying reason, making him forget who he was and where. "Sweet . . . sweet Angel," he murmured.

He'd never tasted anything so perfect as her mouth, and he couldn't get enough of kissing her. He couldn't remember ever being so excited by a woman's scent or the feel of her skin.

Angel's thick lashes fluttered. Her throat flushed, and she gasped for breath. Her lower lip quivered as she gazed wide-eyed and questioning into his eyes.

Her total vulnerability struck him with gale force, and he shuddered with emotion. Her head tilted back, exposing the creamy expanse of her throat.

"Angel," he whispered thickly.

Cradling the nape of her neck with a trembling hand, he brushed his lips against the sensitive spot beneath her ear, her eyelids, and the dimple on her left cheek. Angel's skin was soft and inviting . . . as sweet on his tongue as warm peach honey.

She writhed against him. Her fingers stroked his face, threaded through his hair, and clung to his shoulders. She murmured his name, drawing it out in her soft, almost musical way.

He nibbled the hollow in her neck, rasping his tongue over the delicate skin, thrilling to the quick, hot pulse of her blood just beneath the skin.

Angel made small impatient sounds and strained to find his mouth with hers. And when she did, she caught his lower lip between her teeth, gently nipping and sucking at the sensitive flesh until he thought he would go mad with the joy of it.

"Vixen." He groaned, fighting release. Her teasing caress was a spark to gunpowder. Blood thundered in his loins; his rod ached with wanting her.

But he wasn't ready for this storm of sensations to end. Hungrily, he plundered the velvet cavern of her mouth, thrusting deep with his tongue, claiming what she offered, while his hands sought the swell of her lush breasts.

She sobbed with pleasure as he filled his palm with her soft flesh, and her cry whipped his lust to frenzy. He could control himself no longer. Ripping the thin cloth, he lowered his head and drew the swollen nipple between his lips.

"Mother of God," Angel whispered. She arched her back and encircled his neck with her arms as she pressed against his leg and thigh. He felt her nails cut into his skin, but he found the slight pain exciting. He suckled greedily at her breast, reveling in her soft moans of pleasure while he fumbled with her skirt, trying to remove every obstacle between them.

Without warning, a powerful wave larger than the others surged around them, knocking them both off balance. He and Angel went down in a tangle of arms

and legs and swirling water. Will swallowed a mouthful
and came up sputtering for breath. "Are you all right?"
He gasped and choked, spitting out ocean. "Angel?"

Laughing, she lay on her back in the shallows, foaming water buoying her up. Her red-gold hair hung
around her face like a veil, revealing only her haunting
green eyes. Her scrap of a skirt rode high on her tanned
thighs; her thin bodice hung in shreds, so that both rosy
breasts were exposed by the receding waves.

"All right?" She giggled merrily. "Had I known that
bump and tickle was so gaysome, mayhap I would have
tried it sooner."

Will wiped the stinging salt water out of his eyes and
tried to think with his head instead of his mast. "Best
you cover your . . ." He gestured toward her, feeling
suddenly fifteen and foolish. "I'm but human, Angel.
And the sight of your breasts is enough to . . ." He exhaled between clenched teeth, wishing mightily that he
was a man with less scruples or that the taste of those
taunt pink nipples didn't linger on his tongue. "I'm
afraid . . . *that* . . . was unwise," he stumbled. "Considering our circumstances."

Her green eyes clouded. She got up slowly and tugged
at her ruined garment. "Did I do something wrong?"
she asked him.

"Hell, no." He balled his hands into tight fists. "It
was . . ." He shook his head. "You don't understand,
and the fault is all mine."

Her full lower lip protruded in a delicate pout, and it
was all he could do to keep from kissing her mouth
again and again. The dip in the sea had eased his discomfort, but it would take only seconds to pitch him
headlong into full arousal. He tried to think of something disgusting—maggots, even rotting fish. But the

very available, very desirable woman before him was all too real.

"I don't kiss like those fine ladies in Charleston, do I?"

He shook his head.

"I reckoned that was it." She covered her face with her palms. When she took her hands away, confusion and hurt filled her eyes. "You think me a trull," she declared hotly. For a minute, he thought she would burst into tears.

"It's not . . . ," he began. He felt clumsy, foolish and, because of it, he snapped at her. "I don't know what to do with you."

"Ye . . . you cannot see me as your handfast wife, can you?"

"No. That ceremony was a sham."

She grimaced. "Blast me if you're not the oddest man I've ever laid eyes on." She yanked her skirt down. Wet, it clung to her body like a second skin.

Will felt the back of his neck sizzle with heat. "I've not got the sailor's curse, if that's what you think. I'm a man who likes women."

"So you say."

"Careful," he warned. "You're treading on thin ice."

She sniffed in disbelief. "Are all gentry like you?"

He shook his head again. "No, definitely not." He made for the beach, heading north. How the blazes could he explain it to her when he didn't understand it himself? The need for her throbbed like an abscessed tooth. But he was a man of reason. Since he'd reached his majority, he'd rarely done anything rash—other than go into the ocean to rescue a dead man.

The Falcon family had survived and prospered amid war, floods, and political upheaval because they had acted rationally. Maybe that's why his father's death had come as such a shock. Nicholas Falcon had charted a course in life and never veered from it . . . until the night he'd put a pistol to his head and pulled the trigger.

That had been his father's single act of stupidity. And since he, Will, had already used up his single witless voucher in trying to save Isaiah, it was clear that now he had to be prudent with Angel.

"Will! Wait!"

He walked on, but she soon caught up with him. He glanced at her, then wordlessly removed his shirt and handed it to her. She shrugged and put it on.

"It's the woman in Charleston, isn't it? You do love her."

"Leave it," he answered roughly. He started walking again, and she kept pace.

"You despise me."

"I don't despise you. I simply don't want . . ." He was lying through his teeth again. Hell, yes, he wanted to do it with her, here and now, on this glorious beach. But he refused to be a slave to his cod. "Reason," he muttered. "I'm a man of reason."

"Strange reason, by my way of thinking." She shook her head. "I wait long past anytime I should have taken a husband. And when I do pick one, not only is he an off-islander, but he's a bloody cod's head."

He stopped walking and glared at her. "Mind your tongue, woman. What kind of foul talk is that?"

"Plain speech."

"You don't know the first thing about men."

"Don't I? I've fended off Dyce and his kind since I grew nether hair."

Will swore. "That's the talk that will get you raped in any seaport on the Atlantic. Hell, anywhere. A decent woman doesn't mention her . . ." He gritted his teeth in frustration. Where to start explaining? She was impossible. "Do you make it a habit of walking the beach naked around the men of your Brethren? Of kissing them like you kissed me?"

Her face paled to the color of old bone. "The Lord made women as they are. And if you don't like the way we're formed, take your complaint to Him."

"That's not what I meant, and you know it."

Angel averted her eyes and traced a circle in the damp sand with her bare toes. "Dyce is no better than a shoat," she murmured. "But if he touched me or another unmarried lass, Cap'n would stake him out on the beach for the crabs. He did it to the man who got Tamsey with babe. Crabs stripped him clean. That's why Dyce kept beggin' Cap'n to let him take me to wife. He knew he couldn't have me any other way."

She started walking again, shoulders stiff, and head held high. He knew that if he had any sense at all, he'd let her go, but he couldn't.

"I don't suppose there's a boat on this island?" he called after her.

"If there was a boat, you might escape."

"So you admit it. I'm a prisoner."

"You might could say that."

He ran and caught her by the shoulder. "Why? What's to be accomplished by holding me here?"

She stared stonily at him until he dropped his hand, then said, "Cap'n . . . the Brethren, they all thought that you'd be content to stay and be one of us."

"And you? Do you believe that?"

She sighed and shook her head. "More likely I could hold the wind in my hands." Her green eyes hardened to chips of jade. "The world's not all sky and water, black and white. There's gray in between, like land and the green things what sprout on it. Can't you understand that we're not all villains? Bloodthirsty buccaneers, eager to slash throats and make widows and orphans of off-island folk?"

"You're wrong," he insisted. "It's you that's blind. You won't see what's happening here. My father lost two ships here on this coast. It cost us our company, devastated the families of the crew, and cost my father his life. So you'll get no sympathy from me for your pirate brotherhood."

And none for you, if I had any sense, he seethed silently. He was letting Angel get to him, twisting his values of right and wrong because she had the timeless eyes of Eve, breasts to make a man blind, and a strut that could lure a bishop through the gates of hell.

"You knew your father?"

"Of course, I knew him. Didn't you know—" It was out of his mouth before he realized that she'd take it as an insult.

"Nay. I don't remember my father. Not even his name."

She remembered little of her poppet days. Things just were. Sometimes she had dreams of a man she thought was her father. When she awoke, she could hear his voice crying, "Bett . . . Bett . . . my precious Bett." . . . Almost hear his voice.

She forced herself to be pleasant in spite of Will's picayunish mood. As Bett always said, "Sour bait catches no trout."

"My mother died when I was twelve," Will said. "After that, it was just my father and me. I'm the last of the Falcon line."

"You'll be wanting to breed up sons."

He made a strangled sound. "Is there nothing you won't say? No lady would—"

"No Charleston lady?" Angel wrinkled her nose. "I

don't reckon your Julia would. But I wasn't asking. I was saying what was so." She folded her arms. "No need to go all gentry on me, Will. I wasn't suggestin' that I have your babes. When it comes to your sons and daughters, it's natural you'd want a fancy woman, one of your own kind, to be mother to them."

"A fancy woman."

She could see that he was doing his best to look stern, but the twitch at the corner of his mouth and the gleam in his eyes told her that he wasn't really angry. "Just tell me about Charleston," she urged. "About your father, and your house, and even your Julia, if ye want. Tell it all, and I promise I'll bite my tongue and be still as a beached clam."

"I wouldn't know where to start."

"The beginning is the best." She took hold of his big hand and squeezed it. "Tell about your da," she said.

He gave her a glance that made her go all shivery inside as she walked a little faster to pick up his pace.

"You want to know about my father?" Will asked. "Seriously?"

"Aye," she said, stretching to keep up with him. "I do. I'm hungering to know."

Will's expression turned solemn, but he nodded. "All right, I'll tell you about him. My father's name was Nicholas, and he was the most honest and wisest man I've ever known. He was born on a rice plantation to parents who had given up all hope of ever having a child. From the first day of his . . ."

Once started, Will was as bursting over with words as a cloud full of raindrops. He talked until the sun began to go down, and true to her promise, she listened without asking so much as a single question.

They arrived at camp as the first star twinkled on. Neither had spoken since they had turned inward from the beach. Both she and Will were lost in their own thoughts. It was clear as well-water to her that he'd loved his father dearly, although he'd not said it in so many words.

For herself, she'd seen death aplenty, but she couldn't imagine coming on Bett and finding that she'd killed herself. Hard as life was, it was difficult to figure how a body could come to such an end, especially over a thing like money.

"How long ago since ye lost your da?" she asked, breaking the silence between them.

"A year."

"And you say he did it because of his lost ships and cargo?"

"We've had a difficult time in the last few years. One of our schooners, the *Whippet*, was boarded off the coast of Ireland by the British navy. Our men were pressed into service, and the vessel was seized. And off Saint Kitts, the *Polly Anne* and the *Savannah* were fired on. We lost the *Savannah*, but Jem Howard, the skipper of the *Polly Anne*, made a run for it. He escaped, but when he got his cargo to port, the harbormaster turned him away, claiming it was too dangerous to deal with American merchants. The English are bound and determined to run us off the seas."

Angel busied herself with starting the campfire and fetching fresh water. There was honey in a crock and a bit of cheese. They'd best eat everything perishable right off before it could spoil.

"Things went from bad to worse. Storms, a scarcity of experienced hands. I had a close call with the *Katherine*. A French pirate shredded one of our sails and nearly grounded us on a reef. But keeping good men is the biggest problem. Not many are willing to sign on when they're afraid of ending up as virtual slaves, sailing under the Union Jack." Will crouched beside the fire pit. "I can do this," he said, adding twigs to the small flame.

She nodded.

"We'd flourished after the war, bought more ships than we should have. The shipping business has always been cutthroat, but my father wouldn't compromise. His handshake was as good as any signed contract. Merchants respected him."

She mixed cornmeal, salt, water, and a little bacon grease, then unpacked a cast-iron, three-legged skillet. When the fire was hot enough, she balanced the spider over the coals, poured in a little of her precious oil, and began to fry the mush.

"We weren't alone. Three other small companies were forced out of business in the last two years. There's some who believe all our bad luck wasn't accidental. There's a relative of the governor, a man by the name of Edward Mason. He's well connected with the politicians. Mason and my father disagreed on a lot of issues. Anyway, Mason always seems to benefit by the losses of the other shippers. After . . ." Will's voice grew husky with emotion.

"After my father's death, I sold off what was left to pay the debts. Mason tried to steal our house at a fraction of its worth at the sheriff's auction, but Lady Graymoor outbid him. She owns it now, and I rent it from her."

"So, this man you don't trust, this Edward Mason. He took your ships?"

"No. I sold out to a family friend, Richard Hamilton, Julia's father. He hired me to captain the *Katherine*."

"And you claim you lost two ships here, on these islands. When?"

"A few months before my father took his life."

"What kind of vessels were they? Carryin' what cargo?"

He told her, and she thought back to that winter and spring. There had been a schooner that might fit the description of one, but she couldn't be sure. She did remember helping bury several drowned sailors. "There was a storm," she said. "A bad nor'easter. How can you be certain it was us and not the weather took them? Off these islands, there's many a ship gone under and not seen again."

"Hamilton's lost ships here as well. You'll not make excuses for your Brethren, woman."

She held her tongue and handed him a plate. She didn't want to argue with Will Falcon tonight. He'd hurt her when he'd made it clear that her kissing hadn't been what he was used to. It wasn't fair. She'd had no practice, and if he had just given her time . . . been patient . . . she knew she could learn.

She needed to think through what had happened between them and what she should do next. And she was chock-full of notions about places he'd been and things he'd seen.

She'd thought she was hungry until the food was in front of her, but now her appetite faded away. She moistened her lips, trying not to think of how he'd fondled her and how bold she'd been. Obviously, there was more to kissing than she'd even thought possible.

Things had gone bad for her just when it had seemed she and Will had a chance to be friends. Maybe what folks said was true. Mayhap her pulling Will from the sea had brought on more bad luck than she could deal with.

She hoped that getting him to talk about his father would make things easier between her and him. But now, he'd turned to accusing her folk of piracy again.

"Are you tired?" she asked him when he'd finished his supper.

"Why?"

She shivered at the thread of steel that rang in his voice. It was too dark to read his eyes, but she could feel his wariness, and she knew she'd have to tread softly to get him around to her way of thinking again. "I've a notion to go back to the beach," she said. "There's a moon tonight, and no better time for fishing."

"You want me to come with you?"

"Aye." She drew a ball of fishing line, sinkers, and hooks out of one of her baskets. "No tellin' what we might catch."

"And what did you intend to use for bait?"

"Sand fleas."

"All right," he agreed. "I'll come along on your fishing trip, but what happened earlier . . . when I . . . when we—"

"Kissed?"

"Yes." He stood up. "It was a mistake, Angel. I apologize. It won't happen again."

No? She averted her head so that he couldn't see her lips curve into a smile. We'll see how long you can stick to that, my fine gentleman, she thought. We'll just see.

Chapter 10

When they reached the beach again, Angel led him to a spot at the base of a sand dune, which looked exactly like every other dune, and pushed aside a tangle of wild grapevine. Dropping to her knees, she began to dig.

"What are you doing?" he asked. He didn't trust her. Worse, he didn't trust himself.

Silver moonlight and pearl-gray shadows colored the May night, transforming an ordinary shoreline into a realm of enchantment. Will couldn't remember when he'd ever felt so aware of the slippery feel of dry sand giving way under his feet, or the fecund, almost primeval odors of seaweed, dune grasses, and salt water mingling with the cedar and pine of the encroaching forest.

"You might be giving me a hand," Angel said. "Instead of standing there with your mouth hanging open."

But helping meant kneeling beside her, risking an accidental touch. And he had to keep distance between them, because if he didn't, he couldn't be sure that he could resist her charm.

"You might give me a hand."

Even when Angel was taunting him, he noticed she was making a genuine attempt to improve her grammar.

"I can't understand why you're digging in the dunes for bait," he replied. "Sand fleas burrow close to the—"

"There!" she declared triumphantly. Getting to her feet, she motioned to him. "I found it. Now pry off the lid. Just twist it. And treat it gently, or you'll be cursin' yourself for a hamper-arsed fool."

Will got down and reached into the hole, feeling what could only be the top of a small wooden cask. "What's in it?" he asked. After the episode with the poison ivy, he wouldn't put it past her to have him stick his hand into a beaver trap.

"Flint and steel, a knife, some fishing line and hooks, and something you'll like even better."

"A boat?"

She laughed. "You won't get shed that notion, will you? I like that about you—that you're stubborn. Shows you're more than a fair-weather man."

He wrested open the lid, and Angel pulled out an oil-cloth wrapping and then a small leather pouch. Lastly, she drew forth a crockery jug plugged with a cork. "The rest you can put back in for a rainy day," she said. "And cover the keg as we found it. We've no need of the contents, and some other poor wight may."

"As though he'd have any chance of finding it," Will grumbled.

"It's a Brethren hidey-hole, and we've more on these islands than you'd suppose. There's lots buried here besides Blackbeard's treasure."

"And you know the location of that as well, I suppose."

She laughed again. "Wouldn't I love that? Nay, I do not, and neither does Cap'n, although he tells tales of seven chests of Spanish gold. Guarded by the ghosts of a black dog and three faithful crewmen."

Angel lifted the jug, sipped, then passed the container to him. "Carolina nectar. Made from corn and moonbeams, and clear as well-water."

The whiskey was smooth, and Will held it in his mouth to savor the taste before he swallowed.

"Well?" she asked. "Would you be ashamed to serve that to your grand gentleman friends?"

Will chuckled. "I must admit that I've had far worse on Church Street."

"And is that in your Charleston?"

"It is. A street of fine old homes and the best families."

"Good." She beamed. "I made it."

"You?"

"Aye, Will. I've a touch for making spirits. 'Tis another of my talents, of which I have many you've not seen."

He groaned. "And why do I think I may yet witness these marvels?" And he laughed with her. "I warn you. If your intention is to get me drunk and then have your way with me, there's not enough whiskey."

"Listen to you. Accusing me of all manner of trickery, when my only thought was to put a smile on your face, Will Falcon."

For a moment, he could almost forget where he was and enjoy being here with a lovely woman on a white stretch of sand with the dark waves rolling in and stars blanketing the sky overhead.

"Come on," she urged. "Now that you've had a nip to keep ye awake and to ease the itch of that poison ivy, I'll teach you how to fish."

"You teach me?" He made a sound of derision. "Woman, I was catching whales when you were still a babe trailing wet nappies."

"Bett always says that you can't call a man a fisherman until you've seen the length of his—"

"To hell with Bett and her common talk," Will said.

"His cast," she finished. "Did you think I meant something else?"

"Start digging sand fleas," he said. "We'll see who catches the first fish tonight." He took another drink of the corn liquor and tried not to scratch the spreading rash on his hip.

Three days passed on the island without a repeat of the intimacy he and Angel had shared, three of the longest days and nights of Will's life. He was determined not to fall into her trap, and not to allow her to do something she'd regret once he was gone.

To his surprise, he found Angel a great companion. As long as he would talk about the ships he'd sailed on, the ports he'd put into, and life on the mainland, she appeared content to listen.

If only Aaron were here, Will thought. Would his friend believe half of what he told him about Angel or about the Brethren when he was back aboard the *Katherine*? Somehow, these islands, these people, seemed to be lost in the past, belonging more to Blackbeard's time than to the present. It was hard to keep focused on what needed doing. And it was harder still to look at Angel without thinking of the kisses they'd shared or the way she'd felt in his arms.

One thing he knew: The sooner he was away from her, the better. She was trouble, and he had enough of that to last him. He needed to put distance between them and forget he'd ever seen her . . . all of her.

By day he kept busy. He built a pile of driftwood and dried grass and brush on the beach that he could light as a signal if he sighted a sail. He'd not taken Angel's word that there was no boat. He'd walked the entire perimeter of the island, taking special care to search both sides of the inlet that cut through the north end of Huskanaw. He didn't find what he was looking for, but parts of the isle were so tangled with wild grape and cedar that Angel could have been hiding a fleet of ships.

This morning, she had gone to a cove on the protected side of the island to dig clams for chowder while he'd continued collecting fuel on the beach for his signal fire. He'd already found two good pieces of driftwood and wanted one more before he turned back. Rounding the point, he stopped short and dropped his armload of wood. Not a hundred yards out, just inside the area where the ocean floor dropped off into deeper water, a sloop lay at anchor. And upside down in the surf, he saw a rowboat. One newcomer was already on the beach, while a second, cursing and leaning on an oar, waded out of the water.

"Hallo, the beach!" Will shouted. The first man heard him and turned. Will waved. He didn't know if these two were pirates, but he was ready to gamble that they weren't. He waved again and strode toward them. "Good day to you!"

The pair identified themselves as Jarvis and Archie Gunn, brothers from Philadelphia hauling a cargo to Savannah. A third member of the crew, a cousin of theirs named Martin Hiron, was still aboard the sloop.

Archie claimed salt water had leaked into their barrel of fresh, and they'd come ashore looking to replenish it. From the sly glances the Gunns exchanged, Will was half convinced that they were lying, but he didn't care. He spent the better part of an hour convincing Archie, who seemed to do the thinking for the two, that they'd be well rewarded for transporting him to Charleston. Furthermore, he warned of the danger they were in by sailing so close to islands frequented by the Brethren.

"Best we get that water and get off this island," Archie said, hitching up his single suspender. "Don't want no truck with pirates." Archie was a gaunt, gap-toothed man with a potbelly, thinning hair, and a bad complexion.

His younger brother, Jarvis, the man still clutching the oar as though it were his lifeline, was even dirtier, skinnier, and less attractive. Will wouldn't have allowed either man to set foot on the *Katherine* as passengers or as crew.

"We got to be paid in hard coin," Archie warned. "Don't want none of your paper money."

"Yep," Jarvis echoed. "Hard money. And we want it first."

Will forced a laugh. "I suppose you would. But when I get to Charleston dock, you'll get paid. And not a minute before."

"How do we know you won't try to cheat us?" Archie asked. "Come aboard, get where ya want to, then leave us high and dry?"

"Look at it this way," Will said. "I can provide you with fresh water and a jug of good drinking whiskey. That shows my good faith."

Jarvis tugged at a greasy lock of hair and looked at his companion. "Whadda ya think, Archie? If he don't pay up, we could keep them fancy boots of his'n. They're bound to bring somethin'."

"Exactly," Will said. "But I've given you my word as a gentleman. You're bound for Savannah. Your course takes you directly past where I want to go. And you can always take my boots if I try to cheat you. What have you got to lose?"

• • •

> *"I could have married a duke's daughter,*
> *She would have married me,*
> *But I have returned to Edinburgh Town,*
> *All for the love of thee . . ."*

Angel sang softly as she dropped another clam into the bag tied around her waist. Straightening, she hummed the ballad's refrain as she watched an osprey with a large fish drop into its nest at the top of a dead tree.

She hefted the bag, trying to decide if she had enough. Just one more, she thought. One more, and then I'll head back. It wouldn't do to leave Will on his own too long. No telling what mischief he might get into.

He'd spent most of the last few days finding driftwood and piling it up so that he could light a signal fire if he saw a sail. He thought he'd kept it a secret from her, but she'd trailed him and watched what he was doing from the woods.

Angel grimaced. She'd come so close to becoming a woman. When Will had kissed her like he had and touched her, she'd known he was as near to swivin' her as shell to an oyster. She'd wanted it bad, and she reckoned he wanted it. And why he hadn't done it, she couldn't come close to guessing.

One thing was certain, when Will was gone, she'd miss him terrible. There'd never be another man like him, not in looks, not in his smooth way of talking, and not in . . .

She didn't even have the words to fit what she was feeling inside. Just watching Will made her go all shivery. Lightning-struck, she'd heard Bett call it, when a maid lost all sense and set her mind on a man.

Angel didn't know what being hit with lightning felt like, but one minute she was bubbling with joy and the next near to tears. She was either starving or she couldn't eat a bite, and she had an overwhelming urge to touch him whenever she was close enough.

There was hardly anything about Will that didn't please her. She liked the way he smelled, and the cunning way he arched one dark brow when he teased her. And his smile gladdened her as much as sunrise after a moonless night.

Will Falcon had passed every test she'd given him, even when she'd handed over a jug of her best brew. A jug-bitten varlet would have started on that sipping whiskey and not stopped until the bottom was dry. Not Will. He took a few drinks and set the crock aside for another day, proving he was a man of good sense.

He'd proved his courage against Dyce. Will wasn't lazy, and he seemed game for any task she put him to. The only thing he wouldn't do was what she wanted most—to have him be the one who broke her maidenhead.

She might be ignorant, but she wasn't stupid. She knew that other than in her dreams, she couldn't keep him forever and a day. There was no way an island woman with sand between her toes could be a match for a dashing gentleman like Will. But if he went away, leaving her as virgin as the day he'd first lit eyes on her, it would be her eternal sorrow.

She walked back and forth in the hip-deep water, feeling with her feet for clams. And when she struck something hard that felt like a brick buried in the silt, she ducked under the water and dug it out with her hands.

Coming up with her clam, she gulped air and wiped the water out of her eyes. What she saw made her heart skip a beat. A sloop, maybe a forty-footer, with sail snapping, was making straight for the cove.

It was too far off for her to tell if they were friends or foe, but she knew better than to stand there gawking.

She made for shore as fast as she could. Gulls flew up as she waded through the shallows and ran for the cover of the trees.

"Angel!" Will motioned to her from the game trail. "There's a boat. Is it one of yours?"

"I don't know." Shielded from the water by thick foliage, she paused to catch her breath, untied the heavy bag of clams, and let it slide to the forest floor. "We'd best make ourselves scarce until we can be certain who they are. I know what ye think of the Brethren, but there are worse folk than us on these waters."

He nodded, coming to stand beside her. "You said your friends wouldn't be back for a month."

"Aye. If it's them, there's a good reason. I don't—" She broke off as Will clamped a muscular arm around her shoulder. Instantly, her inner warning alarms went off. "What are you doing?" she demanded, trying to pull away.

In answer, he slipped his free hand under her legs and swept her up into his arms. "They're not your people," he said. "They've come for me."

"Let me go!" Suddenly, everything was wrong, and Will was a stranger. "Put me down!" she cried.

"I'm taking you with—"

Angel knotted her right hand into a fist and punched him squarely in the jaw. Will groaned, and his head flew back. Without uttering another sound, she kicked wildly, swinging another punch with all her might. They went down together with Will on top of her.

She crawled out from under him, leaped to her feet, and darted away. Cursing, he sprang after her, seized her flying braid, and yanked her to a halt.

She spun and kicked him squarely in the knee, following up with a hard left hook to the throat. He came in fast, wrapping her in a bear hug, and pinning her arms.

She stopped fighting. "You're hurting me!"

The instant he loosened his hold, she wiggled her left hand free and slammed the base of her palm into his chin.

"Stop it! Don't make me hurt you!" he yelled, grabbing her wrist and twisting it behind her back.

Panting for breath, Angel brought up one knee, smashing into his inner thigh, missing her target by a thumb's length. "Bastard!" She butted her head into his chin, freed her right hand, and went for his eyes. "Let me go!"

Will grabbed her other wrist, pinned both over her head, and tripped her. They landed in a tangle of berry bushes, and Angel felt the bite of thorns on her arms and legs.

"Be still!" he said.

She sank her teeth into his arm.

"That's it!" he bellowed as he rose on his knees, straddling her, and bearing her to the ground. "I'll swear I'll knock you senseless!"

Trapped, realizing the futility of further struggle, she lay, sucking in gasps of air and glaring at him. "I'll put the *evil eye* on you. I will! I'll make ye wish you'd never been—"

Will clapped a broad hand over her mouth. "Shut up. One more word, and I'll wring your neck." He spat out blood.

She tried to curse him, but she could only make muffled garbling noises. Then she grew silent and nipped him again.

Will whipped his hand away. His blue eyes hardened as he saw the teeth marks she'd left on him. "I'm doing this for you," he said.

She saw to her satisfaction that he was breathing as hard as she was. "I warn you, if I get the chance, I'll put a knife in your back."

"Not a chance in hell," he said. "Whether you want it or not, I'm saving your life."

Chapter 11

"Let me out of here, you black-hearted son of a sea cook!" Angel's muffled shouts, interspersed with loud pounding, seeped through the cracks around the main hatch cover to the underside of the deck.

Martin Hiron drained the last drops from the whiskey jug, belched, and tossed the crockery container over the side. "Sweet temper, yer wife has—from the looks of your face." Snorting at his crude attempt at humor, Martin lurched onto a coil of rope and leaned back against the mast. "What she needs," he slurred, sucking at a rotten tooth, "is a man who'll teach her a few manners."

"The lookers is always bitches," Archie agreed from his place at the tiller. He watched the jug sink with a sorrowful expression. "A waste, wouldn't ye say, brother?"

Jarvis groaned and didn't answer. Then his face turned a deeper blotchy green, and he hung over the rail retching dry heaves.

"True words, cousin, true words," Martin said. "Give me an ugly woman anytime. Ain't no difference in the dark, and the uglies is grateful."

Will snugged off a line and wondered if he'd traded an island Eden for the vessel from hell. Martin appeared to be of no better character than the Gunn brothers. The three

109

together wouldn't make a decent sailor. The sloop was sound enough, but the three men were obviously landlubbers, making their story of hauling cargo to Savannah ring false. None of them looked substantial enough to own a sloop like this, which meant they were thieves or worse.

And he'd brought Angel onto this boat and put her at the mercy of scoundrels. The question plagued him: Had he done it for her or because he couldn't bear to leave her behind?

"Yep, she's a rarin' bitch, all right," Archie said.

Will straightened and fixed him with a steely glare. "I'd take it as a personal favor if you'd not refer to my wife as a bitch." On the streets of Charleston . . . hell, in any harbor on the Caribbean, he would have called a man out for insulting a woman he was with. But he couldn't allow himself the luxury of showing how angry he was. He'd come aboard unarmed, and Martin wore a pistol on his hip. If he acted in haste or recklessly, Angel would pay the price as well as he.

Archie laughed. "What? Them was love taps she give ya?"

"Touchy, ain't he?" Martin pawed through the black hair that matted his exposed chest, captured a fat louse, and cracked it between furred, broken incisors. "Fooken little devils," he muttered. "Worse'n skeeters."

"Let me out!" Angel demanded. "I can't breathe!"

"Let her out of there or knock her senseless," Archie advised. "She keeps up thet thrashin', she'll kick a hole in the hull."

Will looked back in the direction of Huskanaw. Once he'd seen the true state of affairs on the sloop, he'd not wanted to tie her. And had she been able to see her island, he had no doubt it would have taken more than the four of them to keep her from diving overboard. Satisfied that she'd not be foolish enough to try the stunt out of sight of land, he crossed to the hatch and slid back the wooden bolt.

Angel erupted out of the hold, hair tangled, red-faced, and eyes hot enough to melt the brass fittings on the gunnel.

Behind him, Will heard Archie's sharp intake of breath, and he wanted to kill him for thinking just what he was thinking.

Angel shoved the hair out of her eyes and looked wildly around. For a few seconds, Will thought she might fly at him again with fists and teeth, but she surprised him. With almost regal dignity, she turned to the rail and surveyed the empty horizon on all sides.

She was trembling from crown to toe. Her fingers clenched and unclenched. The knuckles of both hands were raw and seeping blood.

"Angel." Will took a few steps toward her.

She glanced at him as though he were a stranger. "How could ye?" Her soft voice cut through him like a cannonball through canvas.

"Try to understand."

"How could you just carry me off, as if I was a side of bacon?"

"I did what was necessary." Will moved closer. "There's no time. We'll discuss it later." His back was turned to the others, so that only she could see his face. Be careful, he mouthed silently.

"Aye." Her eyes narrowed, and Will read not simply a woman's anger, but something darker and more dangerous. "Aye, *husband*," she murmured.

Ice frosted his spine. Maybe she is a pirate, he thought. As ruthless and as capable as any brigand would be of running me through with cold steel.

"Need help?" Martin offered. "The ladies always favors me 'cause—"

" 'Cause he's hung like a Jersey bull," Archie finished.

Jarvis slid to his knees and laid his head against the gunnel. Drool dribbled from the corner of his slack mouth as he twitched and belched.

"These *gentlemen* have promised us passage to Charleston," Will said, ignoring the seasick Jarvis. "Although, if we get a chance, we'll leave them sooner."

Dismissing him with a glance that would have withered iron, Angel retreated to the bow of the boat.

"Strange one, ain't she?" Archie said.

Will forced a nod. "Show me a woman that's not." His knuckles ached to smash that leering mouth.

Martin hauled himself up from the coil of rope, groped his cod, and staggered toward Angel.

Will slammed a hand into the man's shoulder and gripped tightly. "Stay away from my wife," he warned. "You're being well compensated for taking us where we want to go. And she's not included in the deal."

"Didn't say she was." Martin belched again, and Will nearly gagged as a wave of stench enveloped him.

If Martin had ever owned a bar of soap, it didn't show. His woolen breeches were so caked with dirt and filth that it was impossible to tell what color they had originally been or what held them together.

Chalky spots of rage rose on the drunkard's cheekbones, and he focused bloodshot eyes. "Mighty high for an unarmed man." Martin tapped the butt of his handgun. "Don't think I don't know how to use this, neither."

"I want there to be no misunderstanding between us, Mr. Hiron," Will said. "If you so much as speak to my wife, I'll stuff that pistol up your ass, chop you into bite-sized pieces, and use you for chum."

Martin took the better part of a moment to consider the statement, then blinked. "No 'fense, sir. Jest bein' friendly to yer missus."

"Don't bother."

Archie guffawed as Martin wandered back to his coil of rope and plopped down. Jarvis was sick again, hanging so far over the side of the sloop that Will thought he might lose his balance and topple in.

Stepping carefully around Jarvis, Will joined Angel at the bow. "We need to talk."

She continued to stare over the bowsprit. Her expression didn't change, and she gave no indication that she'd heard him. Will seized her hand, yanked her to her feet, and clamped a restraining arm around her shoulder. She moved woodenly, like a ship's figurehead just come to life.

"I know you're angry," he said, "but this is for the best."

"Why? Without so much as a *by your leave*? Without askin' me *would* I go with ye?" Her lilting words came in a whisper, as tightly controlled as her rigid body. Each word struck him another blow.

"You know why." He forced her around to face him, shielding her face from their hosts to keep their conversation private. Then he leaned close and murmured in her ear. "If I left you, you'd suffer the same fate as the rest when the authorities came to settle with them."

She jerked away from his touch and stared full into his eyes. For an instant a shutter raised and he read the full force of her despair. "What do ye mean to do with me?" she begged, tears welling up.

Shame and need warred inside him. "Angel, try to—"

"Nay." She shook her head. "Don't tell me you've decided to have me to wife. I'm not so green as to think that. If you'd not do it on the island, you'll not—"

"No." He frowned, wondering why he, a man who prided himself on always speaking the truth, found this so difficult. "I haven't decided what I'm going to do with you. Don't worry, I'll protect you."

"Why not? A handfast marriage is easily made and easily broken. You owe me nothin'."

"Nothing but my life."

"Then you could have repaid me by leavin' me among my own kind."

"And see you stand trial for piracy? I couldn't do that, Angel, despite this." He indicated his battered face and his voice hardened. "Don't ever raise your hand to me again. Even I have my limits."

"You got what you deserved." She placed her hands on his chest and tried to push him away. "Take me back."

"It's not going to happen."

She made a small sound of distress. "Four walls won't hold me. You have to sleep, and when you do . . ."

Will's gut knotted. "You don't understand what's best for you."

"And you do?"

He'd known this wouldn't be easy. Why hadn't he simply gone with the Gunn brothers when he'd had the chance? He'd almost done it; but in the end, he'd had to go back for her. He'd tried to tell himself that Angel was one more debt he couldn't leave unpaid. But what if that wasn't the reason? And what if his lust got her killed? "When they arrest the Brethren, they won't be particular. They won't spare the women. And the penalty for piracy is death."

She scoffed. "If you're so wary of pirates, how could you bring me aboard this boat? Do ye think these be honest men?"

"I can handle them."

"Can ye now?" she taunted him. "Ye could barely handle one woman."

He stiffened, feeling the red tide of anger sweep

through him. "Curb your barbed tongue, or I'll forget you're a wench."

Her eyes flashed defiance. "I was but askin' a fair question."

"Later. We've bigger problems."

"Three of them?"

"I've seen no weapons on the sloop, other than Martin's pistol and the knife in Archie's belt sheath."

"Three men to one be not the best odds, even for a Charleston man."

"I've faced worse."

"Braggart," she taunted. "Mayhap you mean to do a little buccaneering yourself? Take the ship?"

"I intend to do whatever it takes to get us both home safely."

"Not home for me." Her words came soft but bitter. "I'm island bred. There's no place for me among your fine houses and brick-paved streets."

"I'll not desert you," he promised. "For the sake of what you've—"

"I want no thanks. When I married you, it was as much to gain my own freedom as win ye yours." She pushed his hand off her shoulder. "You betrayed me, Will Falcon, and I won't forget it."

"We'll argue about this when we get to Charleston. Now, I need your help."

"Aye." She nodded. "I'll help ye take the ship away from them if you'll take me back to Huskanaw."

"You're coming with me. Stay close, and keep watch. See if you can put your hands on a knife. There's bound to be one."

"Aye, there is that," she agreed. "I can't tell you what was in the cargo hold. It was dark and packed tight."

"Would you rather I'd tied you hand and foot? You

came to no harm there." She turned her face away, and he took hold of her chin and turned it back. "This is important. If there are weapons, they'll be below in the cuddy."

"All right," she murmured. "I'm with you—for now. But once we land . . ."

"In Charleston."

"When we land, you'd best put chains on me. For if ye don't, whatever happens is on your head."

It was dusk and the wind was kicking up before Angel found the opportunity to slip down the ladder to the small compartment that passed as a cabin. The men were occupied. Will had secured the sails and was taking his turn at the helm. The three rascals were forward. Archie and Martin had their heads together; Jarvis lay on the deck moaning, holding his belly. Angel didn't think she'd ever seen anyone so seasick on five-foot chops.

She hesitated halfway down, waiting for her eyes to become accustomed to the dim light. Her heart was thudding, her breath coming in quick, shallow gasps, not so much from the danger she and Will were in, although she knew it to be very real. It was her husband and what he had done that frightened her. She didn't know whether to be furious with him or glad that he had brought her.

Being close to Will was unnerving. The scent of him— the feel of his hand on her body brought out something wild inside her. Having him near her made her think of lying under him with the weight of his long legs tangled in hers and his fingers touching her most private places.

But he hadn't asked her to go with him. He'd taken her by force. That was what stung most of all. He had simply made the decision. And by doing so, he'd ruined everything. For as much as she valued Will Falcon, she valued herself more. And after a lifetime of making her own choices, she wasn't about to surrender that right to an arrogant outlander.

But thinking that through could wait. Will had sent her to find a weapon, and she couldn't fail him.

The cubby looked as though a hurricane had already passed over it. Blankets and tools were heaped up all catawampus. Rice and dried beans spilled out of torn sacks, and articles of clothing were scattered.

"Where you going, girl?" Archie called. "Ain't nothing of yers down there. Get topside."

Angel began to dig through the mess. She heard Will's voice and then Archie's again. She heaved a pile of stuff off the single bunk and went suddenly cold as her hand brushed a damp, sticky spot on the mattress.

An unpleasant sensation skittered down her spine. She pushed aside the pillow to find a dark, pumpkin-shaped stain on the threadbare mattress. The pillow landed upside down on her foot, and her breath caught in her throat. The underside of the pillow was soaked in the same foul-smelling substance.

"Woman!"

That voice was Martin's, the man with the pistol, and he was right overhead. If he found her here . . .

Swiftly, she scooped up an armload of blankets and dropped them back on the bunk. Then she turned and started back up the ladder. At the last second, she spied a tangle of fishing line, grabbed it, and stuffed it in her bodice.

Will had tied off the tiller and was just outside the hatchway. Archie and Martin, red-faced and hostile, advanced on them.

Will flashed her a grin. "See. She didn't disturb anything."

"That there's captain's quarters," Archie snapped. "You got no business down there."

Angel noticed that his hand hovered close to his knife. "Beg pardon," she said, trying to keep her voice from cracking. "I was looking for something to cook for supper."

"Our agreement was to carry you to Charleston," Archie added. "Nothing was said about feeding either one of you."

She felt the men's eyes boring through her. They know what's on that pillow, she thought. And now, I'm sure of what it is as well. Blood.

She edged nearer to Will. "I meant to cook for all of us," she said. "I didn't mean to cause any trouble."

"This here ain't no tavern," Archie continued. "We wasn't expecting company to feed, let alone no wife . . . if you are his wife, which I got my doubts."

"We're married," Angel replied.

"I don't see no weddin' ring on your finger," Martin said. "Most married women got rings. Hope yer not lyin' to us."

Archie wiped his mouth with the back of his filthy hand. "I can't abide a liar." His fingers tightened on the handle of his knife. The blade hissed from the leather sheath.

"Well, I reckon buyin' me a ring's something my Will can see to when we get to Charleston. Isn't that so, Will?"

"Get back on the tiller," Archie ordered Will. His eyes flicked to hers. "Not you, sweet thing." He reached for her as Martin drew his pistol and aimed it at Will.

"Get back down in thet cabin, woman," Archie said. "I've a hankering to see if you taste as good as ya look."

Chapter 12

Angel dodged Archie, dug into her bodice, and hurled the wad of fishing line and sinker at Martin's head. The lead weight struck him between the eyes as Will dove for the gun.

Angel didn't stop. She tried to put the tiller between her and Archie, but he slashed at her with the knife. A burning sensation seared her left arm.

Sky, sea, and waves seemed suddenly suspended in air. Vaguely, Angel was aware of Will and Martin rolling on the deck, locked in combat. She felt the gusting wind and the splash of spray on her face and smelled the mingling odors of salt and tar and blood. He cut me, she thought. I'm bleeding.

But her fear was gone, replaced with cool reason, reason that did not desert her when Archie's fingers bit into her arm. He yanked her toward him. But instead of resisting, she spun and threw her full weight into his chest.

Archie lost his balance and toppled backward, dragging her with him. His head slammed into the cuddy hatch, slowing him just long enough for her to scramble free.

There was no escape but aft—and barely ten yards from here to the bowsprit. She sprinted down the slippery deck past Will and Martin as the sloop pitched in

119

the choppy seas. And as she neared the mainmast, she heard the pistol blast. Someone howled—an agonized cry that rose above the snap of canvas in the rising wind.

"Will!" she screamed. She glanced back over her shoulder to see Martin flat on the deck, and Will leaping over him to confront Archie.

Without warning, rough arms clamped around her. "Where ya goin'?" Jarvis demanded.

Angel choked back a cry of alarm. He smelled of vomit and sweat. Coarse hands clutched at her, cruelly gripping her wounded arm. She bit back a moan that rose in her throat.

Waves of nausea threatened her unraveling senses as she twisted in his grasp. Jarvis was weak from seasickness, but her own strength was strangely dwindling, and oddly, a cicada had begun to buzz in her head.

"Let go of her!"

Will's command was faint, as though he were a long way off. Pinwheels of light spun and twirled inside her head. And when Jarvis released her, Angel felt herself slipping to the deck.

She heard the smack of muscle and bone driving into flesh. She forced her eyes open to see Jarvis stagger back against the mast. Bellowing like a bull, he lowered his head and rushed at Will in an attempt to headbutt him. Will sidestepped, and Jarvis hit the rail with a hard thud. The force of his charge threw him off balance. Arms and legs waving, he vanished over the side.

Will peered into the choppy sea. "Jarvis!"

Spits of rain splattered Angel's face, but she was so tired that she didn't care. Holding her eyelids open was impossible. All she wanted to do was sleep, but she knew that if she did, she might never wake.

Angel thought she heard Will call Jarvis's name once more. And then a man loomed over her.

"Angel?" Will's voice flooded over her. She couldn't make out his features in the growing darkness, but his breath was clean and warm against her face as he gathered her up.

"Will?" The absolute certainty that she was safe in these powerful arms swept over her.

"I've got you." Raw emotion turned Will's words to a deep rasp. "I've got you."

"Good." Her head fell back, and then she knew nothing at all.

"Angel?" Will's voice was insistent. "Open your eyes. Speak to me!"

She felt his lips on her mouth . . . her eyelids. Warm fingers clasped her face.

"Angel!"

She blinked, trying to clear her mind. "What happened?"

He gripped her hand and pressed damp kisses against her knuckles. "You fainted," he said. "You scared me half to death. I thought you were dead."

"Me?" She tried to laugh, and her voice came out in a cracked whisper. "I . . . I never fainted in my life."

"You did this time."

"Nay . . ." It was raining harder. The drops hitting the deck around them were coming down in sheets . . . soaking her bare breasts. She blinked again, trying to remember when and how her bodice had been ripped away. "I . . . I'm all right," she insisted groggily. But she wasn't all right. She was cold . . . so cold.

"The hell you are. You're bleeding." He drew the torn garment over her naked bosom. "I'm sorry," he said. "I thought you might be stabbed in the chest."

"Not blood . . . rain."

He ripped off the sleeve of his shirt and knotted it around her wounded arm. "I want to get you below while I tie—"

"Not there. Don't put me down there."

He cradled her as though she were a child, murmuring and stroking her hair. "You're safe, but I've got to find rope to bind Archie. And I need to take the tiller before we—"

"Blood . . . blood on the pillow."

Abruptly, it all came flooding back to her: Archie's attempt on her life . . . the gunshot . . . Jarvis rising out of the night to grab her. She began to tremble. "Jarvis, he tried to . . ."

"Shhh, shhh," Will crooned. "He's lost. He never surfaced. Martin's dead, too, shot with his own gun."

"Archie?"

"He's not going to hurt you. It's over."

"I'm all right, I tell you."

"I need to lock Archie in the cargo hold," he explained. "Archie's groggy. He won't cause me any trouble."

She fought to clear her mind of seaweed. "I can take the tiller."

"Are you certain you can manage?" He helped her to her feet, steadying her with a strong arm.

"I can do it," she said. But she wasn't sure she could. Her knees were jelly, her head spinning, and she was suddenly cold. "How did you . . .", she started, wondering how Will had gotten the best of Archie and Martin.

"Later," Will promised.

"Did I hit Martin with the lead weight?" she asked.

"Squarely between the eyes." Will kissed her temple. "You saved my life, woman. Again."

And you saved mine, she thought. She wanted to

thank him, but it seemed too much effort to speak. Her arm felt as though it were on fire, and the odd buzzing had begun again in her head. "Hurry," she managed as he propped her beside the tiller. If he answered, his words were lost in the drumming of the rain, the roar of canvas, and the creaking of wood.

Later—she didn't know if minutes or hours had passed—Will did carry her below. She was so cold and wet by then that she had no energy to protest. When she pointed out the blood, he stripped the mattress and pillow, stuffing them as far away from her as possible.

She watched him with heavy eyes as he stripped her naked, rubbed her bare flesh until it tingled, and wrapped her in an unsoiled blanket. "You sleep," he ordered. "It's the best thing for you."

"But ye can't . . . can't sail this sloop alone. I have to help you. Archie—"

"I tucked him in. He'll stand trial in Charleston for piracy and murder." He covered her with an old coat. "Leave everything to me, Angel."

Her teeth were chattering. "I'm cold," she repeated. "So cold."

Frantically, he looked for something else to put over her. "There's nothing—," he began.

"Hold me," she begged him. "I'm so cold."

"But I'm wet."

Wordlessly, she held out her arms.

For an instant, he hesitated, then swore softly. "All right, Angel." Peeling off what remained of his shirt and breeches he lifted the coat and blanket and crawled in beside her and pulled her shivering against his broad chest.

"I . . . can't get warm," she managed. "I can't . . ."

"Shhh," he soothed, cradling her with his body. "You're in my world now. Trust me."

"Trust you . . . ," she echoed. "Trust . . ." How could she? How could she trust him? But the heat of his flesh and the feel of his fingers stroking her hair eased her troubled mind.

"I'll take care of you," he promised. "No matter what you've done. I'll keep you safe."

Angel wasn't sure how much time had passed from the time they had taken the ship from Archie and his mates. It was the following afternoon, or the day after, that Will carried her off the boat. With her in his arms, he climbed a ladder onto a crowded dock and put her into a painted sedan chair.

She was dizzy with thirst, and her skin was so hot that it seemed on fire. Her head throbbed, and the agony in her arm had become an oven filled with whirling demons poking her with pitchforks.

"Where are we?" she begged him. "Whose chair is this?"

"It will be all right," Will soothed. "The chair belongs to a friend. I'm taking you to my home. A physician has been called to . . ."

His words danced and twirled like gull feathers on a windy beach. Nothing he said made any sense to her. But then he closed the tiny door, and she felt trapped in an airless coffin. She was too dizzy to stand—even if the compartment had been high enough. All she could do was lean against one wall and grit her teeth to keep from crying out in pain.

Then the chair swayed, and she felt herself lifted off the dock. Weakly, she pushed aside the heavy drape and peered out through a tiny square porthole. Two black men in blue coats and breeches with silver piping, wearing silver-colored tricorn hats, had lifted the poles onto

their shoulders and were carrying the chair through
throngs of people.

She couldn't remember ever having seen so many men
and women assembled in one place. She couldn't see
Will, but there were gentlemen in rich clothing, leather-
faced seamen, and red-cheeked ladies in silk and satin.
One elderly woman was trailed by a black boy wearing
a purple turban and purple tasseled boots.

Dark-skinned wenches carried heaping trays of oysters and fried shrimp. Others hawked crabs, meat pies,
or sweet buns. Half-naked slaves rolled monstrous
wooden barrels, sweated under hundredweight sacks,
and drove bleating sheep down the quay.

The noise was as overwhelming to Angel's fever-
sensitive ears as the myriad of odors: fresh-cut lumber,
cinnamon, beer, dead fish, and tar. From the right, a
smithy's hammer rang against an anvil.

A din of voices surrounded her, cursing, shouting,
laughing, chattering in English, French, Spanish, and a
dozen tongues she'd never heard before.

The racket was overwhelming. Angel let the curtain
drop and sagged back against the cushioned headrest.
She felt lost in this buzzing hive of tall buildings, rum-
bling wagons, and painted carriages. Every step her cap-
tors took carried her farther and farther from the sea,
away from the clean ocean wind and trackless beaches.

Tears welled in her eyes, spilled over, and rolled down
her cheeks. I don't belong here, she thought. I don't belong here. She had to make them understand that this
was a mistake . . . that they had to stop and let her go.
She was as much a part of the islands as the birds and
the wild ponies.

"Please," she whispered. "I don't want . . . don't
want to be in this place."

But no one listened to her, and it was impossible to shout loud enough so they would hear. The chair bounced and rattled until Angel clutched the edge of the seat with her good hand. Gradually, the sounds outside the covered box subsided. She still was aware of the clop of horses' hooves, but the clamor of the harbor had faded.

Only half conscious, Angel felt her cage come to a stop, heard the squeak of iron, and then slid back as the compartment tilted and moved uphill. She heard new voices and the sound of a door opening.

"Up here. Be easy with her," a woman's slurred, smokey-soft voice ordered. "You're not totin' a barrel of rice."

More voices filtered through Angel's clouded mind. The chair bumped to the floor, and the door opened. A sympathetic dark face greeted her. "Come out, miss. Don't be afeered of me. I'm Delphinium. Folks call me Delphi. Mr. Will wants us to look after you," she said. "You're mighty sick, and you need to be in bed."

Angel nodded. Somehow she summoned the strength to climb out of the sedan chair, but when she tried to take the few steps to the high poster bed, her legs failed her. She would have fallen if Delphi hadn't caught her.

Pain exploded in Angel's arm. A tide of red swept over her, drowning the vast, high-ceilinged room, the giant bed, and all the folks staring at her.

A fierce undertow swept her away in tumbling waves, finally casting her up on an unfamiliar beach without birds or trees, sun or moon. Bewildered, she lay as still as death. Time and grains of sand whirled silently around her.

". . . Bett . . . Bett . . . Papa's pet . . ."

Someone spun her around, and Angel giggled. "I'll catch you!" she cried. "I will!" Reaching out, she made a dash toward the chanting.

"Over here."

"No, here."

"This way, Bett."

She smelled the roses in the split second before her fingers closed around the leafy stem and thorns pierced her palm. Then pain and the sweet fragrance mingled. She tumbled over and over amid showers of rose petals that turned slowly to shells and finally to drifting sand.

Angel blinked, trying to get the sand out of her eyes. "Bett?"

"It's about time you woke up."

That wasn't Bett, it was Will. His voice was a lifeline, dragging her safely to shore. "Will?"

She shivered as he laid his strong hand on her forehead. "Your fever's broken. Dr. Madison says the infection is nearly gone. He thinks you have a remarkable constitution to heal so quickly. You frightened me, woman. You haven't been fully awake in three days."

"Three days?" She drew in a ragged breath and licked her dry lips. "I've been here three days?" Her lower lip trembled as she tried to recall the lost time. "I thought I heard someone . . ." She trailed off as she realized where she was. Bett couldn't be here. She was back on the islands with the Brethren, while she was here with Will Falcon.

Her head pounded, making it hard to recall what had happened after Will had climbed into her bunk. She wondered if she had lost her maidenhead without knowing it. She'd invited him in, but had he taken what was ripe for picking? She ached all over, so much so that she couldn't tell if she was sore between her legs.

She swallowed. If he hadn't slid between her thighs, he was a man of more substance than she'd ever known before.

"You may have a scar," he said, "but luckily the wound was on the underside of your arm. It won't show."

"How did . . . oh . . ." Angel sighed. "Archie's blade. He . . ."

"Tried to kill you." Will scowled. "Yellow bastard. He's locked up in jail. If he and the others committed murder to steal that sloop, Archie will hang. We give pirates short shrift in Charleston."

She met his gaze. "Did you . . . did we . . . on the sloop . . . after . . . damn me, but my head is all amazy." Trembling, she took hold of his hand and whispered, "Did you futter me while I—"

"Hell, no! What do you take me for?"

"Oh." She swallowed again, feeling foolish. She didn't think he'd do anything she hadn't agreed to, but he was after all a man, and most men thought with their pizzles, didn't they?

"You should know me better than that," Will said.

"Aye. Mayhap, I should. 'Twas not meant as an insult."

"It sounded like one to me."

"All right." Flustered, she stared wide-eyed around her. The room was very large with five big windows, all hung with swathes of rich material. The chamber furnishings were of polished, dark wood, as was the high bed. Leaves and sheaths of rice were carved into each post, and clouds of spotless white netting graced three sides. "Be this the governor's palace?" Angel asked.

"Hardly." His tone was still sharp, and she knew he hadn't forgiven her for asking if he'd swived her.

"It's my home," he continued. "My family owned it for generations . . . until we lost all our money. Now my neighbor owns it, and I rent it from her."

The house seemed a safer subject, and she asked,

"This is but one chamber in your house? And there are more?"

"Many more rooms. Twenty-one, twenty-two, something like that."

"So many, like the castle." She looked back at Will. He was so changed from the husband she'd known on the island that he'd almost become a stranger to her again.

Will's hair had been neatly cut to curl at the nape of his neck, and he was clean-shaven. Knee-high leather boots covered his handsome calves, and doeskin breeches clung to his thighs like a second skin. His coat and vest were robin's-egg blue. His shirt was white lawn, his collar starched, his stock of Irish linen.

"You look like a prince," she said.

"How many princes are you acquainted with?"

"I can't recall none but you."

"Flattery will get you everywhere in Charleston." He took her hand, raised it to his lips, and kissed it gently. "You're a brave woman. I won't forget what you did . . . or the time we spent together on the island."

Won't forget. His words rang hollowly in her ears, and she gripped his fingers as tears clouded her vision.

She bit her lower lip and tried to keep from weeping. She didn't know if it was anger or sorrow that made her so undone. She was still so angry at him for kidnapping her, for treating her as though what she wanted didn't matter.

Theirs had been a temporary marriage. She'd known it must end, that she had no chance of holding him. But she'd never guessed that giving him up would be so hard. Or that the hurt would be as real and painful as the knife slice to her arm.

"What's wrong? Are you in pain?" Will's stern expression became anxious.

"I want to go home."

"Angel, Angel."

He put an arm around her shoulders, and she buried her face in his chest. He smelled of tobacco and leather and other unfamiliar scents she couldn't place, but under it was the clean male odor that was his alone.

"Shhh, shhh," he murmured. "I'll look after you."

"Nay. You don't understand. I won't let you."

There was a rap at the door, and Will pulled away from her. As one, they glanced toward the doorway.

"It's just Sukie," Will said, motioning to the serving girl. "She's awake, Sukie. You can bring in the tray."

Angel wiped her face with the hem of a linen sheet as the black girl entered the room, heavily laden tray in hand.

"You need rest and food." Will gave her hand a warm squeeze. "You'll feel better soon."

"I can take care of myself."

"This isn't the Outer Banks. It's different here, but you'll learn. You'll be fine, I promise."

Angel looked down at her arm. She was wearing a sleeveless gown of pale green silk, and her left arm was bound tightly from elbow to shoulder with a thick bandage. The arm ached, but the devils with the pitchforks had retreated, at least for the moment.

"This is a truce, Will. Ye haven't bested me. Not yet."

The maidservant set down the tray and uncovered a steaming bowl. "This is Miss Delphi's special crab soup," she said. "Awful good." She unfolded a square of white linen and tucked it under Angel's chin, then took a spoon full of the soup and brought it to Angel's lips. "Jest take a taste."

Reluctantly, Angel opened her mouth, then inhaled sharply as another person stepped into the room. Angel knew at once that this slim woman in the high-waisted silk dress was no housemaid.

"Will!" the stranger cried. "Oh, Will, I know it's not proper for me to come uninvited, but I thought . . ."

Pleasure showed on his face. "Julia!"

"We thought you were dead!" Julia flung herself across the room and wrapped her arms around his neck. Will not only welcomed the embrace, he enveloped her in a genuine hug.

Angel clamped her teeth together, spilling the spoonful of soup down the front of the white cloth, causing Sukie to stammer apologies.

But Angel's attention was riveted to the lady in the rose-colored, beribboned bonnet. If Will was a prince, surely this must be his princess. Tall and slender as a reed, she was as graceful as an island doe, with dark cunning eyes that missed nothing.

She was no beauty, Will's Julia. Her nose was too long, her chin too short, her lips too thin. But her skin glowed, and her soft voice was pleasing to the ear.

"I thought I was dead myself," Will said heartily when he and Julia finally parted amid flushed cheeks and more laughter. Her bonnet strings had come undone, and the hat was slightly askew, but Angel saw that each dark curl bounced in perfect twists on either side of her face.

"Don't laugh, it was terrible." Julia averted her eyes as Will caught her hand to brush the back of her knuckles with his lips.

Angel felt the prick of a demon's pitchfork again, but knew it for what it was: not her injury, but plain, unwashed jealousy. The realization made her feel small and mean, and she resolved to give Will's lady a chance.

"But I'm back, all in one piece," he continued. "Eager to organize an expedition to destroy the pirates."

Destroy? Angel stared at Will in astonishment. Destroy the Brethren? The traitorous bastard!

"No more of that now," Julia admonished as she tapped Will's wrist teasingly with her fan. "You must save every word for supper tonight. Father insists you come." She flashed a radiant smile. "I do, too.

"Oh, Will, dearest, you don't know how many tears I've shed for you in the past weeks. And not only me. Half the ladies in South Carolina were desolate."

Then she glanced toward the bed and smiled. "And this must be your mystery woman. Your *angel*? Will, she's lovely."

For long seconds, her intelligent gaze met Angel's angry one. "I'm so pleased to meet a genuine heroine," Julia bubbled, hurrying toward the bed and extending a dainty hand.

Angel caught a whiff of violets. "Were you expectin' a swamp bear?"

Julia laughed. "She's delightful," she said to Will.

"Ye, as well," Angel replied sarcastically.

Julia smiled with her mouth, but Angel could read the wariness in her walnut-brown eyes. "Welcome to Charleston," the woman said, speaking slowly as if to a dull child. "I simply couldn't wait another moment to thank you for bringing Will home safely to me."

Chapter 13

The following morning, Will ushered his neighbor, Lady Graymoor, into the small parlor on the first floor of his home. This chamber, known as the blue room, was his favorite, the place his family had spent most of their private hours together.

He was tired. He'd had little sleep the night before. Angel's fever had risen again, and he'd spent most of the time from midnight until dawn sitting at her bedside. Angel had barely spoken a civil word to him and, by her attitude, she seemed to have taken a dislike to Julia. He couldn't help but wonder if dealing with her would be much more difficult than he'd expected.

Once Lizzy was comfortably seated, Will leaned against the marble fireplace, folded his arms over his chest, and tried to think how best to explain his attachment to Angel.

Lizzy broke the silence. "William, it is perfectly obvious to me that you've contracted brain fever." She waved impatiently at the maid who hovered by the door, waiting to see if they needed anything.

"Go. Shoo!" Lizzy said airily. "Out of here. If I'd wanted eavesdroppers, I would have asked for them."

When Sukie left the room, Lizzy sat up straight in the French gilt chair and turned her full attention on him. "You've suffered an ordeal, poor darling, but that doesn't excuse stupidity. What can you be thinking? To bring this woman here to your home and put her in your mother's bedchamber?"

Will had expected Lizzy to descend on him in full battle mode. He just hadn't expected it so early this morning. No one had ever accused Lady Elizabeth Graymoor of holding her tongue when she had something to say.

When she'd arrived, Lizzy had insisted on seeing Angel with her own eyes. Will had taken her up to Angel's bedroom, but fortunately Angel had been sleeping.

"You must think how this looks," Lizzy persisted.

"Angel saved my life," he said, trying not to lose his patience with the regal woman who was closer to him than any of his living relatives. "Angel is ill; was wounded defending me. I could hardly put her in the servants' quarters, could I?"

What he couldn't tell Lizzy was how raw fury had boiled up in him when Archie had threatened Angel, or how frightened he'd been that she would die of her injury or the fever that followed. It was impossible to relate how deeply he'd become attached to Angel . . . even with the full realization that she might be as guilty of piracy as her comrades.

Heat coiled in the pit of his gut as he thought of Angel lying upstairs, her face pale against the pillow, her shapely form covered by a thin linen sheet. Remembering how she'd felt in his arms, her naked body next to his, was enough to make him stir to life.

Self-consciously, he turned toward the window to hide the evidence of his forbidden musing.

"William! Pay heed to what I'm saying."

He glanced back to see Lizzy—the indomitable Lady Graymoor—glowering at him.

"She's very beautiful."

"As are you." His neighbor was as always the height of fashion, slim and elegant, and looking far less than her seventy-odd years. "You make me wish that I were twenty years older," he teased.

He didn't want to think about Angel, her face or her body. He wanted to shake off the spell she'd cast over him on the islands and get on with his life. Trading words with Lizzy would soon clear his head and prevent him from showing a rising condition that no gentleman should exhibit when entertaining a lady.

"Stop that," Lizzy scolded. "You're as bad as Griffin, constantly trying to manage me. I realize that people think I'm crazy. But I'm neither senile nor foolish."

He smiled at her. "I have the greatest respect for your intelligence. And I've never doubted the state of your mind."

Had she been an American privateer instead of an English countess, Lizzy would have driven the British navy out of the Caribbean. She was smart, and tough, and as business-minded as any man he'd ever known.

"I'm sure you regard me highly," she answered. "You've always seemed to recognize my worth, other than your unreasonable dismissal of my search for my granddaughter as a lost cause."

"Other than that," he agreed, drawing a chair close and straddling it. "Have I ever insinuated that I thought you lacking in wits because you wouldn't abandon your search for the child?"

Lizzy's lips thinned. "There was no need for you to say so, William. I could read it in your eyes." She snapped open her ivory fan and moved it rapidly beneath her chin. "You're very like your father. Neither of you could ever tell a convincing lie."

"Would it help if I could? If I pretended to believe there was a possibility that a five-year-old girl was the

sole survivor of a twenty-year-old tragedy?" He took
her hand gently in his. "I know what it's like to lose
family, Lizzy. My mother. Father. I know what kind of
tricks your mind can play on you."

"You mean well." She pulled her hand free and began
to twist the square-cut emerald ring on her middle finger. It was one of Lizzy's habits, always followed by a
heavy dose of grandmotherly advice.

Will steeled himself.

"In spite of your good qualities, and you have many,
you are a male. You can't be expected to understand a
sixth sense, which we females possess, that often defies
logic. It is my belief that the Creator—who denied to
my weaker sex physical strength—gifted us with special
powers of perception. One of which is—"

"No more," he interrupted. "You've wasted enough
years of your life on this tragedy. Elizabeth is gone. If
she were alive, someone would have collected the reward long ago. God knows, enough charlatans have
tried to deceive you over the years. How many false
Elizabeths have appeared? Three?"

"Four." Moisture glistened in the faded hazel eyes.
"None of them real." Her lower lip trembled, then
firmed. "One babe was too young; another, twice Elizabeth's age." She sighed heavily. "The most outlandish
was by a Methodist minister who produced a mulatto
girl with a port-wine birthmark on one cheek and hair
bleached the color of hemp."

"Five thousand pounds reward," Will said. "You offered too much. A hundred pounds is more than most
Carolina dirt farmers, white or black, see in a lifetime."

"I would gladly have paid a hundred times that. You
know I could. The Graymoor fortune . . ." Lady Graymoor cleared her throat. "But I wasn't gulled by their
foul knavery. I will not be duped by fortune hunters."

"So far."

"Not ever." Lizzy tapped one kidskin slipper firmly. "But we weren't speaking of my personal affairs, were we? We were discussing that exotic creature lying upstairs."

"Angel is attractive," he said, releasing Lady Graymoor's hand. "I will concede that much." Even the fever hadn't stripped away any of Angel's beauty. If anything, her weakness, her vulnerability, made him even more determined to protect her . . . and even more confused.

"What does she mean to you?"

"Honestly?" Will looked away in an unconscious attempt to hide his inner turmoil. "I don't know."

A smile softened Lizzy's overly powdered features. "Yours is the household of an unmarried gentleman. And this is Charleston. I don't need to remind you that word of your exquisite little houseguest will spread through this city in hours."

"I told you, Angel saved my life at great risk to her own."

"Then she must be more precious to me than diamonds. For I could not continue without you, William. I simply could not." Lizzy fixed him with a shrewd stare. "Regardless of how highly you regard her, of how we all must, this arrangement won't do. It won't do at all. Your Mistress Angel must leave this household at once."

"She isn't my mistress!"

"I meant no harm. You mistake my meaning. You are too sensitive."

"I can't turn her out. I feel responsible for her. She's an innocent, and she doesn't know a soul in this town."

Sighing, Lizzy leaned down to scratch behind her spaniel's ear. "You chose an odd way to protect your ward's reputation." The dog laid a feathery paw on Lizzy's knee.

"I realize that your intentions are—"

She cut him short. "Have you thought of what this will mean to Julia? How it will look to her father?"

"I've nothing to hide. Julia and I are not betrothed."

"Not formally perhaps, but can you deny there has been an understanding?"

He stiffened. "I do deny it." He rose. "Julia and I have our differences. She wants a stay-at-home husband, not one who will spend eight months of the year at sea."

"She's a good person. She cares deeply for you. And you are long past the time when you should have chosen a wife."

"I won't tie myself to a desk, Lizzy. Not even for Richard's money."

Lady Graymoor pushed the dog down. "Why do the young believe that wealth and marriage are not compatible? Don't be a fool, William. Don't throw away the best thing that's ever happened to you because she's the answer to your financial problems. You and Julia have been friends for years, long before the Falcon fortune vanished."

"Yes, we've been more than friends. And in all this time, she still can't realize that I'm not a man to be content on shore. I'd be bored senseless in six months. Impossible to live with in ten."

"Don't avoid the subject. Keeping a woman like Angel in your home is a public slap in the face to Julia, so long as there's the slightest chance you two might wed."

Guilt, thick as island fog, washed over him. "Julia doesn't think that way. She was here today. She knows that—"

"Stuff and nonsense. You talk like a green boy." Lizzy

leaned back in the chair, gripping both armrests. "People will assume that you and this woman are intimate."

"I don't care about gossip. I'm not turning her out into the streets."

"Did I say anything about turning her into the street? What do you think I am? A heartless old woman? If I care for anyone in the world, other than my silly dogs, it's you, William. If this brave young creature saved your life, then she deserves our support. But I refuse to allow you to ruin your reputation, and this . . . this Angel's by keeping her here."

"I won't send her back to the island. She'd be in great danger."

"And she's not in danger under this roof?" Lady Graymoor rapped his forearm sharply with her folded fan. "She will stay with me."

"Absolutely not."

"Ridiculous. It's the perfect solution. Looking after her will give me something useful to do."

"You don't know Angel."

"No, I don't. But for that matter, what do you know of her?" She hesitated and went on with a rush. "There's no possibility that she could be—"

"Your grandchild?"

"Elizabeth would be about twenty-five years of age. If this girl Angel—"

"No, Lizzy. No chance. I met her mother. She's little better than a common dockside trollop. Once you've talked to Angel, you would realize that she's not of gentle blood. I'll not have you give a moment's thought that she could be."

Lady Graymoor nodded. "I still want to help."

He hesitated. "Damn it, the truth is, I'm not certain that I entirely trust her. She might be dangerous."

"And I'm not?" Lady Graymoor laughed. "Leave your Angel to me. I'll set her on the straight and narrow."

"She may object."

"What young woman knows what's good for her? She's to come at once. Today. See to it, William."

Will grimaced. It didn't take a shot across his bow to recognize defeat when it stared him in the face. "Yes, ma'am, if you think that's best."

"It's not only best, it's all there is to be done."

"And you're certain you can lead us to this pirate settlement?" Richard Hamilton asked as he tamped tobacco into the bowl of his long-stemmed pipe.

Will nodded. "I think so." After a simple dinner with Julia and her father, during which Will had related an abbreviated account of his adventures, the two men had retired to Richard's library. As was the custom, Julia had excused herself, presumably to do whatever properly brought-up Charleston ladies did for amusement when there were no gentlemen present.

"I can't tell you what a shock it was to see your face," Richard said. "Fletcher was beside himself. He felt at fault, not being able to find you after you went over the side of the ship."

"I searched half of Charleston last night, looking for him. Then I met Reeve Williams. He told me you'd made Aaron master of the *Katherine,* and she'd sailed for Martinique last Monday." If someone else had to take command of the *Katherine,* he was glad it was Aaron. But the schooner was his pride and joy, and he couldn't help feeling regret over losing her.

Richard, a small, dapper man with thinning brown hair and a slight paunch, poured brandy for them both and offered him a glass. Will took it and returned to his seat near the window.

"Did Williams tell you what our cargo consisted of?"

"No." Will kept his expression bland. "Said he didn't have any idea. He saw wooden crates being loaded, but didn't believe the boxes contained chairs or bedsteads. What are we shipping to Martinique?"

"Pennsylvania rifles. Black powder from a small company on the Brandywine. The Indies are about to go up in flames, Will. All this abolition nonsense. Do you know the ratio of freemen to slaves down there? People haven't forgotten the slave revolts of the nineties. Plantation owners and merchants need to protect their interests. And we can command top dollar for what makes them feel safe." Richard lit his pipe.

"Dangerous cargo if the British stop Aaron and search the ship," Will answered. If they found guns, they'd not be content with confiscating them and conscripting the crew into service. Aaron would end up at the end of rope or rotting in some English prison hulk.

"Fletcher has a good head on his shoulders."

"None better," Will agreed. And no better friend. "He should have had his own ship long ago." He frowned. "But I hate to see Aaron and his crew risk their lives for—"

"Profit?" Richard supplied. "Without it . . . you're witness to what comes of running a shipping company without making a profit. When you cut to the core, it's all about—"

"Profit," Will finished. "I'm aware of that. And that's why I'm so anxious to put an end to this nest of coastal pirates. If it hadn't been for them, my father might be alive today."

"And you'd still be helping to run Falcon Shipping."

Will took a sip of the brandy. It was French, very good, and very expensive. It slipped down his throat smoothly, leaving a warm tingling in his mouth. "I need to close that chapter in my life before I can move on."

"Your father was my friend for half a century," Richard said. "No one misses him more than I do. And no one regrets the downfall of your house more." He tapped his pipe against the brick hearth. "This time, we won't be content to throw one ship against these wreckers. We'll send enough men and firepower to be certain that none of them lives to stand trial. I'll speak to the governor. He is—"

"I believe in the law. If I have to kill an opponent in battle . . ." Will left the rest unsaid. He'd killed men before, in the Caribbean, but he'd slain them in defense of his life and those of his crew. It wasn't an act he talked about.

Richard's statement made him uneasy. Will didn't want to consider leveling a pistol at Cap'n or Bett, or even the one-armed Nehemiah who'd conducted the sham marriage ceremony. "I'll go," he said. "I'll do my part to bring the Brethren to justice. But if they drop their weapons and ask for mercy, I'll bring them back here to stand before a judge and jury."

Will's host turned away and extracted a map of the East Coast from a desk drawer. "I'm more convinced than ever that these villains haven't been working alone. They're too organized, and they know too much about shipping schedules. Easily transported, valuable cargoes are most at risk. Tobacco ships are never waylaid. Someone's giving the wreckers information."

"Edward Mason?"

Richard nodded. "He's the only one who hasn't lost ships on the Outer Banks. And he's the only man to argue against organizing a force to eradicate them."

"What about his younger brother George?"

"George is an enigma. He's extremely fond of Julia,

that much I know. He escorted her to Rachel Ridgely's engagement ball last winter. You were on that trip to Boston, I believe. But both George and Edward have influence because—"

"They're nephews to our esteemed governor."

"Exactly. Mason's tried to convince his uncle that going after these wreckers means crossing into North Carolina waters. He says it would be wiser to contact the authorities there and let them deal with the villains."

"We know where that will get us," Will said. "We've been complaining to them for years about the problem." He paused, then went on. "I've never liked Edward, but that doesn't tie him to acts of piracy."

"He's a man with expensive tastes. A gambler." The older man's face hardened. "Mason lost two thousand dollars last week."

"On a horse?" Will asked.

Will and Edward Mason went back a long way. Edward was a bully, older than Will by ten years, and prone to using boots and fists on younger lads. Quieter George had hovered in the shadows, never involving himself in the fights, but standing behind his brother.

While Will was growing up, Edward's age had given him the advantage. Once, Edward had killed a hound pup of his out of pure meanness, and more than once, Edward had beaten him bloody. Everything changed when Will returned from several years at sea. Not only had he had a growth spurt, but he'd gained survival skills in darkened fo'c'sles and the dockside stews.

"Edward put his money on a horse with a weak foreleg, so it happened," Richard continued. "But it's not the first time Mason has lost, and it's not just betting on slow horses."

"Papa!" Julia called from the hallway.

"In a moment, dear." Richard threw him a meaning-
ful look. "We'll talk about Mason later. I think we've
neglected our hostess long enough." He smiled thinly. "I
understand that woman . . . the one who assisted you.
She's staying at your house?"

"No, sir. Lady Graymoor has already taken me to
task for that. She's opening her home to Angel."

"Good." Richard rose and slapped him companion-
ably on the shoulder. "You know what my hopes are for
you and Julia. No." He lifted a hand in protest. "Don't
say anything. I don't want to put you on the spot. What
I want doesn't really matter. Your position with Hamilton Shipping has nothing to do with my daughter. I already think of you as the son I never had, Will."

"I know that."

"Whoever marries Julia will inherit everything I
own."

"Whoever marries Julia will get a wonderful woman.
I'm just not certain I'm that man, the one who will
make her happy."

"What is this about marriage?" Julia smiled radiantly
from the doorway. "Enough of your business talk,
Papa. I won't allow you to keep Will to yourself all
evening. He's promised to walk with me in the gardens."

Richard beamed. "You know I can deny you nothing."

"Nothing but the right to pick my own bridegroom,"
she fussed, taking Will's arm. "Will, pay no heed to
him."

"A partnership in the business and a dowry that will
free you of all debt," Richard reminded her.

"Papa, you are disgraceful. Will and I are friends."

"The best of friends." He smiled at her. And I'm the
greatest of fools not to grasp what's being offered, he

thought. Half the men in Charleston would give their right arm for such a proposition. Julia would make the perfect wife. She was good-natured, sweet-tempered, and rich. And she would solve all of his financial worries.

So why was he walking arm in arm through this magnificent house with a woman like Julia Hamilton and wishing he were wandering a nameless beach with a merry-be-gotten redhead without a copper to her name?

Chapter 14

It was nearly eleven o'clock when Will took his leave of Julia and her father and walked the few blocks home. Despite the hour, people were on the street and carriages rattled past.

"Will!" A well-dressed man on horseback reined in beside him. "It's good to see you alive. Come with me. I'm meeting my cousin Beau and Tom Humphreys at Dixon's."

"No, thanks," Will answered. "I've early business tomorrow."

"Planning another pirate hunt?" Joseph Fisher's ruddy face split in a grin.

"I am."

"Better luck next time. The trick is to catch them before they catch you."

"Thanks. I'll try to remember that. I suppose the tale is all over the city."

"It is. Edward Mason has done everything but place a notice in the paper. He's no friend of yours, Will."

"Obviously. He's still vexed that he couldn't pick up Falcon's Nest for a song."

"He told my Beau that he still means to have it. Wants the place as a wedding present for George."

"Hadn't heard that brother George had found anyone willing to have him."

Joseph laughed. "No, but you know George, always hopeful. But, I'm serious. You should come with me. If Mason's there, you might win back that bay mare of yours. Even my little sister could beat Edward at piquet."

"Another time." Will waved and walked on. He'd known Fisher, Beau, and Tom since he was in leading strings. They were a good lot, but he had no wish to extend the evening with drinks and gaming. And he wasn't in a mood to confront Mason. His garden stroll with Julia had done nothing to settle his mind.

He found her attractive, charming, and witty. But he couldn't shed his reluctance to make their friendship more. He didn't doubt that Julia would make him a good wife. It was his ability to make her a decent husband that caused him worry.

He wondered if he would have felt differently about Julia if he'd never looked into Angel's sea-green eyes or spent time alone with her on the island. Would he have married Julia as everyone expected him to and been content?

He wouldn't be the first man or the last to lose all reason over a pair of perfect breasts and a sweet little bottom that fit perfectly in his hands. Suppose his intense attraction to Angel was purely sexual?

Or suppose he'd let himself be drawn into the web of a heartless wench who could kill as easily as she could shed her clothing?

The problem was that he was beginning to think of Angel as more than just a brave friend or a ripe and luscious body that he longed to bed. She was wise and funny, and she viewed the world in a way that he hadn't done since he was young.

Not that she was a child—far from it. Angel was different, a woman so far apart from others of her kind that they seemed hollow and dull in comparison. He could almost picture her waiting for him when he returned from a voyage . . . or worse . . . see her keeping step beside him as they strolled through the market of some exotic port.

They had nothing in common. She was without education, social position, or respectable family. Hell, the chit could not read or write.

He shrugged, wondering for the first time whether those things were really important or if everything he'd been taught to believe about a Falcon's position in life was nonsense.

His front door opened directly onto Church Street. It was unlocked, as usual. He slipped in quietly so as not to disturb the servants, but chuckled when he found Delphi waiting for him at the foot of the wide staircase.

"Even'n', Mr. Will." Her soft voice echoed in the empty hall passage as she nodded slightly in lieu of a curtsy.

It was hard for Will to get used to the empty feeling. Once these wide planks had been covered with Persian rugs. An Irish hunt table and matching chairs had lined one wall; a tall, Japanese Imari palace vase had stood in the entrance corner. But those items had all been sold to pay debts, and this area as well as many of the other rooms stood empty of all but dour family portraits staring blankly from their gilded frames.

Delphi, however, remained as staunch and cheerful as ever. She had been a member of this household since she was born. Her mother, Sally, had been a wedding gift to his mother when she married his father. And although Delphi had received her freedom at Will's mother's death, this remained the black woman's home as much as his.

"Can I get you anything?" she asked. "I made a fresh kettle of she-crab soup this afternoon."

Will's feelings for his housekeeper would have been difficult for him to dissect, let alone explain to Angel. Delphi was more than a trusted employee. While they were related by affection rather than blood, both maintained a titular master-servant relationship that fooled few. Delphi not only managed Falcon's Nest as she chose, she was not above chastising him when she was displeased by his words or actions. And he, in turn, felt providing for her and her large family was a matter of honor.

One of the reasons losing the mansion would have been such a disaster was that Delphi, her husband, her aging mother, children, and grandchildren would have been left homeless and unemployed. None of them were slaves, but they'd been the property of the Falcons at one time, and Will felt the weight of his responsibility toward them all.

"No, thank you, Delphi," he answered. "I couldn't eat another bite. Miss Hamilton's cook was in fine form." He removed his high-crowned hat, but gripped it by the narrow brim, unconsciously turning it in his hands. "How's Aunt Sally tonight?" he asked, inquiring of Delphi's mother.

"Passable. Thinks she might get up tomorrow, might bake some cherry tarts."

"That's good to hear," he answered. Delphi's mother was blind, and so far as he knew, hadn't stirred from her bed in the room off the kitchen for three years. But every evening Aunt Sally expressed a belief that the next day she'd be up and ready to resume her household tasks.

Will glanced up the stairs and back to Delphi. She

maintained a solemn expression, but mischief twinkled in her dark brown eyes. "Is Angel settled in at Lizzy's?" he asked brusquely.

He knew she was gone. The house felt vacant. Even sick, Angel's vitality had added an intangible excitement to Falcon's Nest.

He swallowed his disappointment, refusing to give in to the irrational need to see her. "Did she protest the move?"

Flickering candlelight highlighted Delphi's smooth brown face. "No, sir. She never made a whimper; walked down those steps on her own two feet."

"Good, good," he replied. What had he expected? That Angel would refuse to leave his house? She was angry with him. Naturally, she would be pleased to take up residence elsewhere.

"Mr. Will? Something troubling you?"

"No. I'm fine. Just tired," he said. "Don't worry about me. You go on to bed."

She lit a second candle from the first and handed it to him. "Good night, Mr. Will. Sleep easy."

He waited until Delphi's footsteps faded away before slowly climbing the winding staircase. What was wrong with him? It was late, too late to go visiting. Damned if he'd make a fool of himself by worrying about Angel when she was snug at Lizzy's.

What he ought to have done was take Joseph up on his offer to go to Dixon's. A few drinks, a few hands of cards certainly would have improved his mood. The trouble was that he hadn't visited Savannah in months. He'd touched in other ports only briefly, not long enough to find a healthy and willing lady of the evening. Perhaps he'd better rethink his policy of never buying the services of a whore in Charleston. A man who set too many boundaries for himself was courting trouble, and who went without release was bound to start thinking with his third leg rather than his head.

Will swore softly. It was his head that had gotten him into his mess. And nothing could alter the fact that since he'd first laid eyes on Angel, he'd wanted to make love to no other woman.

And since having Angel would be like sailing into the eye of a hurricane without a rudder, he doubted that course would do much to ease his confusion.

Will started to open his bedchamber door, then thought better of it. Instead, he went down the hall and entered his father's room.

Inside, he stood still and gazed around. The chamber hadn't changed since the day his father had died. His mother's portrait hung on the far wall. A carved rosewood table held a bowl and pitcher, his father's Bible, and a long-stemmed clay pipe. Furnishings, bed linen, and curtains were as fresh as if Delphi had changed them this morning. And if Will let himself give way to fancy, he could imagine that he still caught a whiff of his father's pipe tobacco in the air.

Heart thudding, Will crossed to the spot on the far side of the bed where he'd discovered his father's body.

"Are you here?" Will called.

The only answer was the steady tick of a mantel clock.

"Why?" Anguish welled up in Will's chest. "Why did you do it?"

He moved the candle back and forth above the floorboards, half expecting to see a telltale stain, but there was no trace of the rivers of dark blood or of the sickly sweet smell of death. His grandfather's dueling pistol was gone as well. Will had hurled that into the Cooper River the morning after the inquest.

"We could have made it right," Will whispered

hoarsely. A hard lump rose in his throat, and he swallowed, trying to ease the constricted muscles.

He waited for his father's voice . . . his deep chuckle. When it didn't come, Will nodded and blinked away the motes of dust he was certain must be the cause of the stinging in his eyes. "Don't worry," he said aloud. "I'll settle your debts, and I'll see justice done. I swear it."

Will left the room and closed the door tightly behind him. If there were ghosts in this house, they weren't lingering there in his father's chamber.

Still, he was too melancholy for sleep. "I wonder if Lizzy's still awake," he wondered aloud. Talking with Lizzy, even arguing with her, always made him feel better.

"Lizzy, hell," he muttered. It was Angel who drew him, Angel who had gotten under his skin so that he couldn't stand being apart from her.

Retracing his steps, he went downstairs, strode through the hall, and followed a passageway that led to the gardens and stables at the back of the house. An eight-foot-high brick wall divided Falcon's Nest from Lizzy's grounds, but the wrought-iron gate was unlocked, the hinge oiled to open easily into her formal garden.

No lights showed on the ground floor of Lady Graymoor's home. On the south side of the house where Lizzy's private suite lay, and on the third-floor servants' quarters, there was pitch darkness. But upstairs, in the oldest part of the mansion, a candle glowed behind shuttered French doors.

A thick mist had drifted in, covering the boxwood and worn brick walks. There were no stars, and the waning moon painted the still garden a ghostly pewter-blue. But Lizzy's property was as familiar to Will as the deck of the *Katherine*. In seconds, he'd doffed both hat and coat, discarded them on a marble bench beside the fountain, and approached the house.

Wooden pillars encircled by wisteria enclosed a porch on the garden level of the original section. The same columns also supported a narrow balcony and ornamental railing outside the second-floor guest chamber. Swiftly, Will climbed up the gnarled vine to the landing.

In a narrow alley, two streets nearer to the harbor, a man in a wide-brimmed hat waited in the shadows. Somewhere off in the direction of McCrady's Tavern a dog barked, but the sound was distorted by the creeping fog that cloaked the shuttered office windows and locked warehouses.

Minutes passed. The seaman thrust his hands into his pockets and shifted his weight from one foot to the other. He could hear nothing but the hiss of his own breath. Still, he lingered, straining for the muffled thud of footsteps.

Without warning, small, cool fingers tapped his arm. The man leaped back, cursing, and slammed into the wall. "What the—"

"Jonah Lapp?"

"I'm Lapp."

"Please, sir. Come wi' me." The black boy beckoned. "This way, sir."

His escort had no torch. Lapp followed as the child turned down one passageway and then another. The stench of rotting fish grew stronger.

"Here, sir." Lapp's guide pointed to a door. The faintest glow of light showed under the bottom.

"Where . . . ," he began, but the boy had melted into the darkness. Swearing, he shoved the door open. The room was small and bare of all but a three-legged table and a single candle stub. Someone stood in the far corner, but Lapp couldn't make out his face.

"If you're lookin' for your money back," the sailor warned. "I ain't about to—"

"You told me Falcon was dead."

"Thought he were."

"I paid for a service that I haven't received."

"It ain't my fault. I cut loose the cannon. And I would have smashed his skull, but a wave took him over—"

"Shut up. I don't want to hear your excuses. I want him dead or you'll return your wages—double."

"Go swive yerself," Lapp replied. "I ain't givin' you nothin', ya tight-arsed . . ." His eyes widened, and he backed up against the door, eyes riveted on the short-barreled pistol in his employer's gloved hand. "Here, now! Ain't no need fer that."

"If this is too difficult a task, I can find someone else. But if I hire another, you're expendable. Do we understand each other?"

"Yeah. All right. I'll do it."

"One chance. Fail me again, and you'll suffer the consequences. Don't think you can escape by taking ship. I'll know it. And I'll have a special reward waiting for you the next time you put into port—any port."

Lapp nodded, his gut twisting. Suddenly, he needed to take a shit. "I'll take care of him."

"Of them. Falcon brought a slut back with him. Red hair. Comely. Do them both and make it look like a crime of passion." He lowered the pistol, just a little, so that the weapon was aiming directly at his crotch. "Unless you're squeamish about the woman."

"Nah. Man or woman. Don't matter to me." He straightened. "You care if I do her last?"

"As you please."

"But I oughta get somethin' extra for her."

"That will be your something extra, won't it?"

"Besides. Hard coin. Murder don't come cheap."

"That's not an unreasonable request. No mistakes this time. Is that clear?"

"Clear as mother's gin."

"Good." He leaned over and blew out the candle. "Wait here for a quarter hour, Lapp. Follow me before that, and I'll blow your head off." He cleared his throat. "Fail me again, and I'll have someone knock you sense-less and sell you to the British navy. I'm sure they'll pay a reward. I understand you had a misunderstanding with a second officer."

"Yeah."

"When you've completed your assignment, wait three days, then go to Carson's shipyard, just after dusk. Your payment will be waiting."

"All right. Three days. I . . ." Hinges squeaked, and Lapp became aware that he was alone in the room. He swore softly, gritting his teeth against the waves of mus-cle spasms.

What he needed was a drink. More than one. He wondered if it was safe to leave and thought the better of it. Still cursing, he dragged down his canvas breeches and emptied his bowels where he stood. "Serve the rich bastard right," he muttered between groans. "Serve him right to have to clean up shit."

"Angel." Will called her name quietly as he swung long legs over the balcony railing. "Are you in there?" He took a deep breath and reached for the bronze knob. "It's Will. Don't be afraid."

A faint tinkling of musical notes came from inside.

"Go away," she called. "I've nothing to say to you."

He pushed open the door. Angel sat cross-legged on

the high bed, her glorious hair spread out around her shoulders, a silver music box upside down in her lap. She wore nothing but a lacy white linen shift . . . a garment so thin that he could clearly see the darker shading of her nipples through the cloth.

His mouth went dry. He drew in a deep breath, feeling heat flood his loins. "Angel . . . ," he began. He wanted her. Honor be damned. He had to have her or go mad.

Her eyes narrowed just before she hurled the music box at his head. "No!"

Sidestepping, he swore and snatched the object out of midair. "Are you trying to kill me?"

"If I meant to kill ye, it wouldn't be with a trinket, you smooth-tongued son of a bitch!" She scrambled up, slid down off the bed, and flung herself at him. The music box tumbled to the floor as he caught her and crushed her against him.

"Angel. For God's sake." Desire spiked through him as she struggled in his arms. "Calm down." His hoarse whisper broke as her unbound hair brushed his face, and he drank deeply of the sweet, intoxicating scent.

"Calm! I'll show ye calm!" Her breath came in short, shallow gasps. Her breasts pressed hard against his chest. He could feel her hips and thighs. She was warm, and soft, and dangerous.

"Be still. Your arm. I don't want to hurt you."

She had no such consideration for him. "Devil the arm, and devil you!" she cried as she kicked him soundly in the knee and pounded at him with a clenched fist. "Burn in Satan's tar pit, ye bloody, lyin' blackguard!"

"Quiet! Do you want to raise the house?" Her blows were more than love taps, but he paid them no heed. He didn't want to rouse Lizzy's servants, so he clamped a hand over her mouth. "Angel, stop!"

Pain shot through his fingers as she bit him.

"Ouch! Damn it!" He bore her backward and pressed her down on the bed. "I'm not going to hurt you."

He threw himself over her, barely avoiding a knee to his groin. Catching the wrist of her uninjured arm, he pinned it to the mattress. His heart hammered against his chest. Heat flashed through his body. "Be still, for the sake of God!" He groaned as raw lust flooded his senses. His sex swelled and hardened, pulsing with sudden, intense need.

But Angel paid no heed to his growing erection. She bucked and thrust against him. "I hate you!" she sobbed. "Let me go. Let me—"

Abruptly, he released her and rolled away, shaken, stunned by his violent reaction . . . shaken more by what he wanted to do than by her forceful blows.

He was no rapist, but he was a man. And having her half-naked beneath him . . . her scent in his nostrils . . . her hair loose and brushing his face was almost more than he could bear. He gritted his teeth and groaned, fighting the urge to capture a reddened nipple in his mouth and taste of her sweetness . . . struggling to keep from parting her thighs and . . . "I'm . . . I'm sorry," he said.

"Sorry? You're sorry?" Bolts of green lightning flashed in her eyes. "You want to hunt down my family . . . my friends, and hang them? And all you say is that you're sorry?"

Not trusting himself to touch her, he rose off the bed and backed away. She sat up, and he saw a red stain flowering on her injured arm. "I never meant to harm you."

"Then you should have left me where you found me!"

"With a nest of pirates?"

"Better for me and mine if I'd let you drown."

"Do you mean that?"

"Aye!" Then she covered her mouth with her hands. "Nay, I don't know . . . I know nothing since I've come to this place." She stared at him, her face pale in the candlelight, her cheeks streaked with tears.

What are you? he wondered. Temptress? Innocent? Murderer?

She shook her head, and gradually the fire in her gaze cooled. "I would not see you drowned and food for crabs," she admitted. "I could not. But neither will I stand by and watch you harm those I love."

His groin ached, and his pulse pounded in his head. "I've no business here," he said. He took a step toward the French doors.

"No. Stay. Throwing the box was a brat's trick. I should not have done it."

"Your aim's good. You nearly brained me."

"Not good enough." She bit her lower lip. "I could not believe that you would betray me so. To plot against the Brethren and turn me—your handfast wife—out of your house."

"You knew all along that I mean to rid the coast of raiders."

She shook her head. "I thought I could make you understand that we are not the murderers you seek."

"I can't let go of this, Angel. My father died because of—"

"Your father took a coward's way out."

Cold fury seized him. "If you were a man . . . ," he began.

"Would you strike me for speaking the truth? It is the truth, and well ye know it!" she flung back. "Have ye not thought as much yourself?"

"My father was no coward."

"Then why didn't he live and face his troubles instead of leavin' them for you to solve?"

"You can't understand a gentleman's honor. There's no way I can make you see—"

"Nay. I cannot. And no way you can make me believe you're not ashamed of me in front of your friends. Or that you didn't send me here to this house to be rid of me."

Don't," he said. "I wasn't trying to get rid of you. I simply—"

She let go of his hand and placed two fingers over his lips. "No lies between us."

His chest tightened as he saw the tears glistening like stars on her eyelashes. "It's not what you think. Lady Graymoor is my friend. She offered to bring you here because it isn't fitting that you remain at Falcon's Nest."

Angel's mouth trembled. "Nay. Another lie," she said. "Julia doesn't want me in Charleston. And I understand that well, because I don't want to be here, either."

"It's not what you think. Julia isn't jealous of you."

"If she isn't, she's a bigger fool than I am, Will Falcon. Her eyes eat you like a spring bear devours honey."

He pulled her into his arms. "I care about you, Angel. I swear I do."

For a moment, she held herself stiffly, and then the tears began to flow. He held her for long minutes while she wept.

And finally, she lifted her head and looked into his eyes. "Don't leave me," she begged. "I don't want to be alone this night. Please, Will. I'm . . . I'm so afraid."

"You?" He didn't think she was afraid of anything, this woman who'd faced down armed men and trod the pitching decks of a vessel in foul weather without the slightest protest.

She wrapped her arms around him and uttered a strangled sob. "I am," she said. "I'm lost without sun . . . or compass in this place."

It was wrong. It was stupid. Yet, he couldn't resist her pleading. He let her draw him back to the bed . . . back to tousled blankets that held her scent, to soft white sheets that bore the imprint of her body. . . .

•

Chapter 15

For a long time, Angel lay cradled in Will's strong arms, trying not to weep, trying not to beg him for what she knew she couldn't have. Her thoughts tumbled frantically, seeking solid earth and finding only shifting sand.

When had she lost her reason and allowed herself to hope Will might love her—she who had never had anyone to call her own? And when had she begun to love him?

Unshed tears as bitter as salt burned her eyes. Never had she felt so weak . . . so unable to choose her own path and follow it, come gale wind or rogue wave. And not once in her life had she looked into the future and seen naught but emptiness.

Finally, Will, a man so beautiful that he might be a merman spun of mist and dreams, leaned down and kissed her tenderly. "I shouldn't be here," he said. "I'm taking advantage of Lizzy's hospitality in the most craven manner."

She moistened her lips and met his gaze with her own. What right did she have to question him as though he belonged to her? To speak as if their wedding vows had been more than a wreckers' handfasting exchanged at sword point.

"I know what I am and what you are," she whispered.

161

"But I must know the truth. Did you lie with your Julia tonight?"

Scowling, he stiffened and pulled away from her. "Julia's a lady! She's not the kind of—"

"Woman that I am?" Angel finished. Terror turned her numb inside, but she would not let him get the best of her. "You need not say it. I know that I am no soft Charleston maiden with pale skin and uncallused hands. But if you haven't gone to Julia's bed, there's no reason you shouldn't be here with me."

"There's every reason." Anger glowed in his eyes. Still, she would not yield, and she would not let him see her fear.

"I don't know what to say to you," he said. "Our being together breaks every rule of honorable behavior."

"Who makes these rules? And who follows them?"

"I do. I try."

"These rules . . . are they written down?"

"They're taught." His features seemed as sharp and lifeless as a ship's figurehead. His eyes burned through her, etching her soul.

"Then you've been taught nonsense." She rose on her knees, struggling to find the words to make him see. "I need you tonight, and mayhap you need me."

"It isn't fair to you for me to be here."

"Let me judge what's right for me." She reached out and touched his cheek, trailing her fingers along his jaw and lower lip. "Can you tell me that you don't care for me?"

"You know I do. But I also care for Julia. And every ounce of common sense tells me that we don't have a chance in hell of being happy together."

"Because you mean to lead men to kill the Brethren?"

"That's part of it."

"You don't have to go, Will. Revenge won't ease the hurt you feel for the loss of your father."

"Maybe not. But it will save other lives. It's something I have to do."

"Even if I beg you not to?"

He nodded. "Even then."

"You found us by accident," she argued. "But many have searched. Mayhap you'll not be lucky again."

"We'll see."

She was trembling inside, but she hadn't given up hope that she could change his mind, make him see the Brethren as she did. "Can ye deny that you brought me here for your own reasons? Not to save me from being hung, but because you could not be parted from me?"

"Maybe I do."

She gave a small sigh of disbelief. "Liar. There is your dishonor, Will. Not in wanting me, but in refusing to see what your heart tells you."

He swallowed. "I wish it were that simple."

"I'm a woman, and you're a man. What else can be more important?" She put her arms around his neck and pulled him down.

Could Will kiss her like this and not love her? Could the sweet coming together of teeth and tongues, the wonder of skin against skin, the rush of overwhelming excitement be nothing more than physical mating?

It was impossible to believe that, and she would never do so again. Even if he left her forever, she would cherish the memory of these moments when she knew that what she'd found was love. "If you want to break our handfast, can we not part friends?"

"Angel." He groaned as he pulled away. "There can't be a future for us. My life and yours . . . they don't . . ."

"Right now . . . at this minute . . . they do," she whispered. And catching his hand, she lifted it to her breast. " 'Twould be a shame to waste this fine bed." Shivers of delight skittered through her at his strong, hot touch.

Leaning forward, she kissed him, slowly and deliberately, lingering at the corner of his mouth, then slipping her tongue teasingly along his lower lip. "Ah, Will," she murmured as she kneaded the muscles at the nape of his neck until he groaned with pleasure.

"Witch," he accused. But this time it was Will who kissed her, who caressed her throat and ran his hands possessively over her body, lingering at her breasts and causing her nipples to swell and harden into tight, aching buds.

"Kiss me there," she begged him, pushing her shift off one shoulder to allow him access.

Gently, he cupped her breast in his hand and nestled his face against it. "You are so beautiful," he murmured huskily, "my wild, beautiful Angel . . ."

Her breathing quickened as his lips closed on her nipple. "Oh . . ." The sweet tugging sensation caused waves of rainbow light to break over her. But it wasn't enough, didn't satisfy the throbbing ache between her thighs.

She couldn't lie still. She had to get closer to him . . . to feel all of him against her bare skin. It didn't matter if he left her before morning. This moment would be all she would ever ask for. "Forget your rules," she whispered. "For this one night, forget everything but what we feel for each other."

Boldly, she sought the source of his power, sliding an exploring hand inside his breeches to stroke the length and breadth of his arousal, making him gasp with need. The feel of him was glorious, hot, and granite-hard beneath the layer of silken-soft skin.

"Take me, Will," she begged. "Make me yours."

"No! I can't do this," he protested, pulling away.

Tears blurred her vision as she stared at him. "Why?" she asked. What manner of man was he to refuse what she offered? She knew he didn't despise her. She could hear his quick intake of breath, feel the hard heat of his need.

Heat scalded her cheeks. "Go," she said.

"I'm sorry," he answered. "This isn't about you. It's me." He rose off the bed, tucking his shirt back into his breeches.

She couldn't tear her eyes away from him. She should hate him, but she couldn't. She would sooner despite the sun for being out of reach. She had no shame.

And as if he had read her mind and misunderstood her thoughts, he said, "You've nothing to be ashamed of. The fault is mine. I should never have let this happen."

She buried her face in her hands, shaking with unfulfilled need.

"Don't cry," he said. "I . . ." Swearing, he crossed the room to where a glass decanter of port stood on a table. He poured two glasses, then carried them back to the bed, and handed one to her. "Take it, damn it."

She lifted the glass to her lips, but she couldn't drink. She felt as though she'd turned to wood. She couldn't speak . . . couldn't even think. All she knew was that Will was leaving her, and she might never see him again.

"I have to decide," he said. "I need to choose which way my life will continue."

"You! Your life?" Without warning, her temper flared. "A pox on you for bringing me here, for making me—" *love you.* She almost said it, but snatched back the word at the last second, and with it saved a fragment of her shattered pride.

She pulled her legs up so that she sat Indian fashion

on the bed again. "I'll trouble you no more." She forced herself to take a sip of the wine and swallow it. "If you won't be Adam to my Eve, I'll find another not so particular."

"Don't talk like that," he said harshly.

She swirled the port in her glass. The thick, sweet liquid was as red as blood. "You've given up any right you might have had to tell me how to act or what to say."

"I don't know why I came here," he said.

"Liar." Angel's injured arm was throbbing, but she ignored it. Her heart was what was broken. The cut would soon heal. But nothing could mend her heart. "Be glad I'm not a witch," she said. "If I were, I'd give you reason—Go, Will. Go before I wake the house with my screams. I release you from our handfast marriage."

His eyes clouded with confusion and regret. "And if I don't want to be?"

She shrugged. "What you want doesn't matter."

"I'll take care of you. I won't abandon you."

"I can take care of myself, Will Falcon. Any of the Brethren could tell ye that."

"I've hurt you."

"Hurt me?" She forced a bitter laugh. "You're the fool. You did what I planned all along. You brought me to Charleston, where I wanted to be. Where a canny wench can make something of herself besides toothless and old before her time. I'll find my own fortune. And none—least of all you, you hamper-arsed cod's head—will say me nay!"

His reply was one that would have made Bett blush, but Angel paid him no heed as he jerked open the louvered double door and vanished over the side of the balcony. Instead, she sank to the bare floor and sobbed dry tears until she could weep no more.

• • •

Back in his own house, Will finished off a bottle of French brandy before retiring. It was late when he rose; his head felt twice its size, and his tongue felt as though it had thickened and grown fur.

Sickened in spirit, he had the feeling he had committed some great crime the night before but couldn't for the life of him figure out what else he could have done.

"Damn you, Angel! Would you rather I took my pleasure and then left you for someone of my own station?" He'd done the only honorable thing. So why did he feel like a man who'd just drowned a sack of newborn pups?

An hour later, bathed, shaven, and fortified with two cups of Delphi's strong coffee, he presented himself at Lizzy's front door with a dozen phrases to soothe Angel's wounded pride.

"You are too late, sir," Griffin informed him. "Lady Graymoor and her guest departed by coach earlier."

"Do you know where they went? When they'll be back?"

Dark Welsh eyes regarded Will with a hint of amusement, but the butler's face remained expressionless, and his tone formal. "I am not in the habit of questioning her ladyship on her comings and goings, Mr. Falcon. And I would not be so presumptuous as to hazard a guess when she might return." Griffin inclined his head slightly. "Would you care to leave a message, sir?"

"No message."

Will's mood had not improved when he turned to walk the few blocks to the offices of Hamilton Shipping near the harbor. Where the hell had the two of them gone? Certainly not to the physician's? If Angel had taken a turn for the worse, Dr. Madison would have come to the house. Where could Lizzy possibly go this morning that she would wish Angel to accompany her?

Will had covered half the distance to Hamilton's, passing people on the street whom he'd known all his life and barely offering civil greetings, before realizing he'd missed an appointment with Richard. Two merchants and clients, Walter Hughes and Guy Albright, were supposed to meet with him and Richard to discuss raising funds for the expedition north to destroy the Brethren.

"Mr. Hamilton waited for you," a sharp-nosed clerk with ink-stained fingers said, when Will entered the outer office. "They left more than an hour ago." The young man frowned. "Mr. Hamilton and the others seemed quite put out."

"Do you know where they went?" Will asked.

"Didn't say. Mr. Hamilton did say that he expects to see you here on Monday morning, no later than eight o'clock."

Uncertain whether he would find Richard at his home, Will stepped out into the street just as Edward and George Mason, and a third man whom Will didn't know, approached on horseback. All three animals were streaked with sweat, giving evidence of hard riding.

Edward was riding Calli, a sweet-faced bay that had been Will's favorite horse before he'd lost her at auction. Calli tossed her head and nickered in recognition, only to have Edward jerk hard on the reins, yanking the mare's head back. Pink foam flew from the corners of Calli's mouth.

Will used every ounce of self-control to keep from dragging Mason out of the saddle and grinding his smug face into the dust. He knew that showing interest in Calli would only tempt the bully to further cruelties.

"Falcon!" Edward touched his hat with his whip. "Heard you were still among the living. Congratulations." Will hadn't seen the big man in months, but he appeared much the same, over-fed and over-sour, with a soft, almost feminine mouth, faded blue eyes, and sagging jowls.

George nodded and mumbled a greeting. Their companion stared pointedly away and did not speak.

"You're ill-suited to that mare," Will said, clenching his fingers into tight fists at his side.

"She's been ruined by poor training. My horses and my slaves learn to obey me, or—"

"It's me you've a grudge against," Will interrupted. "Not the horse. I'll give you twice what you paid for her."

"Your credit's not good enough, Falcon," Edward said.

"Is that an insult?" Will asked.

"Take it for what you wish," Edward answered. "Everyone in this town knows you for a rakehell and a bounder. No better than your father."

Will lunged for Mason.

The stout man reined Calli around and drove his spurs into her sides in an attempt to run Will down. Calli reared, her front hooves cleaving the air inches away from his head as Mason slashed Will's face and arms with the leather crop.

Will didn't feel the pain. With one hand, he seized Calli's bridle and forced her to a standstill. With the other, he'd locked a vise grip on Mason's wrist and wrenched it until the bat dropped from his fingers.

In seconds, he had Mason three-quarters of the way out of the saddle and screaming for help. Releasing the mare, Will delivered two stinging openhanded slaps across Mason's face. "I demand satisfaction!" Will said. "Tomorrow. Pistols at dawn. Reynold's meadow."

George and the third rider were off their horses and coming to Edward's aid as men spilled out of the business establishments onto the street.

"My foot!" Edward howled. "My foot's caught in the stirrup."

"Tomorrow, sir. Be there," Will said, letting him go and stepping back. "If you're not, I swear on my father's grave, I'll hunt you down and shoot you like a rabid dog."

Chapter 16

"You want what?" Lady Graymoor demanded in her most imperious tone. It was midafternoon, and a footman wearing a purple turban had just ushered Will into Lizzy's opulent, private drawing room, where the countess was feeding strawberries to a large green and yellow parrot.

"I want your permission to ask Griffin to stand as my second," Will repeated quietly. "On the morrow."

He'd already regretted his public attack on Mason and the challenge that followed. He wasn't afraid to face him, and he wasn't sorry to have the chance to finish the bastard. It was his own inability to control his temper when provoked that troubled him most. But it was too late for remorse. What he'd set in motion must be finished. If he didn't meet Mason at Reynold's meadow tomorrow, he'd never be able to hold his head up in Charleston again.

Lizzy wiped her hands on a damp cloth, summoned the footman, and ordered both bird and servant away before settling herself in a chair. As though she had all the time in the world, she poured first a dollop of cream into a thin porcelain cup and then steaming black tea. She added three lumps of brown sugar, stirred, and sipped daintily. When she finally raised her gaze to meet Will's, she appeared as composed as if he'd announced

171

that it looked like it might rain. "Sit down," she instructed. "You're not meeting Edward until dawn tomorrow. It is dawn, isn't it? You men insist on rising early for your blood sports."

She pointed to a chair that she'd told him had once graced a French château. "Since you're not shooting anyone today, you may as well take tea with me. And do have a slice of this lemon cake. It's superb."

Tea and lemon cake. Trust Lizzy to take life in stride. But he took a chair, because it seemed rude not to. "No tea." He glanced around the room, half hoping that Angel would be there. She wasn't. It was true he wanted Griffin to stand up with him. But asking Lizzy's permission was only a formality. The real reason he'd come was his fear of what would happen to Angel if Mason killed him in the duel.

"Why my Griffin?" Lizzy asked. She was all in gold today, with enough gold on her throat and fingers to arm a merchant ship with cannon, shot, and swivel guns.

"Why not?" Will answered. "Griffin served king and country for twenty years in the Grenadiers. Who knows weapons any better?"

She took a small bite of lemon cake and fed it to the nearest spaniel. The other dogs raised their heads expectantly. "I don't doubt Griffin's competency or his levelheadedness. But surely custom demands that your second be—"

"A gentleman," Griffin finished.

Will turned to see the Welshman standing in the doorway. He'd come in so quietly that Will hadn't known he was there.

"Beg pardon, sir. I didn't mean to eavesdrop. I merely wished to see if I could be of assistance, and—"

"You can," Will answered. "I want you with me tomorrow. You've done this before, haven't you?"

"Merely as a spectator, sir. It's been years since I've handled a dueling pistol."

"It's not something you forget. Richard Hamilton offered to stand with me. I'd rather have you."

Griffin nodded solemnly. "Very good, sir." Then he glanced at Lady Graymoor. "My lady? Have you objections?"

"By all that's holy, of course I have objections!" Lizzy set her cup in the saucer with such force that cream sloshed out of the silver pitcher. "Have you completely lost your mind, William? To shoot someone? To allow them to shoot at you? Over what? A horse?"

Muscles rigid, Will stood. "How did you learn of—"

"It's all over town." She sniffed. "Griffin told me an hour ago."

Will scowled at her. "Mason insulted me . . . insulted my father's name. I had to call him out."

"Nonsense. When is bloodshed ever the answer to a problem? And what if you kill Mason? Can the act of murder soothe your foolish pride or bring your father back from the dead?"

Anger thickened Will's tone. "Edward Mason is an excellent shot. It's more likely that he'll walk away from our confrontation."

"What does this idiocy accomplish?" Lizzy demanded. "If you lose, does your death clear the Falcon name and satisfy your creditors?"

"I appreciate all you've done for me," he answered. "But I have every intention of fulfilling my financial obligations. If Falcon's Nest is a burden, I'll find somewhere else to live, and you can sell it to Edward at a profit."

Lizzy chuckled. "And have that varlet for a neighbor? I'd sooner sell my spaniels. No need to take offense. I am an outspoken woman. It is one of the few benefits of age."

"I see that it was a mistake to trouble you. I did so only because I was concerned for Angel's welfare, and I hoped you might consent to act as her guardian if anything goes wrong."

"Her guardian? You've taken this girl to heart. Are you certain she couldn't be my missing granddaughter? My late husband's mother was a redhead. Isn't it possible—"

"No, Lizzy. It isn't possible. She's not Elizabeth. And I'll be honest with you, I'm not certain she isn't one of the pirates I went to hunt down."

"And why is that, William? What would make you think that?"

"She was living with them."

"Ah. You always did have a talent for attracting trouble." She hesitated before going on. "Is there any chance that she could be carrying your child?"

"None whatsoever."

"Hmmm." Lizzy sighed. "I'll look after her, of course. But I wish I understood your motives."

"I'm in your debt. As always." Barely containing his ire, Will turned to leave.

Abruptly, the inner door that led to Lady Graymoor's bedchamber opened, and Julia entered the room. "Will."

Will nodded. "Julia."

Angel followed a few steps behind her. When Angel's gaze met his, she stopped and glanced wide-eyed around the parlor, as if seeking a way to escape. Behind her, the rays of the afternoon sun streamed through a multipaned window, bathing her in golden ribbons of light.

For an instant, Will thought he saw the shimmer of an incandescent halo around Angel's head. "I was just leaving," Will mumbled awkwardly. Damn the wench! She must be a witch. How else could she cause him to become tongue-tied as a green country lad by merely strolling into a room.

"Stuff and mustard!" Lizzy exclaimed. "You're not stomping off in a huff. You've just come. And I've barely fired a few shots across your bow." She motioned to the women. "Join us, and pay no attention to our bickering. It's a game we play. I try to interfere in William's life, and he tries to interfere in mine. I'm better at it.

"I'm attempting to talk some sense into William. Perhaps you can assist me. He's determined to get his head shot off tomorrow in a ridiculous duel."

Julia's complexion paled. "Who is it, Will? Who are you meeting?" Eyes glazed with distress, she sank into the nearest chair.

"Edward Mason," Lizzy supplied. "The oldest of the brothers and a marksman of no small order, according to repute." She peered at Griffin for verification.

The butler nodded. "Mr. Edward Mason killed a man named Hancock in a duel over a woman near Savannah, and another, Brantley Giles, here in Charleston five years ago."

Will couldn't tear his gaze away from Angel. Her redgold hair was curled and nearly hidden by a lacy white cap. She wore a simple white spotted muslin dress that accentuated her breasts and clung to her shapely body like a second skin.

He had thought her exquisite when he'd seen her clad

in rags on a beach, but nothing had prepared him for this transformation. Not even the small swelling that must be a bandage high under one sleeve could mar her appearance.

"Angel?" he asked. "How are you? Are you . . ." His words sounded stiff and awkward. "Are you feeling stronger today?"

When she made no reply, he glanced at Lizzy in confusion. He couldn't understand why Lizzy had garbed Angel this way. He was about to ask, when he realized that whatever he said, he'd make a fool of himself. He hadn't expected Angel to wear a gown suitable for a lady. The result was stunning and ethereal.

"Don't you like the dress?" Julia asked. "Emma Jones made it for a planter's wife who thought it too plain and refused it." She shook her head. "Forgive my foolish woman's prattle about gowns when you've brought us such dreadful news. Is there no other way out of your dilemma?"

Will shrugged. "None that I know of."

"I don't understand," Angel murmured. "What is this duel?"

"William and Mr. Mason will appear at an appointed spot and time," Lady Graymoor said in a matter-of-fact tone. "Each will come with a friend—a second, as it were—to insure that the rules are carried out properly. William and Mr. Mason will stand back to back with loaded pistols. At a signal, each will step out fifteen paces. On the count of three, they will turn and fire. One ball each should suffice to satisfy honor."

"Nay," Angel protested. Will's gut clenched when he saw the slightest quiver of her lower lip . . . the mouth he'd kissed only the night before. " 'Tis surely madness."

"Can't Father do something?" Julia asked him.

Will shook his head. "You know better than that."

"I'm afraid I do," Julia answered. Despair clouded her eyes. "Will's honor is at stake."

"Damn your honor!" Angel declared. "Must ye die for honor?"

Julia looked shocked, but Lizzy chuckled and patted the arm of the love seat beside her. "There's a child who knows foolishness when she sees it. Come, sit," she said to Angel. "William may be churlish, but he won't bite."

"Mayhap, he does." Obediently, Angel perched on the edge of the seat with fingers threaded together like a schoolgirl.

Will swallowed, unable to keep from remembering the feel of those fingers brushing his bare skin. Guardedly, he let his gaze slide up over her shapely breasts and slim neck to her face. Although she wore not a trace of powder or paint, he noted the smudges of color highlighting her cheekbones and lips . . . lips that had fitted his own so perfectly.

Her eyes flashed with anger. "Ye cannot go through with this."

He had no answer that she could fathom, so he didn't try. It was but one example of the vast differences between them. But he kept staring at her, thinking how beautiful she was, how much he wanted to kiss her . . . to pick her up in his arms and run from the room . . . to take ship and carry her off to some nameless Caribbean isle.

He swallowed again. The white dress was so right for her, and yet, so wrong. Lizzy and Julia had dressed Angel as something she wasn't. Or was she? Was it something more than birth that made a woman of quality?

"Oh, do sit down, William," Lizzy fussed. "All this hopping up and down is most disturbing." She gestured languidly in Julia's direction. "I kidnapped Miss Hamilton this morning to help with Angel. I'm too old to know what's in fashion for young people. But no one in Charleston has better taste than our Julia."

"Yes," Will said. "I agree. And Angel will need all the friends she can get if Mason kills me."

"I can take care of myself," Angel said. "I'll nay be beholden to any—"

"Now, see what you've done," Lizzy fussed. "You've upset her. But you needn't worry about her welfare. Your Angel is the prime item of gossip in Charleston. Everyone wants to meet the young woman who risked her life to save yours from the pirates. And when they do make her acquaintance, they will be as charmed as I am."

"Lady Graymoor and I are going to sponsor her," Julia said. "We intend to make her presentable to society and to find her a wealthy husband."

"A gentleman of sense who will be more concerned with what she is, rather than where she came from," Lizzy said.

The point hit Will hard, and he wondered if it was his own stupidity that was keeping him from taking what was offered.

Angel shook her head. "I told them it was as likely as making samite out of seaweed. I've no book learnin'. I cannot even write my own name."

Lizzy scoffed. "And what man ever took a wife for her reading?"

"It's a foolish notion," Will said, then regretted his hasty words when he saw hurt flicker in Angel's eyes.

"And why is it foolish?" Lizzy asked. "Have I not told you a dozen times that I was a parson's daughter? If I could secure the hand of a belted earl in marriage on the strength of my trim ankles and wit, why is our plan so silly?"

"I didn't bring her here to be auctioned off to the first squire with a pocketful of cash and an eye for a pretty face," Will answered.

"Then why did you bring her?" Julia asked.

"He can't answer that, my dear. He doesn't have a clue." Abruptly, Lizzy glowered at Griffin. "Go, go. No need for you to hang about and listen to every word we say. Everyone knows you are an incurable gossip."

"You are wrong, madam," Griffin answered in his customary deep timbre. "I never repeat what I hear in this house. I only tell you what occurs elsewhere."

"I don't believe it. Men are always the worst gossips. Far worse than the weaker sex." She waved a hand at him. "Go!"

"As you wish, madam." Griffin's eyes twinkled.

"I still intend to have Griffin with me tomorrow," Will said. "And I'd like your promise on the other matter."

"William, William, you shame me. When I say I shall do a thing, it is as good as done." Lizzy poured herself a second cup of tea. "And as for Griffin, I don't doubt that he will be foolish enough to accompany you. Men love nothing more than an opportunity to play at war."

Julia walked with Will to Lizzy's front door. When they reached the entranceway, he paused. "Are you certain you're doing the right thing? About Angel?" he asked. "What are the chances that any gentleman of means and character would take—"

"Your little island urchin as a bride?" Julia chuckled. "For a smart man, you know so little of your own kind."

"It still seems to me—"

"So you object to us finding her a husband, Will?"

"No," he said. "Of course not, but—"

"But what better way to provide for her?" Julia took his hand. "I know you've been more involved with her than is proper. This is best, believe me. Whether you choose to make a life with me, which is what I'd like to happen, or if you offer to another, you simply cannot throw away your future with Angel. She's lovely. Unique. Some might say a child of nature. But she's not a child, Will. She's a woman, perhaps older than I am."

"I realize that."

"This duel of yours," Julia continued. "It breaks my heart to think of you in danger from such a churl as Edward. He's a disgrace to his family. Even his brother George is shamed by his behavior."

"But you understand why I have to fulfill my obligation?"

"Am I stricken by the thought of losing you? You know that I am. But I understand the code a gentleman lives by, as Angel never could. She isn't our sort."

"Our sort," he repeated. "What is our sort?"

"Don't pretend to be dense. We share the same tastes in music, in literature, in morals, and religion. For all Lady Graymoor's good intentions, you realize that Angel could never be accepted by the people who matter. She's too intelligent not to see the rejection. She'd be desperately unhappy, and she would ruin your career."

"What there is left of it?"

Julia scoffed. "You've been an excellent ship's master—the best, according to Papa. And you'll make a wonderful president of Hamilton Shipping someday."

"If I marry you."

She squeezed his hand. "If, Will. If you ask me . . . if I'll have you. I won't wait forever, you know. You've kept me dangling far too long. I have no intentions of becoming a spinster, content to manage my father's house until I'm gray-haired and shriveled. I want a husband, children . . . my own home. And I want it with you."

"I'd have to be a fool to turn down the offer," he answered roughly.

"There is no offer," she replied. "I'm my father's daughter, Will. I won't go into a marriage with my eyes closed, and I refuse to be a sea widow. If we wed, I want you with me. I want to share quiet suppers with you, go to parties, entertain. I refuse to wait in Charleston, never knowing when or if you'll return safely."

"What would the gossips of Church Street say if they heard such utterances coming from that pretty mouth?"

"Don't patronize me," she replied, trying hard to control her anger. "I care more for what I think of myself than anyone else's opinion. I've seen the life my cousin Eileen lives. For all her financial security, she's lonely with her husband constantly on long voyages."

"And what if I don't relish the idea of spending my days hemmed in by four walls? I'm never more alive than when I am at sea. It's what I do best. It's what I love."

She struggled to keep from losing her composure. "Then I suppose the choice is yours. Either you learn to love another occupation, or you learn to love another."

"Let me deal with Mason. I promise I'll give you an answer soon." He lifted her hand and brushed it with a kiss.

"Godspeed."

"Amen to that."

Julia waited until the door closed behind Will's broad shoulders, then turned back to where she'd seen a shadowy figure on the staircase. "Angel?"

"Aye, 'tis me."

"You heard."

"I did." The girl came down the steps, one hand on the banister to steady herself.

"I didn't intend insult."

"Truth is truth," Angel replied.

"You could never find happiness together."

"I didn't think to," she lied. "Will and I have no ties on each other."

"He claims you saved his life."

"And he mine." Angel sighed heavily, raised one foot, and tugged off the cream-colored kid slipper. "They be too tight." She stood up, the shoe dangling from her fingers, and glanced around the hall passageway, staring at the crystal chandelier, the thick oriental rugs, and the heavy mahogany furniture. "This house is too grand for me, as well."

"Marriage is more than a physical attraction between man and woman," Julia said. "It is a social and family tie. We all have our places in life."

"And Will's is with you?"

Julia shook her head. "It isn't that simple. We have our differences, differences that we may not be able to overcome. I'm not a particularly strong woman . . . or an independent one. I want a husband who will be there for me. Not one who appears and disappears according to tide and weather."

"I know that Will Falcon isn't for the likes of me," Angel said. "But I couldn't bear it if he dies tomorrow."

"You could," Julia replied. "It is the lot of women to bear what we cannot change, especially Charleston women." She returned to the door and put her hand on the knob. "Tell Lady Graymoor I must be off," she said. "Papa has invited guests for supper, and I—"

"You can think of dinner? When Will's in such danger?"

"What would you have me do? Send my servants to knock him over the head and lock him in the cellar?"

"Mayhap. I would, if I were you. I'd do something, if he loved me, something to keep him safe."

Tears welled up in Julia's eyes. "If only life were as simple as you believe it to be," she answered. "You really don't understand, do you? If I kept him from going, he'd be shamed, ruined, considered a coward by one and all. He'd never forgive me, and we'd have no chance for a life together."

"So we do nothing?" Angel demanded. "Nothing?"

"We can pray for him."

"Aye, prayer helps, but by my way of thinking, 'tis better to bail a leaking boat while you pray, lest the good Lord lose patience."

Chapter 17

Lady Graymoor stirred and felt around in the bed beside her. "Griff?" The sheets were still warm. Sleepily, she opened her eyes to find the room dark. "Griff?" Memories of a sleepless night returned.

"Here, love. I didn't want to wake you." Light spilled through into the bedroom as he pushed open the door that led to the dressing area.

"What time is it?" she asked.

"Time enough for me to dress and go next door for young Mr. Falcon. I'm taking that set of pistols you brought from Graymoor Hall. I hope you don't mind. I didn't know what shape his father's would be in. I don't hold with hair triggers and such. More likely to blow his own foot off than to hit his opponent."

"Yes, yes, take anything you wish," she said crossly. "You will do as you please. You always do." Climbing down from the high bed, she drew a dressing gown around her shoulders to cover her nakedness. "Do be careful, Griff. It's bad enough that our William is a fool. Must you be one, as well?"

"Better me go along than some young buck who will allow another to load Mr. Falcon's pistol." He came back into the bedroom carrying a small whale-oil lamp.

Griffin was dressed soberly but elegantly in a black, double-breasted tailcoat, short-waisted waistcoat, black

184

trousers, and good leather boots. The bow on his stock was perfectly tied, but Lady Graymoor tisked at its appearance and retied it twice until she was satisfied.

"Do remember to duck," she advised. "I'll not go to the trouble of training another butler. And don't allow William to be injured in any way." She pursed her rouged lips. "I've never liked Edward Mason. His eyes are too close together."

"I'll do my best, love," Griffin promised. "Go back to bed now. You had little enough sleep last night, and you know how you are without your sleep." He backed out of the room quietly and closed the door behind him.

"Take care," she repeated. "For God's sake, take care."

Twenty minutes later, Angel crept down the stairs and found her way through the darkened rooms to the kitchen. Servants had banked the fire the night before, but a dim glow from the remaining coals cast a faint light on the porch door. She tiptoed across the wide floorboards with her slippers in her hand and reached for the latch.

"Where do you think you're going?"

Angel gasped and spun toward the source of the question. "Lady Graymoor?"

"And who else do you think would be awake at this hour? My lazy staff?" The countess made a sound of derision. "I think not."

"I'm leavin'."

"Don't be impertinent. I can see that with my own eyes. Where, exactly, do you think you're going?" Lady Graymoor demanded.

"To the duel. I don't know where it's going to be, but I thought I could follow . . . Griffin? Is that his name?"

"It is." The countess rose, and Angel saw that she

was fully dressed and wore a hooded cape. "I would have been disappointed in you if you'd not gone after him," she said. "You do realize how furious William will be with us, don't you?"

"I don't care. I can't wait here, not knowin' if he be dead or alive. He's not for the likes of me, but it don't matter. There might be some way I could help, if I were there."

"Exactly my thoughts." Lady Graymoor patted Angel's good shoulder. "Fortunately, I know the location of this farce. Can you harness a horse?"

"Aye. I think so. I've not done it, but if ye know, you can tell me how."

"Good. We'll take the dogcart. Just room for two, but with Squire between the shafts, we can travel almost as fast as Griffin and William." She pointed to a row of pegs with servants' garments hanging from them. "Take a cloak and a pair of boots. Leave those foolish slippers. It may rain. No sense in catching ague when you're recovering from that knife wound."

"I know why I'm goin'," Angel said as she tugged on the borrowed footwear. "But why are you—"

"Don't ask foolish questions, girl. William Falcon is the closest thing I have to a relative on this side of the Atlantic. There's a worthless nephew and his son in London, but the two together aren't fit to cut bait for William." She fixed Angel with a knowing glance. "It's hopeless, you know. A man like William may dally with a fisherman's daughter, but they rarely wed them."

"You've no need to tell me, ma'am. But it's as I said before: If I don't go, I'll not draw an easy breath until I know he's whole and safe."

"Good. Now that that's settled, let's fetch the horse and carriage. If we don't hurry, we'll miss all the excitement."

• • •

Fine precipitation pelted Will's face as he and Griffin rode side by side out of the darkened town and onto a country lane. Griffin had come with both horses and a walnut box containing a pair of French dueling pistols. Neither man spoke. The only sounds were the dull reverberation of the horses' hooves on the wet ground and the creak of saddle leather.

As the track narrowed, Griffin dropped back to let Will take the lead. Without moonlight or stars, it was difficult to see more than a few yards ahead. After perhaps a quarter of an hour, with the rainfall increasing, Will reined in so that Griffin could light the lantern he'd carried from the stable.

"No use breaking our necks on an overhanging limb," Will said.

"No profit in it at all to my way of thinking." Griffin lifted the lantern high and pulled his overcoat closer. Water droplets dripped from the brim of his hat onto his face and neck. "No profit to any of this," he muttered.

The flame cast a faint circle of pale yellow, which seemed to make the trace darker on either side. "I suppose that's better than no light at all," Will said.

"True, sir, but you should have asked one of your friends to act as second. You young bucks don't mind going without sleep to kill one another."

"With luck, we'll finish this and be home in time for breakfast." Will had gotten little sleep, but he'd had nothing to drink, either. He might be stupid enough to allow himself to challenge a noted marksman, but he wasn't dumb enough to come drunk to a duel where real bullets would be flying.

His stomach churned. He hoped he wouldn't lose his nerve when he and Mason began to pace off the distance. He'd seen good men turn and run in less precarious situations. He didn't want to die, but worse, he didn't want to show himself a coward.

Will wished he'd been able to speak to Angel alone. If he died, God knew what would happen to her. For the first time, he wondered if she would have been better off on her island. He could picture her face in his mind and remember each word she'd said to him. The expression in her green eyes haunted him, and he wished he could see into her heart to know if she—

In the woods ahead, a horse neighed.

Will stiffened. "Did you hear that?" He shielded his eyes and tried to see, but the forest was too thick. The huge oaks that lined the dirt road stretched overhead, branches and leaves intertwining, further distorting sounds.

"Mr. Mason must be there ahead of us," Griffin said.

Will urged his mount forward at a walk. The rain was falling harder, and the track had become slippery despite the verdant ceiling that provided a little shelter. "That whinny sounded as if it was off to the left," he said. "The meadow is on the right. There's no trail in that direction—"

A shot rang out.

Will saw a powder flash. Something slammed into his head with the force of a hammer. He waited, expecting pain, feeling only hollow emptiness. "Oh, shit," he said. "I . . ."

Angel's image materialized. For a heartbeat, he saw her running toward him on the beach. Then she was gone, and he felt himself falling. The wet earth swallowed him.

"Will!" Griffin shouted. "Will!"

A second explosion split the silence of the darkened lane. Will's horse snorted and reared. Hooves churned air and mud. From his black retreat, Will felt spiraling pain.

Griffin leaped from his saddle and dropped the lantern on the ground. Will's horse reared again, then charged up the left bank and crashed through the woods. Griffin threw himself over Will's body. The lantern rolled into one rut and continued giving forth a feeble glow.

Tearing open the wooden case, Griffin snatched one of the pistols and tried to find a target as he groped Will's body with his free hand, seeking the injury. Griffin found a rush of hot blood from Will's head, and his heart sank. So much blood. And he feared the horse had trampled the boy as well. "Will!" he whispered. "Hang on, lad."

Griffin heard the clamor of oncoming horses ahead. "Mason! Mason!" he yelled.

He heard shouts too far away to make out the words. A lantern bobbed. Griffin could just make out the figures of several riders. "Help!" he cried. "Help us!"

A twig snapped on his right. Griffin peered through the rain, trying desperately to see the assassin. When the sound of shattering glass startled him, he glanced down the road. Flames shot up, and then there was only darkness and falling rain. Receding hoofbeats told him that the horsemen weren't coming to assist him. They were fleeing.

"Mason! You yellow-bellied Colonial bastard!" Griffin shouted. "It's you, isn't it? Murderer!"

Another crunch of underbrush alerted Griffin to the continued danger. He pressed hard with his left hand against Will's head, trying to staunch the bleeding. Will groaned, the first sound Griffin had heard him make since he'd fallen out of the saddle. That's it, lad, he thought. Stay with us.

Griffin's heart raced. Sweat broke out on his forehead. He heard a sharp snap and twisted, pistol in hand.

Abruptly, a dark form lunged onto the road. Griffin fired off a shot. The panicked doe touched down lightly in the center of the road and bounded on, unharmed.

Cursing his folly, Griffin cast aside the empty pistol and fumbled for the second. Rain pounded his face. His hand closed on the pistol grip. Before he could raise the weapon to shoot, a man leaped onto his back, pinning his right arm in the mud. Griffin squirmed, rolling off Will, trying to throw off his assailant. But the man was big and strong. His sour breath was hot on Griffin's face.

Grunting with effort, they strained and shoved. With a mighty effort, Griffin broke the grip on his wrist, raised the pistol, and squeezed the trigger.

The bullet missed. His opponent drove a knee into Griffin's groin, and pain roared through him. Griffin gasped for breath and moaned as he heard the slick squish of a knife sliding from a sodden leather sheath.

Angel heard a shot. "Faster! Faster!" she urged Lady Graymoor. The countess snapped her driving whip across the gelding's withers, and the horse broke into a canter. The dogcart careened down the rutted road, wheels slinging mud, splattering the women. Angel clung to the side rail. "Hurry!"

As they rounded a turn, another pistol cracked. A light glowed at the edge of the lane, and in it Angel saw two figures struggling on the ground. "There!" she screamed. "Stop the horse!"

"Whoa!" Lady Graymoor yanked hard on the reins, slowing Squire to a trot and then a walk. Seizing the whip from the floor of the vehicle, Angel jumped over the side and ran toward the confrontation.

A fist tightened around her heart as she recognized Will sprawled on his back, motionless, with features as pale as death. "Will!" she cried.

As she rushed toward him, from the corner of her eye, she caught the gleam of a steel blade. Halting, she turned toward the two wrestling in the mud. On top of Griffin was a bearded stranger with a tarred pigtail and seaman's striped shirt, clutching a twelve-inch knife in a dirty hand. Griffin was putting up a good fight, but the burly sailor was younger and heavier. His back and arms bulged with muscles as he forced the weapon down, closer and closer to the butler's throat.

"Here! Here!" Angel shouted, trying to make the killer think there were other men coming to her aid! "All hands!" Reversing the leather buggy whip, she struck the weighted handle repeatedly against the brute's head and neck. "Cap'n!" she screamed. "Nate! To me! There's only one of them!"

Her fourth blow got his attention. With an oath, he turned and backhanded her. Angel tumbled and rolled. The seaman heaved the knife. It hissed past her head and buried into the trunk of an oak tree.

Angel scrambled to her feet, snatched up the whip, and cracked the braided tip across her attacker's face. He let out a howl, spun, and ran into the woods. Angel stood, trembling, heart thudding against her ribs, too stunned to cry.

"Griff!" Lady Graymoor hurried toward them. "Are you hurt?"

Angel dropped the whip and fell on her knees beside Will. "He's been shot in the head!" she said. "Sweet Mother of God. I can't tell if the bullet went into his brain or grazed his skull." She pressed her cheek close to his mouth, trying to feel his breath. His skin felt cold. She laid a hand to his throat, but could feel no pulse. "No . . . no."

"See to Will," Griffin said. "I'm all right."

"Don't be dead," Angel crooned, laying her head on

his chest. "Don't be dead, my puir, prow man." Ripping away Will's sodden stock, she pressed it to the wound. "He's bleeding," she said. "If he's bleeding, he can't be dead."

"Who did this?" Lady Graymoor demanded. "How did this—"

"Ambush," Griffin answered hoarsely. "The shot came from the side of the road."

"Was it Edward Mason?" the countess asked.

"I don't know. It was so dark." Griffin went to Will and crouched beside him. He had recovered the pistol case and one of the guns. Shielding the weapon from the rain with his cloak, he carefully measured powder into the barrel. Next he seated the ball and patch and rammed it down. Finally, he poured fine powder into the frizzen pan. "Is he breathing?" he asked Angel.

"I can't tell." She felt numb, hardly able to speak or think. She stroked Will's face and whispered in his ear. "Live for me, sweeting. Live for me, and I swear I'll never vex ye again."

"We must get him to a physician," Lady Graymoor said. "Take the cart, Griff. You drive. She can hold him."

He pushed the pistol into Lady Graymoor's hand. "Careful, this is loaded and ready to fire. Don't hesitate to use it if you have to."

"I am an excellent shot," Lady Graymoor said. "And there's no one I'd rather send to his reward than that cowardly beast who tried to kill you and William."

Recovering the second gun, Griffin loaded it and tucked the pistol into his belt. "If we take the cart, what of you?" he asked. "I'll not leave you—"

"Help me onto your horse, you bloody fool," she answered. "I can ride as well as you."

He caught his mount and cupped his hands so that

she could thrust her foot into them. "Up you go. Keep close to us. And if you must shoot anyone, make certain it isn't me."

Together, Angel and Griffin lifted Will into the dog-cart. Angel climbed up onto the seat and put her arms around him. "For God's sake, drive as you never have before," she urged him. "Please." Then she clung tightly to Will as Griffin laid the whip over the gelding's back.

She never stopped praying until the butler reined in the horse in front of Will's house. It was already grow-ing light, and curious onlookers stared at the sight of Lady Graymoor riding astride and the three bloody oc-cupants of the dogcart.

"Hallo, the house!" Griffin climbed down and began beating on the front door. Angel stayed with Will.

Delphi appeared and took control. She ordered her two sons and two grandsons to carry Will upstairs to his bed, and she sent another grandson running for the doctor. Both Angel and Lady Graymoor followed the patient up the staircase and into Will's bedchamber.

"Lord give us grace," Delphi said. "You ladies are wet to the bone. You'll catch your death."

Lady Graymoor allowed a maid to lead her to a chair and wrap her in a coverlet. "I'll have tea. Hot. Cream and three lumps of sugar," she ordered.

Angel wouldn't budge from her place by the bed. She held Will's hand as Delphi and another woman stripped him of his clothes, covered him with sheets and blan-kets, and put a warming stone under his feet.

Will lay with eyes closed, lips slightly parted. The ugly wound over his left ear continued to ooze dark blood. His fingers were cool and limp; his chest showed no sign of movement.

Someone touched Angel's shoulder. "You'll have to leave," a man said to her.

She glanced at him, recognizing him as the physician who had treated her arm. "Nay," she repeated. "You'll have to kill me to make me leave him."

"You should be abed yourself," Madison said, not unkindly. "You—"

"Let her be," Lady Graymoor ordered.

Angel smoothed a lock of damp hair away from Will's face and watched woodenly as the physician took a small mirror from his bag and held it over Will's lips.

He removed the mirror and studied it, and then looked at Lady Graymoor. "I'm sorry, madam, but I'm afraid we've already lost him."

Chapter 18

"Oh, no." Lady Graymoor started to rise, and then sank back in her chair. "Not William. Not him, too."

"He's a liar!" Angel lifted Will's hand and pressed it to her cheek. "Fie on ye! I know a dead man when I see him. And Will Falcon's not set foot on the crow road yet!"

Delphi and a serving girl began to weep. Griffin's mouth quivered, and his lined face blanched to the shade of a sun-bleached oyster shell.

"Shhh, shhh, child. It isn't Dr. Madison's fault." Lady Graymoor's voice broke, and she rocked back and forth in silent grief.

"He's not dead, I tell ye! And I'll not weep for him. Ye can see that the ball didn't go into his head. It dug a furrow along his skull. Why don't ye tell them the truth," she demanded of the physician. "He's unconscious, but he'll wake. He'll wake and be well."

Dr. Madison removed his spectacles and tucked them into a vest pocket. "I'm afraid you misunderstand me, madam. The patient does have a weak pulse. Although the bullet struck the side of his skull and didn't lodge in the brain, it caused the brain great shock. He's sunk into a deep coma. With the loss of blood and the patient unresponsive for so long, I can offer little hope of survival."

The physician motioned to his assistant, a serious young man with a moon face and hair so blond, it was nearly white. "Evans. Send servants for a bleeding bowl and hot water. I'll need my folding lancet—"

"You'll take no more blood from him," Angel said.

Dr. Madison looked at Lady Graymoor. "This woman's interference makes my task more difficult."

"Try to put me out." Angel's eyes glittered with fierce determination.

"Her presence only makes my task more difficult," Dr. Madison said. "There are procedures unfit for the eyes of a delicate female that I must—"

"Perhaps," Lady Graymoor replied. "But my concern is William's recovery, not your inconvenience. Angel risked her life to save ours. Any person attempting to remove her must remove me first."

"As you wish, madam." Dr. Madison cleared his throat and scowled. "You are free to call another physician if you have no confidence in my—"

"Don't be tiresome. You are the best in Charleston. Stop fussing and give William something to wake him."

"I cannot. He must wake on his own."

"For pain, then," she persisted. "You must have laudanum in that demon's black bag."

"I do," he replied. "I can administer laudanum, although I believe the patient is beyond feeling pain."

"What can you do for him?" Lady Graymoor asked.

"I shall begin by administering purges to cleanse his body of ill-humors. And finally, he must be bled to—"

"No bleedin'," Angel repeated.

"I agree," Lady Graymoor said. "He's lost enough blood. And none of your foul purging. My dear, late husband suffered terribly in his last days from purging. I'll not have it repeated with our William."

"Madam." Dr. Madison drew himself up to his full

height. "With all due respect, removing excesses in the body is essential to restoring brain function. If he does live, he may be left afflicted or unable to walk."

"No purging," Griffin said.

Dr. Madison sighed heavily. "Very well, against my better judgment, I will refrain from purging the patient. But he must be bled. I cannot, in good conscience, omit—"

"Bleed him at your own risk," Angel said. "For every drop of Will's blood you spill, I'll let a cup of yours."

Lady Graymoor sniffed and waved airily. "No need to threaten our good doctor, my dear. He will neither bleed nor purge our William."

"It matters little what we do," Dr. Madison replied. "William Falcon will be a corpse by sunset."

Julia Hamilton carried the news of Will's shooting to her father in his dovecote. The classical structure, built in the style of a Greek temple, stood in the farthest corner of their formal garden.

"I just heard." Julia was sobbing so hard that it was difficult to speak. "Papa, they say he's going to die."

"Before he reached the meadow, you say?" Her father thrust the pigeon he was holding back into the coop and dropped the latch. "The coward!" He clenched his teeth, barely containing his anger. "How can he call himself a gentleman?"

"Who?" she asked. "It's Will who's been—"

"Edward Mason." He fisted his hands. Striding past her, he headed in the direction of the house. "He'll not get away with this act of attempted murder."

"Papa, what are you going to do?" Julia hurried after him, clutching at his sleeve. "Please. Don't do anything rash. Surely, the authorities—"

He brushed her off and kept walking. "The authorities

have done little to stop Mason yet. He's gone too far! And if the sheriff won't stop him, I will."

"Papa, no," she begged. "Think of Mother, of me."

"Will's been like a son to me. This is too much!"

"But you don't know it was Mr. Mason," she pleaded. "Anyone could have—"

"Anyone? Who would want to murder Will Falcon but the man who had to face him over pistols?"

Trembling with apprehension, she followed him inside to the library. "Jesse!" he ordered.

A male servant appeared. "Suh?"

"Send Moses to Mr. Ridgely's. Tell him it's urgent. He's to meet me outside St. Philip's Church in half an hour. And he's to come armed and on horseback. You're to go to the stables. Have Kojo saddle my roan. Then you are to take the same message to Walter Hughes and to Guy Albright."

"Yes'suh." The man vanished as quickly and quietly as he had come.

"Papa." Tears ran down Julia's cheeks. "This is dangerous."

"I expected Will Falcon to be the father of my grandchildren—to take over Hamilton when I was too old to run it. I'll not allow him to be shot down like a dog and do nothing." He unlocked a cabinet and removed a pistol. "Look after your mother."

Julia flung herself into his arms. For one long moment, he hugged her. "Don't worry, kitten," he said. "I'm not so fragile as you may think."

"I love you, Papa."

"And I love you." Stiffening, he pulled away. "Pray for Will," he said. "But don't waste any prayers on Mason."

The splintering of her back door ripped Peaches O'Shea from a gin-sodden dream. Her heart leaped in her chest. Cursing, she staggered onto her feet to peer blearily at two intruders charging through her kitchen.

"What the hell are you—," she began, but went silent when she saw that the cutthroats—one black man and one white—carried knives. Without hesitation she abandoned Lapp. "I didn't see nothin'!"

Naked, pendulous breasts heaving, Peaches plunged through an open window into the sweltering afternoon heat. Sprinting barefoot down the alley, she snatched a ragged shirt off her neighbor's fence and kept running.

Lapp groaned and rolled off the filthy mattress. He landed on hands and knees and tried to crawl away, but the lean-to was barely large enough to hold the pallet. His head struck the wall at the exact moment a booted foot came in contact with his right buttock. Lapp howled in pain. A second kick smashed into his kidneys.

The black giant grabbed Lapp's pigtail and slammed his face into the dirt. The second seized Lapp by one leg. Together, they dragged him shrieking into the kitchen.

Turning the table upright, they hauled Lapp faceup onto the flat surface. The big man held a knife to Lapp's throat while his snaggletoothed companion retrieved a pillow from Peaches's pallet.

Lapp froze. "What . . . what . . . ," he blubbered. Blood was running from his nose and dribbling out of his mouth. "Yer makin' a mistake!"

"You was paid to do a job," Archie said.

"It ain't my fault," Lapp protested. "I'll get him. I'll get him and the bitch."

"You was warned."

Lapp gasped as the tip of the knife pricked his skin. "No! I'll kill'm both! I swear! I followed'm to the house. But they got guards around—"

Archie Gunn snickered as he pressed the pillow down over Lapp's face. "Too late, sailor."

• • •

The case clock on the landing at Falcon's Nest chimed two P.M. Moist heat swathed Church Street and all of Charleston in a thick woolen mantle, but Will's skin remained cool to Angel's touch. His features were ashen, and his breath so slow and shallow that she was certain it had stopped a half dozen times.

So far as she could tell, the bleeding had ceased. Whether it was too late and he had lost too much blood to live, she did not know. The physician had predicted the worst and had departed, promising to return at evening. Griffin had taken a sorrowful Lady Graymoor home to sleep. But Angel remained, refusing to leave Will's side, lest Delphi or Dr. Madison not permit her to return to the room.

She moistened Will's cracked lips with clean water and spooned a few drops between his lips. When the water dribbled out again, she wiped his mouth and rose from the chair beside the bed. The only sound in the room was the drone of a lone mosquito.

In despair, she went to the nearest window. Below lay an overgrown garden with winding brick paths, ancient magnolias, climbing roses, evergreen shrubs, and masses of bright blossoms. The humid air was pungent with the scent of rich earth, moss, roses, and a myriad of unfamiliar flowers. But butter-yellow trumpets of jessamine grew up to twine around the window trellis and spill their haunting fragrance into the bedchamber.

Angel closed her eyes and inhaled slowly. She had never seen anything to match this. The only gardens Angel had known before were ones like the straggly patch of corn, beans, and onions that Bett scratched out of sandy island soil. Bett's vegetable plot had been a necessity, vital to providing food for the two of them. But this delightful garden of Will's seemed to exist solely for pleasure.

If he hadn't been so desperately ill, she would have liked to explore the yard and wade in the little brick pond. She wanted to taste the water that bubbled out of the stone fish's mouth and ask Delphi the name of each bloom and flowering vine so that she could commit them to memory. And when she had filled her head with all that beauty, she would rest her cheek against the velvety, thick moss that surely must have first grown in the Garden of Eden.

She did not mind the heat of the Charleston summer. The turn of seasons brought hot and cold, wind, rain, and sunshine, each in its own time. This was a house of many wonders, and she wished she were free to linger long enough to see them all.

Reluctantly, she went back to the bed. She took a cloth, dipped it into the basin of water, and washed Will's face. He had shaved this morning before he had ridden to the duel. She hoped he would survive long enough to need shaving again tomorrow.

A shiver passed through him.

A sheet and two covers in this heat, and still he could not get warm. Quickly, she went to the door, threw the lock, and returned to his side. Removing her dress, she slid in beside him and molded close to his body. "I'll keep ye warm," she promised. "I'll keep you warm, Will Falcon, must I follow you to the gates of hell to do it."

He groaned, the first sound he'd made in hours.

"Will? Can you hear me?" she whispered. She had crawled in on the side, taking care not to jostle his bandaged head. Rising onto her knees, she ran her fingers lightly over him, inch by inch. He was covered with bruises, but she could find no broken ribs or other serious injuries. "Ah, sweeting," she crooned. "My darling man. Can you feel how much you're loved? Wake up, can't ye?"

"Angel . . ."

"I'm here," she said.

". . . my Angel."

"Will, open your eyes." She told herself that his eyelids had flickered, that he must be stronger, that he could hear her voice.

He tossed his head from side to side and mumbled her name one more time before sinking into the restless tides that swept him off into a sea of unconsciousness.

" 'Twas my name you called, wasn't it?" The thought warmed her and gave her strength. No matter what she was and how fine his Julia, he had wanted her in his darkest moment. "Will," she asked. "Can you hear me?"

She kissed his cool lips. "I'll make you right as rain," she promised. "Right as rain."

He'd not die of this injury, and he'd not be left with useless limbs. She'd not let him. If there were payment to be made to the jealous forces of the sea, she'd gladly pay the price for him. Until this instant, she hadn't been able to understand why Will had brought her to Charleston, since he obviously didn't want her. Now she knew.

It wasn't Will who'd made the decision that she should leave the Brethren. That had come from a greater force. She was here because the Lord wanted her to save Will's life.

She was not such a fool to believe she could keep him. Once he was well, she would be free to find her own path. But for now, at this moment, in this room, she and Will were joined by something stronger than flesh. "Husband of my soul," she murmured. "We belong to each other . . . for a little while." But these precious hours would be enough to light her nights for as long as she lived.

She rose again, pulled on her clothing, and went to fetch Delphi. The black woman was smart. She'd surely know where to find a bit of willow bark to make a tea for driving away fever. It was clear as ice that the old fool Dr. Madison knew nothing about bringing a man back from the brink. That was up to her.

"Sweet Lord, help me," she murmured. "Put wisdom in my head and healin' in these hands. For this is as good a man as ever walked your bright beaches, and he needs your love now."

Chapter 19

Lady Graymoor, her butler Griffin Davis, Delphi, and a single spaniel descended on Will's bedchamber just before dusk. "Is there any change?" Lady Graymoor demanded. Despite the thick layer of powder and paint that covered her face, Angel could see genuine concern on the older woman's aristocratic features.

Angel shook her head. "He's still in a deep sleep. But if he woke once, he'll wake again. I know it."

"Richard Hamilton and Julia came to Falcon's Nest earlier," Lady Graymoor said. "They desperately wished to see William, but I told them to return tomorrow."

"Mr. Hamilton is all the talk of Charleston," Griffin said. "He's bigger news than the escape of that pirate Gunn whom Mr. Will brought back from the Outer Banks."

"The rascal broke out of jail?"

"He did. Slick as an eel. The jailers say they found his cell locked and empty sometime after midnight. There's more to that tale than they're saying. I warrant someone was paid to let that creature go."

"They'll catch him soon enough. His kind are born to hang," Lady Graymoor replied. "Now, what of Richard? He's not come to harm, too, has he?"

"No, he's well," Griffin said. "Mr. Hamilton and

some friends found Mr. Mason at Dixon's, and I gather there was a bit of a tussle. Threats were exchanged, and not a few patrons of the establishment took sides."

"Violence. Men glory in it," Lady Graymoor proclaimed. "Any excuse for brawling will do." She patted Will's pillows and brushed a straying lock of hair away from his forehead. "Julia is beside herself with worry, and not just for William."

Griffin nodded. "Mr. Hamilton has a serious heart condition."

"Julia is afraid that the excitement might be too much for him. And rightly so. Richard needs to be conscious of his health. One invalid in the family is enough." Lady Graymoor frowned. "Sorry, child, I forgot that you've only just arrived in Charleston."

"Mrs. Hamilton is confined to her bed with a condition," Griffin explained.

"A permanent condition, I fear," Lady Graymoor said. "Quite tragic. Her mind has deteriorated." She tapped her forehead. "Gabrielle Hamilton suffered several miscarriages before Julia was born and more after. The last was the son Richard wanted so badly. The babe lived for nearly a day. Poor woman never recovered from his loss."

"That is very old news, I'm afraid," Griffin said. "I was attempting to inform Mistress Angel of yesterday afternoon's tidings."

Lady Graymoor sighed impatiently. "Richard Hamilton called Edward Mason out, but Edward refused another duel."

"He insulted Mr. Hamilton by calling him an old man," Griffin put in. "Naturally the villain denies any culpability in the attempt on Mr. Will's life."

"When Edward wouldn't meet him on the field of honor, Richard tried to have him arrested." Lady

Graymoor spread her graceful hands, palms up. "Many in the city believe that Edward tried to have Will murdered, but there simply isn't any proof of his guilt."

"Unfortunately, being a blackguard isn't enough to condemn him," Griffin said.

Lady Graymoor stood for a few moments staring down at Will, before taking a chair and addressing Angel. "You look as pale as death yourself, child. Has she eaten anything, Delphi?"

"No, ma'am, not a bite. I brought up biscuits and ham and some of my she-crab soup, but Miss Angel jest let it sit and get cold. I can't get her to take a mouthful.".

Angel nodded. "I'm not hungry."

"You'll do William no good lying flat on your back in a faint."

"I'm strong. I won't faint. But I can't leave him."

"Has Dr. Madison returned?"

"No, ma'am," Delphi replied.

"Hmmp." The countess sniffed. "Absenting himself from the scene of the crime, no doubt. Not that there's much for him to do. Time and God's mercy is all that can help our William."

"He's not going to die," Angel said.

Lady Graymoor glanced around the room. "That chaise longue will do. Griffin, can you move that closer to the bed? Good," she said when he complied. "You can rest there, Angel. Delphi, could you send up another tray? That, I assure you, she will eat. Won't you?"

"I'll try," Angel answered. In truth, she had not the faintest appetite. But if that was the price of remaining with Will, she'd eat what they forced her to.

"We've set stout guards with cudgels around the house," Griffin said. "You're not to worry about Mr. Will's safety."

"Not even Edward Mason would be so stupid as to try to murder William in his own bed," Lady Graymoor said.

"Mr. Hamilton will be leading the expedition to destroy the pirates," Griffin explained. "He challenged Mr. Mason to prove his innocence by accompanying the group with ships and crews at his own expense. If he refuses, Mr. Hamilton is certain that he will find a judge to issue a warrant for—"

"Yes, yes," Lady Graymoor fussed. "That is all well and good, but . . ."

Angel felt suddenly sick. Vaguely, she was aware of the older woman's continuing chatter, but all she could think of was Bett and Cap'n and her friends among the Brethren. A part of her wanted to run from the room, to steal a boat, and sail north along the coast to warn them. But doing that would mean leaving Will, never to know if he lived or died. And to her discredit, she could not desert him . . . not even to warn those who had loved and cared for her all her life.

A single tear welled in her eye and trickled down her cheek. Her place was there on the island. She should be among the Brethren, taking her chances with her own kind. By staying here, she betrayed not only them but herself.

She swallowed, trying to dissolve the lump in her throat. She nodded when Lady Graymoor asked her a question, although she had no idea what she had agreed to. She allowed Delphi to lead her to the chaise lounge. Woodenly, she sat. But each breath seemed a struggle.

Without the Brethren, she would have no one . . . nothing to return to but loneliness and the memories of her own cowardly betrayal. She lay back and closed her eyes, vowing she would not sleep, and cursing her own weakness to surrender everything for a man who could not love her.

"Bett! Bett!" A woman's scream tore through Angel, ripping her out of soft darkness into a smoke-filled chamber. Steel clashed against steel, and she heard the muffled crack of a pistol. The room shuddered, and she tumbled onto the floor in a tangle of blankets. "Bett!"

Heart galloping in her chest, her clothing damp with sweat, Angel struggled free of the imprisoning quilt. The room was as quiet as death. The smoke that had filled her nose and burned her throat was gone. The floor was solid and unmoving.

"Will?" Trembling, terrified of what she might find, she went to his bedside. He lay as she had last seen him. Sinking to her knees, she laid her cheek against his cool fingers and sobbed.

"What's wrong? Angel?"

Will's voice was a grating rasp, but when she looked into his blue eyes, nothing could dim the joy that filled her to overflowing. Her knees were almost too weak to hold her, and she didn't know whether to laugh or to cry.

"Oh, Will, you're yourself again. Ye vexed me . . . near to . . . near to dyin'," she said, all the while showering his face with teary kisses. "Ye hamper-arsed cod's head. Ye frightened us all."

"You . . . you were crying for me?"

" 'Twas nothin'. 'Twas but an old nightmare."

He closed his eyes, and for a second, she thought that she'd only dreamed that he'd spoken to her. But when she shouted his name, he spoke again.

"Easy, easy, woman. Don't . . . don't shake . . . the bed."

Will's words came faint and hoarse. She leaned close. "Did Mason . . . shoot me?"

"No." She needed to touch him, to feel every inch of his body against hers. "You were shot from ambush," she said as she stroked his face. "Some craven varlet tried to put a bullet through your head before you reached the dueling field. Mayhap he was Mason's bawd."

"His bawd?"

"In his hire. 'Twas a seaman. His hair was drawn back in a pig's tail and tarred."

"You saw him?" Will touched the bandage on his head. "How could you see my assailant?"

" 'Tis . . . I mean it is a long story, and one that can be told when you're feeling stronger."

He nodded and glanced wearily around the room. Each movement seemed to take every drop of his strength. "I'm thirsty," he whispered.

"No doubt, with the ocean of blood you lost. You leaked like a rotten skiff. And a horse danced on your arm to boot."

"Are you certain . . . certain it didn't dance . . . on my chest?" Will's crooked smile tugged at her heart.

"Shhh, don't talk. Ye need rest." She forced herself to action in an attempt to regain control of her shattered emotions. Quickly, she filled a cup with water from a blue and white flowered pitcher and lifted it to his lips. "Could you eat a little soup?" she asked him.

"Soup?" His eyelids fluttered, and he drifted off again. But it seemed to her that his breathing was more regular, and his color better. When she pressed her fingers to his throat, she could feel the slow, steady pulse of his blood.

Late in the night, Will's cheeks flushed with fever, but his temperature did not rise dangerously high. And so improved was he by morning that Dr. Madison—who had come to pronounce him dead—found his patient sitting up and sipping spoonfuls of chicken soup.

"He's not out of danger," Madison insisted after examining Will's injuries. "We cannot know for four or five days if laudable pus will form in the wound. If it doesn't, there is no hope. I strongly recommend both cupping and bleeding to—"

"Yes, yes," Lady Graymoor said, sweeping into the room. "If William survives, the credit for his recovery shall go to you. If he does not, you may defend yourself by saying that a deranged old woman and a red-haired wench prevented you from practicing your art."

She glanced at Angel and winked before squeezing Will's hand. "Your father would be proud of you, lad," she said. "Good stock."

"You were to call back last evening, I believe, sir," Griffin reminded the physician.

"I was called away to a case of yellow fever near the river."

"Pray it does not strike nearby," Lady Graymoor said. "Call again tomorrow," she commanded. "Doubtless William will continue to improve. No need for you to trouble yourself over bandaging his injuries. The girl can do it. She has gentle hands."

Griffin opened the bedroom door. "Let us not keep you, gentlemen."

Madison and his apprentice barely made it through the door before Richard Hamilton and his daughter arrived. "Will!" Hamilton cried. "By God, I knew the rascals couldn't keep you down."

Angel retreated to the corner window overlooking the garden as Julia and her father approached the bed. From there, it was only a few steps to the doorway leading to a dressing room. She slipped into the smaller chamber and then found her way down the servants' back stairway.

She was bone-weary, so tired that she could barely keep her eyes open. An aching hollow in her belly reminded her that she hadn't eaten since the day before Will's attempted duel.

As she crossed the kitchen, she snatched a biscuit from a tray that Sukie had just removed from the bake oven beside the wide brick hearth. She tossed the hot bread from one hand to another as she left the house.

A gate led to the garden Angel had admired from Will's bedchamber. She pushed it open and went in. She took the first pathway and then another until she discovered an arch of greenery that opened onto a plot of thick moss. In the center of this space stood the tiny pond with the stone fish spouting water from its mouth.

Angel sat on the lip of the brick pool and nibbled at the biscuit. Yellow butter oozed from the feather-light bread, and it smelled heavenly, but to her it had no more taste than tree bark. How could she eat when her heart—her very soul—was in such turmoil?

Her gaze strayed to the second floor of the grand house. Will was there, living and breathing as she had prayed he might. But she wasn't with him. Julia was. Julia, her father, Lady Graymoor, and Griffin were beside him. They belonged to him as she never could.

Nothing ever changes, she thought. Why should she expect otherwise? She'd always been alone . . . always been different.

When Lady Graymoor and Julia had decided to find her a husband, they hadn't asked her opinion. Protest seemed useless, since she had no intentions of remaining in Charleston. And if she couldn't convince Will that they were man and wife, how could she possibly make Lady Graymoor believe her?

Slowly, she crumbled the biscuit and tossed the pieces to the sparrows that hopped across the brick walk. She was thirsty, but she didn't taste the water. It was warm and had a green cast that warned her it might be foul to drink.

The stone pond was a disappointment. She didn't know how the water moved from the pool up through the hollow fish to spray from the statue's mouth, but it was plain that the body of water had no link to either earth or sea. Could it be that all this grandeur of the outside world was the same? That behind the tall brick walls, gleaming windows, and painted carriages life wasn't as true and real as on her ocean's washed islands?

If she had the slightest bit of courage, now would be the moment to escape—to flee back to the Brethren stronghold and warn them. But she couldn't, not when Will hadn't yet recovered fully.

"Soon," she promised herself. "Soon, I'll go." But the words sounded like a lie, even as she said them.

As Angel wandered away from the fountain and walked the boxwood maze, she trod on the sharp edge of a broken brick. Her shoes were under Will's bed, but she'd not go back to fetch them now.

"You, girl! What's your business here?" a man shouted.

Startled, Angel looked up to see a black-bearded stranger with a belaying pin in one hand striding toward her. She fled down the path into the maze, taking first one turn and then another. The man pounded after her.

She came to a dead end, dropped onto her hands and knees, and crawled through a hole in the hedge. When she scrambled up, she saw a small vegetable garden and, beyond that, a high wooden fence with a gate. In seconds, she was dashing between two rows of turnip greens. As the gate slammed behind her, the cries of her pursuer faded. Without glancing back, she ran down the deserted lane and didn't stop until she was several blocks from Falcon's Nest.

When she did slow down to catch her breath, it was on a narrow street between tall wooden houses. She was sweating from running, and her injured arm ached. It was so hot that she felt as though she were in an oven. No breeze stirred the leaves of the single tree in sight.

"Out of m'way!"

Angel jumped back as a surly-looking man rattled past in a pony cart. Crowded together in the back of the vehicle were a skinny pig, a white goose, and a freckled-face boy about five years old. The child stuck out his tongue at her.

She laughed, stepped over a sleeping dog stretched in the shade of an overhanging balcony, and kept walking. A few doors away, a black girl in a white cap and apron came toward her, carrying a covered basket. "Can ye tell me how to find the harbor?" Angel asked.

The maid pointed. "That way."

Angel nodded thanks and hurried on. She didn't know who had chased her out of Will's garden or why, but finding the docks would be the first step in returning to a world she understood better than this one.

"Give me two weeks," Will said. "Finding the Brethren's hideout will be difficult enough with me along. Without me, your search may end as so many others did—empty-handed."

"It's out of the question," Lady Graymoor insisted. "You might go into coma again. Your recovery may be difficult. Infection—"

"Two weeks, Richard," Will repeated. "If I am not

well enough to stand on a quarterdeck by then, you can sail without me. It will take you near that to fit out the ships, assemble your men, and get backing from our esteemed governor."

"I've told Papa over and over that he shouldn't go," Julia said. "And now I'll tell you the same thing." She drew near Will's bed. "We almost lost you to those scoundrels once. I don't want to risk you a second time."

Will struggled to keep his eyes open. The room kept spinning, and the effort it took to form words was almost too great to overcome. "Water," he murmured.

Julia brought a cup to his lips.

"We need to talk," he said to her.

"Yes," she replied. "I'd like that."

"That woman, what exactly do you know about her?" Richard asked. "I understand you feel you owe her for saving your life. But . . . is there a chance she's one of the pirates?"

"Her name is Angel," Lady Graymoor said. "And I admire her greatly. I doubt very much that she is involved with this pack of cutthroats and brigands."

"I don't believe she's a criminal, Papa," Julia said. "She's rough in speech and manners, certainly, but—"

"I don't trust her," Richard answered. "You know that you are too softhearted when it comes to strays, Lady Graymoor. She could be a danger to you and your household."

"No," Will said. "Not Angel. I'd trust her with my life."

"But would you trust her with Lady Graymoor's?" Richard asked. "Or Julia's." He patted Will's good shoulder. "You rest. As you say, we'll not pull anchor in less than two weeks, perhaps three. Since we'll sail into North Carolina waters, it is only common courtesy that we inform the local authorities of our intentions."

"No more talk of pirates," Julia insisted. "Can't you see how ill he is? We'll leave you to your rest, Will."

"I need to talk . . . talk to you," he said. He let his head sink back on the pillow in an attempt to slow the room's spinning. "Julia, I want—"

"Enough!" Lady Graymoor proclaimed. "Out, everyone. Sleep is what he needs. The rest will sort itself out in time."

Can it? Will wondered as he heard their footsteps moving away from the bed. Then he smelled the faint scent of roses, and a woman's lips brushed his forehead.

"Do get well," Julia whispered.

He forced his eyes open. "Julia, I . . ."

"Tomorrow," she promised. "I'll return tomorrow, and we can talk then. Sleep, dearest. Sleep and grow strong."

He tried to speak, but the words lodged in his throat. And then the waves of pain smothered his determination and pulsing darkness closed over him again.

Chapter 20

Morning turned to afternoon and finally evening. Will slept, awakened, and slept again as his fever rose and fell. Delphi took charge of the sickroom. She ordered the cook to prepare kettles of both beef and chicken broth to tempt her patient, and she kept the maids and her grandchildren busy running up and down the stairs with cool well-water and mugs of willow-bark tea. Dr. Madison did not return. Instead, he sent word to Lady Graymoor that he had been called to a possible case of cholera near Washington Square.

At quarter after eight, Lizzy came to Will's side, her brow furrowed and the corners of her mouth drawn down with worry. "How are you, dear boy?"

"Where is she?" he asked.

"Who?"

"You know who. Angel. Why hasn't she been here? Is she ill?"

"Don't fret yourself. You're still warm. When is the last time this dressing was changed?"

"Angel," Will repeated. A feeling of cold dread settled in the pit of his stomach. "What aren't you telling me?"

"I put her to bed. She's not recovered from her own wound, and—"

"You're a bad liar, Lizzy. Tell me the truth!"

Delphi backed quietly out of the room. Sukie and Delphi's grandson did the same.

"Don't upset yourself," Lizzy said. "The guards Griffin set around the house didn't realize that Angel was my houseguest. They chased her out of your garden."

"Chased her?" He swore. "Where is she? For God's sake, woman! Angel hasn't the slightest idea how to look after herself in a town like Charleston. She could be—"

"This is exactly why we didn't tell you," Lizzy scolded. "I knew you'd overreact. She's a sensible girl. Griffin's out looking for her as we speak. Angel will be fine."

"I'm getting up." Sweat broke out on Will's face. Pain greater than that from his gunshot wound knifed through him. "Turn your back, madam. Lest you see—"

"Do you think the sight of male genitalia will alarm me? I assure you that it won't. And you won't go anywhere. Do you wish to start bleeding all over again?" She pushed him back with surprising strength for a woman her age. "Delphi!"

"Ma'am?" Delphi's anxious face peered around the doorframe.

"Call your sons. Mr. William is delirious. If he gets out of this bed, he'll do himself great harm. You are to keep him here at all costs."

"Delphi," Will said. "Don't listen to—"

"I take all responsibility," Lizzy said. "Tie him to the bed if you must." She shook a finger at Will. "Stay where you are. You don't have the strength to walk to the head of the stairs, let alone search the town for her. Trust us, William. We'll find your little island waif."

"You'd better," he warned.

"We shall," Lizzy answered. "I give you my word." She hesitated and then continued in a rush. "And when you're stronger, you should give careful consideration to the question of why she has become so important to you. And, most of all, what mischief and heartache your attraction to Angel can cause her if you do not mean to make an honest woman of her."

An hour later Will woke to the squeak of door hinges. "Angel?" he called. "Is that you?"

"No, sir," Delphi replied. "It's Miss Julia here to see you."

"Is there any word of Angel?"

"No, sir, not yet. But they'll find her." The black woman backed out of the doorway, leaving Julia alone in the room with him.

"Are you in much pain?" she asked.

He was, but he wouldn't admit it. "It's bearable."

"Delphi told me that Angel was missing."

He didn't answer.

"It's unseemly that I come at this hour, I know," she continued. "Papa would be most distressed. But I couldn't leave without speaking to you. We're going to River's End in the morning. You know how frail my mother is. The MacKenzies' footman died of cholera yesterday, and there are reports of yellow fever near the docks. If Papa hadn't been organizing the force to move against the pirates, we would have left days ago."

"It's wise to go. Charleston was always a pest hole in summer." Finding the right words had never been a problem for him before. He and Julia had always been comfortable together. At this moment, comfortable didn't seem as important as it once had.

"I felt that I needed to explain . . . ," she said.

She drew nearer to his bed, and he smelled her rose scent. Slippers to bonnet, Julia was a lavender vision of the latest fashion. And for the first time in his life, he wondered if she dressed in this manner because she liked the style of the clothing or simply because it was required of a Charleston lady.

"Julia . . . ," he began.

"No, wait. Let me say what I came here to. . . ."

"I understand perfectly."

"Can you?" She straightened and cleared her throat. Bright spots of color tinted her cheeks. "I've been frightened for your safety. First when we thought you were dead, and now this attempt on your life."

"I'm not in love with you, Julia." His tone was brusque, more so than he'd intended.

Her mouth trembled as the flush deepened and washed from cheekbones to throat. "I assumed as much," she said. "And I believe I can say the same. I can't admit to ever being *in love,* but we are well suited to each other. Isn't it true that the best marriages are often based on friendship?"

"Some are." He hadn't wanted to hurt Julia, but he owed her the truth. "Have I wronged you? By word or action, have I ever led you to believe that—"

"Is there someone else?"

He struggled to sit up. "I think there might be." Damn but it was hot in here! Not a breath of air stirred. He would have given his right arm to be standing on deck, sailing into a Caribbean sunrise. "Whatever else I've done, I've never lied to you."

"I see." She dabbed a lace hankie to her lips. "It is this Angel."

"She isn't the reason . . ." He exhaled softly. "Nothing can change the respect I feel for you . . . or the genuine affection. You're everything a Falcon bride should be."

"Except?"

"I said nothing about *except.*"

"You didn't have to."

"If I loved you, Julia, no one could come between us."

"Other than the sea?"

He nodded. "Not someone. Something."

"Papa said that might be a problem, said that I was being foolish. But I know what I want from my marriage. I refuse to be a captain's widow, and I won't accept the possibility that my husband might find other . . . other companionship during our separations."

"You deserve more than companionship."

"I believe that I'm a better judge of what will make me happy than anyone else. And I understand that someone like Angel has a certain primitive allure. But you can't believe that she could ever make a proper wife, a mother for your children."

"Those qualities are of deep concern to me."

"Then . . ." Julia fluttered her hands much in the same manner he'd seen Lizzy do so often. "Nothing is settled between you?" she asked.

"No."

An essence that might have been hope flickered in her eyes. "Good," she said. "Then nothing can be settled between us, either."

"I think it must." His voice rasped, dry as sun-scorched canvas. He wanted water, but the pitcher stood on the table beyond his reach, and pride wouldn't allow him to ask for her help. "We've always been the best of friends. Can we part that way?"

She rose gracefully. "No, we cannot. You're much too ill to make such a momentous decision, to end years of affection for—"

"Affection. Not passion. Not a love great enough to bend. For me to give up the sea. For you to try to live with my absences. Deep affection, but not deep enough for either of us to compromise."

"You're feverish. Doubtless, we've both said things that we shall regret. When you recover, we'll talk again. When your mind is clear."

"Good-bye, Julia."

She smiled, avoiding his conclusion as efficiently as a swordsman blocking an opponent's descending cutlass. "I'll tell Papa that you are making a fine recovery."

"Tell your father that you've changed your mind about me," Will said. "That you've had second thoughts."

"I think not." Her smile thinned. "Do with Angel as you wish. I'm convinced that once you've had your fill of her, reason will prevail."

"Julia . . ."

"If it doesn't, spare me no sympathy. Our agreement was never put into words."

"You said you know what will make you happy," he said. "I envy you that. I don't know that about myself. But I know what I'm not going to settle for. I want more than comfortable. And so should you."

"Will Falcon, you are a foolish romantic. When you're stronger, come to River's End. Our door is always open to you."

Heat pressed around him. The damp sheets tangled his legs, and he kicked them off. The room was heavy with the scent of flowers . . . and of the woman lying next to him. He groaned and reached for her, pulling her soft flesh against his, molding her lush feminine curves against his hardness.

She sighed, a small erotic sound that thickened his blood and made her all the more desirable. Her hair, soft and springy, brushed against his naked chest, and one small hand rested against his upper thigh.

He wanted her. If the room was hot and the air moist, how much hotter and wetter she would be. The thought of thrusting into those slick intimate folds made him throb with need. His growing erection pressed against her silken thigh.

"Angel." He kissed her mouth, parting her lips with his tongue . . . tasting the velvet depths, savoring the sensations of sharp teeth and warm tongues caressing.

He cupped her breast in his hand, teased the nub until it hardened and swelled against his fingertips. Then he bent his head and laved the sweet nipple until she sighed and arched against him.

His cock throbbed with need.

"Kiss me," she begged him sleepily. "Suck me. Hard."

Desire washed through him in bright waves. "Will." She squirmed and took hold of him, sliding her hand slowly down his stiffening length, and lightly stroked his head. He groaned as she quickened her motion, tightening her grip.

"Woman . . ." He gasped when she twisted and took him between her lips.

She giggled, sucking lightly.

Molten heat pumped through him. Desire thrummed in his veins. Much more, and he would explode.

"Witch," he accused. "My turn."

He pulled her up and kissed her mouth. Her arms went around his neck, and she lay against him, heart to heart and breast to breast.

"I love you," she whispered. "For always."

With a groan, he rolled on top of her, bracing his weight with one arm to keep from crushing her. Again, they kissed, slow and deep and hot.

Sweat glistened, slick on his skin as he fought for control . . . struggled to wait for her. "I've got something for you," he rasped.

"Promises, promises." She squirmed against him, urging him on with cries of passion.

Eagerly, he pleasured her with fingers and tongue, slowly, deliberately trailing lower, nibbling at the soft skin on her flat belly, and burying his face in her damp nest of curls.

"Yes . . . yes."

He slipped a finger between her legs, seeking the pulsing source of her need. "Shall I kiss you here?"

"Yes . . . yes."

She tossed her head from side to side as he kissed first the red-gold fluff and then hot flesh. He slid a finger inside her, slowly at first and then faster until she seized his head and pushed him down to taste her slick, sweet honey.

She wrapped her legs around him, and moaned as he teased and licked. "Deeper," she begged him. "More." Her nails dug ridges in his back as he thrust his tongue deep and brought her to shuddering climax.

"I want you," she said. "In me."

He reared up and slipped inside her, probing until he found his way. She screamed in ecstasy as he plunged to the hilt.

The tight, wet feel of her was maddening. Shedding thought and reason, he pulled back and slammed his engorged cock into her again and again. She met him thrust for thrust. And with each plunge his spasms grew hotter and stronger until, when he thought he would die, he felt the sudden gush of release. With a final thrust he carried her to paradise with him, and their excited cries mingled in the hot night.

Gasping for breath, drained of strength, almost in

pain, he fell back onto the sheets. His heart crashed against his ribs. He could still taste her . . . feel the joy of her caress. "Angel . . . Angel," he whispered into the stillness. He reached for her . . .

And found only emptiness.

He sat bolt upright, ignoring the pain that bore through his shoulder. His pulse raced. His mouth was dry. Memories of what he'd just experienced tumbled through his mind.

"Angel?"

It had been so real . . . as tangible as the thick bandage wrapped tightly around him.

The candle had gone out. The room was still. Not even a curtain stirred. He sighed heavily, not wanting to let go of the image of Angel beneath him . . . of her expression when he'd entered her . . . of her sweet cries of fulfillment.

"A dream," he whispered. "Nothing more than a dream."

Hollow, aching loss welled inside him.

His stomach turned over. He was alone, and the woman he wanted beside him was still missing . . . maybe lost to him forever.

Angel flattened her back against the wall as the three men halted long enough for one to take a piss.

". . . get a drink," a harsh male voice said.

She heard a belch, and then the unmistakable sound of spewing. Her stomach clenched as the smell hit her.

"Had yer share, ain't you?" Archie Gunn jeered.

Angel held her breath. How had Archie gotten out of jail? If he found her here . . . her heart thudded, surely loud enough for them to hear.

"You buyin' or not?"

Perspiration trickled down Angel's back.

"Hell, yes. More where that came from," Archie's words slurred. Footsteps moved away.

When Angel could no longer hear voices, she fled in the opposite direction. And after only two false turns, she found herself on the narrow street behind Will's property.

In less time than it would take to dig worms for bait, Angel avoided the guard who had chased her earlier, and reached the deeper shadows of the house.

Treading lightly on the damp grass, Angel moved along the walls until she found what she was looking for. Scrambling up onto a rain barrel, she climbed onto the roof of the summer kitchen. The cedar shakes were damp and moss-covered, but she took her time.

Cautiously, she made her way over the peak to a decorative brick ledge that ran across the top of the first-floor windows. There was barely room for her to get a toehold. In shoes, it would have been impossible. But she moved inch by inch, clinging to the rough wall until she reached the balcony.

Twisting vines growing up the side of the house made the rest as easy as opening oysters. She scooted up over the railing and slipped into Will's chamber.

"Who's there?" he called.

She gave her best imitation of a cat's meow.

"Angel? Is that you?"

She sighed in disgust. She was sorry she'd hadn't pretended to be an owl. She could do a perfect screech owl. "Aye," she admitted sheepishly. "It's me."

He came up off the bed.

She ran to him and caught him in her arms. "Nay. Nay, Will. You'll tear your shoulder. Lie back."

He hugged her tightly against him. "Where were you?"

"Lie back," she said. "Lie back, and I'll lay with ye

and tell you whatever you wish to know." With soothing murmurs, she pushed him back. "You are a terrible
patient."

He groaned.

"I'm sorry." She rounded the bed and climbed up beside him. "I didn't run," she said. "I was chased. A great
fellow with a belaying pin. He said I had no business in
your garden."

Will swore. "You should have known that it was a
mistake."

"I should have?" She sniffed. "So you say. But he
wasn't chasing you." She pushed a pillow behind him.
"Lie back now. I'll not have ye bleeding like a stuck
pig."

"Where have you been? Why didn't you go to
Lizzy's?"

"You're a fine one to talk," she replied. "And me
thinkin' you were dying. Look at you. Feet set on the
crow road one day and standing on them the next."

He caught her hand and squeezed it. "I thought I'd
lost you."

She swallowed. She wanted to kiss him, to say that
she'd never go. But she couldn't. She'd heard what Julia
had said to him in Lady Graymoor's hall. And as much
as she loved Will, she'd not ruin his life.

She wouldn't shame him with her wild ways. He was
a gentleman, and he deserved to have a lady at his side.
Julia had spoken truth when she said that she, Angel,
wasn't fit to be Will's wife. As soon as he recovered, she
would go. But not yet. For now, she could be with him.

She snuggled close and put her head on his shoulder.
Will slipped his good arm around her and kissed the
crown of her head.

"You cost me most of a night's sleep," he admitted.

She held her tongue. It wouldn't do to worry him that

she'd almost stumbled into the arms of Archie Gunn. That could wait until he was stronger. And there was no need at all to trouble Will by explaining how she'd come close to escaping from Charleston by climbing aboard a northbound ship and hiding herself amid the stacked cargo.

"There's sickness in the town," she said. "I smelled it. And I heard people on the streets. Fever, they say."

"You didn't go near them?"

"Nay. Not me. I'm good at hiding." And at changing my mind when I've made a mistake, she thought. When push came to shove, she just couldn't abandon Will. Not yet.

"Give me your word that you won't do that again."

Not likely. "If you'll give me yours that you won't go after Cap'n and Bett and the others."

"I can't do that."

"Then I'll make ye no promises, Will Falcon." And live to regret none, she thought. For when I'm certain of your safety, I'll hie away to somewhere you'll never find me, and leave you to what's rightfully yours.

Chapter 21

Three days later, two of Delphi's sons supported Will as he walked the last steps to a high-backed garden bench. The housekeeper came after them, quilt in hand. Will waved her away. "No blankets. Have you lost your mind? It's hot enough to fry eggs on the bricks."

"Not in the shade, it's not," she fussed. She folded the quilt and laid it on the bench beside Will. "Abraham, Benjamin, don't you go too far. We'll need you to help Mr. Will back upstairs later."

"Yes, ma'am," replied the eldest, a tall broad-shouldered fisherman. His brother Benjamin grinned and nodded as they strolled off toward the stables.

"Sukie will be out with the tea tray," Delphi said, "but I'll be in the kitchen." She surveyed critically a table laden with fruit juices, punch, gingerbread, and small apple tarts. "You need anything, you just shout out." She moved a chair, rearranged the flowered porcelain dessert plates, and adjusted the stack of folded napkins. "Anything at all."

Will chuckled. "I'll be fine, Delphi."

He was impatient to make a full recovery before the fleet sailed. Although his fever was gone, and his appetite beginning to come back, he was still concerned about his ability to travel to the Outer Banks and fight when he got there.

"You oughta be in bed another week," Delphi said. "No tellin' what you'll catch out here. All that sickness in town."

"Go on. I'm fine," he repeated. In truth, his head hurt, and walking downstairs had taken more effort than he'd expected.

A dog yipped. Will turned to see Lizzy coming down the pathway from her backyard, followed by three turbaned footmen, the entire pack of spaniels, and Griffin.

"William!" Lizzy called. "Griffin said you were waiting for us out here. Capital idea. Capital. Sickrooms make people sick. Garden air, that's the cure for you. Garden air and nourishing soup."

One servant set a large glazed tureen in the center of the table. A second added soup bowls and spoons. The third uncovered a silver platter of scones, butter, and jam.

Lizzy settled herself beside him. "I had a visitor this morning," she said. "You'd be interested to know that Edward Mason had the nerve to send his solicitor to my house with an offer to purchase Falcon's Nest at an outrageous sum."

"Maybe you should take him up on the offer," Will answered.

"Impudent upstart. To imagine that I'd receive him." She snapped open an ivory fan and waved it under her chin.

"No, seriously," Will said. "You've no need of a second home. And I've no prospects of making enough money to pay you what you've already put out."

"Unless you marry Julia Hamilton."

"I'm not."

"Does Julia know this?"

"Yes. I've told her," he said. "I've made it clear to Julia that what I feel for her is friendship. That's no basis for a marriage."

Lizzy laughed. "Since when?" She tapped him with the fan. "Many would say that Hamilton is a perfect match for you."

"And you, Lizzy? What do you think?"

"I believe there are times when reason must be abandoned, and a man—or even a woman—must follow their heart."

Will grinned. "I keep telling you that you're the only woman for me. And I am serious about the house. I'll find a place for Delphi and her family. It's foolish for me to go on living like a man of wealth, when . . ." The words died in his throat.

Angel came down the walk accompanied by a maid. "What do ye think?" she cried. "Am I as fancy as a flounder in a petticoat?"

Will laughed. In the days since Angel had returned, he'd seen little of her. Lizzy had sent word that she'd commenced Angel's lessons in deportment.

"It's hopeless," Griffin confided. "She doesn't even know how to walk or sit. Not the slightest clue on how a lady faints, or how one is expected to dissolve in hysterics. I fear Angel has not the constitution to learn."

Will stared at Angel. She was in a white, filmy dress with ruffles along the hem. The material was so thin that he could see the outline of her body through it when she moved from shadows to sunshine.

His instant reaction to the sight cheered him with the thought that he wasn't completely dead. Quickly, to hide the growing evidence, Will covered his lap with Delphi's quilt.

Someone had made an attempt to tame Angel's hair, but pins and bonnet did little to contain the wild, coppery-gold mass. Tendrils tumbled over her forehead and hung loose around her cheeks and throat . . . locks of hair that he wanted to stroke and rub between his fingers.

"Are ye speechless?" Angel demanded. She twirled around, revealing a glimpse of shapely ankles and pink satin slippers. "I've learned to pour tea and to dance."

"Show us." Lizzy clapped her hands, and one of the footmen produced a violin. As the servant drew the bow across the strings, Lizzy nodded imperiously to Griffin.

The butler bowed and offered Angel his hand.

"Nay." Laughing, she yanked a bonnet ribbon and sent the fine straw confection spinning into a boxwood hedge. She shook her head, and pins flew in all directions. The pink slippers followed.

Will started to rise, wanting to go to her and pull her into his arms . . . remembering how it was between them in his dream. But before he could make the effort, she came to him and put her hands in his.

Her touch, her nearness, made his throat constrict with emotion. What was there about Angel that drove all else from his mind when she was present? He'd never felt this way about another woman.

If only he was certain that he could trust her.

Lady Graymoor and Griffin retreated to the far corner of the garden, where the gardener was planting a sapling. The servants followed attentively a few steps behind.

"You are beautiful," Will said to Angel.

"But no Charleston lady." Her eyes sparkled with merriment. "Griffin says that I will find a husband all the same. Do ye . . . do you think I can?"

Will's grip tightened. His pulse quickened. If Lizzy thought to tease him by mentioning other men, she had succeeded. "Do you want a husband, Angel?"

"I had one, but I didn't suit him," she replied,

growing suddenly serious. "If I ever take another, he must have me as I am, not as he wishes me to be."

He was no good at these games, and he had no wish to play. "I've ended it with Julia," he said. "Irrevocably."

"I hope she's not heartbroken."

"It was never more than friendship between us. With you or without you, I never could have married her. We would have made each other miserable."

"Then it's best you part."

"What of you, Angel? Are you heartbroken?"

She pulled back, out of his grasp. "I'm a pirate," she said. "I have no heart."

He pushed himself up to his feet. "Are you?"

"Ye say I am. It must be true." Her emerald eyes glistened with unshed tears. "Send me home, or send me away. I can make do anywhere that the tide washes."

"You're still determined to be rid of me? Is there no chance that you could learn to be at home here in Charleston?"

"As what?"

"I think I—" he began, then broke off as he saw Lady Graymoor and the others returning. "Later," he promised. "When we have more privacy."

"It's useless," Angel replied. "No matter how Lady Graymoor changes the outside, inside, I'm still the same island wench with salt on my skin and seaweed in my hair."

"There, there," Lizzy said as she joined them. "If you two argue, people will take you for man and wife." She chuckled and smiled kindly at Angel. "No one expects you to learn decorum in a few days. It took me years to go from parsonage to earl's ballroom. You listen to me, and I promise to find you a rich husband."

"I don't think I want one." Angel hitched up her dress

and rolled down a stocking. "Who but a cod's head would wear hose in this heat? Or long sleeves?"

Waves of dizziness made Will weak, and he sat down heavily. "We need to talk," he said to Angel.

"Mayhap," she answered. "Lady Graymoor says she means to leave Charleston. That I'm to go with her. But your wound is far from healed. I won't leave you until you're out of danger."

"Of course you won't leave William," Lizzy said. "We're all going together. Cholera is spreading through the town. It's not safe here. I'm moving my household to Nottingham, and you must come with us."

"To your plantation?" It was difficult to carry on a rational conversation with Lizzy when all he wanted was to be alone with Angel.

"Where else?" Lizzy pursed her lips. "I do believe the fever has addled your mind. Did you think I was planning a sea voyage to England?"

"Take Angel," he said. "I'll stay here." He didn't want to remind them that he meant to sail with Richard's fleet or that he'd not be able to rest until he found justice for his father. "The wound is nearly closed."

"You'll gain nothing by staying to die of cholera," Griffin said. "And the road to Nottingham runs two ways. It's not that far."

"I'm not afraid of cholera," Angel said.

"You should be." Lizzy glanced meaningfully at Will.

"If I come, Delphi and her family must come, too. I'll not leave them," Will hedged. "I should—"

"Bring them all." Lizzy frowned. "We'll talk there, William. You're doing our Angel no good, you know. Best to plot a proper course of action before your reputation and hers are utterly ruined."

"Very well," Will agreed. "I'll tell Delphi to pack at

once." He smiled at Angel. "You'll like Nottingham," he promised.

"You promised I'd like Charleston."

"You'll love it. It's on an island."

"Water around it?" Angel's eyes narrowed suspiciously. "No streets, nor rows of houses, and mobs of chattering town folk?"

"Not a single paved carriageway," Griffin assured her. "Nottingham is surrounded by river and swamp, a primeval wilderness of hanging moss, live oaks, and black water."

"Sounds like Eden," Angel said.

"I'm certain you'll think so," Will said. "There are even snakes."

Early the following morning, Delphi, two of her daughters, five grandchildren, and assorted members of the household set off for the plantation with Lady Graymoor's household staff. Will had just locked the front door and was waiting for Lizzy's coachman to bring the carriage from the stable when he was confronted by Edward and George Mason.

"You don't appear deceased," Edward said as he reined in his horse.

Will noticed that the man was riding a flashy bay gelding. "Did you want something?" he asked. "Or did you come by to continue our disagreement?"

"I demand an apology, Falcon. You've made false and defamatory statements about me—publicly insinuating that I ordered you shot from ambush. I could sue you for defamation of character."

"Impossible, you self-righteous bastard. You don't have any character to defame."

Mason's mouth tightened. "I appeared at the appointed hour. You are the one who didn't. Perhaps you had someone pretend to shoot you, because you were too cowardly to face me on the field of honor?"

Will's reply was both succinct and profane.

"I don't like you, Falcon," Mason said. "I didn't care for your father, either. It's men like you who give gentlemen a bad name."

"I've been given to understand that you'll be supplying several of the ships going in search of the wreckers," Will said, ignoring the insult. "I'd think you'd be afraid of being recognized by your comrades."

Mason smiled thinly. "Perhaps when this messy pirate affair is settled, we can resume our appointment. I'd like nothing better than to silence that foul mouth of yours permanently."

"I'm at your service, Edward. Anytime, anyplace. I assure you, the feeling is mutual."

"I understand that the brigand you had arrested has escaped without a trace. Doubtless, you'll blame me for that offense as well."

"Archie Gunn's escaped?" Will asked.

"Ah, something the great Will Falcon doesn't know."

"Let's go," George said. "This exchange is meaningless."

"If you'll excuse us," Edward pulled back on the reins, and his horse moved restlessly. "And for your information," he added, "the mare proved to be unsound. She went lame. I ordered my stable master to dispose of her."

Swearing, Will lunged at him.

Edward laughed and nodded to George. Digging his spurs into his mount's sides, he rode away, disappearing around the corner just as Lady Graymoor's carriage appeared. His brother followed.

Anger, black and deadly, washed through Will. He knotted his hands into fists as he thought of the sweet-tempered mare Mason had destroyed out of spite. "I'll add Calli to your score," he said. "But you'll pay in full, you sanctimonious bastard. I swear on my father's soul."

Angel woke in the lavender-white glow of dawn. For a minute or two, she lay there, remembering yesterday's journey from Charleston by coach and then boat to this great house among the moss-hung oaks.

Rising, she pushed away the mosquito netting and crossed the high-ceilinged room to an open window. Heavy mist blanketed the house, but she could feel the nearness of the river and smell the scents of brackish water and tidal reeds. To her, the smells were sweeter than wild strawberries, and her throat tightened with emotion.

She strained to hear the chorus of frogs and insects and the far-off cry of a night heron. Her heartbeat quickened. She pulled a cambric chemise over her head, and after a few seconds' hesitation, stepped into a pair of silken drawers with drawstrings at the waist and a pearl button just below each knee. Reluctantly, she tied on an unboned bodice that Lady Graymoor's maid had called *jumps*, and topped off her attire with a ruffled underskirt of linen. Shoes would only hinder her progress, so she left those behind as she climbed nimbly out the window and onto a tree branch.

Skinning down the oak to the soft grass, Angel ran lightly across the lawn toward the river. She didn't need to see the water. She could hear it.

Next to a dock, she found a dugout with a paddle lying in the hollowed-out bottom. Smiling, she stepped into the gently rocking craft, slipped the rope, and let the current carry her away.

● ● ●

Will found her two hours later walking away from a tiny cabin nestled in the palmettos. "Angel? What are you doing here?" he asked her. "I couldn't find you."

She smiled at him. "'Twas the river. It called me." Seeing him on his feet and able to walk this far gave her a rush of happiness. "There was fishing line in the bottom of the boat I borrowed. I caught some fish and gave them to the old woman who lives in that house. Her name is Aba Sunday."

"I've been wanting to talk to you since we got to Nottingham."

"Aye. I thought that. But I wasn't sure that I was ready to talk to you." She approached the dugout that she'd secured to a tree root earlier. "How are you feeling? Is the headache better this morning?"

"Most of it. A twinge here and there, but I'll live."

"Good." She inspected him closely for signs that he might not be telling the truth about his recovery. Only a small bandage covered the gouge the bullet had made, but Will's eyes still reflected pain and a bone-deep fatigue. She touched his arm. "Let me take you back to the house in the dugout."

He nodded. "All right."

Taking his hand, she helped him into the boat, pushed it out into the river, and leaped in.

The tide was still incoming, running away from the house. Will didn't protest when she made no attempt to turn the craft.

"Am I being kidnapped?" Will asked after they'd traveled another quarter of a mile, drifting past groups of slave quarters and a green rice field.

"Mayhap," she answered. A great blue heron started up and took flight over their heads. "It's fair country, this place. So much beauty, it hurts a body to look at it."

"Yes, I agree."

She felt his eyes burning holes in her back and turned to meet his clear-eyed gaze. It wasn't the bird or the great, moss-hung trees he was looking at, she realized. It was her Will was calling beautiful. She felt her cheeks grow warm with pleasure. . . .

"I've been thinking, Will. I'd made up my mind to leave as soon as you were out of danger. But now . . ."

"Now, you've changed your mind?"

"If you'd never come . . . if I'd never pulled you from the sea, I would have stayed with the Brethren . . . stayed where I was content."

"But we did meet."

"Aye, and you carried me here."

"To a bigger world."

She nodded, realizing there were things out here that she'd miss if she returned to her island home . . . sights she wanted to see . . . questions still unanswered. "But you took me without asking did I want to come," she continued. "That was hard for me to accept, to be treated like what I wanted didn't matter. It's the same as some of the men on the island. They made the laws, and women lived by them. I thought you were different."

"I am different, Angel."

"Are you?"

"I was wrong not to ask you. But you would have refused. And I didn't want to leave you there."

"Why? When I mean so little to you?"

"Don't say that. I think I'm in love with you."

She scoffed. "No need to tell me lies."

"Angel—"

"Hush, Will. Let me have my say. When I wanted you, you wouldn't have me. We were handfasted, but I wasn't good enough for you to take to your bed."

"It was never that. It was a matter of honor. I care for you, more than I can find words to tell you."

Her heart fluttered like a trapped bird. She turned her back and fixed her eyes on the bow of the boat. Digging her paddle in, she stayed the little craft and spun it in midriver. His words were bittersweet. She thought he meant them, but it had always been too late for the pair of them. They were no more suited to be bride and groom than a doe and a swan.

But, oh, how hope tantalized her, dancing just out of reach. Tears welled in her eyes, and she blinked them away. "You might think different once you're well," she said. "Julia's a good woman. And she's one of your kind. Ye could do far worse."

"I could do far better."

She raised the paddle, staring at the crude carving along the blade and watching as drops of water ran off to drip into the dark flow. The lump in her throat was back, making it impossible to talk and hard to draw breath.

She couldn't hide the truth from herself any longer. She loved Will Falcon, loved him as deep as the sea and as high as the moon. But because she loved him, his happiness meant everything to her. She'd not let him throw away his future for her.

But neither could she stand by and let him destroy the people she loved, those who had raised her and been her friends. She'd have to find a way to convince Will to forget the attack, or she must warn Bett, Cap'n, and the others of the danger. But so long as she could keep Will in Charleston, the Brethren were safe.

And if the Brethren were safe, what was wrong with snatching a few hours . . . a few days of happiness? After all, wasn't that what she'd wanted from the first? From the moment she'd laid eyes on him.

She'd known that she and Will were different . . . that nothing between them could last. But she'd wanted Will to be the man who made her a woman and gave her something to hold close to her heart forever.

Since she was a child, she'd stood in the shadows of other families, never really belonging to anyone. She was no more than driftwood washed up on a beach, a merry-be-gotten child without a name or memories.

"Could we forget Mason and Julia and the Brethren?" Will asked. "Here, in this place, could we try to see what we feel for each other?"

She already knew, she thought. And no space of time or words would change her love for him. Or her realization that even if she could trade her happiness for the lives of the Brethren, Will would only want her until he came to his senses.

How could she make him understand that all they'd ever have was the pleasure they could give each other here and now?

She couldn't.

So she wouldn't waste breath in trying.

Instead, she forced a smile, dipped the paddle, and lightly splashed him. "Ye were right," she said. "I do like this place."

"And me?" he asked. "Do you care for me?"

"That's for me to know, and ye to guess," she answered lightly. Leaning forward, she dug the paddle hard, and forced the dugout against the current back the way they had come.

Chapter 22

At exactly ten o'clock, a tall, lanky footman with close-cropped hair climbed the wide center staircase at Nottingham to deliver morning tea to Lady Graymoor's second-floor chamber.

"Thank you, Coffie," Griffin said as the servant placed the inlaid tray carefully on a table. "That will be all for today. Her ladyship says you may have the rest of the day off. But be back by breakfast tomorrow."

A smile spread over Coffie's dark face. "Yes, sir, Mr. Griffin."

"You are too lenient with your people," Griffin said to Lady Graymoor when they were once more alone. "They take advantage of you."

"Perhaps." She smiled. "But Coffie is the best footman I've ever had. He deserves time to visit his friends and relatives on the island."

Lizzy was a vision this morning in her coral dressing gown. She wore not a trace of makeup, and her thick, swan-white hair was plaited neatly into two braids and hung down her back as simply as a country milkmaid's.

He returned to his seat by the open window that overlooked the wide expanse of front lawn stretching down to the water's edge. He'd already donned fresh breeches and hose, but he was still bare-chested.

Lizzy poured each of them a cup of tea, then set them

241

aside and continued massaging horse liniment into his back and shoulders.

"It's going to be hot today," Griffin said. He groaned. "Lower . . . ahhh, there." The woman was a marvel. She knew instinctively where to find all the sore places.

"This is ridiculous, Griff. My hands will reek of this mess for days."

"It eases the ache, love. What better medicine for an old warhorse than your soft hands rubbing out the kinks?"

She laughed, a highly amused sound that came out much like a giggle. Leaning forward, she kissed the back of his neck. "I imagine you would have a few twinges after last night."

He twisted to look at her. Lizzy's cheeks glowed with color, and her eyes twinkled merrily. He grinned.

"I believe the country is better for more than an escape from fever and plague," she said.

"Hmmp." He rolled his head, first left, then right, and stood up. "Enough of this. I have duties to attend to."

"Not yet. You may put on your finest and huff and puff at the servants at dinner, but we have plenty of time. I want to talk with you about Angel and William."

Griffin examined a spotless lawn shirt for wrinkles, then, satisfied, thrust an arm into it. He'd known it. Things were too calm this morning. They were bound to get into a patch of nettles before the dinner hour. "You know exactly what my feelings are about that subject," he replied. "It's a disaster."

"Don't be such a dragon. Even you must have been young once. Can't you appreciate Angel for what she is?"

He began to button the shirt's single fastening at the

throat. She brushed his hands away and buttoned it herself. Griffin frowned. Dealing with Lizzy was difficult when he didn't agree with her.

"I do know what the woman is," he said. "That's the problem. She's a good and loving soul. And I don't want to see her hurt."

"I agree. My heart goes out to her. She is very secretive about her life, but I'm sure she's suffered great hardship. And she dearly loves our William."

"He is very fond of her, I'm sure," Griffin said. "But Will is a gentleman, a Falcon of Church Street. Wherever he goes, he is welcomed into the homes of quality, given great responsibilities because of his birth and status."

"He asked me last night if I thought Angel could be happy here . . . if she could form friendships, learn to manage a home."

"And what did you tell him?"

"I had to be honest. I said I didn't know."

Griffin frowned. "She will present him with a bastard child if they're permitted to associate with each other for long. Why did you insist on bringing her here? You'll never prevent improprieties on this island."

"What makes you think I want to?"

"She isn't your lost Elizabeth."

"I didn't say she was."

"You didn't say it, but I know you are thinking it—wishing it were so. She isn't. You know I'm right. I was right about the last one, wasn't I? You've wasted far too much money on this hopeless quest."

"Is it hopeless?"

He pulled her into a warm embrace and kissed the crown of her head. He wanted so badly to protect her, but Lizzy's soft heart was her own greatest enemy. "Ah, love, you're such a dreamer. Wee Elizabeth is lost, rocked in the arms of angels. She has been lost for twenty years. She's dead, Lizzy, and the sooner you accept that, the happier you'll be."

"You'd have me completely alone?" She laid her head against his chest. "I'd know if she were dead. I can't tell you how I'd know, but I would."

"You'll never be alone as long as I draw breath."

"Then why won't you agree to make an honest woman of me?"

"Marriage? Between us?" He released her, stepped back, and tapped her lovingly under the chin. "Lady Graymoor wed her butler?" He shook his head. "It simply isn't done. Not even in the godless colonies. It is as impossible as a match between Angel and our Will."

How many times had he daydreamed about such a possibility of running off with Lizzy? But there was nowhere to hide. Italy, Holland, even India would find them out eventually. Lizzy's wealth and her title would be discovered. And doubtless the worthless cousin's son would sue to have her declared incompetent and seize her fortune. No, wedding his little countess wasn't in the cards. Besides, he told himself, so long as he was her butler, he could keep his self-respect. He wasn't a kept man, living on the coin of a rich woman. He was a trusted employee.

"I've reached an age where I care little what others think of me," she proclaimed, retrieving his waistcoat and holding it out to him.

He chuckled. "Can you deny your love of being the high point in Charleston society? Or that you wouldn't miss a card party or a ball? How many doors would be open to you with your hired man on your arm? No, my dear. Our relationship works very well for both of us. Let us not tinker with success."

"You are a stubborn old man, Griffin Davis. Why I've

put up with your impudence all these years I'll never know."

He winked at her. "It's the Davis legacy. Sergeant may be a tad slow to rise to attention, but once his blood is up, there's no finer steed in the British Empire."

Lizzy screwed up her face and prepared to fire a return volley, but he defused her attack by blowing a kiss at her. "Admit it, love. There's no lover like a Welshman, and no Welshman like a Davis."

"You are . . . are impossible," she stammered. "Get out of my room and see to . . . see to your duties."

"Yes, m'lady," he replied with a solemn face and a deep bow. Inside, a warm glow filled him to overflowing. She might pretend otherwise, but Lizzy loved his rough soldier talk within the confines of her boudoir. Last night had been a triumph, and if his intuition was correct, tonight might hold even greater heights to conquer.

At exactly one in the afternoon, the regular dinner hour at Nottingham, Angel, garbed in a fancy dress and wearing shoes and stockings, appeared at the doorway of the formal dining room.

This morning, floating on the river with him, she'd been nearly overwhelmed by her feelings for him. Now, seeing Will rise to greet her, she wanted to weep with relief that he was alive and whole. If he lived and was safe, how could she ask for more?

She hadn't wanted to play this game, to dress and act like someone she wasn't . . . someone she could never be. But Will had asked it of her when they returned to the landing. And knowing they had so little time together, she could deny him nothing.

Now, it was all she could do to keep her knees from knocking out of fear that she'd make a fool of herself.

Lady Graymoor had been so good to her, but the old woman couldn't understand that being a guest here, even an honored guest, wasn't the same as belonging. A quick glance at Griffin's face told her he knew she didn't belong in this room or in this house. She stopped, trying to decide if she should turn and run.

"Angel!" Lady Graymoor called. "How lovely you look. The picture of health. Do join us at table."

Sparkling crystal and silver gleamed on the white linen cloth. The table was laden with enough food to feed a dozen sailors. Overhead hung a large sail of woven reeds. Ropes and pulleys led from the sail to a far corner of the room where a footman fanned the still air, making the room much cooler than it would have been at midday.

In Charleston, she had eaten in her room or with Lady Graymoor in her chambers. There had been no fancy table, no fuss such as this.

Angel looked down at the array of forks and spoons on either side of her plate and felt a fresh wave of fear. So many. How would she possibly know which to use and when?

As if reading her mind, Will glanced at Griffin. "No need to put your staff to such trouble for me," he said to Lizzy. "The table seems set for the governor, rather than just us."

The countess looked puzzled. "Who is more dear to me than you are, William? Why shouldn't we eat off the lovely plates and silver. If we don't, who shall?"

A maid came to the table carrying a silver tureen of soup. Angel watched apprehensively as the girl ladled the steaming liquid into a bowl in front of her. Then, unexpectedly, Angel felt a tap on her ankle. She looked up to see Will wink at her and reach for a large spoon. Relief spilled through her as she followed his lead.

Realizing she had only to study Lady Graymoor and Will and do as they did made the dinner almost enjoyable. The food was delicious, and the conversation kept her wide-eyed with wonder. The countess prompted Will to talk of his journeys in the Caribbean and across the Atlantic to the shores of Ireland and Spain.

As she grew more relaxed, Angel glanced around at the beautiful room. The furniture here was dark and heavy. It looked old, but against the white plaster walls, the effect was startling.

Occasionally, while Will was telling of his adventures, he'd rub her ankle again with the toe of his shoe. And whenever he did, it was all she could do not to laugh. After the fourth time, she decided that what was fair for the gander was fair for the goose. Wiggling out of her slipper, she returned the favor. Will gave no sign that he was aware of her gentle stroking, but she sensed he was excited by it, and she silently vowed to give him more of the same whenever the opportunity presented itself.

At last, a final course was served: a light pudding and some kind of cake that Angel had never tasted before. Lady Graymoor laid her napkin beside her plate and stood up, a signal that the meal was over. But when Angel tried to do the same, she knocked a spoon off the table onto the floor.

Quickly she bent to retrieve the spoon, but as she ducked under the tablecloth, an odd sensation swept through her, making her light-headed. Will's voice faded and she seemed to hear another man speaking over Will's.

" . . . *find you. Where are you, Bett? Fee fie fo fum, I smell the blood of an Englishman!*"

Suddenly giddy, Angel took hold of a table leg to steady herself. For the barest instant, she was a child again, crouching not beside the table, but under it.

"Can't find me!"

A small giggle bubbled up from the child's hiding place.

"Oh, yes, I can!" cried the deep male voice. "Got you!"

"Angel! Angel, what's wrong? Are you ill?" Will's anxious tone drew her back. She felt his arms around her, lifting her up. "What's wrong? Are you feverish?"

"Nay." She gasped. "Nay, nothin' be . . ." She drew in a ragged breath and blinked. Was she losing her mind? Why did she keep hearing Bett's name called? And why the ghost of a child under the table? "Just the heat," she lied.

"Ruby, take Miss Angel up to her room," Lady Graymoor ordered a maidservant. "Tuck her into bed. She may have a touch of fever." She laid her hand on Angel's forehead. "You are warm."

"I'm all right," Angel said. " 'Tis just the great meal and the warmth of the day."

"Nevertheless," Lady Graymoor insisted. "It's to bed with you." She smiled reassuringly. "Or perhaps my lessons on how a lady faints have taken hold."

Ignoring her protests, Lady Graymoor and the slave woman Ruby followed her up the stairs to her bedroom. There, the maid opened the windows and helped her out of the dress. "I'm not going to bed," Angel insisted. "I'm fine."

"Humor an old woman," Lady Graymoor coaxed. "Just lie down for a little while. It's the custom here. We ladies always nap in midafternoon. Besides, I've been wanting an opportunity to talk with you."

Angel perched cross-legged on the bed as Ruby hung up the gown and left the room. Lady Graymoor drew a chair close to the bed and sat down. Angel looked at her warily and waited for her to say what was on her mind.

"Do you like Nottingham?" the old woman asked after a short silence.

Angel nodded. " 'Tis lovely. But awful big."

"The house has a wonderful history. It was built by a Frenchman for his bride and passed through several families before it was renamed Nottingham. There used to be an Indian camp on the land. I understand the native people remained here long after they'd left the surrounding area."

"Yet . . . you did not bring me here to talk about Indians."

Lady Graymoor chuckled. "No, I didn't, did I?"

"You've been good to me, but I won't take advantage of your—"

"Hush. I like you, child. You're much as I was when I was twenty. I imagine it's hard for you to think that I could have been young. I wasn't so beautiful as you are, but I had my share of beaus."

"You have beauty now, ma'am, a beauty of the soul that shines for all to see."

"What sweet flattery." Lady Graymoor chuckled, but Angel could see that she was pleased. "I wonder if you would indulge me."

"More questions?"

"I've asked before, I know. But this time, would you please answer? It would mean so much to me."

Angel shrugged. "If I can."

"Fair enough. Are you certain you can't tell me the month and year of your birth?"

She shook her head. "No, ma'am, I cannot. I told you before. I don't know."

"But surely your mother . . ."

"Bett. Bett took care of me. She loved me like her own."

"Like her own? You aren't her daughter?"

"I am. I just wasn't born from her body. Bett some-times said she was looking for driftwood and found me on the beach. Other times, she'd say she caught me in her crab trap, or dug me up in an oyster bed."

"Do you remember her finding you?"

She shook her head. "Sometimes I think I do, but . . ." She sighed. "In the end, there's naught but fog."

"You didn't ask where you came from? What your name was?"

"Just Angel." She could tell that Lady Graymoor was becoming more excited. The old woman leaned forward and took her hand.

"Do you remember a ship? A mother and a father? A baby brother?"

Angel shook her head.

"Where, exactly, did Bett find you?"

Angel laughed. "You know not the Brethren. They wander the length of the Outer Banks. One month here, the next another island. I doubt even Bett could tell you."

"And you're certain she isn't your real mother?"

"Nay. I'm certain of nothing. Did you know Bett, you'd understand. Bett is a fine piece of work, she is. And she's fond of tall tales. She was between husbands when I was young. Could be I'm her natural child, and she's too canny to admit it."

Lady Graymoor squeezed her hand. "Did you know I've spent twenty years and more searching for my lost granddaughter?"

"Will has told me a little. But I'm not that child, ma'am. I'm an island wench and no kin to the great of England."

"You do understand, don't you? I'm wealthier than you can imagine. And if you were my granddaughter, you'd inherit everything."

"Wish I was. I'd like to be your missing poppet. I never had a grandmother, nor any that I could name my own. But I'd not lie to you or to myself."

"But you can't be sure. If this Bett found you after a shipwreck, it's possible that—"

Angel raised the lined hand and kissed it. "Look for your granddaughter within heaven's gates, ma'am. For what the sea claims, she will not give up."

"So many have told me." She rose, looking suddenly older and weaker. "And perhaps they were right." She started toward the door, stopped, and looked back. "Is there anything you need? Anything I can do to make your stay more pleasant."

Angel shook her head. "No, ma'am, I'm—wait." She swallowed, hesitant to ask, then blurted it out: "I'm fond of the woods and the beach." She pointed to the dress she'd worn earlier. "The gown is lovely, but it's not fit for fishing. Could I have something plain to roam in?"

"You want an old dress?"

"A skirt and bodice will do for me. Or even a man's shirt and breeches." She shrugged. "I am what I am, and no more. Best not to waste silk and satin on the likes of me."

"Very well, if that would make you happy."

Angel couldn't tell if Lady Graymoor was pleased or vexed. "It would, my lady. If it's not too much trouble. I need no shoes."

"No." The old woman chuckled to herself. "I don't suppose you do. I'll ask William's Delphi to find something suitable for you." And then she sighed. "I wish you were my lost granddaughter."

"Not if you knew me better. I'm rough, ma'am. I'm used to island ways. I'm grateful for your kindness. But I know where I belong."

"And so do I," she replied. "So do I."

Chapter 23

Angel did sleep in the afternoon. At seven, when Ruby came to announce supper, Angel asked to be excused, saying she wasn't hungry.

"Mr. Will, he's worried about you," Ruby said.

"Tell him not to fret. I'll be myself tomorrow."

The young black woman cocked her head. "You got the moon misery, miss? Belly troublin' you?"

"No need to mention that to the gentleman or to Lady Graymoor. Just say . . . say I'm in-de-posed."

"Yes, miss, I'll say just them words."

As Ruby padded away down the hall, Angel wondered if she'd been dishonest. Although her pain was more heart than belly, she was sure some of her aching came from her gut. And the moon—rising full and yellow tonight—for certain was part of her maziness. She felt it in her bones.

Later when Will knocked at her door and called her name, she would not open it. Instead, she drew close and asked, "What do you want?"

"I have to see you," he insisted.

"By the dock. When all the house is asleep."

"If you don't come, I'll come for you, locked doors or none."

She heard his footsteps fade away.

And when Lady Graymoor came to check on her,

Angel lay as if sleeping, with her eyes closed and one hand flung out motionless.

"Are you sick, child?" she asked kindly.

Angel stirred and pretended to awaken.

The older woman felt her forehead again. "No fever. Doubtless a good night's sleep will put you right."

"Aye," Angel answered. "I'm certain I'll be more myself on the morrow."

"The boats are yours to use whenever you like," Lady Graymoor said. "But take care. There are bears and alligators, poisonous snakes, and even a few wolves. It's easy to become lost when you don't know your way, and there are places where quicksand will suck you down."

Angel smiled. "I'm never lost, ma'am, not with stars to guide me." She shrugged. "And wild critters don't scare me. Bett always said that because I was born fey, I could charm them with fairy magic."

"Perhaps you can." The countess kissed her on the forehead. "God keep you."

"And you, my lady."

For a moment, as Lady Graymoor swept from the room, Angel let herself think of what it would be like to belong here, to be not just an uninvited guest, but this good woman's lost grandchild. The thought crossed her mind that it would be easy to pretend, to lie and say that she remembered bits and pieces. Hadn't one of the servants mentioned that the child was lost when a ship went down?

I could say, I remember almost drowning. I was with my mother, but then she was gone and I was alone. Bett pulled me from the water. I cried and cried, and then Bett took me home with her and told me that I'd best forget my family. They were gone.

Shame flooded her, disgust that she might even think

such dung. Lady Graymoor had been good to her. She could never betray that kindness with lies and deception.

If she wasn't good enough for the likes of Will Falcon, she couldn't pass herself off as an English lady. She'd not the stomach for such evil.

Elizabeth likely had been a frail child with pale skin and dainty features. She'd never have had the strength to swim to shore in rough seas or to survive if she reached the beach. Washed away, she was, poor mite. And none to hear her dying cries but seabirds on the wing. No cross or stone to mark her grave, naught but a grandmother's anguish. Mayhap the little maid had become a wandering ghost, forever lost, forever weeping in vain for someone to come take her home.

Gooseflesh rose on Angel's arms. Many the times she'd felt the presence of something unexplained in the stillness of a hot afternoon or in the early morning mist. All manner of haunts and unearthly beings roamed the Outer Banks, and those who had the sight, as she did, were wont to see or hear them now and then.

Angel had never seen a spirit child, but she'd witnessed other things that didn't bear repeating, sights that would turn a man's bones cold. She didn't fear the specters, didn't fear much but humans between earth and heaven, but some visions had troubled her sleep and made her wary.

Lady Graymoor had bid her beware of snakes, bears, and gators. Angel chuckled. She'd sooner step gently around a water moccasin or keep upwind of a black bear than face down the likes of a headless pirate or a wailing, soul-sucking banshee. And most wild creatures were peaceful. If you left them alone, they'd do the same by you.

She waited until the house grew silent. The moon rose

over the trees, the horses in the stables ceased their nickering, and the birds went to roost. Then she shinnied down the limb outside her window and made her way to the damp grass below.

When she reached the dock, Angel's heart leaped in her chest. A ghostly shadow waited for her in the dugout. "Will?" she whispered. "Is that you?"

"I was afraid you wouldn't come." He climbed out and took her in his arms, kissing her so passionately that it made her head swim.

"What do you want?" she asked breathlessly.

"You . . . only you." He kissed her again and then murmured, "It's not safe for you to roam the river country alone."

I think I'm in more danger here, she thought, trying to maintain control of her emotions. "So Lady Graymoor said," she managed. "But I told her that I'm used to looking out for myself."

Will held her in the circle of his arms. "Archie Gunn escaped from jail."

"I know," she admitted. "I saw him."

Will's muscles tensed. His gaze pierced hers. "You saw him? When? Where?"

She touched her lips with two fingers and wiggled free of Will's embrace. A hard resolve slipped over the features that had greeted her with such open intensity, and she sensed again the intensity and danger she'd not seen since the night he'd climbed in her window. Affection. "While you were abed at Falcon's Nest," she admitted. "Archie was coming out of a tavern near the docks."

"He didn't see you?"

She shook her head.

"And you didn't think it important enough to tell me?"

Will was angry now. "I did want to tell you," she

said. "But I wanted to wait until you were stronger. Ye could hardly chase him when you were too weak to rise from your bed."

She climbed into the small boat, and he followed, taking care not to tip it as he settled into the stern. She pushed away from the dock without speaking.

For a few minutes there was strained silence between them, and Angel concentrated on maneuvering the light craft in the current.

"When will you learn to trust me?" he asked after a time. "I don't want there to be secrets between us."

"Easy said." She pushed off from the dock and dipped her paddle. "When have ye trusted me? You've accused me and mine of piracy, and you've hidden your thoughts and your actions from me."

"I have my reasons."

"As I have mine."

"I love you, Angel."

His words affected her so much that she nearly dropped the paddle. Gooseflesh rose on the nape of her neck. Suddenly, it was hard to draw breath.

I love you wasn't the same as *I think I love you*. She'd waited so long, hoped and prayed for those words. But now they came too late.

She wasn't as ignorant as she'd once been. And she knew that a man and a woman wanting each other's bodies wasn't the same as a love that would hold you together through storm and fire until age turned your hair to white.

"I said, I love you. Now, you're supposed to tell me the same."

"What do ye want of me?" she asked, not looking back, afraid she couldn't face those relentless blue eyes boring into her soul. "A woman who cannot read or write her own name."

"I want you to be my wife."

A knot twisted in her throat. She paddled harder, unable to speak. She had gone over and over the possibility that this might happen. But hearing the words from Will's lips was different. She prayed silently that she had the resolve to carry through her plan.

"Angel. You could learn to read, if that's important to you."

"Mayhap I could." But she wasn't certain she wanted to try. What if she couldn't? What if she was too thickheaded to ever make sense of letters jumbled together?

"I'm asking you to marry me," he said. "At St. Michael's Church, with Lady Graymoor, Richard and Julia Hamilton, and all of Charleston bearing witness."

Tears stung her eyes, but she forced them back.

"I love you. I want to spend the rest of my life with you." He reached for her, and the dugout rocked.

"Stop that," she said, "unless ye wish to dump us to the gators."

"Pull to shore or I'll take my chances."

Stubbornly, she kept paddling. "Men like you don't marry women like me. They hide them away where they can visit them without anyone knowing." She knew she sounded foolish. All this time they'd been together, and it had been her wanting the swiving and Will too proud to take what was offered.

"What rule says I can't make you my wife?"

They say it, she thought. Everyone. All the world says it.

"We can make our own choices, Angel."

"Do you still think me a pirate?"

"No. I don't. I was wrong, and I'm sorry I accused you."

"What made you change your mind?"

"The way you cared for me while I was hurt . . . the

way you refused to take advantage of Lizzy. Any woman with an ounce of larceny in her heart would have pretended to be her lost grandchild. And you never did, Angel. Your actions proved your honesty far more than words."

They passed the old cabin. No light had burned in the window, and Angel smelled no smoke from the hearth. From far off, inland, away from the river, echoed the faint sound of African drums.

"Do you love me, Angel?"

She swallowed, resting the paddle on the side of the boat, letting the current take them. "I do," she answered finally. That much was true. No need to tell him that she would not wed him in St. Michael's Church or any other. No reason to spoil what might happen between them today by arguing about tomorrow.

Any more than she would try to convince him of the Brethren's innocence . . .

"If we both love each other," he continued, "nothing else matters."

She remained silent, remembering all too well what Julia had said to Will that day in Lady Graymoor's hall. *"Angel could never be accepted by the people who matter. She'd be unhappy, and she would ruin your career."*

If she married Will, his friends would turn their backs on him. She and Will might care deeply for each other now, but in time he would blame her for her base blood and her ignorance. Oh, she could ape the manners and the words of a Charleston lady, but she would come to feel the walls close in around her.

And when Will sailed away—if anyone would give him a ship to captain—when he was gone for months or years, she would be truly alone without a soul who loved her for herself. She would pine for the sea and lonely beaches, for the sight of swimming dolphins and the great flocks of waterbirds. In the end, she would run away and leave him, or wither and die within the cramped streets of Will's city.

What Will was asking her to do was impossible. She had to remain strong, not let herself become bewitched by what could never be. She took a deep breath and dug her paddle in the dark water, thrusting them out into the deepest part of the river.

The beauty of swamp and forest embraced her. The bright moon illuminated great stands of pine, interspersed with yaupon, beech, and walnut. Stately cypress crowded the live oaks draped in Spanish moss that hung low over the water. The banks were thick with ferns, palmettos, swamp privet, and pickerelweed; and the air was sweet with the scent of wild orchids.

Any other time, she would find wonder and delight in such sights and smells. She would listen for the croak of frogs, the splash of fish, and the rustle of wild things in the underbrush. She would look for deer or bobcats, and she would glory in the magnificence of God's kingdom.

But not tonight . . . tonight, nothing mattered but this man and her need for him. Her heart raced, her thoughts tangled, and her body yearned for the touch of his hands.

She nibbled her bottom lip, trying to pretend that her breasts didn't feel heavy and full, and that her swollen nipples didn't rub against the rough linen of the man's shirt she wore in place of a bodice. Heat pooled between her thighs, and aching desire spiraled up from the core of her secret places.

"Angel." Will's voice came soft, but she could no longer ignore his order.

And when she came to a break in the foliage at a natural landing, she nosed the craft against a bank and leaped out. Will followed her. Together, they pulled the boat onto high ground. He removed a blanket and a bottle from the stern of the dugout and caught her hand.

"Find us a clearing free of snakes and alligators," he said.

Trembling, she led the way up a slight rise and into a mossy hollow ringed by fairy tufts of wild rice and jack-in-the-pulpit. Still smiling, she broke away and twirled in the moonlight like one demented. "Will this suit ye, sir?" she teased.

"Perfect."

Her hand tingled where it had touched his. She felt light enough to float above the treetops . . . to soar into the velvet heavens and touch the stars. "Nothing will harm us here," she promised. " 'Tis enchanted. Can't you feel them? The kelpie folk are all around us."

"Kelpies?"

"Pixies. Sprites—the fairy folk."

"I should have guessed." Chuckling, he set the wine bottle down and spread the blanket on the moss. "You're the only charmer I know, Angel. You've put a spell on me, one that I never want to awaken from."

He opened his arms. Suddenly shy, she took a step backward. The moss was cool on her bare feet.

"I love you," he repeated.

The forest beckoned. If she fled, he'd never catch her. She was as fleet as a doe and twice as wary. But she could feel the blood pumping hot in her veins and knew that everything she wanted lay within her reach. He uttered her name once more, and she threw herself into his arms.

Will's kiss was sweeter than hope of salvation, both tender and demanding. The taste and feel of him melted her fears and fanned the sparks of desire within her. He kissed her again and again, until she didn't know earth from sky or her flesh from his.

Will's hands moved over her, touching, stroking. "I want you," he murmured. "I can't live without you."

"Sweet Will," she whispered as she clasped his head to her breast and buried her face in his dark wavy hair.

He kissed her mouth and her throat. She moaned and squirmed against him, wanting more. His hard-muscled arms embraced her, and she wound her legs around his waist and clung to him like seaweed to a mooring post.

Her nipples puckered. Her belly tightened. Her breaths came quick and deep. "Show me what to do . . . how to please ye."

He trembled, powerful shudders that clouded her eyes with tears. "You've really never . . ." He broke off, his tone hoarse, disbelieving. "Never been with a man?"

"Are you sorry?" She leaned back, trying to see his eyes in the semidarkness. "Will it make your pleasure less?"

"No." He lowered her to the blanket and knelt beside her. "I never thought . . . hell, none of that matters now." He tilted her chin up and kissed her again. "Do you know what happens between a man and a woman?" he asked her.

"Aye, I do . . . sort of. What goes where, but . . ." Her face grew hot, and she would have turned her head away, but he leaned close and drew her bottom lip gently between his teeth. She gasped as excitement bubbled up inside her.

How could something so simple, the sensation of Will's teeth and tongue, the heat of his mouth, his taste, make her feel too big for her skin? Or cause her hearing and sense of smell to become a hundred times stronger so that she was aware of each blade of crushed grass and the rise and fall of Will's breath?

He caught her hand and pressed it to his, palm to palm, and finger to finger. "I wasn't alive until I met you," he said. "There's no woman to match you on the face of the earth." He kissed the tip of each pair of fingers, hers and his, mated as one. He teased and gently sucked, then slowly trailed caresses down the back of her hand to the wrist, and from there to the hollow of her elbow.

"I want you," he said. His nostrils flared, and his eyes widened with passion.

Had any words ever sounded so sweet? she wondered.

"I want to show you the beaches of Barbados, the blue water off Jamaica, and the markets of Havana," Will said. "I want you to stand beside me on the deck of the *Katherine* with a fair wind filling the sails, and I want to make love to you beneath a Caribbean moon."

She tried to tell herself that these were only words, that they meant nothing. But, oh, how she longed to believe that they might be true . . . if only for this instant.

Releasing her hand, he undid the top ribbons on her shirt. "Trust me, Angel."

Trembling, she looked deep into his eyes. "I do love ye."

In the silver moonlight, Will's skin was drawn tightly across his chiseled cheekbones. His muscles were taut, his hands more steel than sinew and bone.

The ties parted, and he planted warm kisses on her throat and collarbone. "What happens might cause you pain the first time," he said. "But never again. I promise you."

She gripped his powerful shoulders, shivering in the heat, struggling to breathe while passion's tempest rushed through her. She could feel his barely contained strength, like a ship in gale-force winds straining against a storm anchor, threatening to tear loose at any second.

Will undid another ribbon. Angel moaned when she felt the touch of his tongue on her breast. Pushing back, she yanked the garment over her head and struggled out of her breeches. Then, naked as the Lord made her, she lifted a breast and begged him, "Kiss me here, Will. Please."

He groaned. Swiftly, he stripped as bare as she. The sight of him, huge and male and dangerous in the moonlight, terrified her. Yet, she knew she'd come too far along this silvery path to turn back for lack of courage.

She closed her eyes and waited, then cried out with joy when she felt him draw her into his hot, wet mouth. Something bright and wonderful stirred within her. Tension tightened. Golden ribbons of spun sugar linked the shivery sensations in her breast to her maidenhead.

"Touch me," he said.

Now it was she who trembled and she took his staff between her hands. His breathing quickened as she stroked the silken column until he pushed her back against the blanket.

"No more," he rasped. "Lest I shame myself like a raw boy."

Happiness swelled in her chest as he covered her with his body. Legs met and entwined. His hard sex, hot and throbbing, pressed against her thigh.

She could not lie still. She tossed her head and arched against him. "Now, now," she cried.

But he kissed her mouth and throat and breasts. He nibbled her shoulder and teased her belly with a warm, damp tongue while his long, lean fingers worked magic in her lower curls and lower still.

Angel spread her legs and pulled him closer. She felt the pressure of his sex nudging her, and then she sucked in her breath as he slipped inside. He was big, bigger than she had imagined a man could be. She felt herself stretching. There was a quick stab of discomfort, and then Will slid deeper.

"Love me!" she cried. She thrust her hips up, opening for him. They fit together as perfectly as two halves of a seashell. The feeling was unlike any she had ever experienced, a good feeling, but not good enough. She squirmed beneath him and he pushed deeper still.

"Oh." Her eyes widened as pleasure shot through her. "Oh, Will!"

Laughing, murmuring her name, he kissed her mouth. And then slowly, he began to withdraw.

"No. Don't—," she began. But then, her need flared up as he buried himself to the hilt. He gave one final cry, and the power he'd held so long in check broke free.

He slammed into her again and again. She caught the rhythm, moving with him, giving everything . . . meeting passion with passion. Nothing mattered but Will and finding release from this fierce storm that battered and embraced her. The seas rose higher and higher. The water swirled around her until she forgot to breathe, forgot everything but this wild, fierce mating of flesh and soul.

Until a final surge washed her up and over. Until Will covered her face with kisses and rocked her in his arms. Until she found for a few brief hours a feeling of security and belonging that she had never known before . . . and could never allow herself to hope for again.

Later, Will shared the wine he had brought with him, and the two swam naked in the river without the slightest thought of poisonous snakes or alligators. In the shallows, near the bank, Angel nestled against him, her arms around his neck, her hair loose and unbound, hanging around her shoulders.

"I didn't hurt you too much, did I?" he asked. She seemed so small, so fragile between his hands. He wanted to shelter and care for her, to keep her safe from the world, as he had never wanted to protect another.

She laughed softly and kissed him with so much ardor that he felt himself growing hard again. "Nay, ye cod's head." She slid a palm down his belly to clasp his cock, and then her eyes widened in surprise. "I think I woke it up."

They kissed again, and he filled his head with her smell and taste. He was intoxicated—not by the small amount of wine he'd consumed but by this magical being. "I warned you," he teased.

"And if I do this . . . and this?"

He groaned as white-hot desire flooded through him. He drew her close and lifted her so that he could enter her. The buoyancy of the water, the feel of it on his bare skin, added delightful sensations to their lovemaking. And to his wonder, when he'd brought Angel to climax and found his own rapture, he found himself even more determined to make her his legal wife.

"Have I told you how much I love you?" he asked as they walked hand in hand back to the blanket and dropped onto it.

"Mayhap ye have, but I find it pleasin' all the same."

He wound a wet lock of her hair around his finger and lifted it to his lips. "There's no one like you."

She looked up at him through long, thick lashes. "Do I please ye, Will? Truly?"

"Truly," he replied. "I've never been so happy."

"Good." She curled beside him and laid her head on his shoulder. "They say the moon casts a spell on lovers," she murmured. "Do ye think it's so?"

"You've cast the spell on me. My sweet, sweet Angel."

She lay his palm against her cheek and sighed. "I'm happy, too. 'Tis like a dream, isn't it. But one I fear we'll wake from in the morning."

"We'll be married as soon—"

"Shhh." She silenced him with warm fingertips. "Don't talk, please. I need no words. The night is slipping away, Will. I want to savor every minute."

"But I need to—"

She gripped his hand. "Please! If ye love me as ye say ye do, don't talk to me about tomorrow or the next day. Not of Charleston or churches or even clipper ships. For this night, can we be the only man and woman in God's garden?"

And, of course, on this night, when she had given him the greatest gift any woman can give a man, he could deny her nothing. So he merely held her and kissed her until the yellow moon dipped beneath the treetops and the first purple streamers of dawn spilled across the eastern sky.

Chapter 24

The sun was high by the time Will paddled the dugout around the bend past Aba Sunday's cabin. He didn't handle the boat as easily as she did, but Angel didn't care. She was content to gaze at him, to watch Will's shirt stretch tight as his muscles flexed with each stroke, and to study the way he moved his head and arms.

The reality of daylight hadn't yet washed away her happiness of what they had shared beneath the full moon or dimmed the physical excitement of their love-making. She'd never known such joy, and she didn't want it to end.

Old Aba came from her house with a water bucket in her hand, saw them, and waved.

"Aba told me she was a little girl in Africa when slave traders raided her village. She saw her father and two older brothers murdered."

"She told you all that?"

Angel nodded. "She's free now. Her old master left her the house and an acre of land when he died."

"I've known Aba for years, but she's barely spoken to me. I didn't think her English was that good."

Angel chuckled. "Maybe you didn't ask her the right questions." She waved a final time at her new friend. "She promised to show me where to find sweet grass to

267

weave a basket, and she's going to teach me a new way
to wrap the strands so that the basket will hold water."
If I'm here that long, she thought.

"Do you like Nottingham? Better than Charleston?"

"Aye." It seemed to Angel that Will's smile was
sweeter than berry preserves eaten warm by the spoonful. " 'Tis quiet enough to hear your own thoughts."

She wished she could touch him, but she couldn't risk
rocking the dugout. So, she soothed herself by noticing
the way his thick hair curled in dark ringlets over his
shirt collar. Surely, she thought, Will Falcon must be the
handsomest man in all the Carolinas.

If only she could keep him.

But that was wishing for more than was her rightful
portion. Having Will for a little while, pretending they
had a forever together, was far more than she'd ever expected.

He looked back at her, his blue eyes caressing her.
"There used to be more people here. But Lizzy plants
only a few fields of rice and no indigo. She says she's of
no need of more money."

"Slaves, you mean?"

He nodded. "It takes labor to bring in crops, and
freemen won't do the work. If you're going to grow rice,
you've got to have slaves."

"Then I'll never eat a bite of it again. 'Tis a filthy
practice, slavery. Worse than seeking salvage of wrecked
ships. No man or woman should own another."

"Don't let the good ladies of Charleston hear you say
that. They'll take you for a Yankee."

Angel folded her arms. "Let them think what they
please. I'll not hold my tongue if I think a thing's
wrong."

"No, I don't believe you would."

He nudged her with the dripping paddle, and she went to jelly inside. Shamelessly, she wanted him again already. She hoped they could have more nights together, mayhap even weeks before they parted. Truth was, she had the fire for him. She wanted him, needed him . . . his searing kisses, his strong arms enfolding her, his lean hips thrusting against hers.

She could not deny it. She lusted for him like a dockside trollop for a sailor's silver.

"We think alike there," Will continued. "It seems to me that the practice degrades the master as much as the slave. And my father agreed. Over the years, Falcon Shipping hired crew without regard to color, or . . ." He grimaced. ". . . whether the seaman signing on was free or slave. It gained us few friends among the other ship owners."

"I think I would have liked to know your father." She glanced back at Will. "I'm sorry I called him a coward."

"He should have been stronger. He didn't have to die. Together we could have found a way to repay his creditors."

Just ahead of them tree swallows darted low over the water in search of insects. And off the stern, a spotted turtle raised its head, peered at the dugout, then sank soundlessly into the depths. The air was so rich and warm, so heady with the scents of growing things, that to Angel, it seemed like the Garden of Eden must have been.

"My father would have adored you," Will said.

Angel doubted that that was true, but she didn't want to argue. "You say little of your mother. What was she like?"

"Beautiful. Soft-spoken. Always laughing."

"Not much like Bett."

He chuckled. "I think not. My mother . . ." He trailed off as the great house came in view. "We're going to have to tell Lizzy about us," he said.

"Don't tell her that you've asked me to marry ye, not yet," she begged him. "Wait a day or two . . . to give me time to get used to the idea. I've nay said I would. Not yet."

Angel could guess what Lady Graymoor's reaction would be. One hint of a wedding, and the countess would throw her out of the house. And right now, every minute with Will was too precious to risk.

He flashed a boyish grin. "I'll try, but Lizzy is very perceptive. From the hints I've been dropping, she'll have guessed what's in the wind."

Angel threw out her fingers in the old sign for averting evil. "Don't say it," she cautioned. "You'll jinx us."

Black and yellow butterflies skimmed overhead as they made the dugout fast to the floating dock and walked up the wide lawn toward the house. A pair of orioles fluttered up, and a nesting wren scolded them angrily from the veranda. But except for the thin column of smoke drifting from the summer kitchen chimney, none of the servants seemed to be stirring at Nottingham.

Angel clung tightly to Will's hand. When he smiled down at her, she whispered, "I do love you."

He pulled her close and kissed her. "Are you sorry?"

"For what we did?" She felt her cheeks grow warm. "Never."

"I've wanted you for so long. But I always knew you were special, even before I loved you. I couldn't . . . it wouldn't have been right between us."

"You done it with lots of other women, haven't you?"

He chuckled. "That's not a question to ask a gentleman." Then his eyes caressed her. "But you were different . . . you were always my Angel. If I couldn't have you honorably, I couldn't have you at all."

She averted her eyes.

"And the sooner we set a church date, the happier I'll be."

"I've not said I would."

"You have to marry me," he teased. "Now that you've had your way with me."

No more than an hour later, after Angel had crept upstairs to her room and crawled between the sheets to drift off into a deep sleep, she was awakened by a soft voice and the smell of strong coffee.

"Wake up, miss," Ruby called. "Lady says you got to get up. She's got a surprise for Mr. Will, and she wants you to be there to see it."

Angel opened her eyes as the maid set a breakfast tray on the edge of the bed. "She wants you should eat hearty, miss. Got rice scones, Sally Lunn, eggs, and bacon." Ruby shook out a hunter-green skirt and jacket. "This here's a riding habit. I'll fetch boots while yer eating. Lady Graymoor says you'll need the boots." Ruby's intelligent brown eyes sparked with mischief. "Mistress says she hope you had a good sleep. And she wants you downstairs and at the stable before the clock strikes nine."

Will, Lady Graymoor, Griffin, and Delphi were already at the plantation stables when Angel arrived wearing the green outfit and carrying the tall riding boots.

"Good morning, Angel," Lady Graymoor said.

Angel murmured a general greeting and looked around. By Will's expression, he was as puzzled as she was. He'd changed into clean buff breeches, a spotless white linen shirt, and a buff waistcoat.

Will had shaved, and his still-damp hair was drawn neatly back into a queue at the nape of his neck. But the hint of shadows under his eyes told Angel that he was feeling the effects of a night without sleep as much as she was.

"Lizzy," he began gruffly. "What did you call us—"

Lady Graymoor clapped her hands, and a stable boy came out of the barn leading a pretty bay mare. "I had my horse master acquire this animal last week. She'll suit Angel perfectly, don't you think, William? It's really time she learned to ride."

Stunned, Will stared at Lady Graymoor and back at the horse. "Calli?" He approached the animal, patted her neck, and walked around her in obvious disbelief. "It can't be, but it is."

The bay's ears twitched. She nickered, then nudged Will with her nose.

Will beamed like a candle on a moonless night. "This is Calli! I thought she was dead. Where did you get her? Edward said that he'd had her—"

"Disposed of?" Lady Graymoor chuckled. "Odd how horses can be lame one day and sound the next."

The groom, who'd come to stand respectfully beside Will, grinned. "Yes, sir. That's a fact."

Will wrapped his arms around the mare's neck and hugged her. When he looked up, Angel was certain that his eyes glistened with moisture. "Edward has a good stable manager," he managed. "He wouldn't mistake—"

"A competent manager, but not a wealthy one," Griffin put in. "If this is your Calli, doubtless she passed hands several times before she became the property of her ladyship."

"Edward would never have sold her to you," Will said. "He despises Lizzy nearly as much as he hates me."

"Never say never," Griffin replied. "An important man like Mr. Mason surely doesn't attend to every small decision on his estate. And the horse certainly appears gentle enough for a woman. Wouldn't you agree?"

Will turned to the countess. "I don't know what to say. You've already done so much—"

"Teach the girl to ride," Lady Graymoor replied. "That will be thanks enough." She smiled, obviously pleased with herself.

Angel dropped the boots onto the ankle-deep grass. "I've never ridden a sidesaddle. But if you'll let me take it off, I can—"

"You must learn," Will said. "All ladies use them."

"I don't."

"You're afraid?" he dared her.

"Ye know better than that, Will Falcon!"

"Good, then put those boots on, and we'll have our first lesson."

She did enjoy the riding, once she got the hang of the awkward saddle. Her experience had been bareback, on wild ponies on the islands, and now and then, a turn on a mainland plowhorse. She'd never sat astride an animal as sweet and well trained as Calli, but she would have ridden a swamp bear into hell's harbor to bring that glow of approval to Will's eyes.

Once he was convinced she wasn't about to pitch off the mare and break her neck, Will mounted a spirited black gelding and led her off across grown-over fields and vine-clogged lanes to explore the broad acres of Nottingham.

Delphi packed a flask of sweet cider and a hamper of

fried chicken, cheese, corn bread, and blackberry cake to fill their bellies at nooning. They sat on a riverbank and devoured every bite of food and drop of cider before Will pulled her into his lap and began to kiss her mouth until she was mad for him to make love to her.

One caress did lead to another. And after they'd pleasured one another in a dozen, delightful ways that Angel had never dreamed of, they slept the afternoon away in each other's arms in the shade of a mighty oak tree.

When they woke, they laughed and teased each other, and made slow, hot love again before Will helped her dress so that they could ride home to Nottingham.

And that evening after supper, Griffin had the servants light all the candles in the east parlor and brought in musicians so that Will could teach her the fancy steps that quality danced to.

"You're a natural," Lady Graymoor insisted after Angel had practiced for the better part of an hour.

In truth, Angel had paid little attention to where she put her feet or to whether or not the kidskin slippers cramped her toes. Being in Will's arms while music played and candles flickered was heaven. So sweet was the experience that she could almost imagine they were alone.

At half-past eleven, Lady Graymoor signaled to Griffin to dismiss the musicians and bade everyone a good night. Griffin gave final instructions to the staff, and the maids began to extinguish the candles.

"You two young people are welcome to stay up as late as you like," Lady Graymoor insisted. "But I would like to borrow Angel for a few moments, if you don't mind, William."

"I would be happy to do anything for ye," Angel said.

"For you," she corrected. "And 'tis time we were abed. The day has been a long one."

Puzzled as to what her ladyship might want and half afraid that she'd be reprimanded for her behavior with Will, Angel followed the older woman upstairs to her personal sitting room. Five spaniels and a tabby cat trailed after them.

Peggy helped the countess out of her clothing and into a dressing gown and poured two glasses of blackberry wine. The dogs curled up on the rug; the cat settled on a bed pillow. "Shall I have the bath filled for you, ma'am?" the maid asked as she placed a white linen cover over the parrot's cage.

"Peaches!" the bird cried. "Brandywine!"

"Quiet!" Lady Graymoor ordered. "Be still, you devil-hatched bird, or I'll have cook bake you with plum sauce and sausage stuffing for tomorrow's dinner."

"Your bath?" Peggy repeated, raising her voice over that of the squawking bird.

"I'll bathe in the morning. That will be all," Lady Graymoor replied. And when they were alone and the parrot's grumbling was confined to an occasional outburst of clucking, the countess waved Angel to a chair. "I won't keep you long," she promised. "I just wanted to talk with you about an important—"

"If I've done anything to—"

Lady Graymoor motioned her to silence. "No, no, my dear. It's nothing you've done or haven't done. Please, just listen to what I have to say."

Angel nodded. The thought that she had taken advantage of the countess's hospitality made her uneasy. "If you wish me to leave—," she began.

"No, I do not." The crisp reply was followed

immediately by a softening of the older woman's features. "You give me pleasure, child. Surely, you can see that. You've brought this house alive."

Angel took a sip from her glass. The blackberry wine was warm on her tongue; sweet, but not overly so. Nervously, she took another sip.

Lady Graymoor brought a small teakwood chest from her dressing table and opened the domed lid. Angel's mouth dropped open in astonishment. The box was filled to the brim with glittering jewelry: rings, bracelets, brooches, necklaces—all bright gold, silver, and sparkling gems.

"Do you like my pretties?" the countess asked. She unrolled a velvet cloth and lifted a string of creamy pearls. "These were once part of the dowry of a Spanish infanta."

"They're lovely."

"Stones. Metal," Lady Graymoor said. "Better displayed on a young body than on an old, shriveled one."

Angel looked up, uncertain what to say.

"If you were my granddaughter, these would all be yours."

Angel shook her head. "I'm not, ma'am. I wish I was, but I cannot lie to you."

"There is more, much more. My husband's title passes to a distant male heir, but he left his vast wealth to our Elizabeth."

"It changes nothing. Maybe your Elizabeth's still out there someplace, waiting for you to find her."

"Do you realize what you're turning down?"

She shrugged. "Nothing, my lady. I'm not Elizabeth Graymoor. I'm just Angel."

"Butler, child. My husband's family name is Butler. He was Earl of Graymoor, and my son, Henry Butler, was the Viscount Kemsley."

"But . . . how is it that you're Lady Graymoor, if your husband's name is really Butler?"

Lady Graymoor chuckled. "Silly, isn't it. But it is the way things are done, the way they've always been. But I was born Elizabeth Parker, daughter of a country vicar." Still smiling, she returned the pearls to the chest and closed the lid. "One thing I'm certain of, you're no pirate."

"I keep telling Will that, but I fear he doesn't believe me."

Lady Graymoor yawned. "Go on, then. Go to your bed. It is late and past time this old woman was asleep."

"I'm sorry, ma'am, sorry I can't be her."

"Yes." The countess's eyes looked sad. "Aren't we all?"

When she was in her room and all the house asleep, Will came to her and asked what Lizzy had wanted.

"To show me her baubles, jewels, and such," Angel replied.

"I think she'd like to believe you're her lost grand-daughter."

"I won't, because it's not so."

He kissed her and led her back to the bed. "Did you tell her about us?"

"No."

"It's time." He kissed her throat and trailed kisses down her shoulder. "Lizzy's no fool. She'll be hurt if we don't tell her before she figures it out herself."

"Not yet," she replied. "Just let's wait another day. Just one more."

"One more day, woman, but that's it."

They whispered and teased each other long into the night. But Will refused to take their lovemaking further than kissing and touching.

"Not under Lizzy's roof," he said. "She trusts me. It's bad enough that I've deceived her by courting you without telling her. I'll not seduce you under her roof."

"Seduce me? Is that what you've done, sailor?" she replied when she was light-headed with his kisses. "It seems to me that I've seduced you."

"All the same, wench, Lizzy must know that I mean to make an honest woman of you."

The following day, they rode out on horseback again. Without speaking of it, they had come to an agreement to spend evenings with Lady Graymoor and Griffin and nights alone in each other's arms.

Often, when he came at night, Will brought her foolish little gifts that she treasured beyond counting: a dried turtle shell, a hummingbird nest, a single lady slipper blossom, and a piece of sugarcane. And she would tell him stories of the coast, ghost tales, and accounts of terrible storms, and old riddle games that had been passed down from mother to child from across the Atlantic.

She never tired of hearing Will's seafaring accounts. He told her of hand-to-hand combat with Spanish soldiers, of head-hunting Indians in the Indies, and of water so clear and blue that you could see coral outcroppings ten fathoms deep as easily as if you could stretch out your hand and touch them.

Two weeks passed, and then a third. Will did not press her about setting the date for the wedding, and she did not mention the Brethren to him. And secretly, she began to hope that he had changed his mind about seeking revenge for his father's death.

With each day, the sun grew hotter, until even the rain and the limp breezes off the river seemed heated on God's hearth-fires. But the steaming humidity meant little to Angel. Will Falcon and their time together was everything that mattered.

. . . Until the morning she awoke and looked out her bedroom window to see him leading the black horse out of the barn. "Will! Will!" She waved frantically. "Wait for me!" Snatching up the men's breeches she'd worn riding the day before, she tugged them on and looked for a shirt. Finding it on the floor beside the bed, she pulled the garment over her head and climbed out the window onto the tree branch.

She pushed off and dropped the last seven feet to the ground. Scrambling up, she dashed to Will's side. "Where are you going?" she demanded. "Why didn't you wake me?"

She expected his face to split in a grin. She wanted to see him laugh and explain that he wasn't going away. There was a reasonable explanation for his actions. But he didn't smile. When he looked at her, his face was nearly expressionless, his eyes hard.

"Are you leaving me?" She had been poised to throw herself into his arms. Instead, she took a step backward. "Are you weary of me? Have ye realized you've made a mistake?"

He reached for her, but she shook her head. Icy cobwebs of fear prickled her spine.

"Angel."

"No!" She wanted to run, but she knew that her knees wouldn't hold her. "Just be man enough to say it."

His eyes narrowed. "A rider came last night from Richard Hamilton. The fleet is assembled and ready to sail from Charleston in two days."

"The Brethren. You're going to hunt down the Brethren."

"I never tried to hide it from you." His words sliced sharp as a filleting knife. "It changes nothing between us."

"It changes everything."

"They're pirates. They've sent too many ships, too many innocent men and women to a watery grave. If I don't go, then I take responsibility for the next deaths on my soul."

"I'm one of the Brethren," she answered hotly. "How could you lie with me, if you thought me a murderer?"

Will set one foot in the stirrup and mounted the gelding. "Open your eyes, Angel. See the truth you're so fond of. Dyce, Nehemiah, and your captain are common thieves and cutthroats. No matter how much I love you, I have to see this through. I promise you there will be no wholesale killings. I'm going to see that they have a fair trial."

"And hanging?" she demanded. "What kind of fair trial will they get from mainlanders? It's the gallows for all of them, and ye well know it!"

"Not all. Sometimes even the guilty find mercy under the law."

She swore a foul oath. "Could you put a rope around my mother's neck?"

"If we find them, and if they surrender, I'll bring them back alive. That's all I can promise you. The Outer Banks have been lawless too long."

"If you go, it's over between us!"

"This doesn't have to be, Angel. I want you for my wife."

"Then don't be part of this witch-hunt."

"Ask me for anything else."

"Good-bye, Will Falcon."

Two of Delphi's sons, two tall daughters, and a robust grandson in his teens approached and circled her.

Angel glanced at them uneasily as suspicion curled in the pit of her stomach. "What is this?" she demanded.

"I've hired them to keep watch over you while I'm gone," Will said. "By day and by night, to see that you do nothing foolish."

"You think I'd try to get there ahead of you? To warn them?" she said, realizing with a sickening jolt that she'd made a terrible mistake. She'd waited too long before making her escape, and now the Brethren might pay with their lives for her error in judgment.

Will shook his head. "I think neither God nor Lucifer could stop you from trying."

"Ye cannot hold me prisoner here!" she cried.

"Confine her to the house for three days," Will ordered. "She is not to be harmed, but if she sets one foot out the door, you'll receive not a cent of payment."

Angel's hands tightened into fists at her side. Her nails cut into her palms, but she didn't feel the pain. "Three days," she repeated. "Until it's too late."

Will's only answer was to slap the horse's neck with the reins and canter away down the rutted lane.

Angel watched him until he vanished around a bend, then slowly slipped to her knees in the hard-packed dirt. Her eyes burned, but she couldn't weep. Her pain and sense of betrayal was too deep for tears. Instead, she locked her arms around her knees and rocked silently back and forth until the hollow ache inside had turned to frost.

Chapter 25

Will's ride to Charleston was an uneasy one. He was plagued by memories of the stricken expression on Angel's face and the hurt and angry look in her eyes when they'd parted. His decision to put her under lock and key for a few days had been the final insult, and he couldn't help wondering if she'd ever be able to forgive him.

He'd waited so long for this chance to put an end to a long and bloody chapter of piracy, but he feared the price he'd have to pay for duty would be high. Sailing with the fleet might destroy Angel's love for him and shatter any future happiness.

And if he lost her, he knew he'd never take a wife at all. For loving Angel had spoiled him for any other woman.

He hated to hurt her by placing those she cared for in mortal danger, but there was no altering the course he'd set for himself. As a Falcon, and Nicholas's son, he could do no less than keep his pledge to destroy the coastal robbers.

When he reached Charleston, Will rode immediately to Richard Hamilton's office near the docks. There, Richard gave him command of his heavily armed schooner, the *Santee Lady*. The merchants, militiamen, and captains had assembled with the expectation that

Richard would act as leader. But due to his worsening heart condition, Dr. Madison refused to allow him to accompany the force.

To Will's surprise, those in authority elected him to stand in Richard's place. The vote was unanimous except for Edward Mason's vocal protest. Mason was overruled, and the fleet of nine ships sailed north on a foggy Tuesday morning.

Seventeen days later, the *Santee Lady* and six other vessels returned victoriously to Charleston Harbor. Richard Hamilton, face pale and drawn, was waiting for Will on the dock. Will gave a few final orders to his crew and hurried down the gangplank.

"Richard? How are you?" Will knew he was sorely in need of a bath and a change of clothing, but Julia's father was leaning on a walking stick, looking as if he'd aged ten years.

"Did you find them?" Richard demanded as his servant opened the door to his carriage. "Damned foolish when a man cannot walk a few blocks. But that cursed physician overreacts, and Julia frets over me like a mother hen."

Will followed his employer into the vehicle. "You look as though you should be abed," he said once he'd taken a seat across from the older man. "I would have come to the house."

"I could wait no longer. Speak up, man. Did you take the pirates unawares? What are our losses? Did you bring back prisoners?"

"We suffered two deaths, and four wounded. One of the dead men is a seaman named Brickett, off the *Janet*. He has no family that anyone knows of. Three pirates dead, two wounded, one not likely to survive. We took seven prisoners, two of them women."

"You found no more than that? You scoured the beaches clean?"

Will nodded. "I'm certain of it. Captains Joel McCarthy and Brian Connor stayed behind with their crews to continue the search. I expected more resistance, but I fear they may have been warned and fled beforehand. We burned their settlement. A few women with small children escaped in the confusion, but I doubt we'll have serious problems from them for years to come."

"Where are the prisoners?"

"The men are aboard Thomas Williams's *Triumph*. I have the two women under lock and key in the master's cabin of the *Santee Lady*. I'm acquainted with one of them. The city jail's not set up to provide for female prisoners. I'll try to find suitable quarters to hold them for trial."

Richard's breathing was labored, and he leaned back against the headrest. Will's concern for him grew with every moment's passing.

"You said we'd lost two men," Richard said as the coachman turned the team onto Broad Street. "Who else?"

Will met his gaze. "Edward Mason."

"Mason?" Richard shook his head in disbelief. When he began to wheeze, he took out a handkerchief and held it to his mouth.

"Edward insisted on leading the south attack on the pirates' camp. He was killed saving Guy's life."

"Mason dead? I would have sworn these were his minions. Killed by a stray bullet?"

Will shook his head. "No. He took a cutlass blow to his neck. If he was known to any of the pirates, it wasn't obvious to any of us. Maybe we misjudged him."

"Nonsense. His death proves nothing. There's too

much evidence against him. Someone's been alerting that scum to which Charleston ships are carrying valuable cargo. Only a man with inside knowledge would have that information. And Mason's vessels were the only ones never attacked. Not once in all these years."

"I keep telling myself that," Will said. "I've suspected him all along. But not knowing for certain . . ."

"His death spares us bringing him to trial for piracy."

"True enough." Mason's death troubled him more than he ever expected. "I imagine George will take over the shipping—"

"George hasn't what it takes to run the company. He'll sell out. Doubtless, I can secure a few of his vessels at a reasonable price."

"The only ship I'm interested in right now is the *Katherine*. I want command of her, if I still have a job."

The coachman reined in the animals in front of Hamilton's house. Richard looked at Will. "I can't pretend that I'm not disappointed about you and Julia. You're making a huge mistake."

"The mistake would be to marry. We aren't suited for each other."

"And that red-haired adventurer—"

"Don't say another word, if you value our friendship." Will threw open the door. "I've asked Angel to marry me. If that's a problem, I'll find other—"

"It's because of our friendship that I'm speaking out. Damn it, Will. Think of what you're doing. You can't be blinded by the money. You of all people—"

"What money? What the hell are you talking about?"

"Lady Graymoor's fortune. What else? All of Charleston is talking about it. The countess is making the jade her legal heir."

"There must be some mistake. Angel wouldn't—"

"There's no mistake. Lady Graymoor has sent out

invitations to half the county for this Saturday. She'
giving a ball in honor of her granddaughter's return
from the dead."

Will completed his duties and secured both the
women prisoners and his ship before joining Tom
Humphreys and Joseph Fisher at Dixon's. And there
for the first time in months, he got royally drunk.

Becoming highly intoxicated was difficult for him, be
cause in his years aboard ship he'd learned to drink vas
quantities of bad liquor, go without sleep, and turn ou
for duty before dawn. So taking in enough alcohol to
drown his anger at Angel was a herculean task, but on
he threw his heart into.

Sometime after two in the morning, when the club
had closed and his friends had stumbled to their horses
Will made his way back to Falcon's Nest. He let himsel
in the front entrance and went to the door beneath the
grand staircase that led down to the cellars.

He managed the slide bar on the third try, took a can
dle, and walked stiffly down the steps. At the bottom o
the stairs, he turned left and stopped in front of anothe
door that led to an unused winter kitchen and servants
quarters.

A thick wooden board-and-batten door closed tha
space off from the storage areas and wine cellar. This
door was locked as well. A large iron key hung on a peg
to the left, but he didn't attempt to take it down. In
stead, he banged loudly. "Hey! Wake up in there! Bett!'

"Go to hell in a leaky skiff!" she replied.

"Leave us be," answered his other guest. "Are ye ou
of yer mind? It's the middle of the night."

"Bett! I need . . ." Will cleared his throat and leaned
against the door to maintain his balance. What was it he
needed? He ran a hand through his hair, knocking his

hat off. He didn't bother to retrieve it. "I need you to answer a question for me."

"Go swive yerself!"

"Woman! I warn you. You are in my power. I signed ... signed ..." What the hell had he signed? Something the judge's clerk had shoved at him. Responsible. That was it. "I'm responsible for the both of you. One word from me and you're both in ... in the stocks."

Bett's reply was so originally foul that Will chuckled in admiration.

"Have you ever thought of signing on as a sea cook?" he asked. Few cooks he'd known could produce anything but swill in a ship's galley, but they were all masters of profanity.

"Bugger off," Tamsey shouted. "Ain't ye got no respect fer a wench in mourning?"

The brick floor tilted. Will got his sea legs and swayed with the swells. "One question, Bett, and ... and I'll leave you to your rest."

"He's come to have his way with us," Tamsey whispered from the far side of the door. Then she raised her voice. "We ain't givin' nothin' away, mister. You want futterin', you gotta show me hard coin."

Will grimaced, remembering the girl's greasy hair, rank smell, and dirt-caked face and hands. "Not if you paid me," he answered.

"What do you want?" Bett asked.

"Tell me the truth," Will said. "Tell me ... about Angel."

"Where is she? What did you do with her, you jug-bitten varlet?"

"I've got to know. Is she your daughter or not?"

"Hell, yes, she's mine!" Bett roared. "My blood and bone. And too good for the likes of you!"

"Thought so," Will muttered. "Thought she was." Candle wax dripped onto his hand. "Owwlll! Damn it." He dropped the candlestick, then stamped on the flame. The cellar went dark.

"Where is she?" Bett cried. "Where's my Angel?"

Will didn't answer. Turning away, he returned to the staircase, fumbled for the railing, and walked unsteadily up the steps. "Knew it," he murmured. "Knew she wasn't Lizzy's girl . . . couldn't be. Lied . . . tricked us all."

When he reached the top, he locked the hall door. He continued on upstairs to his chamber, where he fell into bed fully dressed and still wearing his boots. "No angel at all," he rasped. "Not my angel . . ." Will's words faded to sleepy mumbling before he dozed off to dream of Angel lying naked in his arms on a blanket.

She waited for more than a quarter of an hour before rising from the high-backed chair in the corner of Will's bedroom. Creeping barefoot past him and into the hall, Angel had little concern that she would wake him. From the smell of the liquor, he'd not have noticed had Moses parted the Red Sea outside the garden window.

The last fifteen minutes had been easy; she'd sat here for hours. At first, she'd been hurt that Will hadn't come to Briarwood when he'd left his ship. Then, when the day had passed without seeing him, she'd realized he probably thought she was still at the country plantation with Lady Graymoor.

Griffin had come to see that all was well with the house, and that the watchmen they'd hired to protect the property while Lady Graymoor was away were doing their jobs. He'd also wanted to order extra supplies for the ball her ladyship was hosting and to collect more of her formal clothing.

Angel had welcomed the chance to return to Charleston in hopes of learning what had happened on the islands. She'd tried to convince herself that it was worry for Bett and Cap'n and her friends among the Brethren, not fear for Will's safety that had brought her here.

She couldn't forgive him for what he'd done, any more than she'd expect him to understand the decision she'd made, to allow Lady Graymoor to make her her heir.

Losing Will was difficult enough. She simply didn't have the strength to walk away from the countess's offer of a home and family . . . of the chance to finally belong to someone.

Trapped at Lady Graymoor's plantation, she had suffered terribly, not knowing which of those she loved might have been killed or wounded.

But then Griffin had returned to Briarwood and told her of the success of Will's mission. He said that all of Charleston was talking about the arrest of the pirates and their imprisonment in the town jail. And he'd added that their own William had taken charge of two women prisoners and was holding them in his own cellar until the trial.

Angel wasn't certain if Griffin trusted her or not. But when she'd asked him for money that night after supper, he'd opened Lady Graymoor's strongbox. "Take what you like," he'd said, not unkindly. "In a few days, it will all be yours."

She'd helped herself to gold Spanish doubloons, solid English guineas and crowns, Louis d'ors, and Portuguese crusadoes.

"Is this enough to buy passage on a boat to Jamaica?"

"And hire a crew to man it."

"Good." She nodded. "Thank you."

Griffin had given her a look that was part amusement and part respect, and then he'd bowed, locked the chest away, and retired to his own quarters in the servants' section of the house.

She'd wrapped the money in a canvas sack, hid it near the fountain in Will's garden, and climbed the wall to his room to wait for his return.

As she descended the stairs in the dark, Angel tried to tell herself that Bett wasn't one of the prisoners. Maybe she'd escaped in the fracas. Bett was savvy, a survivor. Probably she and Cap'n were sitting by a fire at Haunt's Cove, roasting a shoat, and laughing at their good fortune in avoiding capture with the others.

A candle was still burning in the hall passageway. Angel took it, unlocked the cellar door, and hurried down the last flight. After a single false turn, she found the second locked door and the iron key.

The key was rusty. It took all her strength to turn the tumbler. "Hallo," she called. "It's me, Angel. Who's there?"

Bett rushed from the shadows, a wooden trencher in hand, and enveloped her in a crushing hug. "Angel! Faith, sweeting, I nearly brained ye with this treen."

Angel clung to her. "You're all right? You're safe?" Vaguely, she was aware of Tamsey behind her, sniffling and wailing about their bad luck. But Angel paid her no attention. "Bett, Bett! I was so worried about ye. I was afraid ye'd been—"

"We're right as rain. And ye've given yer old mam a head full of gray hair worryin' over you." She pushed away. "And look at ye! Fair dressed to nines and peart as a cricket! Ye've done well fer yerself among the outlanders. Keeps ye in style, does yer husband."

"Nay . . . aye, I suppose he does." Explaining to Bett

would take too long. "But tell me of the others? Is Cap'n safe? Nehemiah?"

"Safe enough. Six foot under," Tamsey said. "Cap'n took a bullet through the head two days after we left ye on thet island."

Bett's eyes grew teary. "Aye, Nehemiah's gone to his reward as well. Dyce appointed hisself captain, he did. No proper vote. Nehemiah pointed out the wrong of it, and Dyce called him into the circle. Cut his throat, he did, the swivin' bastard."

Angel stared at them in stunned disbelief. "I knew it could happen," she murmured thickly. "Knew it could, but never really thought . . . I hope Dyce got some of his own medicine. Did they catch him?"

"That bugger?" Tamsey shook her head. "Hell, no."

"We got a message from Charleston by pigeon, same as always. But with Cap'n and Nehemiah dead, none could read it. I 'spect it was a warnin' that the raid was coming," Bett said. "That fool Dyce was roastin' all the birds, anyway. I tried to tell him that that's how we knew what ships to hit, but he said he didn't need anybody tellin' him how to run his business."

"Tom was killed in the fight, but Dyce got clean away," Tamsey said. "And he'd promised to handfast with me."

Angel noticed for the first time that the girl was no longer pregnant. "What of your babe?" she asked.

"Born dead," Tamsey answered. "Never drew breath, poor mite."

"I'm sorry," Angel said. "To lose a child must be—"

Bett frowned. "Off alone she was, when it happened. A pretty lass, it was, not puny or sickly lookin'."

" 'Tis luck, I say," Tamsey said. "I don't need no wailin' brat to tend to."

Angel turned to Bett. "I'm that sorry about Cap'n."

Her mother shrugged. "Sad, it is, but it's our way. Cap'n was gettin' old. A man can hold his place among the free brotherhood only so long."

"Do you know who in Charleston sent the messages? Who bought our salvaged goods?"

"Nope, only Cap'n knew," Bett replied. "Someone bigwig, I know that much. Cap'n always kept mum on his name. Said he was a powerful man, and it be worth my life to hear it. You was with Brother once, when he went to a meeting with his buyer on the mainland. Didn't you see him?"

"No. Cap'n told me to wait in the boat. I saw them talking, but it was dark. I couldn't see the man's face."

"That's Cap'n fer ye," Bett said. "He was afraid you'd be in danger if ye knew too much. He didn't even share that with Nehemiah, and he was his best friend."

"I always liked Nehemiah," Angel said. "He was good to me. Always had time to listen to my chatter."

"Aye, he was a listener. And he did favor the poppets. Never could father none hisself, because of his vows. Them Catholic priests can't lie with women."

"Nehemiah was a real priest?"

"Got sand in your ears, sweeting. Said it, didn't I? Who did the prayin' and the buryin' amongst us? I was there when Cap'n dragged him out of the surf thirty year ago. And Nehemiah was wearin' them black robes."

"But why did he stay with the Brethren?"

"Said he was a shepherd. And he'd found a flock what needed one. An odd one was Nehemiah, but sound in a fight. Ye could trust yer back to him."

"So my wedding to Will—'twas real, not just a hand-fastin'?"

Bett grimaced. "Be there a difference? A handfasted man is easier to get shet of, do ye sicken of him. Marry one in the church, yer stuck with him till kingdom come."

Tamsey fingered the satin cloak Angel wore. "Flothery, this," she said. Then she glanced down at her own torn skirt and bodice. "Seems yer luck's better than mine, Angel."

"You can have it, if ye like," Angel said.

Tamsey quickly donned the cape. It was long on her, coming down almost to the tops of her dirty bare feet. "Look good fer a shroud. They'll hang us, certain."

"Neither of you will hang if I have anything to say of it," Angel said. "I've come to free you. I don't know if I can help the men, but—"

"Devil take'm," Tamsey said. "They're a sorry lot. Get us out of here."

"She's right," Bett said. "The one's got caught should have been hung long ago. Most are Dyce's kind. More scum than real men. Not fit to be called Brethren."

"They're charging all of you with piracy," Angel explained. "Even Will believes it. I've told him that we were honest wreckers, that—"

"Shit," Bett answered. "Open yer eyes, Angel. Are ye so fey that ye've gone blind?"

A sour taste flooded Angel's mouth. "What are ye saying? The Brethren aren't pirates. They never murdered . . ."

Tamsey's scoffed. "Yer daft. I seen murder done many a night. Sailor washes up on the beach, him half drowned. No need to cut his throat. Hold his head under; after a while he quits kickin'. Shit, done it meself, once or twice."

Angel felt sick. "Bett . . . you said . . ."

"Softhearted, I was. Still am. Cap'n didn't urge killin', but he didn't make too much fuss if it happened. Me, I steered clear. No blood on my hands." She shook her head, and her gray eyes filled with sadness. "Done things I ain't proud of. Things I reckon I'll burn in hell for."

"How could I have been such a fool?" Angel asked. "Why didn't I know? Why didn't ye tell me?"

"Ye always were one to see a thing the way ye wanted to," Bett replied. "But I loved you, sweeting. And anything I could do to protect you, I did." She shrugged. "And if it meant a few lies here and there . . . no need for a poppet to see the worst in men, be there?"

Gooseflesh rose on Angel's arms. "I . . . never . . . Will was right. We were pirates."

"Shit," Bett replied. "Piss-poor pirates, I'd say. Now ye take Billy Kidd or Edward Teach, they was real buccaneers. We was never more than half-arse pirates." She grinned. "But we give a good run, didn't we?"

"I've got money," Angel said. "You can buy passage south to the Indies. Make a new start there."

"Hell, yes," Tamsey said. "Show me yer coin."

"Ye ain't comin' with us, are ye, sweeting?" Bett said.

Angel shook her head. "No, I'm not. I—"

"Don't blame ye," Bett replied. "Ye got a warm berth here, a good man. Ye'd be a fool to give it up."

"I love you," Angel said. "I'll miss you . . . I'll miss you terribly."

"Like poison ivy," Bett said. "Time we parted, girl. We'll be fine, me and Tamsey. I've always had a mind to go south and find me a young husband. Mayhap I'll open a dockside tavern and make an honest livin' in some port where the sun shines every day."

"We'd best hurry," Angel said. "There's only a few servants in the house, and Will's passed out drunk. But the sooner you get to the dock, the better. I've gold coin hidden outside in the garden. That should buy you passage."

"That, it will," Bett agreed. "Gold talks."

"I want my share now," Tamsey said.

"Shut up, ye stupid cow," Bett snapped. "I'll carry the coin. You've not brains enough to be trusted with it." She hugged Angel again. "Sure ye won't change yer mind and sail with us. T'will be an adventure."

"Nay," Angel said. "Charleston's adventure enough for me."

" 'Tis not this town what's holdin' ye, I reckon," Bett said. " 'Tis that fine young gentleman upstairs."

"I'm through with him. He betrayed me. Locked me up and led the others to you—"

"You're more fool if you let him slip through your fingers," Bett said sharply. "Did you think we'd go on like we always had, livin' the old wild ways? Didn't ye think they'd come with cannon and shot to put an end to the Brethren? If not Will Falcon, then another."

"Hell, he saved our lives, me and Bett's," Tamsey said.

"Aye," Bett agreed. "Them others would have strung us all up on the beach if it weren't for your Will. He stood alone against the pack of them. Said he'd come for justice, not murder. Stopped the killin' and made them take us prisoners."

"He let Maude and Hannah and their pack of brats get away in a longboat," Tamsey added. "Pushed it off the sand with his own two hands. I seen him. Could have been me with'm if I'd dropped my musket and run sooner."

"It doesn't matter," Angel answered with a catch in her voice. "I'm no better match for him than he is for me." And when he finds out what I've done, she thought, I'll be lucky if he doesn't hang me with the rest.

"Bless you, child," Bett said. "Don't let that stubborn

pride of yours keep you from finding real treasure." She grinned. "Now, best we cast off before the wind and tide changes."

"Godspeed," Angel murmured. And pray I'll not regret this scheme tomorrow.

Chapter 26

Angel stood in the garden for a long time after Tamsey and Bett hurried off toward the harbor. She'd given them clear directions. Even if she hadn't, Bett would find a waterside tavern and a ship to carry her to the Caribbean. With her easy way with the men and her nerve, Angel wouldn't be surprised if Bett ended up governor of Jamaica.

Lord, but she would miss Bett.

"I could have done far worse when it came to mothers," she murmured. Whatever common sense she could claim, she supposed that it had come from Bett.

Angel was glad she had freed Bett and Tamsey, and she didn't feel the least bit of guilt for doing it. What troubled her was how badly she'd wronged Will.

She'd blamed him for going after the Brethren and for not believing her. She'd been furious with him. And he had been in the right.

How had she been so blind for so many years? She, who prided herself on her instincts, had been completely deceived. Bett was right. She'd seen what she'd wanted, believed the excuses Bett had given her . . . because she'd wanted so badly to be part of the Brethren.

But it wasn't reason that drove her tonight. It was something deeper. In the morning, when Will found out that his prisoners were gone, he would suspect she'd been the one to free them. She supposed he'd be in nearly as much trouble with the authorities as she would.

Tomorrow, she'd ride home to Nottingham and tell Lady Graymoor what she'd done. She'd leave her old life behind and try to become Elizabeth Butler, granddaughter of a countess, gentry of Charleston, if the lady would still have her.

She'd give over her fey, wrecker's ways, put on satin dancing shoes, and learn to wear petticoats and dresses. Angel sighed heavily. According to Griffin, she'd have to bend her mind to learning reading and writing as well.

But for now, she was still a saltwater wench, a lass with seaweed in her hair and a lust for a man she couldn't have. Elizabeth Butler would think twice about seducing a sailor in his bedchamber. A pirate wench wouldn't hesitate.

Since she, Bett, and Tamsey had let themselves out by way of the front door, getting back into Falcon's Nest was as slick as new butter. In less time than it took to rig a fishing line, she was up the wide staircase and slipping back into Will's room.

He hadn't moved. Will was still lying flat on his back, sound asleep. She smiled, slid the bolt on the bedchamber door, and slipped out of Elizabeth's garments.

Will groaned as someone tugged off his boot. "Leave me alone," he said. He turned over and buried his head under a pillow. He was in the midst of a good dream and didn't want to be bothered.

The annoyance persisted. Off went the second boot. Off came his stockings.

"Go away," he muttered. Angel was drifting farther away. Her image was fading just when he was about to . . .

His trousers followed the boots. He tried to keep hold of them, but it was too much effort to put up a struggle. He felt cool air on his buttocks.

"All right, all right." Will felt a weight on the mattress beside him. A woman's deft fingers undid his stock and pulled up his shirt. "Delphi. If it's you, you're a dead woman," he threatened weakly.

Soft hands stoked his spine, rubbing and massaging, kneading the kinks and aches from his back and shoulders. Definitely not Delphi.

"Mmmm, that's good." He was caught between wanting the back rub to continue and trying to retrieve his dream. "Ohh." He moaned as the strong, supple hands squeezed and pressed against the nape of his neck.

A curtain of silken hair brushed his bare skin, and he twisted to inhale a scent of jessamine mixed with mint. Will turned over onto his back and reached up to touch a soft breast. "Angel?"

"Shhh." Her mouth covered his.

He groaned as she slid on top of him, and her warm tongue teased his lips and slid across his teeth. Her firm, rounded body fitted his like a glove, the heat of her sweet thighs bringing life to his fallen mast.

Was this real or was he dreaming? He didn't know . . . didn't care. He cupped a full breast, closed his lips on a silken bud, and suckled.

Desire hammered in his gut. His breaths came hard and fast. Tension tightened his muscles like coiled springs.

She moved over him . . . teasing . . . enticing . . . wet. "Will," she whispered. "I'm going to . . ." She moved her lips close to his ear and uttered words that sent hot blood pulsing through his veins.

And then his dream became real. Heaven and earth shook, and Angel swept him away to uncharted seas of erotic pleasure, where a man's fantasies came true and the woman he wanted more than anything in the world didn't slip through his fingers.

Time became meaningless. Night faded into day. And Will woke with sunshine streaming across his face. Alone. Hung over. And wondering if what he'd thought had happened really had?

Angel.

He shook his head, trying to clear his mind. Had she come to him last night, or had he wanted her so badly that he'd imagined the whole episode?

Damn her to hell. He knew what she was. How could he still care so much? How could he want her so badly that his insides felt hollow and numb?

How could he still love her more than life itself?

"How dare you come here to my place of business?" Richard Hamilton demanded. "Are you mad?"

Archie folded his arms and leaned against the closed door. "Ye wanted her dead. She's dead. Now I want my money."

"Where's your proof?"

"Proof's lyin' in the alley behind McCrady's Tavern. Somebody will find her before the day's over. Jest another dead whore with her throat cut."

"You're positive it's her. No mistakes?"

"I followed her from her house."

"What was she doing near McCrady's?"

"How the hell should I know?" Archie hawked and spat on the floor near Hamilton's shoe. "You want Falcon killed, it will be twice the price. Cleanin' up yer shit is getting to be a habit."

Richard raised an open palm. "Keep your voice down. For God's sake. There are clerks working in the next room."

"Pay me what you promised."

"I got you out of jail. Have you forgotten that?"

"Lots of folks around here probably like knowin' you hired me to do murder."

"Shhh. I'll get your money. Just be quiet."

"Damn straight I'll get my money."

"If you'd just step aside and let me—"

"You ain't leavin' this room until I've got what's comin' to me."

"You arrogant ass! Do you think I keep cash here? It's in a strongbox in the back office."

"Send somebody to fetch it." Archie hiked up his trousers and pulled a knife from a sheath strapped to his leg. "Wouldn't cause me no lost sleep to do you right here, Hamilton. Ain't bothered to clean my blade yet."

"All right. Don't hurt me. I'm not a violent man." Richard raised his voice. "Dyce. Come in here."

Archie stepped back as the door swung open. His eyes widened as he stared into the barrel of a flintlock pistol.

"Ye needed somethin', Mr. Hamilton?" Dyce asked.

"Shoot him," Richard ordered.

Dyce raised the gun, took aim at the center of Archie's forehead, and pulled the trigger. As Archie toppled backward, Richard shouted, "Help! We're being robbed!"

An hour later, Richard was back in his home. Shaken by the incident with Archie Gunn, he ordered hot water for a bath. His coat and trousers were spattered with the creature's blood. His shoes, made especially for him in France at an astronomical cost, were ruined.

"Burn the clothing," he instructed his man Daniel.

"And take away my shoes. Dispose of them. Sell them. Give them away. I don't care. I never want to lay eyes on them again." Richard shuddered, remembering how Gunn had spat on the floor of his office.

Richard was not a coward or a weakling. Running a shipping business meant dealing with coarse and ruthless men. He'd served in the militia during the Southern campaign of the Revolution, and he'd seen men die. But he'd not tolerate unseemly behavior where he worked and lived.

When the bath was ready, Richard dropped his towel and climbed into the tall china tub, letting the hot water and soap soak away the contamination. "Harder," he instructed when Daniel used a long-handled brush to scrub his back.

He cleaned his hands and nails meticulously, scouring and buffing until his fingertips were sore. And when Richard was certain that his hair and skin were immaculate, he got out of the tub and commanded Daniel to empty the dirty water and repeat the entire process.

It was midmorning when Richard, freshly shaven, hair cut and styled, dressed in new clothing from head to foot, entered his wife's apartment on the second floor of the house. "Good morning, Glory," he said.

The nurse mumbled a few words of greeting, gathered an armful of laundry, and made herself scarce.

Richard approached the bed. "Gabrielle, it's your Richard. How are you today?"

His wife stretched and yawned and rubbed her eyes. She was wearing a pink flowered dressing gown and chemise. Her hair was plaited in two braids with thin, pink ribbons woven into the sections and left to dangle below in a dainty waterfall.

He produced a handful of tiny pink roses. "For you, my precious," he said. "Smell the fragrance." He held the flowers close to her.

She rewarded him with a smile.

"And I brought you these," he added. "One, two, three." He dropped three macaroons into her lap. "Your favorite."

"Like cookies," Gabrielle said.

Richard sat on the edge of the bed, took her hand, and raised it to his lips. He kissed it gently. "You are beautiful today," he said.

"I wanted you to come yesterday." She pouted.

"I did, darling. I had breakfast with you, and I came to read to you last night and tuck you in. Don't you remember?"

"No."

He smiled and stroked the cat. "Puddums remembers."

Gabrielle retrieved her hand and nibbled a macaroon. "Maybe I do." She giggled, and crumbs spilled from the corners of her mouth. "I do," she proclaimed. "You wore a funny hat with a feather and we ate gingerbread."

Richard swallowed, pushing back the flood of emotion that threatened to drown him. "Things are not going as we planned, Gabrielle. That island bitch has been most annoying. I had to pay to have her disposed of. Again. She seems to have lived a charmed life."

"Island bitch," Gabrielle repeated. "Puddums doesn't like her." She took hold of the cat's head and moved it from side to side. "No, she doesn't."

Richard removed his coat, folded it, and hung it over the back of a chair. Then he loosened his stock. "But now that she's gone, Will must see reason. I thought he had to die, but now that Mason's gone, there's no need. Will can marry our Julia, just as you've always wanted."

"Marry our Julia." She giggled and popped another macaroon in her mouth, chewing slowly.

"Nicholas's death was a tragedy. We never wanted that. Either of us." He unbuttoned the cuffs of his white lawn shirt. "If Will marries Julia, he'll inherit everything when we're gone. It will make things right."

Gabrielle nodded. "More cookies?"

"Later. I'll make Glory fetch you some from the kitchen."

"Puddums likes macaroons."

"I hate violence," Richard said. "You know how it upsets my constitution. My bowels won't work properly for days."

"No shit."

"Shh, don't use that word. A lady doesn't know such words, let alone say them in the presence of a gentleman." He removed his shoes and stockings. "She saw me, Gabrielle. That time I left you to go to the Outer Banks. I couldn't take the chance she'd identify me, tie me to the wreckers."

"Kill her." Gabrielle pushed the cat away and bared one sagging breast. "Time to play," she said, giggling.

"He'll marry our baby, and all will be right again," Richard said as he slid into bed beside his wife. "He'll marry her, or he'll end the same way as his red-haired whore."

Gabrielle reached for his stiffening member. "Playtime," she repeated. "Ride a cock horse to Banbury Cross."

• • •

Will stood staring at the half-open door. When he began to swear, Delphi's grandson picked up the breakfast tray and backed toward the cellar stairs.

"Wasn't my fault, Mr. Will. When I come down with the grits and eggs, they gone. I didn't let them out. I swear, I didn't—"

"No, Clyde, it's not your fault," Will said. "But I think I have a good idea whose fault it is." He hurried up to the hall passageway in time to hear loud knocking.

Clyde opened the door. "It's Mr. Griffin, sir."

"I can see who's there," Will said. "Go on. Return to whatever it was you were doing before you fed the prisoners."

"Didn't feed them. They was—"

Will pointed toward the back of the house. The boy picked up the tray and fled. Will looked at Griffin. "What's wrong? Not something to do with Angel, is it?"

The Welshman nodded. "I'm afraid it is. She came with me—to Charleston. She had clothing to purchase. Last night, she asked me for money, a great deal of money."

"Did you give it to her?"

"Yes, sir, I did. Lady Graymoor said that she was to have whatever she wanted."

"Get to the point. She's run off, hasn't she?"

Griffin's forehead beaded with sweat. His lips thinned, and his pale expression grew waxen. "A man came to the house just minutes ago. Concerning Miss Angel."

"What did he say?"

Griffin took a breath, and his chin quivered. Tears clouded his eyes. "He said she's been murdered."

"That's not possible. She was with me last night."

"They say it happened sometime before dawn. Near the waterfront."

"How?" Will asked.

"Her throat was cut. Maybe a robbery." Griffin ran a trembling hand over his head. "What will I tell my lady?"

"I want to see the body," Will said.

The black hollow in his gut expanded, threatening to swallow him. He had the sensation of standing next to hell's gate. And he knew that so long as he didn't accept Angel's death, the blackness had no power over him. "I don't believe it. Have you seen her?"

"No. I came right here. I thought you should be the one to identify the body."

"Where is she?"

"McCrady's Tavern."

Will rushed out of the house. He ran down the street, legs pumping. Passersby stared at him. Twice, acquaintances called out his name, but he didn't stop until he reached the tavern.

A crowd had gathered outside. Will shouldered his way through. A woman's body, covered by a stained sheet, lay on a table near the open hearth. Will's thudding heart skipped a beat when he saw bare feet and the hem of Angel's cloak peeking out from under the linen shroud.

"Hey, you can't . . . ," the proprietor began, then he recognized Will. "Oh, Mr. Falcon, it's you. I've sent for the sheriff, sir. I—"

Will took hold of the corner of the sheet. He gritted his teeth and lifted the covering. He stood still and stared down at the still face of the young woman, then turned away and called for a drink. "Rum. A double."

"Do you know who she is?" the innkeeper asked.

Will took the leather jack from a freckle-faced barmaid and downed the fiery liquid in one swallow. "She's one of the prisoners we brought back from the Outer Banks. She escaped sometime last night. Her name is Tamsey Blunt."

Chapter 27

It took three full days for Will to satisfy Judge Cooper and the council that he'd had no part in the prisoners' escape or in Tamsey's death. At the official hearing, a seaman testified that he'd seen a single woman boarding the *Alma May,* a merchant vessel pulling anchor sometime before dawn on the morning after the murder.

Due to the condition of the body, Dr. Madison estimated the death to be sometime between midnight and six A.M. A rice merchant testified that as far as he knew, the *Alma May* hailed from Rhode Island and was bound for a half dozen small ports in the West Indies.

Since the missing woman seemed the prime suspect in the murder, Judge Cooper issued a warrant for Bett's arrest on the charge of murder. But the general consensus in the courtroom was that the deceased had already received justice for her crimes of piracy. As for the accused, she was well out of the court's jurisdiction and would probably never again set foot on South Carolina soil.

Early on Thursday morning, Will and three of Delphi's relatives were the only witnesses to Tamsey Blunt's burial in St. Michael's churchyard. Will paid for the funeral and a round of drinks in Tamsey's name at McClary's from his own pocket. By noon, Will had borrowed a horse from Lizzy's stable and was well on the road to Nottingham Plantation.

The thought of how close he'd come to losing Angel haunted him. He couldn't imagine a world without her.

But neither could he pretend there weren't obstacles between them. His anger at Bett's escape had cooled with the passing days. Secretly, he was glad she had gotten away, and he had no doubt who was responsible. But Lizzy's decision to adopt Angel and make her her heiress troubled him.

When he'd asked Bett who Angel was, the woman had assured him that she was her natural daughter. And if Bett was telling the truth, Angel couldn't be Lizzy's lost Elizabeth.

There wasn't a dishonest bone in Angel's body. She'd no more deceive Lizzy than he would. So why had Angel changed her mind? Surely if she was Elizabeth, she would have retained some memories of her earlier life, wouldn't she?

He rationalized that the temptation was probably too great. Angel was human. Who was he to accuse her when his own reputation hadn't been spotless? Had he been a bastard runaway at twelve, instead of Nicholas Falcon's son, his own life easily could have taken another course.

He loved Angel.

It was that simple. He was mad for her—couldn't live without her. He didn't doubt that Angel would lead him a merry chase, or that taking her to wife would severely limit his business contacts in Charleston and elsewhere. But the world was wide, and he could always find a ship to command.

And she was more important than anything else. Whatever it took, he would find a way to make her happy.

The hatred he'd felt for Edward Mason had faded away with the man's death. Curiously, he was glad he hadn't been the one to end Edward's life. Whatever he'd done, he would face a higher justice.

Will felt as if a weight had slid off his shoulders. He was free of the need to take revenge for his father and for the loss of Falcon Shipping. Falcon House, with all its family history and memories, no longer seemed reason to fight to hold on to a lifestyle that he couldn't afford. He'd do what he could for Delphi, Sukie, and the other servants. But it was time to shake off the past and move forward with his life—with Angel at his side.

"I don't understand why we're going to Lady Graymoor's party at all," Julia protested. "This is ridiculous. You know that woman isn't Elizabeth Butler. It's a farce."

It was the afternoon of the day following Tamsey Blunt's interment, and Richard, Julia, and Julia's maid were traveling by coach to Nottingham. Richard's man Daniel rode up front with the coachman, and two footmen followed on horseback. The day was hot, the road dusty, and the atmosphere worsened by Julia's peevish mood.

Richard closed his eyes and leaned back against the seat, trying to block out Julia's complaints. The carriage bounced and rattled, making it impossible to relax. They'd gotten such a late start and the road was so bad that he knew they'd be forced to spend the night at an inn and continue the journey in the morning.

". . . Mother doesn't do well in the heat. You know how I hate leaving her in Charleston alone."

"Please, darling, stop whining. You're giving me a headache," Richard said, not opening his eyes. "We owe it to Will to maintain the friendship with Lady Graymoor. Even I'm not wealthy enough or well-positioned enough to snub the countess."

"No one will come. We'll be the only people there. I'll

look a fool. Everyone will think he's throwing me over for a bride with a greater fortune."

"If he wanted you for your money, then he isn't worthy of you. But they aren't wed yet. Anything could happen. Will could regain his senses, or Lady Graymoor could decide against taking this nobody as her heir."

"It's not that I dislike Angel. But she isn't right for Will. Once the—"

"Taste of forbidden fruit?" Richard supplied.

"Father!" Julia flushed.

"Forgive me, that was crude and uncalled for." He clasped her hand. "I wouldn't insist that we go if I didn't think it was the correct thing to do. You know your mother and I love you very much, Julia. I'd never do anything to hurt you."

Her voice softened. "I know that, Papa. Truly, I do."

"Good. Now, pinch your cheeks, or whatever you ladies do to look your best, and carry on. No matter what happens, things will work out for the best. They usually do."

"They didn't with Mama."

"No, they didn't with your mother, God keep her. But she's unaware of how she is. The burden falls on us, I'm afraid."

"She's not a burden. I didn't mean that," Julia insisted. "You know I don't mind caring for her. It's just that you've been cheated of a wife in your later years."

He sighed. "And you of a mother."

Julia dabbed a hankie at her eyes. "No one could have a better father than you, Papa."

Richard smiled. "I hope you'll always think that, my dear. Just remember that everything I've ever done, all my efforts have been to make life better for you."

"I know that." She sniffed. "I'll try to make the best of this."

For the next few miles, Julia was blessedly quiet, giving him time to think, to muse over his conversation, two days earlier, with Dyce Towser. Naturally, he'd been greatly disturbed when he'd learned that Archie Gunn had eliminated the wrong whore, and that Angel was still alive.

"How could Archie have been so stupid?" he'd demanded of Dyce. "To kill a totally different woman and not know the difference?"

Dyce had grinned. "Ye said it. He was stupid and greedy. He followed her from the house, and she was wearing Angel's cloak. It was dark, and he was scared. A man what ain't got iron balls can lose his nerve."

"You'd better not fail me, Dyce."

"I won't. Ye get what ye pay fer. I ain't a fool. Ye should have brought me here in the first place."

"I needed you in the islands. Now I need you here. I want Angel dead," he'd told Dyce. "I'll kill her myself, if I must. But if I do, you're not only out of a job, you'll be occupying the same cell as all your companions."

"I'll do the job." The man had seemed to take orders seriously. "I'll take care of them both for you, Mr. Hamilton," Dyce promised.

He'd threatened to have Dyce emasculated if poor Gabrielle showed any signs of pain or fright. Richard had given Glory and the staff two days off, and no one would expect a substitute nurse to show as much vigilance as a family retainer.

Dyce would steal into the house tonight by way of the servants' entrance, go up to Gabrielle's chamber, and place a pillow over her face. Gabrielle slept soundly at night, since Glory always dosed her with laudanum. She would awake to the sound of heavenly trumpets.

Not only would Gabrielle sluff off her earthly bonds of madness tonight, but Julia would be free. His daughter could enjoy her future as a wife, no longer weighed down by the responsibilities of an invalid mother.

Richard swallowed, trying to dissolve the sensation of thickening in his throat. Letting go of Gabrielle would be hard. But it was for the best.

He hoped Puddums wouldn't miss Gabrielle too much. Cats were so sensitive. Often they mourned longer than humans, refusing food and water until they made themselves ill. He'd never forgive himself if something happened to Puddums.

He'd warned Dyce that the cat wasn't to be hurt. "Not a hair disturbed," he'd threatened.

Richard had faith in Dyce, even if the man was too stupid to realize the value of the valuable racing pigeons he'd eaten. Dyce had proven he could learn from his mistakes. He'd shown enough initiative to rid himself of the Brethren's leader and assume the position. In time, Richard might be able to send Dyce back to the Outer Banks to pick up where he and his wrecker friends had left off.

After all, the shipping business was competitive. A man had to look after his own interests. The arrangement had worked well for a quarter of a century, and there was no reason it couldn't be lucrative again.

"Follow my instructions exactly," he'd told Dyce. "I'll lure Angel into the garden."

"I'll be there, Mr. Hamilton. You can count on me."

Dyce could strangle Angel, throw the body in the river, and let the alligators conceal the evidence. Angel would vanish without a trace.

Richard chuckled at the cleverness of his plan. How fitting it was. The mystery woman disappears in a puff of smoke. With Angel gone, Will would wait a suitable time, then marry Julia.

And Lady Graymoor? She would be forced to leave

her fortune to her dear friend Will and his lovely wife. Absolute perfection.

Richard wiped the dust from his face, removed a silver flask from his inside coat pocket, and took a sip. Then he felt his heart; it seemed to be beating with more regularity. He felt better, stronger. Who knew what the future might bring? Perhaps, in a year or so, he might think of remarrying, himself. After all, he was in the prime of his years. It wasn't too late for him to consider taking a younger bride—perhaps even fathering a son.

Will made poor time on the road. The horse threw a shoe not ten miles from Charleston, and it took hours to find a farmer to replace it. Then, when he reached the landing, there was no boat to take him upriver to Nottingham. He had to spend the night at the home of an acquaintance and didn't arrive at Lizzy's home until Saturday morning.

Griffin seemed overjoyed to see him. Other guests had arrived ahead of him, and the house was overflowing with elegantly garbed ladies and gentlemen. "Lady Graymoor is still abed," the butler informed him. "It will be a great relief if you would organize some sort of entertainment until she rises."

"She's not sick, is she?" Will asked.

"No." Griffin's eyes lit with amusement. "You know how my lady likes to keep late hours. She played cards until quarter to four. Won a tidy piece of change from Mrs. Maude Duane of Proctor's Hill."

"Where's Angel? Is she here?"

Griffin shrugged. "On the river, I imagine, sir. I've seen little of her since the first guests started arriving. Lady Graymoor assures me that Miss Angel has sworn to be on her best behavior tonight." He raised one thick eyebrow. "But that remains to be seen, doesn't it, Mr. Will?"

"You told her about Tamsey Blunt's death?"

"I did. She seemed quite stricken by the news. I gather that the two were not close, but—"

"Did you tell her that I knew she let them out of my cellar?"

"I insinuated as much, sir."

"Her reaction?"

Griffin shook his head. "I'm sure it's not my place to say, Mr. Will."

"Do you know which way she went? Upriver, or down?"

"I really can't say." Griffin turned a sharp gaze on a servant carrying a tea tray. "Stop! Right where you are!" he commanded. "Who prepared that . . ." He glanced back at Will. "If you'll excuse me. I have duties to perform."

"It's all right, I'll look for her myself." Will followed the stable boy into the barn to see that Lizzy's gelding was being properly looked after. The horse needed a rubdown and water, and with so many visitors at Nottingham, Will wasn't certain his orders would be followed.

He was just leaving the stable a quarter of an hour later when Angel rode into the yard on Calli.

"Will?"

For an instant, her features lit up in a smile, and he was struck by just how beautiful she was. Not just pretty, but poised and graceful. Her hair was bound up in a net at the nape of her neck, and she wore a broad-brimmed riding hat with a feather in it. In the blue habit, and the boots and gloves, no one would know she wasn't to the manor born. Until she spoke.

"I was hopin' ye'd come," she said. "I'm sorry if I put you in a bad way, letting Bett and Tamsey go like that."

He caught Calli by the bridle and led her around the stable, away from the barnyard, where no one would overhear their conversation. When he halted the horse and put up his arms to lift Angel down, she came into his arms as easily as if there were no hard feelings between them.

"You're sorry," he replied. He set her feet on the grass, but kept his hands around her waist. "Sorry you did it?"

"Nay. I'd do it again. I'm sorry about Tamsey, but she was a fool. And a bad thief. Someone was bound to murder her, sooner or later."

"Are you sorry for coming to my room?"

She averted her eyes. "Who says I did?"

"I do."

"Maybe you dreamed it."

"You play dangerous games, Angel. If you'd been caught, you'd be in jail. Hell, I could be in jail."

"I had to help Bett. She's been like a mother to me."

"No, Angel. Not like a mother. She is your mother." She pushed free of him, and he caught her wrist. "Did you tell Lizzy that you're her granddaughter?"

"What if I am?"

"You know that's not possible."

Her green eyes widened, and the tears spilled over. Will wanted to kiss them away, to wrap his arms around her, to keep her safe. Instead, he went on. "I asked Bett if she was your mother. She said that she was. She is. Not Anne Butler. No matter how much you want it, Angel, you aren't Elizabeth Butler."

"If Bett said that, she lied to you," Angel insisted. "She was my foster mother. She told me . . ." A dry sob broke her words. "Since I was little. She told me she found me on the beach. A gift from the tide."

Will shook his head and yanked her close. "I love you no matter who you are. But we can't take advantage of Lizzy."

"Ye think that's what I'm doing?" Angel's face paled until light freckles showed on her fair skin. "Ye believe that of me?"

"Not out of greed. But maybe it's something you want so much that you're trying to make it true."

A giant fist closed on his chest. God, but he wanted her. He wanted to hold her, to kiss away the tears, to hear her laughter. "Marry me, Angel."

"Ye think me a thief and a liar, yet ye want to wed me?"

"I never said that."

"But ye think it." She tried to jerk free of him, but he held her tight. "Let me go. I was wrong to think—"

"To think what?"

"To think that I could belong someplace. That I could be somebody. Not just salvage on a beach, but someone real, someone with a mother and a father. Somebody with a last name."

"I'll give you a last name."

"Nay. I'll not take it from you. Not when you think I'm so low as to—"

"You're the fool, William." Lizzy laid a hand on his shoulder. "Let her go."

Ashamed, he released Angel and stepped back. "I love her," he said. "I want to take care of her."

"I can take care of myself!" Angel turned and stalked away, head high, back stiff as any navy officer.

Will started to go after her, but Lizzy stepped in front of him. "No. You'll stand here, and you'll listen to me," she said. "You think Angel deceived me, that she passed herself off as my granddaughter for my fortune?"

"I'm not blaming her," he began.

"No?" Lizzy scoffed. "You and Griffin together don't have the brains to fill an egg. What makes you think I believe Angel is Elizabeth? That I expect miracles? I don't know. Maybe I do. But whether Angel is Elizabeth or not no longer matters to me."

He stared at her. "You don't think—"

"Hell, no." She chuckled. "Well, maybe a teensy bit." Lizzy pinched thumb and forefinger together. "I'm tired of being alone, William. I'm tired of searching for Elizabeth. I'm laying her ghost to rest with Henry, Anne, and little Alexander."

"Why, then?"

"Quiet and listen to me! Did it ever occur to you that perhaps the good Lord took pity on a foolish old woman? That he might have sent an angel to fill her empty heart?"

"You've fallen in love with her, too."

"I have. As of yesterday morning, William, she is legally Angel Elizabeth Anne Butler. My solicitor has filed the papers at the county seat. I've rewritten my will. No pun intended. And I've left everything I possess to Angel."

"You've already done it?"

"I have, with Angel protesting every step of the way." She smiled. "Now, you do your part. Convince her you are the biggest ass that the Creator ever smiled on. Beg her to forgive you and give you another chance. Marry her and take care of her, William. Love her and make her happy. And make me happy. Give me great-grandchildren while I'm young enough to appreciate them."

Chapter 28

Angel closed her eyes and took a deep breath. She was terrified, as frightened as she'd been the first time she'd summoned the nerve to leap on the back of a wild mare, nearly as scared as the morning she'd been caught in a riptide and almost drowned.

Her knees were trembling. Her belly felt as though she'd swallowed a handful of dragonflies. Her heart was broken, and she thought she might burst into tears at any second. She wanted nothing more than to run away, to keep going until she was far away from Nottingham and Will Falcon.

All she had to do was hold her head high and walk down a curving marble staircase wide enough to drive a coach and four. She was supposed to remain graceful and poised, yet pretend that she was balancing a bucket of bait on her head. Lady Graymoor expected her to smile at seventy-eight hostile gentlefolk and a host of servants who'd all come to Nottingham in hopes of seeing her eat live chickens or at least trip on the steps and knock herself simple.

She bit the inside of her cheek until her eyes watered. How hard could it be to face Will's friends and neighbors and pass herself off as the granddaughter of a countess? Surely, it would be no worse than catching a barracuda with your bare hands.

Abruptly, the fiddlers stopped playing. Fifty pairs of eyes stared up at her, and Griffin announced, "Lady Angel Elizabeth."

For long seconds, she remained frozen. And then, in the back of her mind, she heard Bett's sage advice: "*It's too late to cast anchor when your boat's on the rocks.*" She took one more heady breath and began her descent.

Her ears burned as a titter of whispers rose to meet her. But then she caught sight of Will standing beside Lady Graymoor. And he was watching her with the look of a man who dug for clams and came up with gold guineas.

Her heart flipped over, and hope blossomed in her chest. Will began to clap his hands. Lady Graymoor joined in, and soon everyone was clapping for her.

As she reached the bottom step, Griffin touched her gloved elbow lightly and whispered, "You're a vision, m'lady. If I didn't know better, I'd think . . ." He cleared his throat and averted his eyes, but not before she saw the gleam of tears shining there.

Lady Graymoor swept forward to take her arm. "See, darling, it wasn't so bad, was it? They love you." The old woman raised on tiptoes to kiss her cheek as a tide of strangers surged around them.

"This is my dear friend, Mary Pritchett, and her husband Raymond," Lady Graymoor said.

One name and face followed another. Angel gave up attempting to keep them straight. She shook each offered hand and smiled, soon finding that she wasn't expected to reply.

"A miracle," a waspish, middle-aged matron said.

Richard Hamilton approached with Julia. "I can't tell you how happy we are that you've found each other." Julia smiled coolly as her father took Angel's gloved hand and kissed it.

Angel pulled back, trying to remain gracious. There was something about Richard that she found unsettling. And she didn't need witchcraft to tell her that Julia hadn't come here out of friendship.

"You must cut some of my flowers for your mother," Lady Graymoor said. "The Maid Marian roses are wonderful this year."

"How kind of you," Julia replied. "You know how I love your garden. It's the finest in the state."

The musicians began to play again, and Angel slipped away from the three of them. Sets formed for dancing in the long parlor, and servants passed among the guests with all manner of food and drink.

Angel couldn't eat a bite for fear of spilling something on her gold and white silk gown or down the front of the very low neckline. The dress was so narrow that she could only take small steps, and the bodice and embroidered half-sleeves so tight that she felt like a butterfly half in and half out of a cocoon.

"May I have the first dance?"

Angel turned to find Will at her side. "I'd not think ye'd trouble yourself," she murmured.

"I'm an idiot."

"Aye, you are."

He led her away from the crowd to a spot by the French doors that led out on the veranda. "Lizzy told me everything. I was wrong. Can you forgive me?"

She wanted to remain angry with him. He deserved her anger. He'd hurt her badly, and she loved him so much. She loved him with all her heart and soul, and she couldn't have him. She felt herself begin to tremble. " 'Tis nothing, Will. If we could remain friends—"

He took her by both arms and whisked her onto the wide, pillared porch. Lanterns hung from the high ceiling, and in the distance, Angel could see the light of the slaves' bonfire. The cadence of African drums and the swirling notes of strange stringed instruments drifted across the wide lawn from the celebration. The air was thick with the scent of the jessamine and of the river.

"I want you for my wife, Angel," Will said.

She shook her head as tears smeared the light dusting of powder on her cheeks. "Ye know I can't."

"Why not? I know you love me."

"William. Here you are," Lady Graymoor called. "Richard wants to dance with our guest of honor. And I was hoping you'd be my partner for—"

"No," Will said. "Angel and I are—"

"It's all right, Will. We can talk later." Angel moved away, still shaking inside, glad for the interruption. Just having Will close to her made her forget good sense.

"I need to talk with you now," he insisted.

"William. Don't make a fuss." Lady Graymoor tugged at his arm. "One dance to humor an old woman. Surely, what you have to say to Angel will wait."

"Go, please," Angel said. She stood there as Will reluctantly escorted Lady Graymoor inside.

"Did you want to dance, or would you prefer a breath of air?" Richard asked. "Would it be too much to ask you to show me the countess's gardens?"

"Nay, I . . . I mean no." Angel led the way down the steps and around the house. An iron gate led to the formal gardens, thick with boxwood and roses of many colors. "You can see the flowers better by daylight," she said awkwardly.

She was uncomfortable, but didn't want to offend the man Will worked for. She didn't know exactly what was bothering her. It wasn't as if she and Richard were alone. Behind her, near the gate, Angel could hear a woman's voice calling someone, and to her left, murmurs came from the maze.

For a while, they strolled in silence. It was a cloudy night with mist lying thick on the grass. The garden was dark except for the lanterns hanging here and there on posts.

When Richard did speak, Angel nearly started out of her skin. "It would please me if you and Julia became the best of friends."

She glanced up at him warily. He was soft-spoken, a friend of Will's, and he'd made no attempt to touch her. So why did she feel as if a ghost had jumped over her grave? "I'm sorry," she said. "I need to talk with Will. If you will pardon me, I'll—"

Richard barred her way. "I think not."

He whistled, and gooseflesh rose on the nape of her neck. Angel took a step backward. Abruptly, Richard seized her arm. "Your game is over, bitch."

"Let me go." She tried to pull away, but his fingers bit into her arm.

"I wondered where you were," Richard said.

Angel twisted to see a hulking shape materialize on the path behind her. She caught a whiff of sour, unwashed clothing and knew who the intruder was.

"Will!" she screamed. At the same instant, she turned back toward Richard, balled her right hand into a fist, and smashed it into his face.

Startled, he groaned and staggered back. Angel dashed past him. Behind her she heard Dyce's grunt of anger. His boot soles thudded against the bricks.

She knew that in the clinging gown and slippers she wouldn't be able to outrun him. There was no time to rid herself of them. "Will!" she screamed. The house was a hundred yards away. Dyce was gaining with every step.

Shielding her face with her arms, she dove into a hedge of roses. Thorns ripped at her skin and gown, but she wiggled through, darting down another path and diving into the tall, boxwood maze.

"Get her!" Richard cried.

Angel flung off the slippers and pulled the dress up above her knees. When she heard Dyce crashing through the foliage, she ran as hard as she could.

"Angel!"

That was Will's voice. She turned left, then right. A wall of hedge rose before her. She was certain she heard someone coming. Not Will. He was too far away.

Again, she fought her way through the leaves and branches. A woman's scream was suddenly cut off. Then she heard a shot.

"Angel!"

"Will!" She ran, ducked around a lantern pole, and threw herself into his arms. "Dyce," she said. "He's here! He tried to kill me."

A harsh cry made the hair raise on Angel's neck.

"Stay here," Will ordered.

"Nay," she protested. "I'll not leave ye."

People were running toward them. Servants with torches spilled into the garden. Angel spied Lady Graymoor and called out to her: "Here! Over here!"

"William!" Griffin shouted.

"You stay here," Will repeated.

Angel and Lady Graymoor followed close on his heels. Just inside the entrance to the maze they found Richard on his knees beside a woman's sprawled body. He was weeping and mumbling his daughter's name. A pistol lay beside him.

"There's another body over there," someone said. "A man's. I think Richard must have shot him."

"Somebody did," Griffin said. "He's got a bullet through his head."

"That's Dyce Towser," Angel said. "He was leader of the Brethren after he killed Cap'n. Will knows him."

Richard rocked back and forth. "Julia. I'm sorry, so sorry." He looked up at Angel. "He was supposed to break your neck," he said bitterly. "It was supposed to be you. Not her. Not my Julia."

"Why?" Will demanded. "Why did you hate Angel enough to try to kill her?"

"Because I saw the man Cap'n took orders from," Angel said. "The bigwig who sent the messages by pigeon from Charleston. And if I saw him, he must have seen me."

"She's the only person who could identify me as their contact," Richard said. "So long as she was alive, I'd never be safe."

"But you were," Angel said. "I never got a good look at his face. It was too dark. I never could have pointed you out as Cap'n's partner."

Will stared at him. "Then it was you, all along. Not Mason who killed my father. You."

But Richard paid him no heed. It took two strong men to pull him away from his daughter and drag him protesting down the brick path to the house.

Will glanced at Lady Graymoor, and she nodded. "I'm fine, William. See to her. She needs you now."

Quickly, he drew Angel away into the darkness. "I almost lost you," he said. "Again." He held her so close that she could feel the beating of his heart against hers.

"I'm so sorry Julia's dead," Angel answered softly.

"I've loved her for years. But she was more of a sister to me than someone I wanted to spend the rest of my life with. I never felt about her the way I love you."

"She said I wasn't good enough for you. That I'd ruin your life."

"She was wrong."

"Ye still want me, Will? After all the trouble I've caused ye, caused all of ye?"

He kissed her, kissed her so sweetly that reason fled, and she found herself kissing him back. Soon she was weeping and clinging to him and kissing him over and over. "I don't want to ruin your life," she murmured.

"You'll ruin it if you turn me down."

"Your friends . . . other people. They'll blame you for my ignorance."

He chuckled. "You're rich, Angel. You'd be surprised how money opens all doors. And if my friends turn their backs to you, I want nothing to do with any of them." He kissed her again. "Besides, I wasn't planning on making you part of my old life. I thought we'd build a new one together."

"I wouldn't have to learn to be a Charleston lady?"

"Absolutely not. But there's one condition. You have to marry me right away."

"Why?"

"Because it's been months since I've been to sea. I'm a deepwater sailor, love. I need to have a ship under me and a brisk wind filling my sails."

"Ye want to me to wed you and have ye leave me?"

He laughed and kissed her again. "Not a chance. I intend to take you with me. Would you do that, Angel? Would you be content as a captain's wife?"

"Where will ye find a ship . . . with Richard . . . they will put him in jail, don't you think?"

"They'll hang him. Unless he hires a very good lawyer and buys a dishonest judge. So, woman, will you or won't you? How often does a man have to ask for your hand?"

She didn't tell him they were already well wed, that Nehemiah was a true man of God. That could wait until another day. If he wanted to marry her, he could do it up fine, with a gown, veil, and golden ring. "Will I be very rich?" she teased. "Now that I'm Lady Graymoor's heiress?"

"Rich enough to buy me a fleet of ships."

"Good." She kissed him again. "But ye must never leave me behind, Will. Unless . . . what if I give you a child?"

"Then you can stay here on Nottingham. Hell, you can buy your own island and build a house twice as big."

She snuggled against him. "We will sail with you, me and our babes, to see the places where the water is as blue as your eyes and clear enough to see twenty fathoms."

"You'll marry me?"

She'd never looked for so much happiness to come in three wee words. "Aye," she promised solemnly as she cradled his chin between her hands. "But I have my own *one condition*."

"And that is?"

"I get to name our first boy."

He laughed, lifted her up by the waist, and swung her high. "Whatever you want, wench. Unless you plan to call him Dolphin."

"Nay, husband." He kissed her again. And when she could speak, she said, "I'll call him Alexander."

"Why Alexander?"

"I can't tell ye why," she answered shyly. Tears of joy blinded her, and she fought to find the words. "So long as I can remember, 'twas always the lad's name I've loved best."

"Ms. French knows how to make the past come alive and our hearts sing with happiness."

—*Romantic Times*

THE TAMING OF SHAW MACCADE

by Judith E. French

Four years ago, hell-raiser Shaw MacCade departed Missouri for the gold hills of California, leaving behind the bitter feud that had plagued his family for generations. Now he has returned to bring his brother's murderer to justice and put an end to the legacy of bloodshed between the Raeburns and MacCades. But Shaw is not prepared for the changes that greet him at home, especially those in the captivating Rebecca Raeburn. Enemies by birth, the two are soon brought together by a common destiny and an attraction that neither can resist. But will a love as tempestuous as the raw country that reared them heal the sins of the past...and gentle one man's restless soul?

Published by Ivy Books.
Available in your local bookstore.